THROUGH HIS EYES

first novel in the MIND'S EYE *series*

by

DEBORAH CAMP

Contents

Acknowledgments

Cover design by Patricia Schmitt

I owe a debt of thanks to my good and patient friends Joyce Anglin, Jackie Kramer, and Pat Wade for assisting me with getting this book ready for publication.

And thanks to everyone who reads it. Please drop by and say hello to me on Goodreads, Facebook, my website, or my blog. Sign up for my newsletter and get news and freebies! I love interacting with readers and writers.

www.deborah-camp.com
www.facebook.com/officialdeborahcamp
www.pinterest.com/debbycamp44
www.deborahcampwritersdesk.blogspot.com
www.twitter.com/authordebcamp

Chapter One

The six white squares of paper lay like fallen tombstones on the table. Slowly, almost ponderously, Trudy Tucker moved her left hand toward them. Her tapered fingers hovered two or three inches above the table, and then she moved her hand back and forth as she closed her eyes.

Within seconds, the tingling blossomed in her fingertips, but she continued the sweeping movement as the sensation traveled up her arm. *Because she wanted to be certain.* She *had* to be certain. Lives depended on it. A dark substance poured through her mind and she felt as if it coated her face until she thought she might be smothered by it. She sucked in a breath and willed herself not to panic. This was all part of the process, she told herself. She had been schooled in this. She could control this now.

The comforting words she repeated to herself settled her, soothed her, so that she could push through the discomfort and decipher the signals that tingled from her fingertips to her brain. Flickering scenes of horror passed behind her eyelids. She made herself look. She made herself see. Although everything within her screamed for her to turn away, to block out the inhumane scenes, she stayed there. She observed. She witnessed until she was secure in what she was sensing and in what she now knew to be true.

Plucking four of the white squares from the others, she opened her eyes again. The police interrogation room swam into view, reminding her of what was expected of her and that she wasn't alone. She had an audience of two people and she quelled the feeling of being looked at as if she was a circus freak. Methodically, she moved the two remaining pieces of paper farther apart. The tingling remained strong, winding its way along her whole hand and twisting up to her wrist. Yes, she had it right.

"These two are definitely involved," she said, looking across the table at the police detectives who watched her intently. "I feel strongly that the one on the right is the murderer and the other one watched. I . . . I believe they both raped . . . I mean, I *know* that they both raped the woman." She took a deep, cleansing breath to erase the rest of the dark blot from her mind. "But this man . . ." She tapped her index finger on one of the mug shots. "This man strangled her." She pushed the others across the table toward the two detectives, eager to be done with them. The youngest officer, Ramon Martinez, reached out and flipped over the pictures.

"Well, I'll be damned." Detective Hal Bernardo chuckled. "Look at that."

Martinez eyed Trudy with dark brown eyes that called her everything but honest. "How'd you do that? Who you been talking to out there?" He jerked his head in the direction of the squad room.

"No one," Trudy said, keeping her voice and gaze level. "Are these two men your prime suspects?"

Martinez nodded and ran a finger along his closely cropped mustache. "They're in lockup right now. We're waiting for forensics to do their thing." He glanced toward the photos. "Why don't you look at their faces when you do that?"

Trudy swallowed against the tightness in her throat. It was never easy. Would it ever be for her? "It's too distracting to see them. I don't want to be prejudiced by how they look or by their expressions." She rubbed her stinging fingers and then ran her hands up and down her bare arms. "There isn't any goodness left in them. They should be locked up or they'll kill and rape someone else."

Martinez's smirk was purely sarcastic. "Is that a prediction?"

"I don't make predictions," Trudy said with a tight smile. She didn't like Martinez and he didn't like her. One needn't be a psychic to figure that out. "It's just an opinion."

"Don't pay any attention to him." Bernardo extended a beefy hand across the table to her. "Hey, thanks for your help. I figured since you were already here in Houston working on the Finnmore murder, I might as well pull you in on the tail-end of this one."

"Good luck, Detectives." Trudy stood, glanced at the two stark faces in the photographs, and braced against another shiver of revulsion. Yes, they did it. No doubt.

"I hear you've broken open the Finnmore investigation," Bernardo said, clearly fishing.

"I looked over the case file and told them what I could. An arrest has been made and Kirby's body has been found," Trudy said, edging around the table to make her way out of the room that had suddenly become too cramped. Being hired by people as a psychic was still new to her and she felt strange taking money for it. But now that she'd sold her share of her granddad's pawn shops to her brother and sister, she had to find a way to make money. And this was it.

"The family called you, right? They hired you," Martinez said around the toothpick he'd stuck in his mouth. "Are you their fortune teller?" He snickered and elbowed Bernardo. "Lots of rich folks hire their own personal fortune tellers."

"That's enough, Ramon." Bernardo sent him a quelling glare.

Martinez opened the door leading to the squad room. Although she wanted to escape, she hesitated as words burned her tongue. "Like I said before, I don't read fortunes or predict future events." She looked squarely at Martinez. "But if I did, you know what I would predict for you, Detective?"

He grinned around his toothpick. "I'll bite. What?"

She leaned in closer. "That you'll never make lieutenant. You're too dense." She waited only long enough to see his smile fall away from the toothpick before she left the interrogation room.

Hurrying through the large area that was dotted with desks and cubicles, Trudy was aware of the curious looks slanted her way. She flattened her hands against the double doors and sent them swinging forward. Anxious to be away from police officers and murder cases, at least for a little while, she shot down the hallway toward the bank of doors that gave access to the street.

Outside, she stood still for a few moments to let leaves of yellow and pale green whip around her ankles and tangle in her short, auburn hair. The September air was cooler than she had expected and she wished she'd worn a jacket instead of a sleeveless blouse.

She crossed the street and sat on a concrete bench in the sunshine, hunching her shoulders against the breeze. Sunlight warmed her eyelids as she turned her face up to the sky and took in a deep breath. Exhaust fumes tainted the air and she coughed to clear her throat, wishing she could clear her mind just as easily. She scolded herself for smarting off to Martinez. If she was going to continue working as a psychic, she had to make nice with cops. *All* cops. They would be her main source of any word-of-mouth advertising.

For the umpteenth time, she wondered if she should have sold her third of the pawn shops to Derek and Sadie. The money had come in handy, but it was dwindling. She had to find more work. No, that wasn't true. She had to start *accepting* more work that paid well. The freebies had to stop.

The cell phone in her jacket pocket vibrated. She fished it out, flipped it open, and held it close to her ear. "Yes?"

"How is it going down there in the Lone Star State?"

Trudy sighed expansively. Just the person she needed to hear from in this moment of doubting. "Oh, Quintara, I just smarted off to another cop." She closed her eyes for a few moments, picturing her psychic mentor dressed in her usual flowing caftan and carnival bead necklaces.

"Trudy, you're going to slice up enough lawmen with that sharp tongue of yours and they'll stop calling you about any case anywhere."

"I know, I know. I have to stop being such a smart-mouth." She sighed. "Sometimes I still worry that I'm not cut out for this." When a woman walked past her and looked at her with a mixture of annoyance and amusement, Trudy realized that she was almost yelling into the phone in an effort to be heard above the traffic noise. "Ummm, can you still hear me?" she asked, lowering her voice and twisting away from the street.

"Loud and clear. I think you should come to Florida. There is a serial killer in the Keys. You've heard about that?"

"A little. But I can't. I need to watch my money. I'm not a famous writer like you with book deals and magazine editors begging for articles."

"But you could be. This Florida case will open the door for more cases to come your way," Quintara said with her usual confidence. "You have a gift. You have a duty to use that gift responsibly. Believe me, you'll get more comfortable with your abilities as you learn how to use them instead of letting them use you. Do you really think you won't have all of these feelings and visions if you stop working on murder cases?"

"I know they won't go away." Trudy pinched the bridge of nose between her thumb and forefinger. Darkness swam at the edge of her mind and she tried desperately to deny it, conquer it, vanquish it. It had appeared the moment Quintara had mentioned Florida.

"Listen, dear, Levi Wolfe and I are in Florida working on this case. Since, he can only channel the deceased, he thinks you should come here and help track the killer. Working both sides of it, you and Levi could locate the lunatic in no time so that no one else is murdered."

Levi Wolfe? The Casanova of the psychic world wanted to team up with her on a case? Suddenly, she was hot. Just the mention of his name made her breathe faster and instantly picture his brooding, fuckalicous face. His midnight, unruly hair, his soulful blue eyes, his full lips, and that smile. That slightly lopsided, bad, *bad* boy smile. She swallowed and cleared her throat, wondering what was up. It just didn't make sense that he'd want to work with her. He was extremely talented and famous, so why would he want to team up with someone who was just starting out? She'd met him about a year ago in Tulsa when he'd visited Quintara's Psychic Roundtable where fledgling psychics honed their skills and perfected their techniques under Quintara's patient and skillful tutelage. She'd seen him a few times after that and he'd always made her skin prickle with longing and her thoughts scamper to all things sexy.

She smiled, thinking that the scornful Martinez should get a load of Levi Wolfe! Wolfe was a true showman with his dark good looks, raspy voice, devilish grin, and all-black ensembles.

"Another body was discovered yesterday and this murder was especially grisly," Quintara said, cutting through Trudy's musings. "Levi says the woman was tortured for several days before being killed. That's different from the other victims. They were killed almost immediately."

"Quintara, I'm going home to Tulsa. Not to Florida." She shook her head. Levi Wolfe was sexy as hell and *way* out of her league.

"Trudy, listen to me," Quintara suddenly sounded less breezy and more determined. "This will be your turning point, dear. Do you know how many young psychics would jump at the chance to partner with Levi? Wrap it up there. I expect you to join us at the end of next week."

"I really can't," Trudy said, laughing a little at the older woman's tenacity. "Your crystal ball is on the blink."

"I know what's best and this is your time to shine. See you soon."

Trudy realized that Quintara had broken the connection. Rolling her eyes, she pocketed the cell phone. Guilt nudged her. She owed so much to Quintara, so how could she refuse her?

At her lowest point three years ago, when Trudy had wondered if she might need to check into the psych ward, she'd met Quintara at the Tulsa State Fair. Quintara had a booth in the exposition center where she was selling her books and promoting her work with the area ghost hunter and psychic groups. The minute she'd met her, Trudy had known that Quintara had been placed in her path for a reason and she'd grabbed onto her like a life line. Because that's what she was then and now. A life line.

Glancing around at the whirling traffic, Trudy pondered her next step. Now that she was finished with the Finnmore case, she'd need to find another one to keep her bills paid and continue to bolster her reputation. For the past two weeks, she'd worked closely with Cher and Brad Finnmore and had helped identify their daughter's slayer. She'd been able to slip into the murderer's mind and get information about who he was and where to find him. She'd also seen through the killer's eyes where he'd buried Kirby's remains, which had been found only a few hours ago exactly where she'd told the police to look for it. Near a yellow barn on the killer's uncle's property.

Working with Levi Wolfe certainly would further her reputation and give it more gravitas . . . but could she keep her mind on work with him around? He was sex personified and she could barely think rationally when she was in the same room with him. She'd experienced that every time he had visited the Roundtable. When he looked at her, her skin heated up and her heart raced. When he spoke to her, she replied in a breathy voice that didn't even sound like hers! It was weird. The man was dangerous.

No. She couldn't work with him. She could rip his clothes off with her teeth. But she couldn't work with him.

*

Two days later Trudy sat at the dining room table in her home in Tulsa and scanned a newspaper article about the discovery of the most recent murder victim in the Florida Keys. It was the case Quintara and Levi were working on.

Her interest piqued and she read the information more carefully. Suddenly, a black veil descended over her mind and then the thoughts and visions of a stranger bombarded her with a ferocity she hadn't experienced before. It blotted out everything else in her world. She saw bright sunshine and the backside of a girl in a bikini.

Nice ass. Shake that thing, slut-baby. Turn around and let me see your tits.

His voice was a purr. He saw the woman as an object. Not sexual. Contemptuous.

A beach. He was at a beach. He sat in the shade at a table. A beer in his hand. He was casing . . . looking for the next one. The last one hadn't been satisfying. She'd been passive and dull. So strung-out on drugs that she hadn't even known her life was ticking away. He'd kept her at his place for a couple of days, hoping she'd snap out of it and make it more interesting. But she'd been a dishrag, a disappointment. He wanted a lively one this time. Someone who needed to be taught a lesson about appreciating and respecting what God had given her.

His mind latched onto a woman he'd met. She worked at a bar in Key West. He thought of cutting her. She had fake tits and he wanted to cut them open and watch the silicone spill out.

Trudy sucked in a breath and managed to jerk out of the twisted thoughts. She threw down the newspaper and ached to talk to Quintara. But Quintara was in Florida . . . in the same place where the man who'd just given her a glimpse of his depravity was planning his next murder.

Damn it! Trudy pushed aside the newspaper sections and buried her face in her hands. She couldn't hide in Tulsa. She had insight about the next victim that she couldn't keep to herself. And she had connected with the killer, so she couldn't ignore this! If she went to Florida, the connection would strengthen. Proximity always did that.

She grabbed the phone and jabbed in Quintara's cell phone number. She got the outgoing message.

"You've reached Quintara. I'm busy with other things right now. Be so kind as to leave your name and number and I'll return your call. If this is Trudy, we're staying at the Conch Motel in Key Largo, dear. I've reserved a room for you."

Trudy disconnected without leaving a message. Why bother. Obviously, Quintara was way, way ahead of her.

*

The RV was sweet. The dealer had called it a "25-foot Class A Holiday Rambler." Trudy decided to call it "Gypsy Spirit." She relaxed her grip on the steering wheel and settled more comfortably in the roomy seat, recalling her siblings' hot debate about the wisdom of such an investment. Sadie had said she was crazy to spend so much of her money on it, but Derek had seen her reasoning.

"Trudy will be traveling more now," her brother had explained to their older sister. "In the long-run, an RV will cost her a lot less than plane tickets and hotel bills."

She glanced over at the passenger seat. "I bought this thing mostly for you, I hope you know."

Mouse opened her big, gray eyes briefly, gave a little whine, and snuggled back into sleep. Trudy directed her attention back to the highway. She'd adopted the Chihuahua two years ago and she didn't like leaving her with her parents or siblings for weeks at a time.

"Good decision," she murmured, happy with herself. Forking over the dough for the RV was almost painless. Almost. She'd received the pawn shops' pay-out from her siblings a year ago and she only had about twenty thousand of it left in her bank account. Not good. And she was once again taking on work that would pay her nothing. Nada. A big goose egg. She rolled her eyes, questioning her decision for the hundredth time to strike out for Florida. But she would gain the experience of working with Levi, she thought. A shiver skipped through her at the prospect of spending time with him. Alone.

Her cell phone began playing "Stronger." Mouse's small body jerked all over as she emitted a single bark before going back to sleep. Trudy grappled for the phone inside the console and flipped it open.

"Yes?"

"Dear, where are you?"

"Oh, Quintara," she said on a long sigh. "I just crossed the state line into Florida. I'm going to drive a while longer before I pull into an RV park for the evening. Why? Has something happened?"

"No, no. I just wish you'd flown here like a normal person."

"Normal? Me? Us?"

Quintara's laughter floated through the phone. "So true. When will you finally arrive?"

"Tomorrow."

"And where will you park that thing?"

"I've reserved a space in Stirring Palms RV Park on Crescent Key."

"Crescent Key? Where in heavens is that?"

"It's near Duck Key."

"What Key? Did you say Fu—?"

"Duck," Trudy said, laughing. "It's close to Marathon. It sounds lovely. Full hookups, shady sites, and a fishing pier. *Trailer Life* gave it four stars."

"I think you're speaking Latin. Anyway, it's a language I don't quite understand. Levi connected with the latest victim and she revealed that she didn't know who killed her. He's also been in contact with Gregory."

"And who is Gregory?" Trudy asked, unable to keep the sarcasm from her voice.

"You know perfectly well that Gregory is Levi's spirit guide," Quintara said in a lightly scolding tone. "Just because you don't use a guide, doesn't mean that they don't exist."

Trudy made a face at the phone. Two of the psychics in the Roundtable also claimed to have spirit guides. They were constantly one-upping each other on whose spirit guide was the best, the oldest, the wisest. Blah. Blah. Blah. Trudy rolled her eyes. They were full of hooey. What was the point of having a guide? Shouldn't they be able to do the work on their own? Especially a hot shot like Levi Wolfe!

"This case must be special for Wolfe to take time away from his frequent appearances on all those talk shows and radio programs," Trudy said. "Especially that one with the former prosecutor that he's on every time you turn around . . . Sissy Franklin on Court TV." She couldn't keep the irritation from her voice. Whenever she'd seen Levi on that show, Sissy had seduced him with her eyes and fawned all over him. It was disgusting.

"Sure you're not just a teeny bit jealous?"

"Wh-what?" She sputtered wordlessly for a few seconds. "Of what? Making a spectacle of myself is the *last* thing I want!"

"He's sleeping with that Sissy Franklin woman. Oh, he won't admit it to me, but I know. You can tell by the way she looks at him when he's on her program. She's got it bad."

Trudy sighed. She didn't want to engage in more Levi Wolfe gossip. The Roundtable participants never tired of wondering who he was or wasn't sleeping with and if he would ever settle down with one woman. Everyone – including the two men in the group who happened to be gay – gushed over him and went on endlessly about how ripped he must be under his clothes.

"You still there, Trudy?" Quintara asked.

"What?" Trudy shook her head. "Yes . . . um, Levi Wolfe is just weird."

"Aren't we all? The thing is, he's accurate." Quintara waited a few beats to let that sink in. "He's one of the most gifted psychics around. You can't deny that. Showman, flashy, handsome as the devil, and probably a dynamo in bed, yes. But you can take what he tells you to the bank. He's the genuine article."

"And you're all hot and bothered over him," Trudy said with a wicked smile. "You've always wanted to get him in the sack."

"Well, of course. I may be white-haired under this red dye job, but I'm still breathing!"

Trudy laughed. "And I'm coming up to a toll booth."

"Dear, the more cases you work, the quicker you'll learn to trust yourself. Given time, you'll be as successful as Levi."

Trudy wagged her head back and forth, wanting to believe, but thinking that Quintara was overly kind. "Thanks for the pep talk. I really must hang up. I have to look for change."

"Very well. Call me tomorrow after you're settled in at Spinning Palms."

Trudy laughed. "*Stirring* Palms. Okay. Will do!" She closed the phone, dropped it back into the center console, and dug through the cup holder for quarters. She paid the toll and urged the RV back up to sixty-five miles an hour as her thoughts meandered to how she was going to keep her focus on the paranormal instead of on her womanly urges when she was in close proximity to Levi. But then again, he had women melting all over him, so he probably wouldn't give her a second glance.

*

Trudy stood on the broken concrete slab and looked at the scraggly, crooked palm tree that leaned drunkenly toward her. Her RV stood out like a cherry on a sundae in the nearly deserted Stirring Palms trailer park on Crescent Key. She was surprised that there were electricity and water hookups. Free cable TV was probably out of the question. "This place must have been hit by a hurricane since *Trailer Life* bestowed four stars on it."

"Nah. Changed hands is all."

Trudy jumped and pivoted around, one hand flying up to cover her heart. She hadn't heard the stocky, older man approach her. She recognized him from when she had checked in a little while ago. He ran a hand over his balding pate and grinned as he shifted his weight to his cane.

"Howdy. You okay?"

"Yes, I didn't know you were there."

"Oh." He shrugged and looked around. "Yeah, well, I bought this place two years ago and then my health took a downward spiral. I've been in the hospital more than out of it since I sunk my retirement money into this RV park."

"Oh, I'm sorry. I didn't mean . . ."

"You're not the first one to say that this place has gone to the dogs." He paused to eye Mouse before continuing. "I got it up for sale, but no takers yet. I forgot to give you the washroom key." He held out a silver key attached to a big, plastic palm tree.

"I probably won't need it, but——." She took the key from him.

Suddenly, the world grew fuzzy around the edges as if it was going out of focus on her. She glanced around quickly, jarred by the odd sensation. She'd never felt it before and . . . the vision of a woman filled her mind. The woman smiled and mouthed one word – Ethel. But there was no malevolence in the vision like there had been with all the others. No. Just the opposite. This woman was pure kindness. Almost angelic. The image faded away and Trudy realized that the man had moved closer to bend over and pet Mouse.

"Is your wife around?" Trudy asked, not even sure from where the question had originated.

"No, she died six years ago."

"Oh, I'm sorry." Trudy blinked her burning eyes, disturbed by what had just happened to her.

He chuckled warmly when Mouse licked his fingers, then straightened with some effort and obvious discomfort. "I don't know if I introduced myself when you checked in. The name's Yardley. Mike Yardley. So, you're staying at least a week? Are you on vacation?"

Trudy managed a smile, her mind still reeling. "No, I'm – I'm meeting some friends here in the Keys."

He squinted at her through his bifocals. "You're meeting friends here, but you're not on vacation?"

"That's right. My friends and I are working on a project together."

He tapped his bulbous nose and winked. "Sorry to be a buttinski. I've still got a reporter's nose."

"You were a reporter?" She tried to concentrate on the innocuous chatter, but she still felt shaken. She made a mental note to ask Quintara about the vision of Ethel and what it might mean.

"A coon's age ago I was a newshound. I was a college professor before I came here." He laughed at her widened eyes. "Yeah, that's right. I taught journalism at the University of Nebraska for twenty-five years. I was a goddamned institution! My son works for the Associated Press out of Miami. My late wife was a copy editor when I met her. Ethel was fresh out of college and the prettiest girl I'd ever laid eyes on."

Ethel! Trudy stared at him. Ethel? A mist seemed to float through her mind and then out of it. She blinked. The spirit was back, but this time she wasn't in Trudy's mind. She stood beside her husband.

Oh, no. Oh, no. Trudy shook her head, denying what her eyes were witnessing. Quintara had said that she might see spirits someday. Why was this happening? Didn't she have enough to deal with? Did she have to add ghosts to her repertoire?

"Ethel called me Coach," he said. "I taught her the ropes. We worked together on the copy desk." He glanced beside him, following Trudy's gaze. "Hey, you okay? What are you looking at?"

"Oh. Nothing." Her voice sounded high and girlish – not like her at all.

He drilled her with his gaze again. "Nothing, huh? The color has drained from your face and your lips are quivering. Something's got you upset."

"You'll think I'm crazy if I tell you." Trudy placed her hands to her cheeks. Yes, he was right. Her skin felt unusually cool.

"Try me."

"Well, you see, I'm psychic and I think I'm seeing . . . your . . ."

"Ethel?" He grinned. "You see Ethel?"

Trudy sucked in a breath, stunned for a moment by his insight. "I . . . how?"

"You look like you've seen a ghost and suddenly I can smell Ethel's perfume. Every now and again I get a whiff of it. *White Shoulders.* That's what she wore." He grinned, but there was a hint of mischief in his eyes.

Trudy focused on him, trying hard to ignore his wife. She suspected that Mike didn't believe a word she was saying and was just pulling her leg.

"So, you see dead people?"

"Not exactly. I think I see your wife, but . . ." She shrugged. "I don't usually commune with spirits."

He pinned her again with his cagey stare. "You're here sniffing around after that serial killer! I saw some psychic guy on the news last night. Said he was talking to the dead girls about who killed them. What a load of horseshit."

She didn't take offense to his opinion of her abilities. She was used to it. "That was Levi Wolfe."

"He's one of your friends, I guess."

"Well, we're . . . uh . . . acquaintances." She glanced at her wristwatch, mainly to look at something besides Ethel, who was mouthing words Trudy couldn't hear. She didn't know how to deal with it – with her.

"I won't keep you. Me and Ethel will be moseying along." He chuckled and shuffled off, shaking his head.

Ethel was beside him, walking through picnic tables and palm trees. She glanced over her ghostly shoulder once to wave at Trudy. Before she could stop herself, Trudy waved back.

"That pretty much makes it official," Trudy whispered to herself and Mouse. "I'm nuts."

Chapter Two

"Now that you're here, I know we will make tremendous progress," Quintara said, hugging Trudy close for a few moments. "Where's the dog?"

"Back at the RV park. I was afraid she'd be bored listening to us drone on about dead people and murderers." Her gaze moved of its own volition to the man standing quietly, unnervingly behind Quintara. His thick, black hair lay in tousled waves, and the lower half of his face was shadowed by tomorrow's whiskers. He wore perfectly tailored black trousers and a gun-metal gray shirt, the sleeves rolled up to his elbows. His blue eyes glinted at her, framed by sooty lashes. He towered above Quintara's five-foot-two frame.

Trudy's mouth went dry and she knew she was staring at him, but she couldn't tear her gaze away. It was a sin for a man to be that pretty, she thought with a twist of malice. His winged black brows brought more attention to the arresting blue color of his eyes. His nose was perfection, his jaw line was square and infinitely masculine, and his chin bore the barest hint of a cleft. He oozed sex appeal like it was part of his DNA.

"Hello, Tru," he said, his voice husky and deep.

Tru? She bristled a little. "Hello, Leviticus," she rejoined, arching a brow in an effort to appear on equal footing with him even as nerves erupted in her stomach.

He frowned for a second at the use of his Christian name, but then his lips slid into his trademark, slightly lopsided grin that made her stomach do a somersault.

"Children, be nice," Quintara said.

"I thought I was." Levi stepped away and motioned to the bar. "Care for a drink, Tru?"

Grudgingly, she decided she liked the way he said her shortened name, even though it made it sound as if he knew her well – which he didn't. "Is there juice?"

"Of course. Orange, Papaya, Pineapple—."

"Pineapple sounds good." Trudy sat beside Quintara on the rattan sofa. The living room faced a sliding glass door that gave a view of white sand, palm trees, and a slip of the ocean. The doors to the bedrooms that flanked the dining area were closed. Levi handed her a tall, frosted glass of juice. He smiled at her as his long fingers slid against hers on the slippery glass.

Trudy drew in a breath and told herself to chill out. He sat in the rattan chair to her right, crossed his legs, and flicked a white thread from his black trousers. He was the picture of calmness and she felt as if her chest was full of butterflies.

"Do you two have separate rooms?" Trudy asked, trying to drive past her nervousness and get Quintara's goat.

Levi smirked and glanced at a cackling Quintara.

"Levi's too busy seducing all the pretty television anchor women to want to share a room with a well-rounded, older enchantress like me. Isn't that right, Levi?"

"You're the one who was announcing your room number to every waiter and barkeep we ran into last night."

"And a lot of good it did me," Quintara said, flipping her string of red beads and puckering her lips in a pout. "But let's talk about murder." She glanced from him to Trudy. "Have you felt anything, dear? He's been talking to you, hasn't he?"

Trudy fidgeted on the sofa. "Yes, a little. I don't know . . ."

"You *do* know," Quintara said, her tone scolding, scalding. "You have felt him?"

"Yes." The word almost stuck in her throat. She glanced toward Levi and flinched when she saw that he was completely focused on her. Talk about intense! It was like she was being blasted by a laser beam. "He's thinking of murdering a barmaid that he knows. But I'm not entirely sure—." She caught the rapier-edged glance Levi and Quintara exchanged. "What?"

"You have the right person, dear." Quintara nodded to a folded newspaper on the coffee table. "A barkeep was murdered last night. He mutilated her."

"Oh, no!" Feeling as if she had been socked in the gut, Trudy reached for the newspaper and located the front page article easily. The details were sketchy. No clues. No leads. Used a serrated knife. Mutilation. Worked at the Gold Lagoon on Canal Street. A shiver ran through her and guilt brought hot tears to the back of her eyes. "I should have told you about the vision sooner."

"And what? We would have cased out every bar in Key West and warned the potential victims?" Quintara shrugged. "We must have more to go on than that, dear. We'll put our heads together and create a profile of this killer. We'll get to know him so well that we can predict his movements. Eventually, we'll be ahead of him and be able to identify him and help catch him."

Trudy turned toward Levi to find that he was still studying her, one brow slightly arched. "What have you been getting about this guy?" she asked.

He lifted one broad shoulder. "The victims haven't given me much to go on yet. They didn't see him coming and were knocked out. The woman before this one – Janie Fullbright was her name – was blindfolded, gagged, and when she came to, her wrists and ankles were tied. She was a heroine addict." He held out a hand for the newspaper. He wore a silver ring on his middle finger and the square black onyx in it glinted in the sunlight.

When he moved, Trudy caught a whiff of lemony lime. One cool customer, she thought. Everything about him was controlled, calculated almost. But there was an undercurrent of turmoil just below his polished surface. She'd always felt it and that intrigued her about him – more than his abilities or his reputation as a womanizer.

"Janie Fullbright had burn marks, rope burns, cigarette burns. She was tortured before her throat was slit. Nothing sexual with any of them, other than he sometimes ejaculates on them. The latest woman was Shelly Farmer. The other two – Barbie Allen and Debra Williams – were strangled and then stabbed in the heart over and over again. They were knocked out cold from behind."

"He doesn't want them to look at him while he's killing them?"

"So far," Levi confirmed, his gaze moving from her hair down to her breasts and then back up.

Trudy forced herself to concentrate on the case and not the shape of his mouth. She noticed that he called the victims by their names, making it more personal. It was oddly touching and admirable since Trudy always tried to view these things from a distance. It seemed safer and less painful. She became personally involved with the survivors, but she needed a buffer between her and the murderers and their victims.

She realized that Levi was still studying her, one brow arched. Feeling as if she was under a microscope, she cleared her throat again and wondered if this was a new tic reserved for when she was around Levi Wolfe. "Is it the same killer then?" she asked him.

"The police think so."

"It has to be the same person. Two serial killers in Key West?" Quintara cut in, frowning. "Not likely. I'm surprised even one could elude police for so long. You can't kick a cat there without someone seeing you and reporting it."

"I think he knew the last victim," Trudy said. "So, had he met the other women before, too? Or did he just stalk them and then pounce?"

"You tell us." Levi tented his fingers and his navy blue eyes issued her a challenge. "Can you read him now?"

She stiffened her back and looked away from him. "I don't work like that. I'm not a light switch."

"Remember our lessons?" Quintara placed a hand over hers. "How we gathered our energy and sent it out like feelers?"

"Yes, but I didn't have success with that."

"You were improving. The images were coming to you when you concentrated."

Trudy reached for her drink and downed it in a few large gulps. She felt like a woman caught in the glare of the desert sun and she was blazingly aware of Levi watching her. "I don't . . . I'm not comfortable working in front of an audience."

"Audience?" Quintara repeated, clearly perplexed.

"She means me, I suppose." Levi's smile was pure indulgence. "You don't approve of how I conduct my business. You don't like that I appear on television and that I'm a guest on radio programs."

"No, I simply—."

"Trudy, let's not play games with each other. Not that kind of game, anyway."

Her gaze bounced to his and the intensity radiating from him told her that he could read her like a book, damn him.

"What I meant was that I don't work well with people staring at me and waiting for me to do something like I'm performing a magic act." She hated that her voice held a slight tremor. "Why don't you ask *Gregory* if he can't wriggle the name of the killer out of the last victim since she knew him?"

He narrowed his eyes. "That's not how it works between us."

The mention of his spirit guide brought to mind the spirit she had seen earlier that day.

"Is something wrong?" Quintara asked, leaning toward Trudy. "Your aura is disturbed."

"My aura?" Trudy shook her head. "I hate it when my aura rats me out." She paused and the memory of Ethel strengthened in her mind, refusing to be dismissed. "I saw someone at the RV park earlier."

"Who, dear?"

"A ghost." Trudy glanced toward Levi. He was still watching her as if he found her fascinating. "The man who owns the RV park . . . well, it was his wife's spirit. I think Ethel was trying to say something to me."

"What?" Quintara perched on the edge of the cushion, her brown eyes glowing with embers of excitement.

"I couldn't hear her. But her husband? He could smell Ethel's perfume."

"Interesting," Levi said, pursing his lips for a moment. "Could you *sense* what she was trying to convey to you?"

"No. I was so weirded out by it that I was just trying not to scream in front of the old guy."

"I knew this would happen to you," Quintara said, sitting back with a sigh of utter satisfaction. "I told you, didn't I? Your powers are great, Trudy. You must simply learn to trust them." She looked at Levi. "It's what we were talking about earlier!"

"You've been talking about me?" Trudy asked, instantly on guard.

"I was telling Levi that you might be his match psychically if you keep coming to the Roundtable and practice what I'm preaching."

"Or if she simply dives in and gets completely wet instead of dipping her toe in the water over and over again," Levi said.

Trudy looked from him to Quintara, miffed to be talked about as if she had disappeared, but also interested. The room suddenly felt charged in the standoff that transpired between them. It was like watching a silent movie with only the performers' faces to glean information from and understand what was going on. Levi frowned at Quintara and she tipped her nose in the air in a show of haughtiness. Trudy looked from one to the other. What had been going on before she'd arrived? Obviously, they'd been quarreling or, at the very least, disagreeing about something that had to do with her.

"The next time you see Ethel, don't try to hear with your ears," Levi said, dragging his gaze from Quintara to confront Trudy again. "Listen with your mind."

Trudy bristled at his high-handedness. She could never take his criticism well. Levi always seemed to be speaking to her from his ivory tower in the clouds. He had a way of barking orders that grated on her. She had a feeling that he was used to being obeyed.

"Listen with your mind," Quintara repeated. "Good advice."

"I might have to scare up a spirit guide to translate. Does Gregory have any pals who are out of work?"

Levi accepted her quip with a quick scowl before he directed his attention to the patio doors that gave a view of the restless ocean. Trudy sensed restlessness in him, as well, and she figured he was reining in his patience. It was easy to see that he didn't care much for her sassy mouth. Seconds ticked by with only the faint sounds of pounding waves and screaming gulls to fill the silence. Trudy glanced toward Quintara, who shook her head in a scolding gesture. Feeling justly chastised, Trudy rolled her eyes and drew in a breath to launch an apology when Levi spoke up.

"Gregory says that Ethel showed herself to you out of concern. Beyond that, he can't help you." Levi ran a hand down his face and sat straighter in the chair. "So, Trudy, let's get something straight." He pinned her with his steady, don't-you-dare-look-away-from-me gaze. "If we're going to enter into a partnership, we need to respect how we each work and what we believe. You think I'm a showman and that's fine." He shrugged. "I am and I make no apologies for it. I've learned to work with what I have, but that doesn't cancel out my innate talents. Any more than your lack of faith in yourself and your penchant for sarcasm diminishes yours."

She blinked, feeling as if she were emerging from a shouting match, although no one had been shouting and only one person had been talking. So, why did she feel drained? She leaned away from him, needing distance, and looked to Quintara for help.

"Now that the air has been cleared, we can get to the real work ahead of us," Quintara said, smiling with satisfaction. "We have been given precious gifts that should be used for the betterment of the world."

Trudy shook her head, amused by Quintara's grandiose pronouncement. Her bright spirit was a beacon to troubled, confused souls. Quintara had been a lighthouse, guiding Trudy through choppy, dark dreams to calmer seas. She had shown her how to steer her own course, to avoid obstacles instead of crashing into them to end up bruised and broken. Now if she could only show her how to navigate around Leviticus Wolfe!

"Zelda," Levi said, out of the blue.

"Who's that?" Quintara asked.

"Gregory says that Zelda visited with the last victim at the bar earlier that evening. A customer, I think, but someone she liked. They laughed together. They were new friends."

"Zelda." Trudy let the name rest in her mind and it did seem familiar, although also strangely distant. "We should go to that bar tonight. People there might know Zelda and we can talk to her. Do you think it will be open?"

Levi nodded. "It's not a crime scene. I imagine it will be business as usual. You're old enough to drink, aren't you?"

Trudy scoffed at him. "Your false flattery is wasted on me, Wolfe. I'm twenty-seven and you damn well know it."

Quintara laughed. "We should all go tonight. It will give us a chance to work on our sense memories."

Trudy eyed her, wondering when she'd developed sense memory. As far as she knew, Quintara professed to read minds, auras, and palms and occasionally see spirits, but that was it. Sense memory was specialized, giving the medium the ability to experience trauma or other extreme emotions that happened in a place. She glanced at Levi. If anyone in the room had the gift of sense memory, it was him. He smiled indulgently at Quintara as if he also thought she had claimed something that was beyond her capabilities.

"What sense memories?" Trudy asked, shrugging. "She wasn't killed at that bar."

"That's right," Quintara allowed, her lips curving into a confident smile. "But her ending began there."

*

The bar was a bust. Trudy couldn't feel anything except claustrophobic. She tried to catch Quintara's eye, but the older woman was fascinated with something the cute bartender was saying. Levi was nowhere in sight. The last time she'd seen him he had been heading for the restrooms at the back of the bar.

Feeling smothered in the crush of sun-kissed flesh and beer breath, Trudy elbowed her way outside. She was met with more people, some sitting on car hoods and others straddling motorcycles, laughing too loudly at bad pick-up lines. Stepping around a braying bottle blond and a couple of guys in short-shorts and tank tops, Trudy made her way across the parking lot. The soles of her sandals crunched loudly on the crushed sea shells.

Near the street, she leaned against a light post and gathered clean air into her lungs. A breeze, redolent with salt and sea, flirted with the hem of her skirt and shimmied up her bare legs. A sinus headache bloomed behind her right eye and she didn't know whether to blame the stuffy bar or the stuffier Levi Wolfe. The man could be so dark and domineering! Did he have a sense of humor? Did he ever laugh? Jeez! Yeah, they were chasing a serial killer, but Levi's intensity made it all the more tedious. Still, she couldn't imagine Quintara being so hot for him if he didn't have a lighter side. Quintara loved a good laugh and she could be bawdy as hell.

Cars whizzed by and one slowed to a crawl. A grinning college boy leaned out of the passenger window and motioned for her to come closer.

"Hey, babe, wanna party?"

Trudy turned her back on them. The car's tires squealed on the pavement, almost drowning out the shouted, "Fuck you, bitch!"

She flinched and shot them the finger. Suddenly, she felt deflated and weary. She had expected to glean something from the bar and its customers. She had hoped she would channel someone or even zero in on the mysterious Zelda. But all she had felt was sweaty and edgy.

Crowded places were like that for her, even back when she was a kid. She had memories of her mind going fuzzy when she'd tagged along with her mother and sister to buy school clothes or Christmas gifts. Sensory overload. That's what it was, she thought. Like being caught in a rainstorm of feelings, thoughts, and visions.

"Hey, don't be that way, sugar!" a man shouted from behind her. Trudy turned to see a tattooed guy stomping across the parking lot, the silver studs on his boots winking back at the street lights. He headed toward a group of people. "Sugar! Come back here."

Trudy turned to face the street again, tired of the bar scene.

"Zelda!"

She spun back around, her breath whistling down her throat. A pickup truck zipped past her — a dark blur, so close that Trudy stepped back just to be on the safe side. She looked for Zelda, but

21

only the man stood the middle of the parking lot, looking utterly defeated as he stared toward the street. He snatched off his cowboy hat and threw it to the ground in a fit of juvenile rage.

Trudy whirled back around, realizing that Zelda must have been in that speeding truck. "Crap!" She walked toward the man, who was fitting his hat back onto his floppy, blond hair. Cussing under his breath, he glared at Trudy when she stopped a few feet from him.

"I know you, darlin'?" His drawl came straight out of Dallas.

"No, but I heard you calling after Zelda."

"Yeah. So?" He had a ruddy complexion, but he wasn't that old. In his 20s, probably.

"How well do you know her?"

"What's it to you?"

Trudy shrugged. "I came here to talk to her, but I just missed her. Do you know where she was headed?"

"Hell if I know." He grinned, showing off dingy teeth.

"You think she's going home?"

"Do you know where she lives?" he asked, hopefully.

"You don't?" Trudy countered.

The hope blinked out of his expression. "Hey, don't jerk with me."

"What kind of truck was she driving?" She had to get some kind of useful information from him!

"I don't know and I don't rightly care."

"I need to talk to her."

"Then give chase, sugar." He extended a hand to the street. "She's as free as the breeze. Good luck to ya." Reeling about, stumbling, righting himself, walking sideways, stopping, stumbling, and then giving a lurch in the direction of the bar, he set off, ready for another round. This time without Zelda.

The bar door opened and Levi filled the threshold. He held out a hand to steady the listing cowboy. The minute his fingers touched the man's arm, his expression froze and his intense gaze locked like a laser onto the cowboy's face. Trudy didn't know if the cowboy could feel the magnetism of Levi's focused attention, but she sure could.

"You know Zelda," Levi stated. "Where did you meet her? How long have you known her?"

"Whoa, whoa up there! What's with all the interest in Zelda?" The cowboy looked over his shoulder at Trudy. "Y'all ain't her friends. Does she owe you money or somethin'?"

"We need to talk to her. It's a family emergency," Levi said, glancing toward Trudy.

"Zat right?" The cowboy didn't look convinced. "She peeled outta here and she's long gone." He placed his shoulder against Levi's to shove him aside, but couldn't budge him. The cowboy grunted and tried again to forcibly move Levi and failed a second time.

Arching a sardonic brow, Levi butted him with his shoulder, sending the man stumbling back a step or two so that he could cross over the threshold and allow the cowboy to enter the bar again. Trudy smiled to herself. Levi Wolfe was no pushover, she thought. Obviously, the Roundtable folks were right about the muscular physique under his clothes.

Levi sent Trudy a speaking glare. "Did you get a look at her?"

Trudy drew in a shaky breath, feeling like an underachiever. "No, but she was in a dark pickup truck."

"Which way did she turn?"

"She hung a right."

Levi rested his hands on his hips, his long fingers splayed across the dark material of his trousers, and surveyed the parking lot. He shrugged and then reached out one hand to squeeze her shoulder. "Don't sweat it. It's been a long night. I'll get Quintara."

Trudy trudged to the car and settled into the backseat. Within a few minutes, Levi and Quintara joined her. Levi steered the car out of the parking lot and turned right.

"How disappointing," Quintara said, twisting around to look at Trudy. "You didn't see her profile or anything?"

"No. It was a blur. She was driving like a bat outta hell."

"Let's look for a dark pickup," Quintara suggested.

"Yes, there shouldn't be more than a couple of hundred around here," Levi noted.

Trudy turned her face into the shadows so that Quintara wouldn't see her grin at Levi's droll observance. He *did* have a sense of humor, she thought. Dry and brusque, but intact!

They toured the streets for half an hour seeing numerous dark pickups, but with no results. Trudy sat forward, touching her fingertips to Levi's shoulder. "Let's call it a night."

"Fine with me. We should work on a profile of the killer in the morning and then we'll discuss our next step."

She met his gaze in the rearview mirror. "What did you sense when you touched that guy at the bar?"

"Sense?" His dark brows knitted together. "Oh, I see. I just knew he'd been with a woman named Zelda."

"But no vision of her?"

"No, just the name."

"Too bad."

"Sorry to disappoint you."

She felt him still looking at her in the rearview mirror. Wanting to tell him to keep his eyes on the road, she quelled the urge. "It's just that Quintara said that you went to Arthur Findley College in England to study this stuff. I figured you must be way ahead of the rest of us amateurs."

"Oh, I *am* way ahead of the people in the Roundtable." He glanced at Quintara and they shared a smirk.

He's so arrogant, Trudy thought. In the flash of the street lights, she caught sight of Quintara's rapt expression as she looked at Levi. Enthralled, Trudy thought. His most devoted fan. And she knows him. Quintara knows him well. Envy speared her and she caught her breath, stunned by the unexpected feeling. She shook off the momentary lapse in good sense.

"Do you have control over your — what do you call him — your guide?" Trudy asked, hearing the skepticism in her tone and feeling instantly contrite. She shouldn't be a Doubting Thomasina because she knew how hurtful that could be, but it was so difficult to take some of the hocus pocus seriously. She kept thinking of Billy and Jerrod, the guys in the Roundtable and all their eye-rolling and chanting as they summoned their guides. She glanced at the rearview mirror. Levi's expressive eyes glittered darkly. She couldn't see his mouth, but she knew he was frowning.

"I don't control Gregory, no. Why does it bother you so much that I occasionally consult a spirit guide?"

She looked away from him, hiding her face in the shadows again. "I don't know."

"Tell us, dear," Quintara insisted. "You *do* know why you think guides are hogwash, so please enlighten us."

Trudy worried her lower lip between her teeth and stalled for a few seconds, wishing Quintara would quit putting her on the spot. "I don't understand the concept, that's all. From what I've seen in the Roundtable . . ." She shrugged, not wanting to besmirch Quintara's other fledglings.

Levi drove into the parking lot and whipped into a space next to Trudy's car. He killed the motor. "Come inside for a little bit, Trudy." His voice was tight, almost biting.

Trudy was out of the car in the span of a few seconds. She slammed the car door and turned to make a getaway. "No, thanks. I'll call it a night and——." His firm grasp on her elbow cut off the sentence.

"Come inside," he said in a tone that brooked no argument. "I won't keep you long." Levi didn't let go of her, but guided her along the sidewalk to the suite he shared with Quintara.

Stunned to be manhandled by him, Trudy glanced at Quintara and widened her eyes in an appeal. Quintara pursed her lips to keep from grinning and shook her head at Trudy.

Levi fished his key card from his back trouser pocket and unlocked the door. Stepping back, he waited for Quintara and Trudy to go in first. Trudy wrenched her elbow free of his slackened grasp and, as she passed by him, her arm brushed against his chest. He was solid. He must work out, she thought. And, lord, he smelled delicious! What aftershave *was* that?

A lamp had been left on and the air-conditioner hummed. Trudy went farther inside and dropped her purse on the coffee table. Turning around, she caught Levi giving Quintara a conspiratorial smile.

"I'd like to talk to Trudy alone. Do you mind?"

"No, not at all." Quintara's eyes sparkled with mischief and she gave a little two-fingered salute as she glided toward her bedroom. "I planned on retiring with a good book anyway. See you tomorrow, children." She closed the bedroom door behind her.

Feeling as if she'd been trapped, Trudy faced Levi. "Is there a problem?"

He dipped his head a little to seek her gaze. "You seem to have a problem with me."

She huffed out a breath of exasperation and reached for her purse. "I'm glad we had this talk."

"Wait." He grabbed her purse by the strap and pulled her closer to him with it. "Sit down and have a glass of wine or a Diet Dr. Pepper with me."

"Really?" She gave him a cagey look. "You have Diet Dr. Pepper?"

His smile lit up his face, showing off perfect, white teeth. "I do. Quintara is addicted to it."

With that megawatt smile turned on her, Trudy felt her knees wobble. He obviously knew she shared that addiction with Quintara. What else did he know about her? "Okay. You successfully bribed me."

"That was easy."

"I *can* be easy," she allowed, then couldn't resist adding, "Spread the word."

He laughed, a deep, husky sound that made her pulses throb. *Whoa, girl!* But she couldn't help thinking that the Roundtable members would be so *completely* jealous of her right now.

Reaching into the mini-fridge, he grabbed a can of soda, popped the tab, and poured the dark caramel beverage into two glasses of ice. He handed one to her and sat down on the sofa before he took a sip of his. "Good stuff," he said, smiling again.

"Hits the spot," she agreed, but trepidation trembled in the corners of her mind. What was he up to? What did he want?

"I want you to feel that you can discuss things with me," he said. Patting the cushion next to him, he nodded his head, gesturing for her to join him. "Sit."

She looked at him, sharply. "Did you just read my mind?"

"No." His lop-sided grin was back in place. "I don't need to. Anyone with eyes and ears can tell that you're jittery and on guard around me. Sit."

She shook her head. "I'm jittery because we're on the trail of a serial killer."

"It's more than that." He arched a brow and his all-seeing, all-knowing gaze drifted over her, leaving flesh bumps in its wake. "You're attracted to me."

She had taken a sip of the cola and almost spit it out. "Wh-what?" Her eyes watered and she swallowed hard.

"And I'm attracted to you."

"You're attracted to me," she repeated because she didn't think she could have possibly heard him right. "I thought you wanted to work with me.'

"That, too." Sighing, he stood up and set the glass on the table. He shoved his hands into his trouser pockets and smiled. The air between them seemed to sizzle.

26

Trudy drew in a deep breath, feeling like she was at the wheel of a car that had no brakes and it was downhill all the way. "Why me?" she asked, her voice emerging breathy.

"Why what? Why am I attracted to you or why do I want to work with you?"

"Work," she said, trying to keep the car from going over a cliff.

"I can teach you things and you can teach me things. Simple."

She shook her head. Nothing about him was simple. Feeling as if she was about to crash and burn, she decided she needed to head for the RV park. Moving a little away from him, she placed her glass on the table next to his.

"Trudy, I contact the deceased and you are contacted by the living. That can work in our favor." He angled closer to her and dragged his index finger down her arm from her shoulder to the back of her hand. "I've often thought that you and I might make a great team because we come at problems from different perspectives, but our abilities can sync with each other."

She tried valiantly to concentrate on what he was saying and not on why and where he was touching her. "You've *often* thought that?" she scoffed. Yeah, she thought. Get real.

"I have."

His simple confession made her heartbeats slow and then pop into overdrive. She rubbed her hand up and down her arm, trying to erase the shadow of his touch. She was suddenly hyper aware of him and the tension curling through her, making her skin heat and her senses quiver. She glanced at him and saw him smile as if he knew exactly what she was feeling. "I have to go."

"Why?"

Trudy shrugged and shook her head, unable to tell him the truth. That she'd thought of him often, too. That he made her wet between her thighs.

He regarded her and waited. His shirt hung slightly open at the neck and she could see dark hair curling on his chest. He was lean and lithe – and predatory.

His smile became knowing as if sensed – or read – her thoughts again. "Do you know how special you are?" he asked, his voice dipping to almost a growl that made her toes curl. "Do you have any idea how sexy you are?" He lifted his hand and his fingers floated through the side of her hair. "There's something about you, Trudy. I felt it the moment I touched—."

He whirled around to stare at the sliding glass door at the same moment she felt the light change in the room and alarms blared inside her head. In two long strides, Levi was at the glass door. He slid it back and stepped out onto the patio. Trudy was right behind him. He stopped suddenly and she stumbled into him, her breasts flattening against his back. He reached one hand behind him, his long fingers curving around her hip to steady her, his palm pressing warmly against her.

"Someone was out here," she whispered, tipping up her chin to speak close to his ear. "Someone was watching us!" She was blazingly aware of his hand on her butt.

"Yes, he was listening to us," Levi said. "But he's gone. He must have jumped over the wall and headed for the beach."

"I got the sense it was a man, too . . . I think."

His fingers caressed her hip before falling away. Levi turned to face her.

"Stay here tonight."

"H-here?" She shook her head. "I need to get back to the RV."

"I'll go with you."

"Go with me?" she parroted as her pulses drummed in her ears. "No. I'll be fine."

He cupped her elbows in his palms and leaned close until his mouth was next to her ear. "You must know that I want you, Tru. If there had been any way I could have cleared the room at the Roundtable sessions, I would have fucked you right then and there." His lips grazed the curve of her ear and then he bit her lobe gently.

Trudy jerked away from him and felt her eyes grow wide. She blinked. Had she just heard him right? Had he *actually* just said that? His roguish grin told her that she could trust her hearing.

"Of all the arrogant pricks——." But the rest of her retort was smothered by his mouth on hers. He took advantage of her parted lips and his tongue slipped right in as if it belonged there. He growled into her mouth and the sound set fire to her resistance.

He pulled her up against him and ran his hands down her back to cup her backside before sweeping up again to curve around her neck. His mouth lifted and then took hers again, his tongue moving deeper inside to stroke and solicit a sound that was part whimper and part moan from her.

She reached up and hung her fingers on his solid biceps. He was heat and hard and everything carnal and she was helpless to resist him. She had known that if he ever touched her, ever kissed her, she'd melt like candle wax.

"Stay here," he murmured against her mouth. "In my room. In my bed."

She shook her head and his lips traveled silkily from her mouth to her neck. The tip of his tongue darted out to moisten her skin and she closed her eyes and wondered how such a small thing could make her want to tear his clothes off.

"Okay, then I'll drive you back to your place and your bed," he said against her neck.

"No."

He looked at her and his eyes were smoky blue. "Where then?"

Trudy managed a shaky laugh and wiggled to get some distance between their bodies. "I'm not sleeping with you tonight."

"Why not?"

"Why not?" she repeated, incredulous. "Because I came here to *work* with you. That's it. I'm not your booty call."

He looked at her with a mixture of amusement and pity. "You can delay this for a night or two, but understand that it's inevitable."

"What's inevitable?"

He kissed her mouth again, softly, quickly. "That you're going to feel like a wildcat under me and you're going to purr my name when I make you come."

She pressed her hands against his chest and shoved him away from her. She'd never in her life had a man speak to her with such . . . such . . . words! "I'm afraid you have me confused with one of your slobbering fans. I'm a professional medium just like you."

"I know that."

"Then show some respect." She ran her hands down the front of her blouse and tried to gather her senses, but she also winced at herself for sounding like a nun who had just had her ass pinched.

He chuckled. "I'll walk you to your car."

"No need."

"Get your purse. I'm walking with you."

Trudy whirled away from him. It was better to just do as he said than argue with him. The main thing was to get away from him.

He went outside with her to where she'd left her car – a Ford Fiesta she towed behind the RV – and opened the door for her. Before he shut it, he leaned down and waited for her to turn her gaze to his.

"I'll see you tomorrow." His face was lit by the blue lights of the dashboard. His eyes smoldered. "Think about what I said. It's inevitable. It's kismet."

Trudy grabbed the door handle and yanked it closed. Pulling out of the parking lot, she looked in the side mirror to see that he was still standing where she'd left him.

A shiver of pleasure scampered through her. Jesus! Was he serious? Did he think all he had to do was tell her he wanted her and she would start stripping off her clothes? Did other women do that around him?

Yeah, they probably did. And . . . she probably would, too. Eventually. Inevitably.

He's a hot tamale, she thought with a trembling smile, and she'd always had a taste for anything spicy.

Chapter Three

Sitting at the picnic table beside her RV, Trudy sipped a cup of coffee and waited for Mouse to complete her morning ritual. Seagulls circled and shrilled overhead and palms rustled in the cool, fragrant breeze. It was as close to Paradise as one could get without crossing over.

A big, black Dodge truck ruined the idyllic peace, barreling into the RV park, its tires grinding to a halt in front of Mike Yardley's trailer. A man dressed in jeans and a Hawaiian print shirt, looking sort of like Tom Selleck back in his Magnum, P.I. days, sans the mustache, opened the door and went inside.

Mouse barked, drawing Trudy's attention. She studied her ferocious watch dog. "Better late than never, I guess. Thanks for the warning." Mouse tilted her head and looked past Trudy. She barked again.

Twisting around, Trudy froze. Ethel the friendly ghost stood behind her. Ethel waved. Trudy faced front and gulped down the rest of her coffee before slowly turning back around. Ethel was gone. Trudy relaxed, but tensed when she saw the apparition had simply moved to stand near Mike's trailer. She waved to Trudy again.

Levi's advice floated back to her, stiffening her resolve to see what this ghostly vision wanted from her.

"What's with the waving?" Trudy asked.

Ethel's lips moved. No sound except for noisy seagulls overhead. At least none that Trudy's ears could pick up. She glanced at Mouse, but the dog was paying no attention to the transparent intruder. Gathering her courage, Trudy closed her eyes and concentrated on mentally communicating. She sent her energy out like an arrow to Ethel. *Speak to my mind. What do you want?*

Mouse barked and Trudy opened her eyes. The guy in the Hawaiian print shirt and Mike Yardley were striding toward her. Ethel was gone.

"Good morning," Mike said, smiling and leaning on his cane. "I saw you out here and I wanted to introduce you to my son. Jay, this is Trudy."

Jay held out his hand. He was shorter than Tom Selleck, only about five feet nine. His grip was warm and strong. Smiling, he showed perfect teeth and deep dimples. Just like Selleck! Oh, and come to think of it, Ethel had dimples, too, Trudy noted.

"Nice to meet you. My dad says you're here about that serial killer. That makes two of us."

She remembered that he worked for the AP news service. "You're covering it?" The morning sun tangled in the waves of his brown hair and sparkled in his hazel eyes. He was very attractive. Not the darkly dangerous good looks of Levi Wolfe, but a friendlier, boyish attractiveness.

"Among other news, yes. Do you have any good tips for me? Have you made any progress yet?"

"No, sorry. I just arrived yesterday."

"Are you working with law enforcement?"

"We're cooperating with the police, but they didn't invite us here."

"But you've worked with local police forces before?"

"A few times before." She picked up Mouse, who was barking and growling. "Hush now." She kissed the dog's apple-sized head. "I'd better get going. I'm meeting friends for breakfast."

"It's her psychic friends," Mike said, giving her a wink. "Hope you have a good fishing trip and hook the big one." He slapped Jay on the back. "Then you can give the scoop to my son."

"If only it was that easy," Jay said with a wry laugh. "If I can help in any way, give me a shout." He pulled a business card out of his shirt pocket and handed it to her. "That has my Miami office number on it and my cell phone." He nodded toward Mike's trailer. "Come on, Coach. You promised to make pancakes and sausage for me."

"Okay, let's go." Mike ambled off, following his son, but he paused to look back at Trudy. "Tell Ethel hi for me if you see her again." Chuckling, he moved on.

Trudy smiled sarcastically at his departing figure, not finding it amusing that she could see his dead wife. It complicated things that were complicated enough already. She nuzzled Mouse's head and received a doggy kiss from her.

"What do you think, Mousey? Do you think Jay is cute?" Trudy looked toward Mike's trailer again and sighed. Ethel was walking through picnic tables and trees, following her husband and son.

*

"Was she hit by a car?"

"Yes!" The woman's voice crackled across the phone line. "Yes, it was a hit-and-run and the police said—."

"No, don't tell me anything else." Levi squeezed his eyes more tightly shut and sank deeper into the scene. "It was a red Jeep Wrangler with a California plate."

"California? We live in Omaha."

"I'm asking your aunt if she saw the driver. She didn't see the license plate. She just knew about it because she knows who's driving."

"She knew him?"

"Not him." Levi took in a deep breath and the dead woman's image blazed in his mind. She was middle-aged, shoulder-length brown hair, wearing a long, green skirt and a brown sweater. She said one word to him. "Linda? It starts with an L."

"Huh?"

"Do you know a young woman named Linda . . . or Lynn? Maybe Lynnie?"

"Well, yeah. Lindey is my niece."

"She has something to do with this." The scene in his head faded and Levi opened his eyes to find Quintara sitting across from him at the table. She smiled like a proud parent. "She might have been driving."

"She has a Jeep," the woman's voice on the phone sounded weaker, full of uncertainty.

"Talk to her. She probably needs to unburden herself."

"Oh, my."

"Good luck with that," another voice cut in. "We have to wrap this up, folks. You've been listening to the amazing Levi Wolfe. It's been great having you visit us today on the Tony and Lana Madhouse Mash here on Seattle's top radio station."

"It's been a pleasure, Tony," Levi said.

"We'll try to get Levi back here soon, folks. I know we have a lot of calls on hold. Better luck next time. Hey now, here comes Jake with a traffic report. How's it hanging out there, Jake?"

There was a series of clicks on the phone. "Hi, Levi. It's Lana. That was great. The phone lines sizzled, man."

"Good."

"When can we get you back?"

"I'm up to my eyeballs in work right now, Lana. I'll have my people give you a call in a couple of weeks to get on the schedule again."

"Okay, but make it sooner than later. And stop by here in person next time you're in town." Her voice became a little breathless. "I, for one, would love to see you."

"Thanks. Goodbye, Lana." Levi touched a button on the cell phone to end the call. He ran a hand down his face. "That's never easy."

"Sounds like Lana has the hots for you."

He stood up and stretched. "You say that about every female who sets eyes on me."

"And am I ever wrong?"

He shook his head at her, giving her a chastising frown. "I'll be back in a minute."

Striding to the bedroom, he headed for the bathroom, closed the door, and ran water into the basin. He splashed his face, trying to wash the images from his mind. Every time he did a radio or television show and he had to reach out to one after another victim, the pictures and scenes that came to him clung like spider webs in his mind. It would take a few minutes to clear them out. He felt drained, limp.

Bracing his hands on either side of the basin, he stared at his reflection in the mirror, but he didn't see his own face – he saw Trudy Tucker's. Ever since he'd met her a little more than a year ago during one of his visits to the Psychic Roundtable, he'd been drawn to her – couldn't get her out of his mind. He rarely attended the biweekly meetings because he didn't live in Tulsa. He only visited Quintara there, and when he did, he would drop in on her Roundtable just to see how her students were progressing. Most of the people in the group were moderately, even sporadically, gifted. Trudy was different.

She brimmed with possibilities. He'd wanted her the minute he'd met her. Later, the idea had struck him that they might make a damn good investigative team. The more he'd thought about it – and about her – the more excited he'd become. But Quintara had insisted that Trudy wasn't ready. Respecting Quintara's knack for bringing along psychics gently and successfully, he'd backed off and waited – a whole, damn year.

Closing his eyes, he wallowed in his disappointment at not talking her into bed last night. What was the problem? She wasn't a prude and he knew she was attracted to him, so what the hell was the hang up?

"Levi!" Quintara called to him. "Trudy's here!"

He swallowed the knot of tension in his throat, toweled off his face, and went to join Quintara and Trudy in the living room. His gaze went instantly to Trudy and held on for a few seconds before she looked away. Flags of pink color unfurled in her cheeks. She wasn't the first woman who'd blushed under his scrutiny, but it was the first time he'd enjoyed it so much. Everything about her fascinated him. The shape of her body, slim and curvy, and that way she had of glancing at him and then tipping up her chin as if she were squaring off against him.

Bring it, baby. He smiled to himself, looking her over and guessing that she was about one-hundred-and-thirty pounds of feisty sexiness.

"Trudy says it would be more convenient if we relocated to one of the middle Keys in the chain," Quintara said. "Driving back and forth from Key Largo to Key West wastes a lot of time."

"She's right." He checked out Trudy's shapely legs, exposed by her white shorts. He dragged his hungry eyes away from her delectable body. "Good morning, Tru."

"'Morning, Leviticus."

He glanced at her. Did she *really* want to go a round with him? Sounded like fun, he thought, sending her a grin. "You don't want me to call you Tru?"

She shrugged. "It's okay, I guess."

"It seems to bother you."

"Why would you think that?"

Her gaze flicked to his and she did that chin jutting thing that made his cock stiffen. "Because that's the second time you've snarled 'Leviticus' at me."

She bobbed her shoulders again. "It's your name, isn't it?"

He smirked at her. "Call me Levi."

Her olive green eyes warred briefly with his. "Whatever, Wolfe," she said, snappishly.

He shrugged. "You know, I have a better use for that smart mouth of yours—."

"Trudy says the RV park she's in now has a couple of cottages for rent," Quintara spoke up, calling a truce for them. "It's in the Middle Keys. But a cottage? That doesn't sound like maid service or a nice bar and restaurant to me."

"You're right," Trudy agreed, turning away from him. "But it's quiet and bars and restaurants are only minutes away. As for maid service, I won't tell anyone if you don't make your bed every morning."

"It's an option, I suppose," Quintara said, obviously not impressed. "We'll look around and see what we can find. This is a lovely place and the service is good, but we should consolidate."

"So far the psycho's hitting the Key West area, so you do need to be closer to that action," Trudy noted.

"Do you want a cup of coffee and a croissant?" Levi asked.

"We ordered a breakfast tray earlier," Quintara said. "Help yourself to the leftovers." She waved a hand toward the dining area.

Levi went to the table and poured coffee from the carafe into a cup. "There's also fruit."

"Yum!" Trudy stood beside him, plucked a strawberry from the bowl of fruit, and popped it into her mouth.

He watched her savor that berry, much the same way he wanted to savor her mouth again. Slowly, succulently. He could almost taste her and it was almost making him crazy.

"Do you have any half-and-half?" she asked around the berry.

He forced himself to tear his attention from her delicious mouth and went to the fridge to remove a bowl of individual servings of creamer. He set it before her on the table. "Do you desire anything else?"

"No, thanks." She sat down at the table, pretending to ignore him and his loaded question. He knew she was pretending because he could see the more rapid rise and fall of her breasts beneath her red-striped blouse.

Levi sat in the chair beside her. She glanced at him and started to look away – but didn't. Her eyes widened slightly and she ran the tip of her tongue along her upper lip. Blood flooded to his groin, making him hard. Jesus, did she do that on purpose?

He looked past her to Quintara and raised one brow as he sent her a smile. Quintara glanced from him to Trudy and then grinned. She winked at him.

"I'm going to walk to the gift shop and ask them about nice lodgings nearer to Key West," Quintara said, grabbing a big straw hat from off the top of the credenza and tugging it over her flame-red hair. "I'll be back in a little while. Enjoy your breakfast, dear."

Trudy twisted in the chair, her mouth full of strawberry, and watched Quintara leave. She turned back around, but didn't meet his gaze. Grabbing a croissant, she busied herself with slathering butter on it.

"I'm glad we're alone," he said, and received exactly the reaction he expected. If she'd been a cat, her back would have arched and she would have hissed at him. As it was, her brows arched and she cleared her throat.

"What can't you say in front of Quintara?" She wiped her fingertips on a napkin.

"Oh, that I still want to fuck you."

She sighed and dropped the croissant. "You have to stop saying that."

"Why?"

"Because if you don't, I'm going to pack up my RV and go back to Tulsa. I came here to work with you." She glared at him.

Staring into her flinty eyes, he realized that it had been a long time since a woman had fought against her attraction for him. His notoriety afforded him plenty of willing females. Hell, even before that he'd all the pussy he wanted. Trudy, however, was actually *turned off* by his public persona. That, in itself, made her all the more attractive and challenging to him.

"Okay, so let's work." He issued a sigh and tried to focus on something besides how her mouth would taste like strawberries. "I don't suppose you've had any communication with the killer since yesterday?"

"No."

"Have you tried?"

"I don't try."

He frowned. "Why not?"

She shrugged. "When he begins to hunt, his thoughts will come to me."

Her stubbornness was beginning to piss him off. He drew a circle with his forefinger on the table top over and over again as he chose his words and drew on the reserves of his patience. "You seem pretty set in your ways for someone just staring out." He shook his head and chose a different tact. "You *need* to believe in yourself and develop more confidence in your abilities. Working together will help with that."

"You're right, but I want to be clear that I'm not interested in impressing the masses. That's your thing. The whole entertainment part of being a medium is too much like a freak show to me."

Freak show? Her words lit the fuse on his temper and he landed a hand on her forearm, making her gasp. "Watch your mouth, Trudy. You're coming perilously close to insulting me and you really don't want to do that." He gentled the grip he had on her arm but didn't remove his hand from her warm skin. Taking a deep, calming breath, he tried again to make his point. "No one is asking you to make public appearances. I don't mind the spotlight because the more people who know about me, the more high-profile cases will come my way. That's what *I* want. Now, please tell me what you want. I'm dying to know."

She eyed him, cautiously, and swallowed hard. "I've given this some thought and I want to gain more experience. Of course, I can see that working with you will give me that along with bolstering my credibility. It's your *other* agenda that has me worried."

He sat back in the chair, giving her more space. She wanted to talk shop? They'd talk shop. Shifting slightly, he sent an urgent plea to his dick to behave. "Okay, so putting that aside for now, tell me about your specific gifts. Do you have sense memory?"

She popped the rest of the croissant into her mouth and stood up from the table. "You mean pick up on things at a murder location? That sort of thing?"

"Yes."

"No. I think that works more for channeling victims than for getting in touch with the perps." She strolled into the living room and sat on the sofa, curling her legs up under her. "Being in the vicinity of the killer makes their thoughts come to me more often, though. And they seem clearer. I can hear more nuances in their thoughts and see more details." She angled a glance at him, watching as he came to sit on the sofa beside her. "So, you can pick up vibes by just touching someone?"

"Yes, sometimes. Touching objects owned by victims is how it works best for me."

"Psychometry."

He smiled, hearing her test out the word. "That's right."

"I've been reading about all of the different forms of parapsychology, trying to see where I fit in."

"I have sense and place memory. I can tell if something tragic has happened in a house, a building, or even outdoors. That sort of thing. But it isn't as reliable because, unfortunately, bad things happen all the time everywhere."

"What if you can't touch anything?" she asked.

"If I don't have anything to touch, like when I do radio guest spots, then it's much harder for me," he admitted and then paused for a few moments as he searched for a way to explain it to her. "I can't hear the spirit nearly as well and I can't feel what the spirit feels. It's more distant and not as accurate. It's like they're under water or something." He remembered an encounter he'd experienced earlier. "By the way, I ran into a guy in the gym this morning and I knew he was the one who had been watching us last night." He nodded at the sliders. She sat bolt upright.

"Who is he?"

Levi shrugged. "Mark somebody. It's not important."

"But he was wat—."

"He asked for my autograph for his wife," he cut in to put her mind at ease. "When I shook his hand, I knew he'd been out there snooping around last night. He's harmless. He and his wife are fans of mine. That's all."

She let out a sigh. "Obsessed fans follow you around. Great." She tipped her head to one side for a few moments of silent assessment. "Can you read minds?"

"Not in the classic sense."

"What's that mean?"

"It means that I'm very observant and I can often tell what someone's thinking by picking up on body language."

"That's how most people read minds," she said. "It's trickery."

"Not always. And being observant is no trick. It's a skill."

"Are you totally in control of your gifts?"

He sent her a baffled glance. Was she serious? "No one is, Trudy. We can learn to harness them, use them, but total control isn't possible because no one completely understands the spirit world and how it works."

"That's good to know because I usually feel like I have no control whatsoever." She let her head fall back onto the couch cushion.

He admired the thrust of her breasts. Her lashes were long, her nose tipped up slightly, and her lips looked pouty, the upper lip slightly fuller than the lower one. She had the sexiest mouth on the planet. He was sure of it. He wanted that mouth to know every inch of him – intimately. He forced his thoughts away from his wanting and toward work again. "Do you see the murders as they happen – in real time?"

She closed her eyes for a few moments and he thought he saw her shudder slightly. "I have, but now I block them out."

"Why?" he asked, dumbfounded by such a tactic.

She spread out her hands in a gesture of helplessness. "Because there isn't anything I can do about them and I don't want to see the whole ugly thing."

"You can block out the visions?" He blinked at her, wondering why she would choose to do that.

"I can *now*. That's something I've learned how to do since I've been in the Roundtable."

He frowned. *Goddamn it, Quintara!* And he hoped Quintara felt his aggravation wherever she was. They had that kind of connection. Or she did. She could pick up on his most primal emotions when it suited her. That was one thing Quintara was good at. In truth, she wasn't all that psychic. She was a good teacher, though, and she had a huge heart. She had a knack for communicating techniques and bringing people along slowly, carefully, lovingly. But Trudy didn't need her wings clipped, damn it! She was ready to soar.

"I'm not sure that's a good technique," he said.

"It keeps me sane."

"You probably miss important information that could help track the murderer. You might be able to tell where the murder is taking place or more about the murderer if you stayed there with him."

She squeezed her eyes shut for a few moments. "It's too horrible, too raw. Before I could remove myself from it, I used to be in bed for days afterward with a splitting headache. Back then, I was looking for a way out. I was beginning to think I didn't want to live if I had to live like that."

"Suicidal?"

"I was getting there fast," she admitted in a voice that was barely a whisper, barely there. "It was scary."

His heart wrenched. He'd had no idea it had been that bad for her. He covered one of her hands with his and she tensed. Her gaze flew up to him and there was a warning in the green depths. He refused to let her go. "You've struggled with this for a long time, haven't you?"

"I didn't feel gifted, if that's what you mean. I felt cursed."

"Then you met Quintara."

Some of the tension tightening her mouth faded away. "That's right. She saved me from drowning in all the visions I was having."

"She's done that for a lot of budding psychics. But even Quintara doesn't completely understand the enormity of your gifts. The moment I met you, I could sense the power in you. I knew that I'd met my match."

"Your match?" She eased back from him. "You're bullshitting me again, Levi. And I . . . don't . . . like . . . it." Her tone was menacing and her eyes spit anger at him.

"And I . . . am . . . serious."

When she made a move to spring up from the sofa, he clamped a hand on her shoulder and shoved her back down. "No! Wait." He locked gazes with her and it felt as if he was locking horns with her. He pushed her with his mind. It was something he had learned to do when he had studied in England. She sucked in a quick breath and her eyes widened. "Yes, that was me," he assured her with a confident grin. "You listening to me now?"

"How did you do that?" she asked, clearly stunned. "It was like you'd poked me . . . but in my brain!"

"Someday I'll teach you how it's done. Hear me out. The others in the Roundtable are talented, but they're like a faucet, drip, drip, dripping." He saw her watch his lips move and fought back his smile. "You are a goddamned waterfall. Just like me." He leaned closer and rested his hand on her knee. Her skin felt deliciously warm and smooth under his palm. "I can help you more than Quintara ever could or ever will because I understand what you're going through."

"Quintara knows, too." Her voice had become breathy and it skated across his nerve endings and made his cock twitch.

"No, she doesn't. She can't. Look, I adore Quintara, but she doesn't know how it feels to be taken over and dragged along a dark path by an unknown entity. She can sympathize and help guide you toward better techniques, but she has no earthly idea what you really experience." He met her gaze and hers softened a little. "I do, sweetheart." He could tell that she didn't trust the endearment, but he didn't give a damn. He ran his hand along her silky thigh. "What we can do *accurately* is what matters most. Notice I said *accurately*. I've been keeping an eye on your progress and you're right on target the majority of the time. There are many psychics who can get snatches of information about murderers and victims, but a precious few who get it right as often as we do."

She captured his gliding hand with hers, stopping him from sliding his fingers under the fabric. "Quit putting the moves on me, Wolfe."

He grinned and he knew it was wolfish. "Let's put aside our petty differences and see what we can accomplish together." He waited for her to look at him. "Why are you fighting me? I don't think you detest me as much as you want to." He leaned closer and nuzzled the side of her face. She was wearing perfume . . . something musky. She wet her upper lip with the tip of her tongue and he hardened so quickly it made his breath whistle out of him. Christ! She was dangerous!

"Did I ever say that I detested you, Wolfe?"

Fuck it. He was going to kiss her senseless and take her right there on the couch. "God, Tru. I want inside—."

Quintara chose that moment to return. She was now sporting a large pair of bright orange sunglasses. "It's a beautiful day in Paradise, children. Before the bad man starts murdering again, let's go find somewhere else to pitch our tent, shall we?"

Chapter Four

"I'm glad that's settled," Quintara said, standing in the middle of the "shabby chic" room on the second floor of the Blue Coconut Bed & Breakfast. "This will do fine. What Key is this?"

"Big Pine," Trudy answered. She couldn't imagine that Levi would be enamored with the place. In fact, the rooms were probably far too feminine for him. "You're only about twenty miles from Key West."

"Oh, that's good. Levi, just drop those by the bed," Quintara said as Levi came in, his arms and hands full of luggage.

"Here . . . let me help you," Trudy said, bounding toward Levi, but she stopped dead when he sent her a quelling glare. "What?"

"I can do it," he said between gritted teeth. "Just relax." And he hauled the luggage toward the bed and set three bright yellow pieces beside it. He took the black and silver wheeled duffel and matching suit garment bag with him as he went across the hall to his room. He kicked the door closed behind him.

Trudy looked at Quintara. "What's with him?"

Quintara sighed. "He's a man of many moods and right now he's chaffing because we're wasting time moving about when we should be trying to connect with the murderer."

Trudy narrowed one eye. "Did you know that he planned to hit on me?"

Quintara laughed. "Dear, he's Levi Wolfe and you're a lovely, talented, young woman. Of course, he's going to pounce on you. But didn't he also tell you that he's glad to finally work with you?"

"Yes."

"That's good. He's been after me to hook you two up for months."

"He said something about that . . . wait. Hook us up?" Trudy repeated, aghast. "What? You're his procurer of women now?"

"Don't be ridiculous, Trudy. Hook you up to work together, but I know that he finds you very attractive."

"I think he finds nearly every woman with a pulse very attractive. In fact, I think he probably views most women as fairly easy conquests." She eyed Quintara with suspicion and grinned. "So, you're not pimping for him?"

Quintara released a throaty laugh as she fondled the string of beads around her neck. "As if he needed that! When he's in his element before an audience, he's a sexy beast and women line up for him after every show. It's like he puts them in an erotic trance!" Some of the amusement faded from her expression. "He used to be quite a rounder when I met him, screwing every woman who rubbed up against him—."

"Oh, my God! TMI, Quintara."

"What's that?"

"Too much information," Trudy translated. "But you've just confirmed what I said about him. He treats women like sex toys."

"I said he *used* to be like that. He's more discriminating now because he's matured. Also, he works entirely too much. The man is *driven*, I tell you." Quintara flapped a hand at her, scowling good-naturedly. "You know so little about him."

Trudy pressed her lips together as the truth of that resonated in her. "Pretty much all I know about him is what I read in the newspapers," she quipped. "And see on television and hear on the radio all the damn time."

"He's flashy and can be brooding and dramatic, but he's serious about what he does – and what he does, he does to perfection."

Trudy shook her head, knowing that she was speaking about more than Levi Wolfe's work as a psychic. "You're his biggest fan."

"Maybe I am." She smiled warmly. "I'm a big fan of *yours*, too. Take the time to get to know him, Trudy dear, instead of assuming things about him. You could have a wonderful relationship and do extraordinary things together."

"How long have you known him?"

"Oh, let's see.' Quintara glanced up, thinking. "Six years, I guess. Seems longer than that. Maybe seven years."

She tried to picture him in his early twenties, fresh from college, but it was difficult. Quintara was right. She knew virtually nothing about him. Just gossip and innuendo.

"Who wants a drink?" Levi strode into the room, looking irritated. He was dressed in black jeans and a slate gray, linen shirt that was open at the collar. "I could use a Scotch and water."

"I'm in," Quintara said, rising from the sofa. "But I want something fruity."

"I could go for a beer," Trudy admitted. Actually, she thought, she could go for something stronger, but a beer was safer this early in the day.

"Could you now?" Levi sent her a half-smile, making her wonder once again if he was reading her mind. "Then let's blow this pop stand, ladies."

*

"He's not any older than forty," Trudy said, shifting on the bar stool in the quiet, dark tavern as she tried to picture the serial killer who had been in her head recently. "More like thirty or thirty-five."

"Yes, that's sounds right. Around my age. Maybe a little older." Levi carried a netbook, not much bigger than a paperback novel, and he opened it and typed something into it.

"How old are you?" Trudy asked, figuring she'd start getting to know him better.

He looked up from his notes and something changed on his face and in his eyes. In a nanosecond he went from concentrating on the case to concentrating on her. "Almost thirty."

"Almost?" she said.

He nodded.

She raised her brows. "So, your birthday is soon?"

"Not very far off. Birthdays aren't important to me. Age isn't important to me."

"What *is* important to you?' Trudy asked, playing along.

"What you do with the years you're given."

She told herself to look away, but she couldn't. Her gaze was riveted to him. He had spoken a deep truth that shed light on her own shortcomings. In the handful of seconds that passed, she realized that she'd wasted great chunks of her time cowering from life and not taking chances that might have given her thrilling experiences and dangerous liaisons. The man standing near her – this dark-haired, devilishly handsome man – had never backed away from a dare. She knew that about him. It was apparent in his stance and in the way he held her gaze boldly and made her break the bond first.

Her heart climbed into her throat and lodged there. Trudy gathered in a deep breath and refused to succumb to her new tic of clearing her throat. The tinge of regret shadowing her heart bedeviled her. She hitched up her chin and he smirked.

"Got an idea about coloring? Caucasian?" he asked, bringing her gently back to the task.

"Uh . . . yes, Caucasian."

"Fair or dark?"

"I don't know about that yet," Trudy said, finding her center again, her purpose for being there. "He speaks about women as objects. He notices how they're dressed, the size of their breasts and hips, the color of their hair and if it's natural or bleached." She watched him from the corner of her eye as he typed quickly, his silver ring flashing in the dim bar lights. He looked up from the page and waited for her to continue.

"He curses a lot. He says ugly words. Words most women hate."

"Such as?"

"Cunt. Fat bitch. Whore. Slut. Fuck."

"He sounds fairly typical," Quintara said. "Men love to debase women and put them in their place."

"I beg your pardon?" Levi drawled, his voice taking on an edge. "Would you care to rephrase that?"

Quintara regarded him in the greenish, neon-tinged light and then nodded in agreement. "You're right. I was painting with broad strokes. Present company, excluded, of course."

"Thank you." His lips quirked. "And what's wrong with 'fuck'?"

Quintara released a deeply naughty giggle. "You scoundrel. Nothing. Absolutely nothing is wrong with it! You say it and do it enough!"

"Right, and you don't? And I'm rather fond of cunts," he added getting another laugh from Quintara.

TMI, Trudy thought, rolling her eyes, but drawn by their delight with one another. She felt a stab of envy. She didn't have close friendships like theirs. She had her family, but lifelong friendships had eluded her. Her psychic abilities had made her wary, caused her to not open herself up to acquaintances so that they were able to become friends. She regretted that and never as keenly as she did watching Quintara and Levi nudge each other and share another quick laugh when Levi whispered something in Quintara's ear. He was definitely more relaxed with her — more himself. She wondered if Quintara knew him better than anyone.

Still grinning, Levi returned his attention to the netbook and its softly glowing screen. "Okay, then. Trudy, do you sense any reasoning behind his decisions? Any motive?"

She steered her thoughts back to the case and only then realized that she resented him having fun with Quintara and sticking to business with her. But that's how she wanted it, right? No monkey business with Levi?

"Motive, Trudy?" he asked again.

"Oh, sorry. No, but I've only heard him once. It's early."

He nodded, grabbed the shot glass in front of him, and swallowed the Scotch in one long gulp. His eyes didn't even water. "Good. It's a start."

"You feel more in control now, Levi?" Quintara asked, motioning the barkeep to make another drink for her. It was something called The Blue Bomber and it smelled like coconut.

"Yes, I think so." Levi closed the netbook and held it out to Quintara. "Be a love and slip that into your purse for me."

"Certainly." Quintara shoved it inside her large, straw tote. "Now *you* be a love and dance with Trudy," she commanded, sweetly.

"What? No. I . . . no." Trudy shook her head as she looked from Quintara to Levi and back to Quintara. A shocked laugh tumbled out of her.

"Go ahead, children," Quintara said, almost smugly. "I want to watch."

"*You* dance with him and *I'll* watch," Trudy said.

"No, my feet hurt." Quintara shoved Levi's shoulder. "Go on. You dance so divinely."

"We're in a bar, not a —what are you doing?" Trudy stiffened as Levi captured one of her hands in both of his.

"Let's go. One dance."

"No, thanks. Really, I—."

He tugged hard and she slipped off the bar stool. "Come on. Quit being such a baby about it."

"A baby?" She glared at him, but she was already in his embrace. He circled her waist with his arms and tightened them around her. Her breath caught in her throat. He felt warm and taut and she was staring at his mouth.

"Yeah. Baby."

Oh. My. He had a great mouth, she thought, disjointedly. A curvy, upper lip and a full lower one. Wide, generous, and so very expressive. She snatched her gaze away from it and realized that her hands were on his biceps and he had quite a pair of guns under his cool, linen shirt. His lips touched the top of her ear as he rubbed his cheek against hers.

"Just follow my lead." His breath was perfumed by Scotch.

He was close. So close. She had trouble breathing. He spread his large hands across her back and his touch scorched her skin through her blouse. She looked toward Quintara as Bonnie Raitt sang about giving them something to talk about. Quintara was watching and she lifted her glass in a salute.

He *is* a good dancer, Trudy thought, having little trouble matching his steps. He didn't just do the sway-back-and-forth thing. He actually moved his feet and spun her around the small area that they'd made into a dance floor. He rocked his hips and thrust his pelvis to the sensuous beat of the music. Fast. Slow. Glide. He grasped one of her hands and sent her twirling away from him and then back into his arms, back against the solid wall of his chest.

"Who taught you how to dance?" she asked, letting go of a delighted giggle. He smiled and seemed to be enjoying himself.

"You really don't want to know."

"I really do," she insisted. "Otherwise, I wouldn't have asked."

He shook his head and lights danced in his eyes. "An older woman."

"Your mother?"

At the mere mention of the woman who'd given birth to him, she felt him tense and the pleasure glowing in his eyes was doused like a candle flame killed by a swift gust of breath.

"No," he said, pressing his cheek against hers so that she couldn't see his expressive face. "Just a woman I knew for awhile."

"Well, whoever she was, she knew what she was doing." She felt him relax against her and then his lips touched the curve of her neck. A shiver of pleasure shot through her as potent as a swallow of Scotch.

"Who taught you?" he asked, his voice a raspy whisper.

"My brother." She closed her eyes, loving the feel of his lips barely touching her skin when he spoke.

"Kudos to him."

"He's not nearly as smooth at it as you."

He dipped her, his arms holding her fast, his face poised above hers. "Oh, really?"

She laughed up at him and then he righted her, but the world was still a little off-center.

"You okay?" he asked as his hands splayed across her back to steady her. His thumb skimmed under the band of her brassiere and she sucked in a breath.

"Sure. I'm okay. Why?"

"Well, you're still swaying and the song has ended."

"Oh." Trudy glanced around and heard the deafening silence. "Right." She stepped away from him. "Fine then."

"Yes, it was very fine. Thank you for the dance." His voice was deep, scratching her nerve-endings. He bent his head and his lips brushed hers and then he was still, his mouth hovering an inch from hers. His eyes glimmered with a challenge.

Trudy stopped breathing and she knew he was waiting . . . daring her to kiss him. Well, she wouldn't. Not here in a bar while Quintara sat there and watched and . . . oh, to hell with it. She'd take that dare!

Lifting up on the balls of her feet, she pressed her mouth to his, parting her lips and stroking his tongue with hers. His arms cinched around her waist, pulling her against him and she felt his hardness nudge her. She ran her hands through his thick, soft hair and opened her mouth wider, letting his tongue caress hers hungrily. It was as if she'd caught fire and everything around her fell to ashes. There was only him and her and the frantic strokes of their tongues and the feel of his hands caressing her back and cradling her head. God, oh God, she wanted him.

She heard someone clapping and then Levi's mouth lifted from hers. She opened her eyes to stare into blue pools of naked lust. He gave a little shake of his head before his hands fell away from her.

"You are one devious witch, Trudy Tucker," he whispered. "If I don't watch out, you're going to have your way with me."

"Lovely, children," Quintara cooed, still applauding them. "I used to cut a rug, I tell you. I could samba and make your eyes pop out of your head."

"You'll have to teach me the samba some time," Levi said, turning toward her and smiling gently. "I've always wanted to learn."

Quintara returned his smile. "I'd be happy to. Of course, I'm so out of shape now, it's not the same. I used to be a knockout."

He dropped a kiss on her rouged cheek. "You still are to my eyes."

"Oh, you flirt!" Quintara shook a finger at him, but she was lapping it up like a kitten going after a bowl of cream.

Trudy touched her flaming lips. Good grief! Had she just deep-kissed him in a bar in front of Quintara, who had applauded their performance? She had lost her ever-loving mind!

"Let's take a walk," Quintara suggested. "Maybe we can pick up some vibes. At the very least, we can get to know the area – and each other – better."

Trudy grabbed her purse to poke around for her wallet.

"This has been my pleasure," Levi said, handing the barkeep his credit card.

Oh, he's smooth, Trudy thought. But she had to admit that she liked a man who paid more than just compliments.

*

The beach was small, but not crowded. Sitting in an Adirondack chair, Trudy watched as the sun slowly began to extinguish itself in the ocean. Beside her, Levi watched the same scene, but he was having trouble keeping his gaze on the sun and not on Trudy. On the other side of him, Quintara was fast asleep in her chair, her straw hat covering her face and muffling her snores.

"She's really sawing the logs, isn't she?" Trudy asked, a laugh lacing through her voice.

He chuckled. "Do you snore?"

"I don't think so. Sometimes I make sounds. Maybe I say a word or two. I wake up and I know I've said something, but I don't know what." She turned her head to look at him. "Do you snore?"

"Only when I've had too much to drink." He paused, realizing it had been a long time since he'd been that sauced, thank God. "I have been known to talk in my sleep. And I have nightmares sometimes."

"Me, too." She turned wide eyes on him. "About murders?"

"No." He shut his eyes. Now why did he bring that up?

"About what then?"

He shrugged, closing his mind to painful memories he preferred to keep buried. He rolled up his shirt sleeves to his elbows. "Let's talk about you. Are your parents still living?"

"Yes, but I think we should talk about you. Quintara gave me strict orders to get to know you better."

"She did?" He glanced at Quintara, making sure she was asleep. "Why?"

"Because we're supposed to be entering into a partnership," she said, giving him a "duh" widening of her green eyes. "It's only fair since it's pretty obvious you've discussed me at length with

50

Quintara." She turned to lie on her side and look at him. "Are you close to your family?"

"No." Irritation blasted through him. Quintara damn well knew that he didn't like to talk about his upbringing or personal things. Most of it was just too sordid to dwell on. He went to shrinks to sort all that out and help him deal with it. To everyone else, he liked being a mystery. It was safer that way. He could keep people at arm's length. But, did he really want to keep Trudy that far away? he wondered, and his heart seemed to know the answer that his head wasn't quite ready to accept.

"That's it?" she asked after a few more moments ticked by. "You're going to answer my questions with yes or no?"

Well. Hell. "What do you want to know?"

"Where do your parents live? Where did you grow up?"

"I grew up in a lot of places," he said, resigned to his fate. He gathered in a deep breath. Might as well get it over with, he told himself. She's not going to let it go and Quintara would eventually spill the beans anyway. "My father is a fire-and-brimstone Evangelical minister." Her silence made him look at her again. Her expression was the epitome of shock. "Close your mouth, Trudy."

Her teeth clicked and she blinked. "No shit?"

He smiled at her response. "No shit."

"Wow. So, what does he think about what you do for a living? Has he come to grips with it?"

He stared at the sunset, but it had lost its allure for him. A humorless laugh tumbled out of him and it almost hurt his chest and throat, it was so dry, so lifeless. "He thinks I'm a liar, a black-hearted sinner, and a spawn from hell. He believes that I make my living by fleecing poor, searching, tortured souls. So, yes, I suppose he's come to grips with it in his own way."

"Oh, Levi." All the compassion in the world seemed to coalesce into her voice. "I'm so terribly sorry." She drew in a short, harsh breath. "That really blows."

Before he closed his eyes, before the tenderness in her voice squeezed his heart to the point of pain, he saw her hand lift ever so slightly off her thigh as if she wanted to reach out to him, but then she thought better of it. He found himself wanting her consoling touch and that sent him mentally scrambling back from her. God! What kind of spell had she cast? And why the fuck was he spilling his guts to her?

Clearing his throat and shaking off the strange reaction, he aimed the conversation away from him and safely back to her. "What do your parents do?"

"My dad owns an auto repair shop and my mom works for a catering company."

"And they're supportive of what you're doing," he said, not bothering to pose it as a question. He could tell by the easy way she'd answered that her parents were there for her.

"Yes. They don't understand it, but they know that there's something odd about me. I mean, I've been out of step my whole life, so now my parents are relieved I seem to have found some answers."

He smiled, relishing the complete opposites they represented. "And you lived in Mayberry next to 'the Beav'."

She laughed. "Yeah, sure, and my mother wears pearls, a dress, and heels when she does housework or cooks."

Tipping back his head, he chuckled at that image. It came to him in black-and-white-and gray just like on the old television shows. He watched clouds skate across the cerulean sky for a minute and appreciated the cool breeze and the smiling girl beside him. "I thought Quintara said something about your family owning pawn shops."

"My granddad owned them," she said. "He died a couple of years ago and left his three shops to me and my sister and brother. But I sold my share to Derek and Sadie last year." She propped her head in her hand. "How did you end up going to England to study?"

He glanced at her, surprised at her question. He'd thought she would keep grilling him about his misspent youth. "I read about Arthur Findlay College, so I applied for a scholarship there and got it."

"That must have been a wonderful time in your life. To be in Essex, studying the paranormal with like-minded people."

He noted the dreaminess in her eyes. Mediums loved to hear about Findlay College. It was like Hogwarts to them. "I was lucky to go there. I learned a great deal," he allowed, then his thoughts moved unerringly to the temptress who had betrayed him and set him on a path of self-destruction and he frowned. He felt Trudy's gaze sharpen on him. He erased the frown from his face, but it was too late.

"But?" she goaded.

Aw, hell! He tried for a light, careless tone. "I had a great time the first year, but then I met a girl, fell for her, and she broke my heart. Shattered it to bits, actually."

"Ouch. Was she a student there too?"

"Yes, but we weren't into the same things. She was studying ghosts. She wanted to know why they haunted places and she loved it when she thought they were evil or dangerous."

"She loved the danger," Trudy said. "That's why she was attracted to you."

He shifted to look at her, full on. The setting sun gilded her face and set fire to her hair. Her piquant beauty made his heart skip a beat. "Do you think I'm dangerous, Tru?"

She bobbed her head once and her green eyes narrowed. "Oh, yes."

"Dangerous good or dangerous bad?"

"Good, I hope. You're dangerous around the edges." She shifted and her blouse tightened against her breasts. "What was her name?"

Around the edges? Hmmm. He'd have to think about that. His gaze moved lower where the material of her blouse strained.

"Her name?" she repeated. "What was the heartbreaker's name?"

"Uh . . . Lizzie. Elizabeth." He tore his thoughts from imagining the shape and feel of her breasts.

"She was British?"

"Yes. *Veddy.*"

"I can't imagine you having a shattered heart."

"Oh?" He lay on his back again and saw a cloud that was shaped like a reclining lion morph into a train engine as he watched. Sometimes, he thought, it was also difficult for him to recall that he'd once had such tender feelings. That he'd been so awkward and shy around girls. That he'd worshipped an English lass with long, blond hair and laughing, brown eyes. But just saying Lizzie's name felt like the quick nick of a knife in his heart. Stupid, he thought. It was years ago and they'd both moved on.

Trudy was quiet. So quiet. Too quiet. He glanced at her. "Are you—Trudy?" His heart froze at the sight of her far-off expression and unfocused gaze. He swung his legs over the side of the chair and leaned toward her. She had sat up to face the ocean again. Staring off into the distance, her eyes were glassy, her breathing rapid. She was gone, stolen from him by a madman.

53

Levi reached for her hands. They were cold. *Jesus H. Christ! The bastard has her!* Determinedly, he kept himself calm, his voice soft when he asked, "Do you hear him? Is he there?"

She nodded.

He slid off the chair and knelt before her in the sand, sliding his hands up to her elbows and then down to clasp her chilly fingers. He wished he could climb into her head and protect her, support her. "Breathe, Trudy. Breathe. That's it. Let him in. You're strong. You can control this."

Her eyes moved, tracked, and then settled on a distant point.

"What's happening? Talk to me," Levi whispered, warming her hands in his. Should he encourage her to talk or would that hinder her? It didn't help him when he was channeling, but what about Trudy? He glanced over his shoulder at Quintara, wondering if he should awaken her and ask her to assist him, but then he shook off that notion. No. He'd follow his own instincts.

"He's casing," Trudy whispered. "He's watching. Waiting."

"Where is he? Where are you? Look around," Levi instructed, trying to guide her into getting more information, more clues for them to mull over later. She obeyed him, her lovely green eyes tracking something only she could see. He released a sigh of relief, thankful that his prodding had worked.

"Gallery," she said. "A museum? There are pictures hanging on bare walls. He's looking at a woman now. She's standing in front of a portrait . . . a framed artwork. He's sitting on a low bench behind her. Behind. You've got a great ass, honey. How many men have fucked that ass? You like it in the ass? I bet you do. I'd like to rip open that ass and come all over you. You haughty bitch."

Levi stared at her, wincing at the words spilling from her lips.

"Oh. *Shit.*"

Levi squeezed her hands. "What?"

"She's pregnant! *Goddamn, fucking preggo bitch!* If I wanted a tub of lard, I'd go after a big, fat cunt. There are plenty around. Fat guts spilling over bikini bottoms. No, this bitch won't do. Have to shop some more and — huh?" She sat up straighter, blinked, and slumped forward.

Levi caught her shoulders, keeping her from pitching face first into the sand. He gave her a little shake and she stared at him for few moments before life flooded back into her eyes. "You okay?"

She nodded.

"What happened? Is he gone?" Levi asked, rubbing her arms to comfort her.

"Someone . . . something interrupted him."

He gathered her to him for a quick hug. That was fanfuckingtastic! The way she had zeroed in. So much detail! "You did great, Trudy. Great."

She cringed and hunched her shoulders as if she wanted him to remove his hands from her, so he did.

"What? What's wrong?"

"Nothing." She cleared her throat and shook her head again as if flinging her thoughts into order. "I think we should keep this a professional relationship, Levi. It will be much safer for me that way."

He sat on his heels, feeling like he'd been slapped. Safer? Pushing up to his feet, he felt stung beyond all reasoning, but clung to a feeble notion hat she wasn't rejecting him outright, but that she was still reeling from the danger she'd seen and sensed from the psycho who'd invaded her mind. He didn't like the expression on her face — guarded, assessing, and tremulous. Like she was looking at a heartless beast.

He glanced toward Quintara. What crap had she been feeding Trudy about him? Fury suddenly mixed with his stinging feelings and he strode to Quintara and whipped the hat off her face. "Wake up," he said, his voice as gruff and unforgiving as a drill sergeant's. "Trudy has made contact."

Chapter Five

When Trudy pulled into a parking space at the Blue Coconut B&B the next morning Levi was pacing in the parking lot waiting for her. Looking edgy in dark blue jeans, gray t-shirt, and a dark blue denim vest that he'd left unbuttoned, he carried a small laptop case. He scowled, opened the passenger door, and slid into the seat.

"Good morning to you, too." She breathed in the scent of him and noticed that his hair was still damp from his shower. He smelled faintly of a citrus grove. Bracing and clean. When he said nothing to her, she wilted a little inside. Great. He was still sore about yesterday. "So, what's up?" she asked, placing cheeriness into her tone.

He slammed the door shut and fastened his seat belt without sparing her a glance. "The police have cleared the last murder scene. They've given us permission to go check it out."

She digested this. "You're in contact with the police here?"

"Yes."

Interesting. One of the topics she had wanted to talk to him about was cooperating with the police. Of course, he'd already handled it. She glanced at him. What did he need her for? Oh, right. To channel the killer. "The cops are cooperating with you?"

"The lead detective is a good guy. His name is Tom Sinclair and he's glad for any help with this we can give him."

And he was already familiar with the lead detective. Natch. "That's good to hear."

"I'll introduce you to him at the next opportunity."

"I suppose I should be grateful for small favors," she said, abandoning her fake cheerfulness and not caring that her tone had become snappish.

Finally, he looked at her, taking in her lavender tank top and jeans. She wondered idly if he approved and then wondered why she cared. His expression gave nothing away. "Let's go."

Grinding her teeth at his command, she looked at the B&B. "Where's Quintara?"

"She's not coming. She's having breakfast. Let's go."

"You know how to get to the victim's house?"

"Yes, I've been there. I wasn't allowed in then. They were still fingerprinting and stuff. Let's go."

"Do I remind you of a dog?"

He lowered his black brows and glowered. "If you have a point to make, make it."

"Don't speak to me as if I'm supposed to obey your every command. The next time you do, I'm stopping the car and you're getting out and hoofing it. *That's* my point." She slapped the car into reverse, whipped out of the parking space, and headed toward Key West. From the corner of her eye, she actually saw him smirk! The bastard.

"Is this your car or a rental?" he asked, looking down at the floor mats that were littered with sand, bits of shell, and grass and then up at the pine tree deodorizer that swung from a string on the rearview mirror.

"It's mine. I tow it behind my RV." She glanced at him again. He stared out the side window and his moodiness made her edgy. "So, you're mad at me, I take it."

"No. But you do owe me an apology and I'm waiting for it." He propped an elbow against the window and tapped his index finger against the center of his mouth.

"An apology for—?"

His gaze slid to her, as piercing as a knife blade. "That you have such a low opinion of me and no reason for it."

"Oh, Levi, come on!" She slapped the palm of one hand against the steering wheel. "You can't blame me. You know you have a reputation as a ladies' man."

"Run that by me again? A what?" He turned his face away from her again and his chest moved against his shirt with silent laughter. "I haven't heard that expression except in old romantic films. If you mean that I like women, then I will own it, but I don't think that's what you meant yesterday. I'm pretty sure you said you wouldn't be safe around me like I'm some kind of uncontrollable beast."

"No, that's *not* what I meant." She glanced at the speedometer and saw that her agitation had put lead in her foot. The little car was zipping along at seventy-five miles an hour. She eased off the accelerator. "It's just that I've heard about how you don't hang around long, that's all. You have a short attention span."

He lifted a shoulder in a careless shrug. "So what? So fucking what, Trudy? You're either attracted to me or you're not. Why do you have to make it so damned complicated? Jesus!"

She wanted to reply with a furious, well-aimed volley of wise words, but for the life of her, she couldn't think of any. "I'm sorry." Had she said that aloud? When she saw the glimmer of a smile on his lips, she knew she had. Well, crap. He'd won that round. She shook her head, conceding that she probably owed that one to him. "So, are you still dating the Court TV anchor lady? She's very attractive."

He frowned. "Sissy Franklin and I don't date. We've attended a few industry events at the same time."

"Quintara was certain that you were seeing Sissy and . . . you know, that you're involved with her."

"Quintara's right. I have seen her. I do see her. I've just said that."

He shifted restlessly in the bucket seat, irritation stamped on his chiseled features and in his every move. She felt his gaze on her, burning her, branding her a nosey gossip.

"Now if you think I'm going to tell you whether or not I have carnal knowledge of Sissy, then you're barking mad." His voice was even with an underpinning of barely controlled anger. "I don't discuss such things because it's none of anyone's goddamned business."

Trudy flinched. *Bastard.* "Apologizing to you sure is a barrel of fun," she rejoined, sarcasm dripping from each word.

He arched a sardonic brow, then straightened and pointed ahead. "At the next traffic light, take a left. We're almost there."

*

Shelly Farmer had lived and died in a garage apartment behind a large, two-story house. Levi went to the front door, rang the bell, and collected a key from the woman who answered.

"Detective Sinclair called and asked the owner to let us in," he told Trudy when she gave him a quizzical look. "Housekeeping will be here this afternoon, so this is our only opportunity to see the rooms before they're wiped clean."

He led the way up the staircase at the side of the garage, up to the apartment. He slipped the key into the lock and opened the door.

It took a few seconds for Trudy's eyes to adjust to the change from bright, morning sunlight to the dim interior. She sniffed, catching the scents of blood, chemicals, and booze. Across from her, liquor bottles lay on the floor, toppled from a two-tier table set against the wall. A whiskey bottle had broken, the shards of glass glinting darkly in the nap of the beige carpet. A large circle of rusty brown stained it. A fine dust lay on almost everything. The fingerprinting specialists had been thorough.

The living room was furnished with a couch and two chairs, a coffee table, some lamps. A big, pink, plastic S hung on the wall behind the liquor table. Nothing special. She leaned forward, looking into the next room. A kitchen and a bedroom beyond that.

Levi opened the laptop case and removed a camera and his electronic notebook from it. He set the netbook on the breakfast bar, and then moved slowly from room to room, taking snapshots. He returned to the breakfast bar a couple of times to type something into his netbook. She followed, taking in the furnishings and personal touches. Framed photographs of smiling friends and relatives. Frog figurines sitting on a table. A guitar propped in a corner. A fluffy, pink robe hanging from a peg on the bathroom door. The bedspread was purple and cream and a big, pink, heart-shaped pillow sat in the middle of it. A similar one graced a chair in her own home.

The realization that she shared something with the victim sent tears to prick the back of Trudy's eyes and also made her a little homesick. She blinked rapidly and looked around for Levi. He was in the living room, staring at the blood stain. Something in his posture made her heartbeats sputter. Suddenly, he flung back his head and a low moan escaped him.

Trudy was beside him in the next heartbeat. "What's wrong?" she asked, not liking the thread of panic evident in her voice.

He stared at the ceiling and shook his head. Blindly, he reached out, grabbed her by the shoulder, and pushed her away from him.

"Stay well back," he said, his voice hoarse. "I might hurt you if I get too deeply into this. I'm fine. Don't talk to me. Just listen. Watch."

She obeyed, retreating a few steps. There was a distinct sensation quivering in the air around him. His arms and hands trembled slightly. He took a deep breath that stretched the t-shirt more tightly across his chest and stomach, parting the front of his unbuttoned vest. A scowl crossed his face and then slipped away as his expression tensed and his eyes focused straight ahead. The charge in the air intensified and the sensitive hairs on Trudy's arms and at her nape lifted as her skin pebbled. Running her hands up and down her arms, she knew that he'd tapped into Shelly's spirit and was searching through her final memories of this place.

"She's with someone, but not him. A woman. They're laughing as they come inside. The woman says it's a nice place. Shelly says it's cheap. She's lived here a couple of years now."

Trudy looked at the front door and could almost see two women crossing the living room, laughing, smiling, a little tipsy, a little naughty.

He closed his eyes and gathered in a deep, calming breath. "They're going to have another drink." He opened his eyes and they were dark and swimming with someone else's memories. Reaching out, he ran the tips of his fingers along the edge of the two-tiered table where the liquor was kept. With a jerk, he looked past Trudy to the kitchen. She realized he was about to move and might just mow her over if she didn't get out of his way. She was right. He headed for the kitchen and his shoulder bumped into her hard, sending her stumbling back. She toppled into an upholstered armchair. He never gave her a glance. She was invisible to him.

Transfixed and fascinated, Trudy drew in a sharp breath. She'd never seen anyone work this way. Some of the Roundtable crew had appeared to take on the personae of spirits or commune with them, but she'd never been sure they were actually in a trance or simply wanted to be in one.

With Levi, she didn't have any doubt that he was living and breathing with someone who was no longer flesh and blood. It was thrilling to watch – thrilling and chilling. Would he experience the actual murder . . . the death?

Scrambling from the chair at that thought, Trudy joined him in the bedroom. He stopped and she almost ran into him. He whirled. She skittered back, hurriedly getting out of his way. He returned to the kitchen and stood in front of the refrigerator. He tipped his head to one side as if he were listening.

He massaged his temples, his long, blunt-ended fingers making slow circles. The silver ring on his middle finger threw out meager sparks.

"The other woman wants to use the restroom," he whispered. "Shelly tells her to go ahead while she heats up some egg rolls in the microwave." He leaned his forehead against the refrigerator door. "I can't see her. Shelly won't look at her. Come on. Please." He rocked his head back and forth in abject misery. "The woman is in the bathroom now."

Gripping the edge of the counter, Trudy tried to follow his process. She looked toward the bathroom and crossed to it quickly. There wasn't much to see. It was a small, cramped space. The tub was shallow and wouldn't be comfortable. A screen-printed ocean scene on the shower curtain provided a splash of color to the white walls and white tiled floor. All of the fixtures were old, but clean. The fingerprinting team had been in there, too.

When Trudy joined Levi in the kitchen again, she found that he hadn't moved. His eyes were closed, but his lids twitched and his sooty lashes lifted slightly and then dusted his cheeks again.

"She likes the woman. I'm not sure she knows her all that well. Shelly is wondering what the hell she's doing in the bathroom. Did she fall in? She's laughing at that." He straightened, opened his eyes, and shrugged.

Leaning sideways to get a better look at him, Trudy noted that his eyes were still unfocused and his pupils were large, almost covering up the blue of his irises.

He drew in a breath and his eyes widened. But then in the next second he was retreating, holding his hands out, shaking his head as he back-pedaled into the living room.

"What the hell is this?" He sounded scared, his voice containing a tremor. "How did you get in here? Get out, damn it! Get out. Where is—? Oh, Jesus." He doubled over and moaned, low and guttural, as he sank to his knees, just missing a jagged piece of glass. He clutched at the table and the liquor bottles clinked against each other. Then he flung his head back as if his hair was gripped by someone and jerked hard. He stared at the ceiling and stark fear stamped his features.

Trudy looked away, unable to witness that on his face. When he made a guttural sound, she moved hesitantly toward him, but his warning rang in her ears. She was supposed to just watch. But, oh, she didn't like witnessing the fear twisting his handsome face or hear the pain in his low moans and short, sharp breaths.

Suddenly, his hands came up and he gripped the sides of his head and bared his teeth. "No, no!" His eyes popped open, wild and wide. He looked around, saw Trudy, and released a long breath. "I'm okay, I'm okay," he whispered, and she knew he was talking to her, consoling her, and she found it infinitely touching that he would think of her emotional state when he had been gripped by searing mental pain only seconds ago.

Thank God. He was back.

He staggered to his feet and stumbled to the couch. Sitting down, knees spread apart, elbows propped on them, he rested his head in his hands and his fingers ran over and over again through his inky hair. "Christ. Christ. *Christ.*"

Her heart constricted as she watched this tortured son of a preacher. She knelt in front of him and wrapped her hands around his wrists to stop his restless, almost frantic movements. "Levi? Are you sure you're okay?"

His throat flexed as he swallowed and when he spoke again, his voice was roughened by emotion. "He cut her throat to shut her up, but not before he mutilated her breasts."

Trudy nodded, seeing the murder in her mind. "She had silicone implants," she said. "He took them out and squirted the silicone all over her before he ejaculated on her. That had been his plan all along."

His head snapped up and his pupils focused on her with sharp intensity. There were dark circles under his eyes that she didn't think had been there an hour ago. "How do you know that?" he asked. "Did you receive it just now?"

"No." She shook her head, confused. "When he killed her."

"You saw him kill Shelly?" His gaze grabbed hers. "You didn't tell me that before. You acted like you didn't know that he'd taken another victim when we showed you the newspaper."

She let go of his wrists and sat back on her heels. He was right. How *did* she know? Why was the murder so clear in her mind? It didn't make sense. She stared at him, trying to find an answer. "I don't understand how . . . when did he kill her? What time do they think?"

"Between midnight and three or four in the morning."

"Could I have dreamed it? Did his thoughts come to me while I was asleep?"

"Did you have a nightmare that night?"

The memory of the night she had camped outside Jacksonville returned. "Yeah, I did," she murmured as it came rushing back to her. "I woke up suddenly and I was drenched in sweat. I thought that I'd been talking in my sleep, having a nightmare. You know how you get that feeling? Mouse had heard me, I guess, because she was barking at me. I'd felt woozy and kind of sick to my stomach, so I took a shower and a couple of aspirin before I went back to bed. My God, he must have been in my head and that's why I was feeling so out of it."

"And watching me just now brought it to the forefront of your mind." He sat back on the couch, arms akimbo, looking bone-weary. Turning his head, he stared at the collection of frog figurines. He brushed his fingertips over the top of one and then pulled his hand back as if he'd been burned.

"Goddamn it!"

"What?"

His eyes widened as he sprang to his feet, swaying slightly before he found his center. "Zelda."

"Zelda?" she asked, glancing around, her heart kicking into overdrive. "What about Zelda?"

"She was here." Holding out his hands to her, he helped her to her feet. "Zelda admired those frogs." He nodded to them. "I sensed her. Felt her. I know she was here."

"When?"

He squeezed his eyes shut as if scouring his mind for the memory. "The night of the murder."

Realization hit her hard. "Oh, my God! She was the other woman?"

He let go of her hands as he looked down at the floor, his gaze unfocused as he thought back to what he'd been shown by Shelly. "I didn't feel the woman anymore after she went into the bathroom. I never could see her very well. I tried, but Shelly was always looking the other way."

"So, if Zelda was in the bathroom, she must have witnessed . . ."

"Or maybe she knew the man who was waiting there." He spun away from her and paced, clearly exasperated. "Oh, *fuck!* I hate this. I hate when I can't grasp what's important, what's needed."

"Why don't you ask Gregory?" It was out before she could stop it and she winced when she realized that in his fevered, overwrought state he had taken it wrong.

His gaze was as sharp as the kiss of a whip. She actually felt it and sucked in a breath. "Don't!" That one word landed on her like a blow. He took one stride and was flush up against her, his fingers closing around her upper arms. She had to tip back her head to look at his face. "I'm only going to tell you this once and that's it. You understand me?" There was a low, pulsating tremor in his voice. "Don't make fun of me – of what I do. Of how I work. Do you understand?"

"I wasn't—."

His grip on her arms tightened. "Do you understand?"

"Yes," she whispered, and he let her go, but he didn't move away.

"And don't lie to me. I'm not a stupid boy. I can tell when you're placating me, cajoling me, jerking me off." He closed his eyes for a few heartbeats and when he opened them again the blazing anger was gone, but the intensity wasn't. "I trusted you to be here with me. You were laughing at me. You think Gregory is a pile of shit and you just threw it in my face."

"No, I didn't. You took it all wrong." Her mouth had gone dry. Her heartbeats were loud in her ears, almost deafening. She brushed the back of his hand with her fingertips and ran the tip of her tongue over her parched lips. His eyes smoldered.

"And don't touch me unless you're ready to be touched back."

All those times when she had faced a dare and turned away from it bombarded her and she smiled thinly at him, accepting his challenge again. She wouldn't back down.

She curled her fingers around his hand and saw surprise flicker across his face. "I wasn't making fun of you, Levi," she said, proud that she didn't sound as shaky as she felt inside. "I was actually being sincere. *You* misunderstood *me*."

He looked down at their joined hands and squeezed hers. "I overreacted. I do that sometimes – especially when I think I'm being mocked. As you can imagine, that's happened to me a lot and I made up my mind a few years ago that I wasn't going to stand for it any more."

She could barely breathe. She could barely think. She nodded.

"Gregory isn't here," he said, softly as he looked into her eyes. "He only comes to me when I need him and I need him less and less these days."

"Oh." That's all she could manage.

"Let's go." He released her hand and stepped back from her. "My brain is fried, I'm spent, and we're done here."

Chapter Six

Back at the B&B, Trudy walked behind Levi down the hall to his room. He had said not one word to her during the drive back. They'd even stopped at the RV park so that she could let Mouse out for a scamper and Levi had remained slumped in the car seat. He'd leaned the side of his face against the window and watched her and Mouse, a slight smile flickering across his mouth every so often when she caught his gaze. Back in the car, she noticed that he actually nodded off until she'd steered the car into the B&B's parking lot.

"We're here," she'd announced, parking the car.

"Hmmm?" He'd opened his eyes and yawned. "I feel better." Glancing at her, he'd shrugged and then had given a jerk of his head. "Come inside."

Scowling at his back as they neared his room, a plan formed in her mind. She suspected he intended on getting her naked and this time she'd take the risk, accept the dare, and play the game the way he played it. Just sex. No feelings. No emotional ties. Because he was right. She was attracted to him – obsessively attracted. She wanted this, so why not take what he offered? If she kept her wits about her, she could guard her heart and not allow him to shatter it.

He removed the card key from his back pocket and shoved it into the slot. Green lights flickered across it and he opened the door. He paused to glance at her, then stood back to allow her to enter first.

She had a brief glance of a round table and chairs off to her left and a large bed straight in front of her before she found herself pressed against the closed door and confronted with a pair of cobalt eyes. His hands clasped her shoulders, pinning her in place.

"Yes, I can see you're feeling much better," she noted, smiling.

"After something that intense, it sometimes takes me a little while to clear my head of the images," he said, staring at her lips. "You can understand that, right?"

She nodded. Oh, yes. She knew all about disturbing scenes that played over and over in her head until she thought she might go crazy if she couldn't stop them. His hands moved up to frame her face and he brushed his thumbs gently beneath her eyes. His eyes asked her one big question: are you staying? She nodded again, this time answering his silent query.

A sigh escaped his parted lips before he pressed them to hers, softly, beseechingly. "Thank you," he murmured against her mouth as he grabbed the hem of her top and pulled it up and over her head.

She was spun around, lifted, and placed on the bed, all so swiftly and precisely that it made her dizzy for a few moments. Propping herself on her stiff arms, she watched as he removed her shoes and then he shrugged out of his vest. He smiled at her, shaking his head a little as if he couldn't believe his good luck. He reached over his shoulder, grabbed a handful of t-shirt, and peeled the garment off, mussing his hair as it cleared his head.

Muscles rippled in his arms and chest and she was instantly aroused at the sight of him. She squirmed and her fingers gathered in fistfuls of the duvet. Black hair dusted his pectorals and then arrowed in a straight line down the center of him, disappearing under the waistband of his jeans. Good Lord, he was freaking gorgeous, she thought, not even trying to disguise her erotic delight.

After kicking off his shoes and yanking off his socks, he unbuckled his belt as a slow smile teased his lips. He placed a knee on the mattress beside her and leaned into her, making her fall back onto the bed. His mouth took hers in complete domination, his tongue swirling and caressing until she moaned and drove her fingers through his hair. She arched against him and felt his arousal straining against his fly. Moving her hands down his waist, she telegraphed her intent and he shifted to one side so that she could get her fingers around the buttons on his fly and yank them open, one by one. He groaned appreciatively and kissed her neck and shoulders and throat.

Reaching into the opening, she curved her hand around his erection and smiled when he sucked in a noisy breath. He pulled down her bra cup and latched onto her nipple, sending her arching up again as desire shot through her like white lightning. The man knew how to work a nipple, she thought, incoherently, closing her eyes and relishing the hot sizzle of his mouth and the flicking of his tongue. He slipped a hand beneath her and lifted her up so that he could deftly unhook her bra. It fell away and his mouth moved to her other breast, sucking and stroking, and sending her into mindless bliss.

"You taste delicious," he rasped, his tongue circling and then giving the hard nub a long, lavish sweep. "And you're fucking beautiful."

"Oh, God," she whispered, threading her fingers in his hair again and watching the inky strands caress them. His big hands cupped her breasts and kneaded them, stroked them. Could she orgasm just from him sucking and fondling her breasts?

He unbuttoned and unzipped her jeans and she lifted her hips so that he could jerk them off her. Her panties were gone in a flash and she was naked, staring up at him as he stood by the bed and pushed his own jeans and briefs down his lean hips and muscled legs. He tossed them aside.

She couldn't take her eyes off his erection, bold as brass, hard as steel, just bobbing there and winking at her. He was big.

"You like?" he asked.

Her gaze traveled from his impressive cock to his cocky grin. "I like," she said.

He held out his hands to her and pulled her up off the bed. Reaching behind her, he grabbed a corner of the duvet and pulled it and the shammed pillows off to reveal an expanse of cream-colored sheets. "It likes you, too." He molded his body against hers, flesh to flesh. His chest hair teased her hard nipples and his cock was hot against her belly.

His mouth swooped to hers again and their tongues tangled as he hugged her around the waist and lifted her back onto the bed. He stretched out on top of her and Trudy gloried in the feel of him – the ripple of muscles in his back as she stroked him, and the touch of his hands moving restlessly over her as if he wanted to chart her every curve.

She'd never been kissed with such authority or in so many different ways. His mouth was a sex organ all on its own, plucking and tasting, sucking and stroking, caressing and ravaging. Just from matching him kiss for kiss, she felt herself go from damp to wet. He felt it, too, because his hand moved down and he slipped a long finger into her folds.

"Ummm," he growled, appreciatively. "You're ready for me."

She wasn't at all sure she was, but she was certainly ready to give it a try. He inserted two fingers inside her and made slow, lazy circles. Then a third. Trudy shoved her head back into the mattress as intense feelings corkscrewed in her belly and spread down her thighs until she was all atremble. His fingers thrust in and out of her.

"Feel good?" he asked between sipping kisses across her breasts.

She didn't want to talk about feelings. She didn't want to talk. That would prolong it and make her believe it was something more than just sexual release. "Let's do this," she said, moving her hand down to circle his cock. God, he was big and thick and hard.

He lifted his head and a frown line appeared between his dark blue eyes. She thought she saw a flicker of confusion there. She tightened her hold on him and the fingers inside of her stopped their seduction. He closed his eyes for a few moments and didn't breathe. She gripped him tighter and ran her thumb over the glistening, moist tip, letting her nail slip inside. His eyes flew open and he bared his teeth.

"Fuck, Trudy!"

"Yes, please," she whispered, opening her mouth and biting his chin right where the barest of a cleft tempted her.

His gaze hammered her for a few, heart-stopping moments, and then his mouth thinned to a line of pure determination. "All right then." He ground the heel of his hand against her clitoris and she bucked and released her breath in a hiss. A bolt of desire shot through her, pooling between her legs. His smile was rakish, knowing. He stroked her again and she writhed as a moan worked its way up her throat. Her hand fell away from him and he rose to his knees.

She opened her eyes and saw him rolling a condom over his erection and then he positioned the crown of his cock against her opening. His chest lifted on a huge breath. "Easy," he whispered, and then sank into her.

"Oh!" She let out a little yelp of surprise. Her body tightened around him. Too tight. His momentum stopped and he held himself in place, halfway inside her. Slowly, he pulled out. "No, don't stop," she gasped, her inner muscles revolting.

"Shhh," he hushed her. "Let's try this again." He leaned down and his mouth melted over hers. The tip of his tongue stroked the slick walls of her mouth as his cock nudged her and then slipped inside, further this time. "Uh-huh," he said against her mouth as he pulled out again. "Very tight, but I can work around that."

She felt him gather himself, his back muscles tensing under her stroking hands. She stared up into his face, transfixed by the dark desire in his eyes and the determined set of his jaw. This man knew his way around a woman. In that moment she was certain that she would never regret this decision. She would take it to her grave as one of the best choices she'd ever made. She was in good hands.

One of those hands skimmed down her leg and his fingers slipped around her knee, pulling her leg up to give him more room between her thighs and tilting her pelvis at a different, more generous angle. His mouth plucked hers once, twice, and then the hard length of him plunged inside all the way. For a moment, she thought she could feel him in her throat – he filled her up that much.

He wasted not another second, but began moving, setting a rhythm that her body knew instinctively. With his hand around her knee guiding her, she arched up to meet his thrusts, and her muscles grasped him and stroked each long slide. A sheen of perspiration slicked their bodies as he increased the tempo, driving into her with more force, pulling out slowly, sensuously, letting her feel every smoking inch of him.

Laving her nipples and teasing them with little bites, he let go of her knee and his arms slid beneath her. He curved his hands around her shoulders, giving him more leverage and more command over how he wanted her to move. He was the absolute conductor and she let him maneuver her, guide her, control her. She felt him shift subtly and then the tip of his penis rubbed higher and she felt her orgasm spike. Her breath whistled down her throat and passion blinded her for a moment.

"Found it, didn't I?" he rasped in her ear. "Here we go . . . come on. Come for me. Now, Trudy, now!"

And right on cue, she exploded. "Levi!" Her voice shook out of her, propelled by the intensity of her orgasm. No place in her body was spared. It seemed that every muscle quivered and her heart hammered so hard she was afraid it was going to shatter like glass. He continued ramming into her, his breath coming out in harsh grunts, and then she felt him grow even harder inside her. She knew he was close.

"Aaah, Trudy. I can't . . . I'm there . . . we just . . ." His incoherent words buzzed in her brain.

Opening her eyes, she gazed at the utter look of rapture on his gorgeous face. A trickle of perspiration ran down his cheek to the corner of his wide mouth. His eyes were closed and he tipped his head slightly to one side as his lips thinned to expose his straight, white teeth. He bucked once, twice, and then all tension left his face and she knew he was releasing inside of her.

"Oh, Jesus," he moaned and buried his face in the side of her neck. "You feel so good. So fucking good."

He settled more completely on her and ground his hips against her, rubbing her clitoris and making her shiver with pleasure. It was uncanny how he knew just how to touch her and where!

"Come again?" he whispered against her neck and his chuckle warmed her skin. He circled his hips, grinding, pressing, his cock hardening inside her. Then his hand slipped between their bodies and his fingers slid in to find the pulsing nub and caress it.

The build up began, white-hot and all-consuming. Impossible, she thought, even as she flung her head back into the mattress when the orgasm burst through her belly like fireworks and lit her up from inside.

"Oh, oh, oh!" She let out a little scream and he rocked his hips into her, giving her another burning spasm of sizzling sensation.

"Good girl." He lifted his head and kissed her eyelids, then rested his forehead against hers. A sigh whispered past his lips. "So good." After a minute, he slid off her, lying along her side, one arm resting across her belly and his fingers spread across one breast.

Relaxing with him, softly simmering and replete, felt good. Way too good. Tears stung the back of her eyes, alarming her, engulfing her. Trudy shoved up from the bed and padded across the carpet, bending down to snatch up her clothes along the way.

"Where are you going?" he asked in a sleepy voice.

"To the bathroom." She went in and shut the door. Not wasting time sorting through her tumult of feelings, she dressed and ran her hands through her mussed hair, then emerged from the bathroom, intent on gathering up her purse and getting the hell out of there.

"Trudy?"

She stopped, her hand on the door knob, and closed her eyes for a few moments. Strengthening her resolve, she turned to face him. He was sitting on the bed, the condom gone, but his penis still perky. Really? Still?

"Where are you going?" he asked in a deceptively soft tone, although there was a crease of worry between his eyes. His hand slipped up and down his energetic cock.

"Back to the RV," she said as casually as she could while trying not to stare at his erection.

"Now? Just like that?"

She shrugged. "We've had our bit of fun and now I'm leaving."

"Is this how it goes down with you every time?"

She hitched her purse strap over her shoulder and tried her best to look calm and cool. "What do you mean?"

"I mean, are you a hit-and-runner? You hit it and run?"

Glancing away from his confused look, she heaved a sigh. She forced a smile and blew him a kiss. "Thanks. I'm glad we did it. What time did you want to meet up with Quintara this evening?"

"You're glad we did it, huh?" He rolled his eyes. "You want to have dinner together?"

"Uh . . ." She shook her head. "I'll grab something at the RV."

His eyes darkened and a frown tugged at the corners of his lovely, giving mouth. "Okay. Seven-thirty?"

"Great. See you then!" And she made her escape.

Once she was behind the wheel of the Fiesta and barreling back to Stirring Palms, she let out a shaky breath and fought back the tears that were crammed up against the back of her eyes. Could she do this? Could she have sex with him and turn off her feelings? Just enjoy the moment and not allow any oooey-gooey romantic feelings to creep into her heart?

Her body still hummed with the pleasure he'd rained all over it. Her nipples tingled and tiny muscles clenched deep inside her. Her lips felt swollen from his drugging kisses. The man was magic.

But could she do this?

*

"Levi took me to a beautiful restaurant and we had a lovely dinner," Quintara said, motioning for Trudy to come into Levi's room. "You should have joined us, dear."

"I'm glad you had a nice time," Trudy said, looking at Quintara but utterly aware of the man standing by the round table by a set of windows. At the RV, she'd taken a walk with Mouse, eaten a peanut butter and jelly sandwich, and then had gone online to get a list of museums in Key West. She'd narrowed her quest to three that she planned to visit tomorrow. Then she had tried to take a nap, but had failed. Instead, she'd remembered every second she had spent in bed with Levi Wolfe. Even being in the same room with him now made her pulses thrum. She glanced at the bed and was relieved to see that the duvet and pillows were neatly in place again.

She realized that Quintara was dressed smartly in a white and gold caftan, gold sandals, and full-on makeup. Trudy felt underdressed in her V-necked pullover and jeans. Then she made the mistake of looking at Levi and her knees wobbled.

In a black, perfectly tailored, suit and pale gray shirt, he was beyond good looking. He was expensive eye candy. His silk charcoal and silver patterned tie had a tiny smatter of red running through it that drew the eye. He opened his netbook and glanced up, then held her gaze. He arched a brow and sent her a little frown.

"Come on, ladies. Have a seat," he said. "Let's get cracking." He motioned for Trudy and Quintara to occupy two of the chairs he had placed there. After they were all seated, he sorted through pages and files on the netbook screen until he found what he wanted.

"Okay. First of all, I don't know what the murderer looks like because he was wearing sunglasses and a baseball cap pulled down low. All I could see was his chin and mouth. He was clean shaven. He was average height and build. Shelly didn't know him. He wore a long-sleeved pullover, blue jeans, and boots. Since his arms were covered, I don't know if he has tattoos or any other identifying marks."

Trudy stared at him and then at Quintara, who was smiling supremely. He was so "all business," so organized and thorough. She sat straighter, impressed, and her mind sharpened.

"Now we come to Zelda . . ."

He sat back and unbuttoned his suit jacket, letting it fall open to reveal the crimson inner lining. It was surprising and Trudy wondered what other surprises were in store for her. Levi Wolfe was adept at throwing curve balls, making her feel as if she were swinging wildly most of the time. He ran a hand down his tie in a distracted gesture and it distracted her, as well. She recalled in vivid detail what was under that tie . . . under that shirt.

"I don't know if Zelda knew the man was there. She might very well have been working with him. I just don't know. But she figures into this, so we damn well need to talk to the police about finding her. That has to be a priority of ours."

"What are the other possibilities concerning Zelda's presence there?" Quintara asked.

He consulted his notes before he answered. "He could have been hiding in the closet and he could have known Zelda was in the bathroom, but since she wasn't his chosen one, he didn't care about her. He ignored her. That would mean he's very arrogant and focused. Or he could have decided that if she stayed in the bathroom, he'd spare her, but if she came into the living room, he'd kill her. She hadn't seen him, so she couldn't I.D. him, but if she'd come into the living room, she would've left him no choice."

"And she stayed in the bathroom," Trudy noted. "She must have heard the commotion. I'm surprised she didn't bolt out of there to see what was going on."

"Maybe she did peek out and see him and was frozen with fear, so she locked herself in the bathroom until he was gone," Levi said, consulting his notes again.

"She didn't call the police," Quintara said.

"No. She left her new friend dead, murdered, and didn't even bother to call the police and report it. That seems to make her guilty instead of an innocent bystander." Levi closed the netbook and sat back in the chair. "We could learn more about Zelda's role in this through the killer, but that's not my territory." His gaze swiveled to Trudy and she felt as if she'd been speared by a hot poker. "I hope you don't mind, but I shared with Quintara the revelation that you appear to have seen this murder while you slept and have recalled bits and pieces of it."

"Oh. Right. No, that's okay."

Quintara regarded her. "That's quite an interesting development, Trudy. Usually, when this kind of thing happens, the psychic is awakened with a jolt and recalls the scene. It's amazing that you slept through it and then didn't even remember the nightmare when you woke up."

Levi responded before she could. "I believe . . . and please don't take this as a criticism, Quintara . . . but I believe that she did that because you've taught her to block out the grislier aspects of the murders."

Quintara's gaze snapped to Levi and it was as if a thunderhead formed between them. Trudy stared in rapt fascination at the silent, powerful exchange.

"How else would I take that, Levi?" Quintara asked, her voice taking on an edge.

"It's an observation," he said. "A theory. I could be wrong."

"I thought we agreed on a different approach . . . a gentler touch," Quintara said.

"We're in agreement on that."

"Helping her to block out the actual minutes of death and the ugly aftermath protected her," Quintara asserted. "She was very fragile when she came to the Roundtable. You recall being fragile, don't you, Levi?"

"Yes. Yes, I do." A shadow passed through his dark blue eyes and he lowered his gaze for a few moments. "And I understand why you did what you did. However, she's more in control now. Not seeing the whole thing through could hinder investigations and her ability to catch killers more quickly."

Trudy looked from one to the other, blazingly aware that she'd disappeared, although she was the topic of conversation. Finally, after another few tense seconds ticked by, she cleared her throat. "I hate to butt into this fascinating tug-of-war in which I appear to be the rope, but I *am* sitting right here. Flesh and blood. Not a spirit or a vision."

Levi turned his attention to her, his gaze sweeping down her body and then moving back up to linger on her legs, her breasts, her lips. "So you are."

Silence stretched like a rubber band — almost to the point of breaking. And then it was there again — that undeniable sexual chemistry. It wrapped around her and shot out to him. She knew the second he felt it because his eyes narrowed to smoky slits. For a moment, Trudy thought that she saw the super-charged air between them waffle, but she marked it up to her overworked imagination. However, the flexing of muscles in Levi's jaw and the way his breathing changed from normal to deeper breaths wasn't imagined. Oh, yes, she thought with satisfaction. He felt it and his thoughts were meandering down a particularly naughty path right along with hers.

"Children, I'm leaving you now." Quintara rose from the chair, a Cheshire cat grin spreading across her face.

"What?" Trudy ripped her gaze from Levi to stare at Quintara. *Oh, crap.* She and Levi weren't the only ones who had felt it.

Levi stood quickly and he also looked confused and shaken. "Is something wrong?"

"No, it's getting late and I need to pack," Quintara said, still smiling as if she had a delicious secret. She laid a hand on his sleeve. "And I need to book a flight back to Tulsa."

"We're leaving?" Trudy asked, and almost felt relieved because she was beginning to think that she might combust if she and Levi were left alone together again.

"*We* aren't," Quintara said with a soft chuckle. "But *I* am. I have my Roundtable work waiting for me and a couple of magazine articles I must finish and send off before the end of the month. I wanted to get you two settled in. You're well into this now and you don't need me."

"I wish you would stay, Quintara," Levi said. "I'm afraid I've offended you and I certainly would never—."

"You didn't," Quintara said, resting a hand alongside his face in a gesture that tugged at Trudy's heart, especially when he smiled and rubbed his cheek against Quintara's palm. "We understand each other on this. It's time for you to take the lead now."

"But this is so sudden and we could use your help," he said, trying to persuade her to change her mind.

"That's kind of you to say, but I can be of more use to more people back in Tulsa than I can be here. You don't need me. You have each other now."

Trudy's gaze slipped hesitantly to Levi and his to hers. She quelled a shiver that started in her stomach and spiraled upward to her heart.

"At least allow me to make the travel arrangements for you," he said to Quintara as he escorted her to the door of his room. Her brightly colored caftan flowed around her, the hem brushing the tops of her sandals. "Are you sure you won't stay a day or two longer?" he asked so quietly that Trudy could barely catch his words. He dipped his head toward Quintara. "You don't have to do this."

"I know, dear heart." Quintara placed a hand on his tie and adjusted the Windsor knot. "I'll only be a phone call away. You can ring or text me anytime you need me."

"I'll hold you to that." He opened the door.

Trudy stepped forward. "I don't know what's going on, but there isn't any reason why you should take a powder on us, Quintara. I think things will go better all around if you'll stay for a few more days."

Quintara wrapped her warm fingers around Trudy's wrist. "I'm so proud of you. You've come such a long way in such a short time. Now, it's up to Levi to guide you the rest of the way up the mountain."

Don't desert me, Trudy mouthed, and Quintara laughed and shook her head.

"Good night to you both*,* " Quintara said, wiggling the fingers of one hand as she sashayed out of the room and across the hall to her own.

"I'll book you on an afternoon flight, Quintara," Levi called after her.

"Yes, darling, not too early. You know how I hate mornings."

Trudy heard the door across the hall close before Levi shut the one to his room and turned around to face her. His eyes were hooded. He looked coolly dangerous in that dark suit, she thought. Like an ad in *GQ* or *Vanity Fair*. She glanced around and was suddenly acutely aware that the bed they'd had sex in earlier took up a good portion of the room.

"You have a cell phone, don't you?"

She stared at him. She hadn't expected *that!* God, she'd never be able to know where he was going next or what was going to come out of his mouth. "Yes."

He held out his hand. "Let me have it, please."

"Why?"

"Because I want to program my cell phone number into it. We need to be able to communicate better."

"Oh. Right." Yes, communicating better would be good, she thought, collecting her purse and pulling her cell phone from it. "Here you go."

He took it, flipped it open, then turned it over and over. "Wait a minute . . . this doesn't have a camera . . . or a keyboard." He looked at her, incredulously.

She nodded. "That's right. It's just a phone. It's all I need. I hardly ever use it."

"No, no, no." He flipped the phone closed and gave it back to her, a disgusted look on his face as if he was handling road kill instead of her trusty, little phone. "We're going into Key West tomorrow to confer with Detective Sinclair. While we're there, we'll get you a proper cell phone. You need a netbook, too."

"I don't need any of those things." She shoved the phone back into her purse. "What do I need a camera for? You have one."

"Because I won't always be with you. You need the ability to snap photos of important things that trigger something – places, people, and objects. Then, you can file those photos on your netbook."

"That's how *you* work. That's not how *I* work."

He shook his head in denial, refusal. "Although you believe I can read your mind, I can't. Therefore, you need a system for storing and filing things that I can share. You're purchasing a new phone and a netbook." He held up a hand to block her protest. "What is it with you and modern electronics? You worked in a pawn shop, so I know you were around the latest gizmos all the time."

She shrugged. "I've never been interested in those things. I . . . like antiques."

He chuckled. "Well, I'm here to drag you into this century."

"My expense account is obviously a lot smaller than yours for this little adventure." She folded her arms, mirroring his posture, and tapped one sandal for good measure. Then she wished she hadn't when the action drew his lambent gaze from her face, down, down, down her. She moved, trying to escape his sight, but there was really nowhere to hide, so she sat at the table again and drummed her fingers on the top of it. She sensed him moving, coming closer, standing behind her.

"You know, I can buy those things for you."

"You can go to hell, too."

He chuckled. "Do you have a credit card?"

She puffed out a breath. "Of course, I do! Several, in fact." She turned in the chair to glare at him. "Will you sit down and quit lurking behind me?"

He complied and lowered himself into the chair next to her. The room grew quiet as the air-conditioner cycled off.

"I'm going to check out a few museums while we're in Key West tomorrow."

"Oh?"

"I made a list this afternoon. There are three I want to go to and see if I can locate the exact one the killer was in yesterday."

"I'll go with you."

She glanced at him through her lashes as questions crowded her mind. There was so much she wanted to know . . . to learn . . . and he had the answers.

"What?" He regarded her, intently as usual. "What's wrong?"

"I want to ask you something."

"Go ahead."

"I don't want you to take it the wrong way and get all pissy with me."

The corners of his wide mouth twitched with amusement. "I'll withhold my pissyness. Ask me."

"How does it work between you and Gregory?" She saw suspicion tighten his features and she reached out and grasped his sleeve. "No, really. I want to know what he does for you. Does he give you clues or does he speak to other spirits and tell you things? How long has he been with you? You said he was real old, right?"

He settled back in the chair and his gaze dropped to her hand on his sleeve. Trudy let her fingers slip away to rest on the table top. She thought she saw him hitch in a quick breath.

"It's a strange relationship," he said, his words emerging hesitatingly, as if he wasn't sure how much he wanted to reveal to her. "I don't actually get clues from him, although he does manage to give me insight. Sometimes I can ask a direct question and get a direct response from him, but not often." He tipped his head, his gaze sliding to her again. "How long has he been with me? Since I was nine."

"Nine!" She blinked at him. "Since you were a child?"

"Yes. He came to me when I was in crisis mode and on the verge of spinning out of control."

"At nine years old?" she repeated, shocked, incredulous. What the hell could have happened to him that would send him over the edge when he was nine? It must have been something to do with his paranormal abilities, she thought, and hoped he would be forthcoming with the details, but she suspected he wouldn't.

"Gregory was there for me. He counseled me and showed me there was a way out and a better path to take. And that's primarily what he does for me. He settles my mind, mends my feelings, and reins in my emotions so that I can think clearly and rationally. Then I'm able to do the work that's important and vital to me." He lifted one broad shoulder in a shrug. "He guides me back to spiritual sanity."

"Your spirit guide."

He smiled. "That's right."

"And he's very old?"

"That's the sense I get from him. I believe he lived centuries ago."

"Why did he pick you to guide? Why *is* he a guide for mortals?"

"I don't know." He frowned. "I'm not sure if it's a penance or simply his task as a spirit. He hasn't shared that with me, so I assume it's none of my business. I think it has something to do with his understanding of how it feels to be an outcast."

"Oh? You felt like that, too?" The insight of their shared experience bound her closer to him.

"Yes. Most of my life. Up until I met Quintara, I suppose."

"Were you ever suicidal?" she asked.

"No. Although, I'm sure I was drinking myself to death when I met Quintara, but I didn't see it that way. My ego is too huge for me to ever seriously consider offing myself."

She shook her head, smiling at his honesty. "So, you think Gregory was an outcast?"

"He hasn't told me he was. I just sense it. I believe he's homosexual. Back when he lived, that would result in instant death."

"One of the reasons I haven't been able to believe much in spirit guides is because of how Billy and Jerrod act in the Roundtable. They have spirit guides – or so they say – and they are *very* dramatic about them."

"Oh, right. Billy and Jerrod." He chuckled. "They've talked to me about their guides. They're full of shit."

Trudy giggled. "I'm glad we agree on that."

"Anything else I can help you with?"

She gave a little shrug. "That's all for now."

Flicking back his cuff, he consulted his Rolex. "We'll go to the police station and museums tomorrow after we see Quintara to the airport. Are you staying here with me?"

"No." Trudy rose and gathered her purse.

"Why not?"

"I need to get back to Stirring Palms."

"Why?"

"Because I do." She started for the door, but he grabbed her by the arm and pulled her around to face him. The hint of vulnerability around his mouth sent longing through her.

"What were you playing at this afternoon?"

She ran a hand down his tie, opting for coyness. "I thought I was playing with you."

"You know what I'm talking about," he rasped. "Why did you rush out of here?"

"I told you . . ."

His grip on her arm tightened and he cupped her chin in his other hand and brought her gaze up to his. "I wanted to spend the afternoon in bed with you."

"I had things to do, Levi. We're here to work. Remember?"

He lowered his mouth to hers slowly and placed lingering kisses on her parted lips. "I remember how you feel underneath me and how you sound when you come. That's what I remember."

Passion simmered in her belly and she closed her eyes, feeling the weakness steal through her, robbing her of her good sense. He lifted his mouth from hers and tipped his head back to stare at the ceiling.

"Jesus God, I want you," he groaned. After taking a couple of breaths, he looked down into her eyes again. The resolve stamped on his features made her shiver. "And you want me, too. You're staying."

Chapter Seven

With a nod, she loosened his tie and unbuttoned his shirt while he shrugged out of his jacket and pulled her shirt up over her head. In a matter of minutes, they had their clothes off and were on the bed again. Trudy clutched at his hips and he clamped his lips around her straining nipple. She drew in a shuddering breath and felt the wetness between her thighs. One touch and she was ready for him. Amazing.

She parted her legs, wanting no more preamble. What was it about him that made her crave his closeness and yet feel that she could never get close enough to him? "Inside," she panted. "I want you in me."

"Wait one sec." He reached across her to the side table and opened the drawer, withdrawing a condom from it. Ripping the packet with his teeth, he sheathed himself with practiced ease, grinning down at her.

"Hurry," she ordered and then groaned his name as the fullness of him consumed her. Her body clamped around him, creating a friction that was delicious and daunting, all at the same time. He was big and powerful and her body felt stretched to its limit. It felt so good she wanted to cry. But then he moved and she wanted to scream as an orgasm twisted in her stomach and burst forth. She trembled and heard his rasping breath near her ear. There was nothing in the world but him and how he made her feel. He was magic.

"Jesus, Trudy." He moved inside her like a surging tide, increasing the tempo with each thrust and retreat, thrust and retreat.

As she came down off her orgasm, she opened her eyes and stared into Levi's gorgeous face, which was a study in erotic concentration. His cobalt eyes blazed with pent-up passion as he continued the relentless rhythm, lifting her up, up, up. He was a connoisseur of orgasms, she thought, incoherently. Finding previously undiscovered erotic triggers on her body to touch and rub and suck, he made her tremble with longing and burst with passion.

The wide crown of his penis rubbed incessantly on a spot inside her that sent flames shooting through her. She opened her mouth and garbled sounds escaped.

"Ah, yes," he growled, opening his eyes to slits to watch her. "Explode for me. Just for me. Let me see it."

Trudy's body quickened and clutched violently at him and then she knew she was going to come apart and the shattering came, scattering her like ashes. She heard herself chanting his name in a hoarse, primal cry, begging him to stop and pleading with him never to stop. Never, never, never stop!

"That's right, that's right," his voice drifted to her like from a fevered dream. "Sweet. Feels so fucking good, doesn't it?" The words poured over her like warm honey. He grew still, waiting for her body to cease its throbbing and desperate clutching.

"Oh, my God, Levi," she whispered, sweeping her damp bangs off her forehead. "That was incredible. I never . . . I don't know what to say." She knew she wasn't making sense and she didn't care. Her body hummed happily and her mind was nice and foggy so that she didn't have to think clearly about what had happened and that she was naked and slick with perspiration and that she'd all but screamed his name over and over again. What power did he have over her? How could she ever think that she could be with him like this and not want more and more? Not cringe when she thought of it being over?

He sandwiched her upper lip between his and sucked gently, then nipped it. "I love your mouth, Trudy. Someday I want to fuck it . . . but right now –." He slipped his arms beneath her and pulled her up to sit on his lap so that they were face to face. "Ready?"

She stared into his stormy eyes and realized he was still hard, still primed.

"For what?" she asked, dubiously. Hadn't he come yet? After all of that? Every man she'd been with had ejaculated before she came or maybe right after. Actually, the majority of the time, they didn't even care if she'd come or not. But Levi paid attention. He made sure she was satisfied. It was important to him.

"I'm going to take you higher, Trudy."

She shook her head, not believing that she could experience anything more and worried that she wouldn't be able to live through it. But then he wrapped one arm around her waist and lifted her and let her settle back down onto him. She convulsed around him, feeling him sink deeper into her. Impossibly deep. Her eyelids fluttered down and a firestorm of sensations burned through her. God, had she ever really had sex before? Did she actually have another orgasm in her? This was . . . was . . . crazy and oh! He rocked his hips, pumping into her faster and harder, driving in and out like a relentless, flesh-covered piston. She wrapped her arms around his neck and held on, her breath escaping in choppy huffs and little moans with each powerful thrust.

She squeezed her eyes shut as the intensity of her climax climbed higher and higher. When she felt him slow to a long, quivering caress inside her, she shuddered and came again and again, her insides on fire and melting . . . melting.

"Ahhh, Christ," he bit out, his face pressed against the side of her neck, his breath hot and rapid on her skin. "Too much. It's too goddamned much."

She draped herself over him, her bones liquefied. After a minute, she managed to raise her head and look at him. His eyes were closed, but opened slowly to smoky blue slits.

"I think you just blew off the top of my head," he said, his mouth quirking.

Trudy laughed under her breath and leaned her forehead against his. "I've never had that many orgasms. I don't know how you do that, but you're very, very good at it."

"Why, thank you, Miss Tucker. I aim to please." He cupped her breasts in his big hands and ran his thumbs over her tight, sensitive nipples. He blew gently on them and they stiffened and strained to find his lips.

"Oooh," she breathed and strove to steady her voice. "I'm not even sure that I *ever* climaxed before today."

His eyes sparkled and she knew she'd pleased him. He kissed the tip of her nose and lowered her back onto the bed. He pulled out of her slowly and stretched beside her. She was vaguely aware of him removing the condom, tying a knot in it, and dropping it into the waste basket beside the bed. And then his hand smoothed over her belly and he drew her closer so that he could nuzzle the side of her neck. "You smell so damned good. What is that? Euphoria?"

She nodded. "Yes."

"When I smell it from now on I'll get an erection."

She laughed as her body and breathing resumed normal functions. But her heart still raced a little and she glanced at Levi from the corner of her eye. From the look on his face, he was satisfied, but had she reached any other part of him besides his penis? She wanted to know him. She wanted him to really know her. And that was dangerous thinking. She knew it, but she couldn't help it.

He pulled her closer and his mouth claimed her lips as he kissed her deeply, ardently. His tongue caressed hers in long, slick strokes. She twisted her fingers in his hair. God, she loved the ebony silkiness of his hair! And his hands. Those big, commanding, tender, tormenting, consuming hands of his! They covered her breasts possessively, urgently. He tore his lips from hers and fastened them on her straining nipple. Instantly, fire shot to her groin and she moaned. His mouth and fingers were everywhere, sucking and tweaking, licking and flicking until she could not bear it another second. She arched into him.

"Levi!" she breathed his name.

"I can't get enough of you, Trudy. I just can't." He ran a hand over her belly and between her legs. He pushed two fingers inside her. "So fucking wet," he murmured, and then he was on his knees and he had another foil packet. "Turn over onto your stomach."

She blinked up at him, not sure she liked the idea. He was suddenly assertive and terse. "What are you . . . what are we . .?"

"Don't worry. You'll like it." His eyes were dark, dark blue and his lips curved into a tense and predatory smile. He tore open the packet and removed the condom. "Flip over," he instructed again and he sheathed his lengthening cock.

Unsure of her next move, she stared at him, amazed that he was erect again. "How can you still be hard?" she asked, shaking her head.

"This is what you do to me, Trudy. I was still hard when you left me this afternoon." Impatience drew his brows together. He gripped her hips and unceremoniously flipped her over.

"Levi, wait!" She propped herself on her elbows as panic billowed through her. "What are you going to do?" He wasn't going to . . . She shuddered. No!

"Take it easy," he whispered, running a hand down her spine and cupping her behind. "We're going to do it doggy style. You've done it like this before, right?"

She shook her head. She'd actually only had sex the old-fashioned way, front to front, and she wasn't at all sure she wanted to experiment yet. But he was already leaning over her, kissing and sucking all the way from her nape down to the small of her back where his tongue drew lazy circles.

"No? You're such a novice! Up on all fours, baby," he said, pulling her knees up until she balanced on them and her elbows. "That's right. It's deeper this way." He gripped her hips and then he thrust hard into her.

Trudy cried out, startled by the quick invasion and his sudden mood change. This was definitely all about sex. Nothing seductive and coaxing going on between them this time. She felt herself expand and then contract, gloving him.

"Oh, my God, Trudy." His voice was hoarse. Awe and surrender threaded through it. "Take all of me. Every fucking thing."

She felt tears sting the corners of her eyes. She understood – knew what he was feeling . . . the overpowering sensations and the helpless sense that this was so incredibly perfect that it was terrifying.

He started to move then, really move and he took Trudy right along with him. Her thoughts scattered and she bowed her head as passion built within her. Reaching out, she grabbed the edge of the mattress and held on for dear life as he worked himself in and out of her, rocking his hips, thrusting, pushing her to her limits. Suddenly, all of her senses were in sharp focus. She could smell sex in the air and she could hear the slapping and slippery sounds as their bodies collided and glided. She could taste blood on her tongue where she'd bitten down on the inside of her lip. Looking over her shoulder, she watched Levi stare intently at the joining of their bodies, beads of sweat rolling from his temple to his jaw. He gripped her hips more tightly and drove into her faster, harder.

She could feel his own orgasm building as his body grew hotter and hotter and his breathing became harsher and harsher.

He went in deep, right to his root. She thrust back to meet him and he groaned. Matching his tempo, she gritted her teeth as the friction of their hot, slick bodies became a tad uncomfortable. She was tender inside and her flesh trembled. He was almost too big, almost too deep, but Trudy bit her lower lip and tasted blood again. Her discomfort gradually gave way to another inner explosion that had her crying out again. Black spots floated across her vision and she shut her eyes and let the orgasm find her.

"Yes, yes," he bit out, almost savagely. "Get there . . . I'm there!" He came in a driving, hip-rocking force that sent a deep, deep spasm through her. His fingers dug into her hips as he rode out his orgasm. His breath escaped in a long, hissing, groan. She fell onto the mattress, her muscles suddenly jelly, and he collapsed on top of her, his chest rising and falling and his skin hot and shimmering with perspiration. "Jesus, that was good," he whispered, clearly awed as he caressed her arms and laced his fingers with hers. "I am wrung out. I don't think I can even move."

"You have to," Trudy said, squirming. "I can't breathe."

Laughing a little, he rolled off her. "Aren't you glad you stayed?"

She rolled her eyes. The arrogant ass. "Yes," she conceded.

"So am I." He discarded the condom and then flung a leg over hers. "Stay the night."

"No."

He lifted his head and looked at her. "Why the hell not?"

"Because I have to get back to the RV."

"Why? Mouse isn't going anywhere. She'll be fine."

She started to move, but he flung an arm across her. "Levi, just swing by and pick me up on your way into Key West tomorrow."

"I have a better idea. You keep your sweet ass in this bed next to me and we can have sex again in the morning." He nuzzled her ear. "What's with the brush off after we fuck?"

She winced, hearing him call it that right after she'd had multiple orgasms diminished it for her. Obviously, it hadn't meant as much to him as it had to her. She patted his arm. "Let me up."

"No can do." His breath was warm against her neck.

With a burst of strength, she wiggled free and bounded from the bed.

"For Christ sake, Trudy!" he bit out, clearly ticked off.

She snatched her clothes off the floor and began dressing under his scowling regard. When she glanced at him, she winced again. He was furious. His black brows bridged his stormy blue eyes and he rested one muscle-defined arm on top of his bent knee, the sheet pooling between his legs.

"I'll see you tomorrow," she said, trying to appease him.

"Shouldn't you leave some money on the nightstand?"

That brought her to a halt. She turned slowly toward him. "Don't be that way. We had fun, right?"

"Right, and now you're done and you can't stand to be in the same room with me. But I'm not supposed to feel like your man whore?"

She let her hands fall limply to her sides and her shoulders slumped in defeat. "Levi, please! Are you going to sit there and tell me you've never had sex with a woman and left shortly afterward to go home to your own bed?" She held his gaze and when he looked away, she knew she'd won. "Seriously?"

"Go on then." He fell back on the bed. "Drive carefully."

Seizing the meager victory, Trudy let herself out of his room, needing to get away from him so that she could think clearly. Her plan to keep her heart guarded from him wasn't working. His heart seemed to be well-protected, but her defenses were weakened. Severely weakened.

*

The police station on Roosevelt Boulevard looked like a wedding cake to Trudy — all pink and white with soft, rounded edges. Inside, it was tougher looking. Bustling with uniformed officers, there were also a lot of regular folks milling around and most of them looked as if they wished they didn't have to be there.

She and Levi went through a metal detector and were issued "visitor" lanyards which they hung around their necks.

Levi led her up a flight of stairs, down a hall, and into a big space full of dividers and desks. A sign on the double glass doors read: Detective Division. He stopped at the first desk where a dark-skinned, young woman was speaking to someone via a headset.

Dressed in his usual — black upon black upon black — Levi had added a pair of tortoise shell sunglasses which he now took off and slipped into his jacket's inside pocket. In the Keys where "casual dress" was the dress code almost everywhere, he stood out in his suit and tie. But, then he'd stand out in jeans and a t-shirt, too, she thought, giving him the once-over and remembering how gorgeous his body was without clothes.

He was back to being cool, in control Levi, she thought, and she was glad. She'd been nervous when they'd set off for Key West in the Nissan to take Quintara to the airport, unsure of how to act around him after last night. But she needn't have worried. He'd greeted her as if nothing had transpired . . . as if he hadn't made her come over and over again and she hadn't cried out his name until she was hoarse.

Feeling a little flushed by her meandering thoughts, Trudy was thankful for the blast from an air-conditioning vent as they waited for the receptionist to address them. It was a hot day and she was glad she'd opted for a light blue sundress with spaghetti straps. Moderately-high heeled strappy sandals hugged her feet. The afternoon was heating up.

"Hello," the receptionist said, ending the call. "How can I help you today?"

"Hello. I'm Levi Wolfe and this is Miss Tucker. We have an appointment with Detective Sinclair."

"I'll let him know." She punched some buttons on the telecommunications console and waited a few seconds. "Detective? Mr. Wolfe and Miss Tucker are here to see you. Will do." She smiled up at them. "Do you know which cubicle is his?"

"I do. Thank you." Levi grasped Trudy's elbow and ushered her around and through the crowded room to somewhere in the middle of it. "Hi, Tom. Good to see you again." He reached out to shake the man's hand who had stood up from behind a cluttered desk. "You haven't had the pleasure of meeting my associate Trudy Tucker. Trudy, this is Detective Tom Sinclair. He's heading up the case we're interested in."

Tom Sinclair was in his early thirties, Trudy guessed, and his blond hair was beginning to thin and recede, but he was still a handsome man. He reminded her of a young Prince William. He shook Levi's hand, then hers. His fingers were gentle as he gave her hand more of a squeeze than a shake.

"Good to meet you," he said, his brown eyes moving up and down her frame. "Won't you have a seat? Where are you from, Ms. Tucker?"

"I live in Tulsa. Please call me Trudy."

"Okay, but only if you call me Tom." When he smiled, the skin in the corners of his brown eyes crinkled. "Oklahoma, huh? Is that where you live, too, Wolfe?"

"No."

Trudy looked at Levi in momentary surprise. Where *did* he live? She realized that she had no idea. She had assumed he lived near Tulsa, maybe Oklahoma City.

After they were seated, Tom Sinclair opened a green file folder on his desk. "We've made some headway," he said, flipping through a few pages. "I talked to that guy this morning – the one you said was at the bar with Zelda. Your description helped a lot and the bartender was able to zero in on him and find his credit card receipt."

Swiveling her gaze sharply to Levi, Trudy hitched up her chin in a show of irritation. When had all this happened? Levi unbuttoned his suit jacket and sat forward, obviously eager for more information. Trudy would have liked nothing better than to give him a swift kick in the shin.

"What did he say? Is he a local?" Levi asked.

"He's a truck driver out of Marathon and El Paso, Texas," Tom said, his eyes moving back and forth as he read from the file. "His name is Hank Booker or Henry Booker. He's divorced." Tom's gaze lifted to find Trudy and he smiled. "Like me." Then he looked down at the file again.

Trudy shifted in the chair, wondering if Tom Sinclair was flirting or simply being friendly.

"Booker met Zelda that very same night and he hasn't seen her since," Tom continued, reading from his file notes. "Doesn't know where she lives or her phone number. The barkeep couldn't remember much about her, but hopefully we will be able to jar his memory." He closed the folder and grinned at Trudy. "Are you attached? Divorced?"

Trudy smiled. Oh, okay. He was definitely flirting. "Neither."

"Really?" Tom wiggled his eyebrows, making her laugh under her breath.

Trudy looked away from him and felt her face and neck grow warm. She had the distinct feeling that Levi was glaring at her. She glanced at Levi and censure was evident in his expression. He lifted one, winged brow and set his mouth in a firm line of disapproval. She shrugged him off. Jeez! Stand down, Wolfe, she thought. It's just a harmless, little flirtation!

Sinclair opened the folder again. "Booker gave a description of Zelda to Wanda, our sketch artist, and Wanda's putting finishing touches on it now. He described her as having black, shoulder-length hair and she's tall and has broad shoulders – kind of like a swimmer, you know? She has a good figure. Couldn't remember the color of her eyes. She wore a tight, black mini-skirt and a long-sleeved, red blouse that night. Oh, and really high heels." The detective's gaze drifted to Trudy's shoes and the ghost of a smile flitted across his lips. He closed the folder and tossed it onto the desk. "Anyway, we'll check on how Wanda's doing. She's probably done by now." He looked at Trudy. "So, you're psychic, too?"

"Yes."

"Wolfe says you get into the murderer's mind. That must suck."

She laughed. "Yeah, that's a good description of how it is." She shared a few more moments of mirth with him before a colder presence made her glance sideways. Levi was *not* amused. His glare was downright glacial as he looked from Tom to her and back to Tom again.

"Could we see that sketch now, Tom?" he asked, low and clipped.

The detective blinked. "Sure. This way, folks."

"Did you get my e-mails, Tom?" Levi asked, motioning for Trudy to walk ahead of him, even though he didn't spare a glance for her.

"Yeah, I did." Tom checked his stride, looking over his shoulder and the top of Trudy's head to Levi. "Thanks. That gives us a lot more to consider."

"I e-mailed my notes from yesterday to the detective," Levi said for Trudy's edification.

"Did you now?" She bristled, feeling left out. What else had he been doing? Who else had he e-mailed about his findings?

"Hi, Wanda," the detective greeted a middle-aged woman sitting by a sunny window. She looked up from the computer screen. "Got anything yet?"

"Yes, I think so. Let me print it off." She hit a button on the keyboard and a printer on her desk buzzed and began to vibrate as it spit out a sheet of paper. "Here you go." She handed the page to Tom, then smiled at Levi and Trudy. "How are you today?"

Levi held out his hand. "Fine, thank you, Wanda. I'm Levi Wolfe and this is Trudy Tucker."

"Oh, 'scuse my lack of manners," Tom said with a chuckle, handing the paper to Levi. "She's a pretty good looker. I'd buy her a drink."

Levi accepted the drawing and angled it so that Trudy could see it, too. The woman staring back at them had a chiseled nose, square chin, big, luminous eyes, thick hair, combed back from a widow's peak, and a wide mouth. Her lips weren't full, but they weren't too thin either. She wasn't smiling, but she was giving a kind of come-hither stare from the page. Trudy looked at Levi. He gaze was devouring the image before him and she knew he was committing it to memory.

"You can keep that," Tom said. "Print me off another for the file, Wanda."

"Sure. No prob." Wanda hit the button again, bringing life to the printer.

"We'll take copies of this around to the bars in that area to see if anyone knows her," Tom said. "And I'll show it to the bartender at The Gold Lagoon to see if he recalls seeing her around and if she's been back since then."

"You'll call me if anything important is uncovered that might help us?" Levi asked.

"You got it." Tom gave a wink that he directed mostly at Trudy.

Levi motioned for Trudy to precede them as they wound their way back to Tom's cubicle. "I wanted to ask you something, Tom."

"Sure, shoot."

"Sissy Franklin of Court TV wants me to do a remote to discuss my interest in this particular case. How do you feel about that?"

Trudy stopped in her tracks and spun around to face Levi. He studiously avoided her blazing glare at him, but Tom Sinclair didn't. He looked, bemused, from Levi to Trudy and back to Levi.

"Well, uh . . ." Tom ran a hand around the back of his neck and grinned at Trudy. "I guess that would be all right with *me*," he said with great emphasis, "so long as you don't reveal anything that hasn't already been in the newspapers and on television. I mean, you know things that we haven't released to the public because we—."

"You keep some details to yourself so that you can use them to validate anyone who comes forward and says he or she has something to add to it," Levi finished for him, nodding. "Yes, I know that tactic and I'm fine with it. So, it's okay?"

Tom nodded with a shrug and cut his eyes at Trudy again. She could barely keep from screaming at Levi, she was so irritated. Oh, he'd get an earful as soon as they were out of this building and out of earshot!

"Great. Thanks." Levi edged around Trudy as if she was a pillar that was in his way. He confidently made his way to the exit.

"You okay?" Tom asked.

Trudy blinked and forced a smile to her lips. "Yes. It was nice to meet you." She held out her hand.

"Nice to meet you, too. Hey, could you give me your phone number in case – well, in case I want to call you?" His brown eyes sparkled with good-natured interest.

Trudy nodded, glad to have a friendly cop on her side for a change. "Sure."

He pulled a small notebook and a pen out of his breast pocket. He pressed the button at the end of the pen and grinned. "Blast away. I'm ready."

She told him her phone number and he recorded it in his notebook.

"Thanks. Now, is this your home number in Oklahoma or your cell?"

"Cell."

He winked. "Good."

"Well . . . see you later."

"You betcha."

Trudy walked quickly away from him. She found Levi waiting for her just outside the building. He sent her a dark scowl.

"What was that all about?" he asked.

"He wanted my phone number."

"What for? He has mine."

She looked at him from beneath her lashes. "Really, Levi? Three guesses and the first two don't count." When he continued to glare at her, she rolled her eyes. "Quintara has been on me to be friendlier to the police."

Still fixing her with an ominous scowl, he pushed his sunglasses on to hide his steely blues from her. "There's a big difference between being cordial and being flirtatious. You two were flirting."

"So what? I'm unattached." She shrugged.

His head jerked as he stared hard at her. "You were attached to me a few hours ago." He shook his head, clearly irritated. "Christ, Trudy." He held up a hand to stop her from saying anything. "Look, all I'm going to say about this business with Sinclair is that you shouldn't get personally involved with the police or anyone else connected to a case you're working."

"That includes you?" she asked, quietly, and she couldn't keep the smile from touching her lips.

A curse she could barely hear above the traffic sounds whispered past his lips. "I'm your partner, Trudy. They are on one side . . ." He gestured, motioning away. "And we are on the other side." He brought his hand back to his chest. "Got it?" He tilted his head sideways, silently telling her to follow him. "Let's find a good electronics store."

Trudy walked with him across the plaza and along the street to where he'd parked the Nissan. She waited until they were strapped in and merged into the traffic before she launched into what *she* wanted to talk about.

"Sissy Franklin?"

A muscle flexed in his jaw line, but he said nothing.

"You don't think I should have been told about that before Sinclair?"

"Sinclair wants to play slap and tickle with you."

"Sissy Franklin already plays slap and tickle with you. So what?" She set her back teeth and counted to ten. When she spoke, she was proud of her lighter tone. "Tell me something. When, exactly, are we going to begin working together?"

Scowling, he didn't look at her, preferring to concentrate on Key West traffic. "I don't understand the question. We're working together already."

"But you didn't tell me about the Court TV thing."

"Did you want to appear on there with me?"

"No!"

"That's what I thought. You've made it clear that you don't work that way, so I didn't tell you about it because you wouldn't appear on the show with me anyway."

"That's not the point. You should have *asked me first.*"

His scowl deepened and she wished he wasn't wearing sunglasses. She could tell so much more about his moods when she could see his eyes.

"Ask you *what* first?"

She gritted her teeth, irritated with his dense act. "You should have asked me if it was okay for you to appear on Court TV."

He released a short, harsh laugh. "Are you joking? Tell me you're joking. Why the hell would I have to ask you for permission to appear on that show? I've been on it many times before *without* your permission."

"I know that, but we're working this case *together*, Levi. Therefore, we should make decisions about it *together*. You didn't even tell me that you'd e-mailed your notes to the detective."

"Well, since you can't e-mail anything because your phone can't access e-mail or the Internet and you have no e-notebook yet, that task was left up to me."

"I have a laptop and an e-mail account, for your information. Back to the point, if you would tell the truth, you would simply say that you didn't tell me about the Court TV appearance because you knew I would advise against it."

"I know what I'm doing, Trudy." He set his mouth in a firm line and his jaw tensed, the muscles bunching and flexing. "When I appear on a show like Sissy's to shed light on a specific case, people call in with tips that often pan out and help us catch the killer. I mainly want to shake the tree and see if anything falls out if it."

They pulled to a stop at a traffic light. Suddenly, his chin bobbed up and he smacked one palm against the steering wheel. "Now we're talking!"

Perplexed, Trudy followed his gaze and saw a Best Buy store straight ahead of them. She slumped down in the seat, resigned to spend more of her disappearing savings.

Chapter Eight

"Do you think you've got it now?" Levi asked.

Trudy looked from her confusing new cell phone to him. He sat across from her at the picnic table beside her RV. The afternoon sun threw shadows, engulfing them. A cool breeze combed his jet black hair off his forehead and then let it fall back again. She knew how soft his hair felt sliding through her fingers and that he liked for her to tug on it when she came or when she wanted to direct his mouth to a different part of her body. She knew so much, so why did she feel that she didn't know him at all?

He'd removed his jacket and loosened the knot of his tie. His blue eyes moved as he read something on the screen of his own cell phone, concentration settling over his handsome face.

It was a sin for a man to look that sexy with little or no effort, Trudy thought. No wonder he had women falling all over him. Did he take it for granted? Or did he gaze in the mirror every morning and thank God for his good genes?

He'd been fiddling with his cell phone for several minutes, typing messages, hitting buttons, typing something else. What was he doing? He could be sending sex-texts to Sissy Franklin for all she knew. The very thought of that made her cringe.

"Trudy, are you going to answer me?"

"Yes! Yes, I think I can figure it out from here," she said, forcing herself to focus on the stupid phone instead of the jealousy poisoning her mind and making her even more aware that her feelings for him were deepening and that was dangerous for her heart and her head. She knew she should make more use of electronic gadgets. "I liked my little phone. This one is much bigger."

"Believe me, bigger is almost always better."

A delightful shiver arrowed through her. She glanced at him through her lashes and wasn't surprised to see a devilish smile tip up the corners of his mouth. "How do I get on the Internet?"

"I'll show you that in a minute. First, I'll send you an e-mail. Let me know when it appears in your Inbox." He typed a few letters and then pressed a button with his thumb. His gaze lifted to hers. "Is it there?"

She looked at the phone. It made a little "bing" noise. "The light has gone off and I can't see anything on the screen. It must be broken."

He sighed. "Press the button on the side. The *other* side. The left button is the volume control, remember? The right button turns your screen on and off. Is my e-mail there?"

"Okay, okay. It's just that my other phone lit up when a call came in," she grumbled.

"I'm not calling you. I'm e-mailing you," he reminded her, and she could tell his patience was wearing thin.

She studied the screen and the number "1" blinked on the envelope icon. "Yes, it's here!"

"Good, open it and send it back to me."

She read the e-mail's message. *Test Levi Wolfe.* Keeping the smile from her lips, she typed, *Don't you mean Testy Levi Wolfe? I agree!* She hit send.

The phone in his hand, an identical one to hers, "binged" and he touched the screen with his forefinger and read her e-mail. His gaze bounced to her for a second, then back to the screen. He grinned.

"How do I get on the Internet?"

"Touch the globe icon."

"Right. Same icon as the one on my computer."

"Same one," he agreed.

"This had better be worth it," she said. "My other phone only cost me twenty bucks a month. This thing costs three times that a month!"

"It's a valuable tool and you can write off the expense."

"What did you do with my other phone?"

"I donated it to a battered women's shelter."

"You . . . you did?"

His gaze met hers briefly. "Yes, that's what I do with mine every year when I change phones. The shelters wipe them clean and program in emergency numbers for the women in the shelters to use."

"I see," she murmured." Levi, the socially aware benefactor. Hmmm. She liked that. Then the other part of his statement hit her. "Wait . . . you buy a new phone *every year?*"

He grinned at her shocked expression. "Yes, almost every year."

Shaking her head at the consumer-gone-wild aspect of that, she pressed the button at the bottom of the screen to return to the "home" page. Another question crept into her mind; one she had contemplated before. "Is Leviticus Wolfe your real name or is it a stage name you made up?"

He whipped his head from side to side as if watching a race car zip by. "You should issue a warning before changing subjects that fast." He rubbed the back of his neck and grimaced. "You gave me whiplash."

She smirked at him. "Such a showman."

He shrugged. "Believe it or not, Leviticus is my given name," he answered. "Wolfe isn't, but it's my legal name now."

"You changed your last name – for theatrics?"

"Mainly to spare my family further embarrassment."

She saw the cloud descend again in his eyes. His family was a very touchy subject. His family or his father? "Why Wolfe?"

His smile was back. "For theatrics, of course." He arched a brow. "Do you know the Bible fairly well?"

She wrinkled her nose. "Not as much as I should, I suppose."

He shrugged. "Leviticus was quite vocal about the evilness of mediums. He preached that people should never consort with a psychic or necromancer."

"No kidding? That's ironic."

He smirked. "To say the least. The whole reason for naming me Leviticus backfired on my old man."

She examined the bitterness tingeing his smirk, but decided to steer clear of his family for now. "Where do you live?"

He regarded her for a few seconds as if he thought she were teasing him. Finally, he said, "In Atlanta."

"Atlanta?" she repeated, stunned.

"Yes. Why are you looking at me as if I said I live on the moon?"

"I thought you lived somewhere near Tulsa. Oklahoma City, maybe." She'd actually had sex with him and she hadn't even known what city he lived in. Unbelievable. She really knew next to nothing about him. "Why Atlanta?"

He shrugged. "It has a good vibe about it, a big airport, and the seasons are fairly mild – except for summer, of course. They don't call it 'Hotlanta' for nothing."

"Did you have friends there? Family? Is that why you ended up there?"

"No. I went to college there."

"Which college?"

"Georgia State."

"Do you live in a house?"

"No, an apartment." He slipped his cell phone into his trouser pocket. "I'm not there all that much. I travel a lot." He waited a few seconds and then arched his brows. "Any more questions, Miss Tucker?"

"That's all for now, Mr. Wolfe."

"Good. I prefer to be a man of mystery."

"Oh, really?" She told herself sternly that she needed to stop sleeping with him if he wasn't going to let her get to know him. Now if she could only convince her libido of that.

He squared his shoulders and grabbed his jacket from off the picnic table where he'd placed it. "Okay, you have your cell phone and your netbook, so we can keep in touch." Flicking back his shirt cuff, he glanced at his watch. "I'm going to——." His words were chopped off by Mouse, who chose that moment to bark furiously.

At first, Trudy thought the dog had awakened from her nap, saw Levi and had forgotten that he'd been there a few minutes ago. On their arrival at the RV, she had introduced them, allowing Levi to give Mouse a treat and get on her good side.

"Mouse, hush! This is Levi. You remember him, don't you?"

Levi looked away from the dog and surveyed the empty RV lots behind him. "She's not barking at me. She's barking at something back there."

Trudy followed his eye line and her heart sputtered. Ethel was back. She stood no more than six feet away, a sweet smile on her face.

"Do you see her again?" Levi asked, his voice soft and calm.

"Yes," Trudy groaned. "Can you see her? Please tell me that you can see her."

Levi shook his head. "No. She's for your eyes only, Trudy. What's she doing?"

"What she always does — she's waving and trying to talk to me." Trudy spread out her hands to Ethel in a helpless gesture. "I can't hear you!"

"Speak to her with your mind. Concentrate."

"That didn't work before."

"Try it again."

Sighing, she drew in a deep breath and then released it in a quick sigh. "Okay. Here goes." Staring at Ethel, she imagined her words to be small darts. She took careful aim and threw them at the vision before her. *I can't hear you. Talk to me this way.*

Ethel's smile wavered and Trudy knew a moment of triumph. Did she make contact with her at last? But then Ethel's smile turned upside down and she even looked a little afraid. In a blink, Ethel was gone, replaced by a dark veil that floated over Trudy's mind.

This is my favorite, so far.

Everything inside her froze. Those thoughts were not hers. Ethel? No, they weren't Ethel's. She was sure of that. Bad feelings were attached to them. Fog filled her head and blocked her vision.

Took it off that college cunt. What was her name? Oh, yeah. Janie. Stupid cow, but she was fun. I liked hurting her.

An inner vision suddenly speared her. A red, cardboard box in the shape of a valentine. Inside she caught sight of a passport, a bracelet . . . what were those? Charms? Keychain. Frog figurine.

What will I add to my collection this time?

The black mist in her mind lifted and the sinister feeling blinked out. Trudy heard a whimper and realized it had come from her as she went limp.

"Tru? Trudy!"

She felt bands close around her waist and then her head cleared like she'd been zapped and she found herself staring into wide, navy blue eyes. Levi was holding her in his arms.

"You with me? What just happened? Did you hear Ethel?"

"Ethel." She looked to where Ethel had been, but was no more. "She's gone."

"Did you hear her? What did she say?"

"It wasn't her." She swallowed and closed her eyes, her head spinning. "It was him. The killer. He has souvenirs from each one of them. He had one of Shelly's frogs." Tears burned her eyes. "He's so proud of his collection, the sicko!"

"Shhhh." He placed one hand at the back of her head and pulled her to him. She rested her cheek against his tie and breathed in the scent of him. He always smelled so good. "They usually always take souvenirs. You know that."

"I know." Her voice sounded small to her ears.

"Was he thinking about his next one?"

"Yes, but I don't think he's made a selection yet."

"That's good. That gives us more time."

She felt him move against her and she knew he was staring down into her face.

"You okay?"

"Yes." With some reluctance, Trudy gently pushed out of his embrace. "It just snuck up on me. I was trying to tap into Ethel and he was there – bam! – in my head."

"What else did you see besides the frog?"

"A charm bracelet and a passport. Oh, a key chain! I think the key chain was shaped like a four-leaf clover."

"Good." He smoothed her hair and then rested his hand along the side of her face. "Now, you know what I want you to do?"

"What?" she asked, loving the tenderness of his touch.

"I want you to type in your new notebook everything you recall from what you just experienced. Every little detail you can remember. Then I want you to eat something, take a long shower, and get some rest."

"What are you going to do?"

"Well, for starters, I'm going to move my stuff from the B&B to one of those cabins over there by the boat dock." He smiled and his hand moved from her face to her shoulder, giving it a gentle squeeze.

"Really?" She turned her head to look at the four small cabins lined up along the shore. "You're moving here?"

"Yes."

She wondered if he'd expected to move into the RV with her. It was tempting, but she knew that it would be disastrous. "Have you talked to Mike? They might already be rented."

"I've already taken one for a week."

"When did you do that?" she asked, looking at him again.

"A few minutes ago while you were learning how to use your cell phone."

Oh, so *that's* who he had been e-mailing! Sneaky devil. "Those cabins probably won't be as comfortable as the B&B."

"It'll be fine." He narrowed one eye when she smiled at him. "What are you grinning about?"

"You don't like The Blue Coconut."

"No. It's not my style."

She nodded. Maybe she *was* getting to know him, after all. "Didn't think so."

"The cabin isn't my style either, but it will be more convenient for us."

"What *is* your style?" she asked before she could stop herself. She suspected he liked modern, sleek, contemporary lines.

He gave her a measured look. "Someday I'll show you."

"I thought we were going back to Key West to check out the museums."

"Later. Maybe tomorrow. Record this latest vision into your notebook and then get some rest. If you need me, I'm only a phone call, e-mail, or text away. All my digits are stored in your new Samsung."

"They are?"

"Yes. I'm at your beck and call, twenty-four-seven. And you're at mine." He shook his head and gave her a gently teasing smile. "Welcome to the Twenty-first Century, Miss Tucker."

*

I'm at your beck and call, twenty-four-seven.

Trudy smiled as she emerged from the bathroom after her shower and recalled Levi's declaration. Wow. How many women did she know personally who would absolutely swoon at being told that by Levi Wolfe? Just about every single one of them. Probably even Billy and Jerrod from the Roundtable, too!

Belting her fluffy bathrobe, she leaned down to peer out the RV's windows to the cabins. Earlier, she had sat at the kitchen table, her netbook switched on, and had watched Levi move his things into Cabin Four. He had parked the Nissan right in front of the cabin, beneath a lamp pole. She had seen him look toward her RV a couple of times and she had been tempted to open the window and shout to him, "I'm writing down the details of my vision in my netbook!" She knew that's what he'd been wondering. He was such a task master!

What was he up to now? She squinted, trying to see the outline of his car under the light pole. Wait . . . his car wasn't there. Had he gone out for dinner? By himself? Why hadn't he asked her to go with him? How rude! She glanced at the microwave's digital clock. Seven forty-five. When did he leave? His car had been there at four o'clock when she'd decided to take a nap.

Immediately, she thought of her cell phone. She sat in one of the living room chairs and picked up the phone. Should she call? E-mail? Text? Text! She hadn't done that yet.

Your car is AWOL. Hope no one stole it!

She snickered, imagining his reaction. Drumming her fingers on the table, she waited for what seemed like a loooong time, but was probably only a minute. Her phone binged and she jumped.

Car's with me. Busy now. Hang tight.

Trudy stared at the screen and the words seemed to pulsate. Busy? Doing what? She pressed the button on the side of the phone and the screen went dark. She dropped it onto the table beside her, not liking it anymore. What was he up to? Where the heck was he that he was so damned busy he couldn't . . ! An answer blasted through her and she hoped to God she was wrong.

Hurrying to the television in the bedroom, she grabbed the remote off the top of it and switched it on. Frantically punching in numbers, she finally found the right channel. A commercial was ending. She sat on the bed and waited, tapping one bare foot on the carpet.

And then, there she was in all her platinum blond glory – Sissy Franklin. And there he was in all his black-suited smolder – Levi Wolfe.

"We're back," Sissy announced with a big, beauty pageant smile. She looked to be in her thirties. She had a voluptuous figure and wore necklines to show off her cleavage. A few years ago, she'd been a hotshot prosecutor in Austin, Texas.

"Tonight our special guest is the always *fascinating* Levi Wolfe," Sissy said, glancing down at her notes. "He's coming to us tonight from Florida where he's chasing down a vicious serial murderer."

The picture divided in half to show Sissy on one side and Levi on the other. His features were set in his "I'm a mysterious, paranormal, sex god" visage that he reserved for TV audiences. Trudy hated that particular mask of his because she knew it for what it was – a façade. She guessed that she'd always known that about him.

"Before we cut away for those commercials, you were telling us about how serial killers keep souvenirs," Sissy said. "Do think the madman who is murdering women in the Keys is doing that?"

Oh, no, he didn't! Trudy stared at the television, her mouth dropping open. That two-timing rat!

"I wouldn't be surprised if he does," Levi said, lowering his brows to make his eyes seem even darker, his expression more ominous. "It's sick, but most of them do take something that belongs to the victim. It gives them a perverse thrill."

"That sends chills through me," Sissy said, rubbing her hands up and down her arms and, in the process, squeezing her breasts together to show more cleavage. Could Levi see her? Trudy wondered. Of course, it didn't matter. She was fairly confident that he'd not only seen Sissy's ample breasts but they'd also been in his hands and mouth on more than one occasion.

"Are you confident that you can assist the police in finding this monster?" Sissy asked, her blue eyes wide with hope.

"Sissy, this person *will* be stopped," Levi said, his voice low, each word clipped for full effect. "I've made this my top priority. But, I could use the help of your viewers."

"Of course! What can we do for you, Levi? *Anything.*" Sissy leaned closer to the camera, her pink lips shiny with gloss.

Trudy placed her hand over her mouth, afraid she might barf. The woman was shameless.

"If anyone out there knows anything about this case, please come forward. We showed that sketch earlier of the woman we're calling Zelda. If anyone has seen her or even heard about her, please call the Key West police. It's imperative. These murders must end tonight."

"Absolutely, Levi!" Sissy's eyes were bright with excitement – or maybe with raging hormones. "Have you talked to the spirits of the murdered women?"

"I have." Levi nodded and sadness blanketed his features. Trudy wondered if he was putting on an act. Was this all just for show?

"Did they know their attacker?"

"No, I don't think so."

"But Zelda knows him?"

"Zelda is involved, yes, and she could be in danger."

"Levi, my viewers are fantastic and I *know* they will come through for you."

The sadness lifted from him and he nodded. "Thanks, Sissy. I appreciate that." He looked directly at the camera and gave his trademarked, all-out, dazzling smile. Trudy was amazed that the television screen didn't melt.

She aimed the remote at the TV and switched it off. "Bastard," she hissed. She leapt up and paced, fighting off the stab of jealousy and clutching, instead, to her anger. Why did he sneak off like that? Did he hold no regard for her feelings whatsoever? She jumped when the cell phone rang in the next room. Was that him already?

Bounding into the kitchen again, she grabbed the phone and stared at the screen. Tom Sinclair.

She pressed the phone to her ear. "Hello?" Nothing. It rang again. "Oh, for pity sake! How do I answer this stupid thing?" Punching the screen over and over again and not able to make the phone stop ringing, she paused and tried to remember Levi's instructions. Oh. Right. She ran her index finger across the screen to unlock the phone and then tried again. "Hello?"

"Hi, there! It's your friendly neighborhood detective."

She walked into the bedroom and sat on the bed again. "Hi, Tom."

"You busy?"

"I was watching TV."

"Yeah, I saw Wolfe on Sissy Franklin just now. On her show, I mean."

Despite her sour mood, Trudy had to grin, sarcastically.

"Are you there with him?"

"No. I don't like to appear on those shows." And he didn't ask her to go. She was just his fuck buddy.

"Roger, Dodger. Do you like to eat? Because I'm starving and I could use a pretty dinner companion."

A refusal rose automatically to her lips, but she stifled it. Rebellion blazed through her. "Yes! I'm ravenous!"

"Well, then I'm one lucky guy. Where are you staying? I'll pick you up."

"My RV is parked at the Stirring Palms on Crescent Key. Do you know it?"

"I sure do. Back when I was a rookie, I set up a mighty fine speed trap near that place. Let's see . . . it's eight. I'll be there in about half an hour."

Trudy nodded, listening intently. "I'll be ready." She pressed the button on the side of the phone to increase the speaker volume because she had barely been able to hear Tom. Punching the button a couple more times, she slid the phone into her purse. How long would it take Levi to drive back here? Then she frowned. What did she care? But that was the problem. She *did* care.

*

After dinner at a nearby restaurant, Trudy stood outside her RV and knew that Tom Sinclair was going to kiss her. With a deft move that surprised her, she was able to turn her cheek just as Tom moved in to kiss her on the mouth. He froze, clearly disappointed.

"Was it something I said?" he whispered against her cheek.

"I had a nice time. Thank you for dinner."

He straightened away from her. "You're not going to invite me in for a nightcap?"

"Not tonight. It's late . . . after midnight. Maybe next time?" She rested a hand on his arm, then turned and fitted her key in the lock on the RV's door. "I'm beat. It's been a long day."

"Guess I'll take a rain check. Be sure to let me know how it goes tomorrow with your museum search."

"I will." She opened the door and climbed the two steps, then turned to look at Tom's expectant expression. "Good night, Tom. See you soon."

He grinned. "You can count on it."

She went inside and closed the door. Standing in the living room, she watched out the windows as Tom got into his sporty car and drove away. She took Mouse outside for a few minutes and looked toward the cabins. The Nissan was back and there were no lights inside the cabin. Good, he's asleep. He sure had made it back fast from Miami! She had assumed she would arrive at the RV park before him.

She took Mouse inside and put her in her crate for the night, smiling when the dog circled three times on the cushion before finally settling down.

The rapping on the door swung Trudy around and she felt her eyes stretch wide. "Who's there?" Was Tom back?

"Open the door, Trudy."

She sucked in a breath. Crap! Levi.

Responses flitted through her mind. *Go away, you bother me. I'll see you in the morning. I'm not decent.* She shrugged them all off, knowing they would be useless against him. She could hear the heavy resolve in his voice. He would not be denied.

105

Unlocking the door, she opened it to a frowning Levi. The sight of her changed his frown into a dark scowl. He was still wearing his dress shirt and suit pants, but the jacket, tie, and vest were gone. His hair was mussed as if he'd been running his hands through it, and there was a bruised, haunted look in his eyes that she found very disturbing.

"You went out with Sinclair?" he asked without a how-do-you-do.

"Yes. We had dinner." She jutted one hip. "Do you need something, Levi?"

"Yes, I need to come in for a minute." He took both steps at once, making her back up or be run over. Pulling the door shut behind him, he looked right and left, his eyes taking in the RV's interior. It was the first time he'd been inside it.

Trudy moved toward the living room area, thinking that the motor home had never seemed so confining before. Levi loomed large in it.

"I finally realized that you might have gone out with him, so I called him, but he had forwarded calls to his work phone at the station."

"Why did you call him instead of me?" she asked, irritated that he had tried to phone Tom. Who did he think he was . . . her lover? Her man? Well, he was, but he didn't want to be, so he could damn well quit acting as if he had some claim on her.

"I *have* been calling you all evening – and leaving texts – and e-mailing."

Blinking at him, stunned, Trudy shook her head. "I didn't hear anything . . . I must have . . . I guess I messed something up."

"May I see it, please?"

"The phone?"

He tipped his head to one side in a gesture that was becoming familiar to her. "Isn't that what we're talking about?"

"Um . . . yes." She grabbed her purse off the end table and fished the phone out of it. "Here you go."

He examined it and nodded. "Yes, you've silenced it. It's fairly useless this way other than to be used as a *goddamned doorstop*."

She winced, only then realizing that he was fuming. He was really, really, royally pissed. He pressed his thumb against the side of the phone and it beeped, the volume of the beep increasing with each flex of his thumb.

"I'm switching on the GPS tracker, too. It will pinpoint your location – or, rather, this phone's location. It's a safety precaution that can come in handy. You'll also be able to see where I am."

Trudy swallowed the tickle of nerves in her throat. "I didn't realize . . . What did you want?"

"I wanted you to answer me. I wanted to be sure you were all right." His voice was so gentle that it was chilling. "There's a serial murderer roaming around here, you know."

"Right. Sorry if I worried you."

"Sorry if you worried me?" he repeated, ever so softly. "Wasn't that your goal?"

"My goal?" she asked. Was he accusing her of silencing her phone on purpose just to annoy him? She planted a hand on her hip. "No, it was not! It was a mistake."

"I agree. Going to dinner with Sinclair without extending me the courtesy of a note or a call or a *goddamned smoke signal* was a colossal mistake!" His jaw flexed with bunched muscles as he gritted his teeth.

"And leaving here and appearing on that show tonight without a note or a call or a *goddamned smoke signal* was a colossal mistake, too!" she bit out at him.

He stared at her, eyes shooting blue fire. "You knew I was going to be on that show."

"I knew because you told Tom Sinclair about it and I happened to overhear your conversation, but I didn't know that you were going to be on it tonight! I didn't know where you were or what you were doing until I happened to see you on television. I texted you and you texted back that you were too busy to deal with me. So, climb down off your high horse, Wolfe. You're going to give yourself a nosebleed."

He drew in a deep, deep breath, banking the fiery anger in his eyes. "I didn't think you cared when I was going to be on the program. You said you didn't want to be part of it."

"I *didn't* want to be part of it. But you could have told me you were leaving."

"You were supposed to be taking a shower and resting. I didn't want to disturb you."

"When did you know that you were going to tape the remote for Sissy's show?"

Wariness flitted across his face. "A couple of days ago."

She gave him a tight smile. "Right."

He spread out his hands. "You didn't want to have anything to do with the show, Trudy, so why do you give a damn when I was going to be on it?"

"You should have told me where you were going," she shot back.

He raised an index finger to stop her from saying anything else and his eyes were suddenly ablaze again. "And you should have told me where you were going. Women are being killed, Trudy. Women like you!" Pivoting away from her, he pushed his fingers through his hair. "Not answering your phone. Not answering your e-mail. Ignoring my texts. I was fucking scared for you!"

What he said and what he didn't say curbed her sharp tongue and squeezed her heart. Trudy stared at his broad back, her mouth going slack and emotion tightening her throat. He hadn't insisted on that new cell phone just so that they could communicate about the case – although it *would* make it easier. He wanted her to have it so that he could be sure she was safe. He *did* care for her. Damn him.

"Did you catch any of the show?" he asked, his voice low and strained as if he were trying hard not to shout at her.

"Just the end of it when you were telling Sissy about serial killers collecting souvenirs. That really chapped me."

"Why?"

She gave him a dubious look, then shook her head to dismiss that whole discussion. A different thought struck her as she recalled feeling something during her dinner with Tom – a sense of urgency, of something not being quite right. She had kept thinking about Levi and had wondered if he was thinking about her. "Did you try reaching out to me – you know, psychically?"

"No!" He glared over his shoulder at her. "I've told you that I can't read your mind, Trudy."

"I know, but I thought that maybe . . ."

"If I could have reached you that way it would mean that you were dead. So, no, I didn't give it a try."

"Oh." She swallowed, wishing she hadn't gone there. "I didn't think about that."

"I did," he snapped. "Endlessly."

She rolled her eyes, surrendering. "I'm sorry I worried you, Levi. It was *not* my goal. I was hungry and Tom happened to call and ask me out to dinner. Of course, I accepted."

"Of course," he repeated in a sarcastic way that made her want to strike out again.

"You could have asked me to dinner, you know," she said. "In fact, you *should* have. You should have told me you were driving to Miami – I assume that's where you went for that remote – and asked me to come along and we would grab dinner on the way. But you didn't want me there."

He turned sideways to look at her. "You told me you didn't want to participate in the show."

"I didn't!"

"Then what the hell are you talking about? Why would I ask you to join me when you made it abundantly clear that you weren't interested? You aren't making any sense."

"You should have checked in with me. You could have called me and told me you were headed for Miami. You aren't the only one who might worry, you know."

He turned to face her, imposing in the narrow space. "Okay, damn it! I'm sorry I didn't tell you I was driving to Miami." He waited a beat. "Now you're supposed to tell me that you're sorry you had dinner with Sinclair and you had a lousy time and you wouldn't let him kiss you good night."

She felt a smile tug at her lips. "I'm sorry I didn't let you know I was going out to dinner."

"And?" he prompted.

"And Tom was a good dinner companion."

"And?" His eyes darkened.

"And he did kiss me good night. On the cheek," she added quickly when she saw the fury in his eyes. She brushed a finger against the right side of her face. "Right here."

"Right where, exactly?" He stepped closer so that she had to tip back her head to see his face. He was suddenly so solemn!

"Here." She touched her fingers to the spot.

"I'm going to erase that kiss," he stated.

"What?" she asked, looking up into his face and laughing nervously. Oh. He wasn't kidding!

"I'm going to obliterate it."

Her mouth went dry and she couldn't have moved if a bomb went off right beside her. Passion uncoiled in her belly and spread down to between her thighs as he dipped his head and his lips hovered above the spot on her cheek.

"Did you say . . . right here?"

"Yes." She could barely make a sound, her heart thundered and her knees suddenly began shaking.

His lips touched her cheek with feather lightness. The tip of his tongue wet the spot and then he sucked gently before his mouth lifted. "All gone," he whispered against her fevered skin. But he wasn't finished. His lips found the spot again and then slipped sideways until they covered hers. She moaned and brought her hands up to clutch his forearms, using his strength to keep her upright as his kiss flamed from longing to voracious in the space of a breath.

He framed her head between his hands, holding her still so that his tongue could slip inside and ravage her mouth. She moaned again, her emotions whirling, swirling around inside her head and then spiraling down to her belly. He gave an answering moan and rocked his hips into her, making her blazingly aware of what she was doing to him. And, oh! What he was doing to her. How could this be happening to her? So fast! Around men, she'd always moved slowly. But not with this man. With Levi, he couldn't move fast enough to suit her. She wanted him naked and inside her. Not now. But ten minutes ago.

When he lifted his mouth from hers, she was breathless. So was he. He leaned his forehead against hers and closed his eyes. "I don't want to share you, Trudy." His hands fell away from her and he stepped back. Then took another step back, as if for good measure. "I *won't* share you."

"Share?" she asked, her head still buzzing. She was fairly certain that he kissed better than most men made love. "Do you have the right to make that demand?"

He seemed confused, uncertain. "It's never been an issue with me before. With others . . . well, I didn't give a damn, but you—." He shook his head and his mouth firmed in a line of determination. "If we take this further, I don't want another man touching you."

The buzz was gone. She pulled herself up and felt her lips part in astonishment. "And what about you? How will that work for you? Will you tell every other woman to keep her hands off you? That you're taken?" When he didn't answer immediately, she knew she'd made him think, made him reassess his stipulation. "You're not going to answer my question?"

He drew in a deep breath and shut his eyes, suddenly looking defeated. "Look, just keep your phone ringer on and make sure you charge it every night." His voice was hoarse. "I never again want to experience what I just went through during the past few hours. Never. Never again." Then he turned away from her and pushed open the door.

"That's it?" she asked, making him pause in the doorway.

"That's it for now," he rejoined. "I need to sleep." He stepped out into the night and it swallowed him. "Lock this door behind me." His voice floated into the RV, but Trudy stood still, irritation rising in her at his brusque command. "Now, Trudy. Lock it now."

She held her ground. "I'm waiting for a 'please.'" Tense, stubborn seconds ticked by.

"Oh, fuck it. Please."

She turned the knob on the door, sending the bolt home.

*

An hour later, Trudy lay in bed with the cell phone and fought back another wave of remorse as she re-read his text bubbles.

Bubble One. *Hey, I'm back. Sorry. Doing that remote for Sissy's show. What's up, Buttercup?*

Bubble Two. *Trudy? U there? Answer me.*

Bubble Three. *If you can't figure out how to text me back just e-mail me.*

Then she read his e-mails.

#1. *Dear Cell Phone Challenged; U need something? Want me to pick up something for dinner or have you already eaten?*

#2. *Trudy, answer me, please.*

#3. *Okay. I've waited ten minutes. Answer the e-mail or call me. Now.*

Then she listened to the phone messages. They were the most difficult for her to bear and they brought an ache to her heart.

"Trudy, it's Levi. Pick up. Tru, I'm not amused. Please . . . answer . . . your phone. Call me. Just hit the callback button. I'm sitting in my car on the side of the highway and I'm waiting, so hurry."

"Stop messing around with me and answer the fucking phone!"

She squeezed her eyes shut, her heart constricting at the sound of worry and anger lacing through his voice. He had really been upset! She could imagine him sitting in his car, so mad at her that he was shaking.

"When you get this message, call me. I don't care what time it is or what the hell you're doing. You call me. I'm driving ninety fucking miles an hour back to

that fucking RV park because I'm scared shitless that something's wrong . . . that something's happened to you. Call me, goddamn it!"

No more calls from him. His voice had been rife with panic on the last one. Ninety miles an hour! Jeez, he could have had an accident and . . . and . . . all because she had accidentally silenced her stupid phone.

She turned on the bedside light and checked the phone to make absolutely sure that it was on and the ringer volume was turned up. It vibrated and played a few musical notes in her hand and she dropped it with a little squeal. Then she snatched it back up. A text! She had a text! She touched the screen and the text floated into view in a yellow bubble. It was from Levi.

Turn off the light and go to sleep. Please.

She looked around the room, half-expecting to see him standing near her. She texted back. *Where are you?*

Bing! A new text. A new bubble.

Cabin 4. I can see your light from my window. Go to sleep.

She shook her head and typed, *I thought you wanted to sleep.*

Bing! *I do. Desperately. I'm waiting. Pretty please? Does that do it for you?*

Rolling toward the lamp, she switched off the light.

Bing! The phone screen lit up with another bubble. *Thank you. Sleep well.*

Trudy lay back in the bed and stared up at the ceiling. She had never in her life met or known such a man as Levi Wolfe. She wasn't quite sure she had it in her to handle him. He was all fire and raging testosterones and smoldering sex!

And he cared for her. He didn't just want her for sex. She could see that stamped on his handsome face tonight and she could definitely hear it in his voice when he'd left those phone messages. She needed to give him some space and time to realize it for himself. When he did, he'd either run for the hills or run into her arms. Either way, she was in for it.

Chapter Nine

The next morning they drove into Key West and had breakfast at a diner near the police station. Looking across the table at Levi, Trudy sipped from a mug of hot coffee. It was delicious. Almost as delicious as the man sitting across from her. He finished off the last of the pancakes and sausage and sat back with a smile of satisfaction.

"How's the cabin? Comfy?"

He made a face of resignation. "It will do."

"They have no kitchen. I don't mind preparing meals for us. It's a lot less expensive than going out or ordering in."

His gaze became speculative. "You know that I can afford to eat out? That my penny-pinching days are behind me?"

How did she answer that? "Actually, I don't know much about you at all. And that's the way you like it, right? A man of mystery so that you can keep everyone at arm's length?"

One of his eyebrows lifted fractionally. "Nice little lecture. Can't say that I enjoyed it . . . but . . ." He shrugged. "I'm well off. I have a successful company."

She drank some more of the coffee. If he was in the mood to talk about himself, she decided she'd better take advantage of it. "What kind of company?"

"Real estate and construction, primarily."

"That's nice."

"Nice," he repeated with a scowl. "And I have my paranormal work and my books, but I couldn't live as well on just that. Have you read my books?"

"Yes. Why?"

"Just wondering."

The waitress filled their cups again and then laid the ticket on the table. Trudy reached for it, but Levi snatched it away, sending her a thunderous glare.

"Why can't I pay for our breakfast this time?" she asked.

"Here's the thing, Trudy. I'll probably be picking up the bill and paying for things as we work together and I don't want you pitching a fit every time I do. Your fits won't prevent me from doing it." He shrugged. "You'll just piss me off and I'd much rather be in a good mood when I'm around you."

Oh, so that's where this was going . . . She shook her head, not liking it one bit. "I want to pay my own way."

"So, you want to fight?"

"No."

"Then . . . let . . . it . . . go," he said, enunciating each word with force. "You can pay your way, but there will be times when I'll pay for something *for us* and I don't want to argue about it."

She puffed out a breath, hating his logic, and decided to change the subject since she wasn't going to win this one. Besides, she liked the way he had said "for us." He deserved a break. "I want to talk to you about last night."

His expression was suddenly guarded. "What about it?"

"I read your e-mails and texts. I listened to your phone messages and I'm sorry for worrying you so. It wasn't on purpose. I wouldn't pull a trick like that. Do you believe me?"

He looked out the diner window and she thought he might be embarrassed.

"Yes," he said, tightly.

She let out a long sigh. "Good. Thank you."

"It's not like me to become so unraveled," he murmured, almost as if he'd forgotten she was sitting across from him. "It's disturbing."

Now she was disturbing? She frowned, not liking that description.

He leveled his navy blues on her again. "I want to discuss something with you."

"Oookay," she said, drawing out the word.

"I'm booked as a guest on the Lexie Patterson Show. How do you feel about that?"

She set her jaw, but then forced herself to relax and answer breezily, "What? They've run out of baby daddies and paternity tests? Or is that the subject of the show you're going to be on?" She widened her eyes in mock excitement.

He smirked. "Ha. Ha."

"Are you going to talk about the case?"

"I don't think so. I imagine I will focus on answering questions from the audience. That's what I usually do on that show. People ask me to help them with cold cases or to find their loved ones' remains."

"Can you do that?" Trudy shoved aside the empty dishes. "Find bodies without touching something of theirs?"

"Hardly ever, but on that show people bring items for me to hold. Scarves, necklaces, rings. Things like that. I can tell people where a murder took place and sometimes that helps them find the burial site."

"I can do that, too."

He gaze sharpened. "Oh? How does it work for you?"

"I can sometimes get into the killer's thoughts and he will tell me where he buried the victim."

"So, you *can* reach out to the perpetrator."

Trepidation skittered through her. "Not really," she said, hedging. Rats! She wasn't ready to talk about that. It was new to her, this ability, and she wasn't sure she wanted anyone to know about it. But he was looking at her expectantly and she suspected that he wouldn't let go of it. "Once I'm in contact, I can sometimes steer them to certain victims and get them to relive the murder. Then I can see the area or what they did with the body. I've only done it a couple of times."

He rested one arm across the back of the booth and spun the coffee mug around and around with his nimble fingers. "Quintara doesn't know about this, does she?"

Trudy looked at his smug expression. "I don't . . ." She rounded her shoulders. Dread oozed through her. She could tell from the animated glint in his eyes that he was like a dog with a particularly juicy bone. "Maybe not."

"Why have you kept it from her?"

"I haven't. I just . . . I haven't done it much and . . . it might be a fluke. I might not be able to do it again."

He leaned toward her to drive home his point. "You didn't tell her because you didn't want her to know that you can do yet one more amazing, astounding thing. You scare yourself, don't you?"

She tried to laugh, but the sound of it was about as genuine as his last name. "Don't be silly." She rested the flat of her hands on the table. "You should go on that TV show."

Giving her a knowing smile, he folded his arms on the table. "We'll revisit this conversation later. I want to know more."

"How long will you be gone?" She stared at his lips and was transported to last night when he had obliterated Tom's kiss and told her that he didn't want to share her with any other men.

"I'll leave this afternoon on a four o'clock flight and return late tomorrow night, unless the airlines screw me over, and then it might be the next morning before I can get back here. The show is taped in Los Angeles."

"Go ahead, then." She looked at his arms – tanned, muscle-defined, and covered in a dusting of dark hair. He must workout often, she thought, and then realized that he had no tattoos. How lovely that his body was unmarked by cartoons, icons, names of past loves or relatives, or snatches of lyrics or poems. God, she was tired of skin covered with strange images and cryptic messages.

He angled a glance at her. "So you're okay with me appearing on Lexi's show?"

Lexi, is it? Was he romancing Lexi, too? So many women, so little time, she chanted. No wonder he didn't respond to her question about becoming a one-woman man. "If I told you I wasn't okay with it, would you cancel?"

"Yes."

She stared at him, wondering if he was pulling her leg. "You would not."

"Yes, I would. Is that what you want? You want me to cancel? Tell me now so that I can call Lexi and let her know. Her team will have to come up with another guest."

Studying his serious expression, she realized he was primed and ready to cancel on Lexi Patterson. "No, it's okay," she said, her voice coming out a little breathy because she was actually flabbergasted that he would do her bidding on this. "You should honor your commitment."

He studied her for a few moments and then nodded. "Good." He leaned back in the banquette. "If that psycho gets into your head again, I want you to let me know immediately."

"I will."

"Immediately. Not an hour later . . . not the next day . . . not until we see each other again. Immediately."

"Okay, okay!" She scowled at him. "Don't get your panties in a wad! It appears to be hard for you to comprehend, but you're not my boss, so please don't bark orders at me. If you're leaving this afternoon, we should get going."

He gave her a smirk. "Yes, ma'am."

*

They hit the jackpot on the third museum they visited. The moment Trudy walked inside, she knew she was in the right place. Instinctively, she grabbed Levi's hand and pulled him with her to the correct gallery, standing with him before the paintings of the Madonna and Child.

"This is it," she whispered, glancing at him, then angling her head back a little when she found him looking at her with blatant admiration and . . . what? Affection?

He tightened his fingers around her hand. "You have no idea how remarkable you are, do you?"

Stunned into silence, she could only give a little shake of her head as her heart grew wings and flew up into her throat. He had no idea what it did to her when he said such things. He gave her hope – gave her foolish heart something to latch onto. Past his shoulder, she saw a museum guard and she gave a nod, signaling Levi to take a look for himself. He turned and they walked toward the uniformed woman.

"Excuse me," Trudy said, releasing Levi's hand as she approached the stern-faced guard. "I'm Trudy Tucker and this is—."

"Ohmygosh!" The woman's chocolate eyes widened and her dark face split in a huge grin. "You're Levi Wolfe!"

Levi hit her with his lopsided, drop-your-panties grin and she released a girlish giggle.

"I've seen you on television. I love that Sissy Franklin show." She glanced around and took a deep breath as if trying to control her enthusiasm. "I heard you were in Key West helping to find that serial killer. I just love you and all the cool stuff you do."

"Thank you," Levi said, still slaying her with his smile. "I appreciate that. Maybe you can help us with our investigation." He zeroed in on her name badge. "Ms. Talbert."

Her grin grew bigger. "I'll try, but only if you call me Kenya and let me take a picture of you so I can prove to my friends that I met you."

"It will be my pleasure, Kenya, as long as you're in the photo with me."

Watching the exchange, Trudy was impressed and chagrined all at once. The man was in his element and he was amazing. When he turned on the charm and that megawatt smile, he could pretty much have whatever he wanted. She cleared her throat to remind them that she hadn't disappeared.

"Kenya, were you working here Saturday?" Trudy asked.

"No, I don't work on weekends." It was all Kenya could do to yank her gaze away from Levi for a few seconds to acknowledge Trudy.

"Trudy is also a medium," Levi said, turning his shining cobalt eyes on her before looking at the grinning guard again. "Were any of the other guards here today working on Saturday?"

"Uh . . . well, let me think." Kenya directed her gaze to the ceiling for a few moments before latching onto Levi's face again. "Yeah! Stan worked on Saturday. Want me to go get him for you?"

"If you don't mind . . ." Levi said.

"I'll be right back." She reached out to touch his shoulder. "Don't you go anywhere."

"I'm planted right here," Levi assured her.

As the guard hurried away, Trudy tilted her head and scrutinized the virile virtuoso before her. Feeling her regard, he glanced at her from the corner of his eye and then took a step back.

"What?" he asked, innocently.

"You really have learned to work it, haven't you?"

For a few moments, she thought he was going to continue the innocent act, but then all artifice fell away and self-contempt took its place — and that disturbed her more than his cocksure mannerisms. He made a dismissive, sweeping gesture that encompassed his face and body.

"The package?" he asked with unconcealed disdain. "It gets me in places, around tough spots, and introduced to the 'right' people, but I know it for what it is."

"And that is?" she asked with a little shake of her head.

"Attractive wrapping paper. Nobody really sees me."

She held his gaze for a moment as his words plunged into her heart and guilt tasted like bile on her tongue. She'd done that. She'd only seen his handsome face and fit body and had presumed to know him. But not anymore. Now she glimpsed his heart and feelings that ran deep and true.

"I see you." It was out before she was even aware she'd spoken. He had started to glance away from her, but his gaze swung back and locked on. The hard intensity in his eyes and on his face softened slowly and his lips parted. She saw his chest expand with a quick, full breath and she thought he was going to say something, but then the *thump, thump, thump* of advancing footsteps shattered the connection between them.

"I found him," Kenya sang out, still grinning. She was followed by a short, bald man with a big, black mustache. "This is Stan Meyers. Stan, this is him! Levi Wolfe!" She extended her hands, palms up, proudly presenting Levi to his audience of one.

Levi shook the man's hand. "Nice to meet you. So, you were here on Saturday?"

"Pleasure," Stan said. "Yeah, I worked on Saturday."

"Hi," Trudy said, getting Stan's attention. "I'm Trudy Tucker. Levi and I are working together."

Stan shook her hand and smiled. "What can I do for you, ma'am?"

"Did you notice any man who seemed to be watching women more than he was actually looking at the art exhibits?"

He rubbed his chin in a thoughtful gesture. "Can't say that I did."

"He would have been in here," she said, turning to point at the long bench set before the wall that displayed the Madonna and Child artwork. "Sitting there. We think he's in his late twenties or early thirties."

"No . . . I didn't notice anyone peculiar." He shrugged. "It was busy that day. Lots of people. Sorry."

Trudy gave a little shrug. "If you think of—."

"I was telling Kenya, though, that I did see that woman on the news."

"What woman?" Trudy and Levi asked in unison.

"The picture of that woman the police say might have some knowledge about the killer. I think her name is Zelda?"

Trudy looked at Levi and saw her own excitement mirrored in his eyes. "She was here? On Saturday?"

"Yes, ma'am. I called the police and told them about it."

"You told the police," Levi repeated. "When and who did you talk to?"

"I called them on Monday and some gal took down my name and number and said they'd get back to me. Nobody's called yet."

Trudy shared a frown with Levi. "You're sure it was Zelda?"

"Looked just like her."

"Was she alone?"

"I think so. I saw her several times and I never saw her with anyone. She smiled at me. She was real friendly."

"How tall was she?"

"Oh, about my height. I'm almost six feet tall, but she had high heels on."

"Shapely?" Levi asked.

Stan grinned. "Yes, sir, she had a nice figure. Sort of like Joan Crawford. You remember her?"

"Who's that?" Kenya asked with a frown, earning chuckles from Levi and Stan.

"So, would you say she was stately? Good posture?" Trudy asked, trying to recall the late, great actress's figure.

"Yes, that's right." Stan nodded. "And she was all made up. Penciled eyebrows, fake lashes, red lipstick. Real dolled up." He leaned sideways toward Trudy and said in sotto voce, "Not a natural beauty, like you, ma'am."

Trudy felt color wash up into her face and Levi's warm gaze on her. "Well, thank you, and thanks for that information, too."

"Can I get my picture now?" Kenya asked.

"Certainly." Trudy held out her hand for Kenya's cell phone. "I'll do it."

"Let's go to the entrance. We can't take photos in the gallery." Kenya led the way.

In the sun-splashed entry, Trudy waited for Levi to step closer to Kenya and place his arm around the guard's shoulders. Kenya grinned and looked up into his face. Trudy snapped two photos. "Got it." She turned to Stan. "Would you like a photo with Levi, too?"

Stan shrugged. "Sure. Why not?" He wrestled his phone out of his trouser pocket and held it out to her.

"Tell you what . . ." Levi took the phone from him and gave it to Kenya. "Why don't you take the picture for us, Kenya?" He grasped Trudy's hand. "You want Trudy in the picture, don't you, Stan?"

"Absolutely!"

Trudy gave Levi a quick grin, touched by his smooth directions to include her. Stan motioned for Levi to get on one side of him and Trudy on the other. They took their places and Kenya snapped the shutter.

After thanking the guards again, Trudy and Levi made their way out of the museum. Levi paused on the steps and slipped on his sunglasses.

"I'll leave it to you to contact Sinclair to see why no one has followed up on this Zelda spotting," he said, glancing at his Rolex. "We need to get back to Stirring Palms. I have to pack and zip to the airport to catch my flight."

"No problem. Do you think Zelda was here with the psycho?"

He sighed. "It's hard to say. Maybe he's following Zelda. Maybe he was here with her and the guard just didn't notice. Maybe it's all a huge, fucking coincidence."

"I'll enter all of this into the case file," she said, "along with what Tom says."

He nodded, cupping her elbow in his palm and moving down the steps with her to where they'd parked the Nissan. "By the way, Trudy . . ." He stopped, turning her around and nudging her chin up with his knuckle until she was staring at her face reflected in his sunglasses. "I see you now, too." His kiss was light and gentle. "And I like what I see."

*

"Would you like another Scotch and soda, Mr. Wolfe?" the pretty flight attendant asked, leaning across the empty seat beside Levi.

He turned away from the window and his moody contemplation of clouds. "No. Two is my limit."

"May I get you anything else? Candy? Cashews? An extra pillow?"

"No, thank you."

She smiled and her eyes were a warm shade of brown. "Very good, Mr. Wolfe. Are you flying to Los Angeles on business this evening?"

"Yes."

"I hope it goes well."

"Thank you."

"I think what you do is simply fascinating." Her eyes widened. "I saw you on the Sissy Franklin show last night."

He nodded and turned his face away from her to stare out the window again. She took the hint and left him alone. Any other time he would be glad to chat with an attractive flight attendant while he whiled away the hours in first-class, but not now. He closed his eyes, feigning sleep, and let go of a long sigh. God, he was tired! Tired, wrung-out, spent. Trudy Tucker was exhausting.

His thoughts shuffled back to last night when he'd been frantic, racing back to the RV park, his heart lodged in his throat, images of Trudy facing the serial killer because the psycho had found a way to locate the woman who could ensnare his mind, share his demented thoughts and plans. Quintara had said that was highly unlikely, but who could say for certain? It could happen, and that was all he could think about as he had sped back to her, desperate for the phone to ring and it would be her and she would say she was safe.

Sometime between midnight and dawn, when he was sure Trudy had finally gone to sleep in her RV, he had phoned Quintara. She had answered on the first ring.

"This is Quintara."

"You weren't sleeping."

"No. I'm working on a magazine article. Why aren't *you* sleeping?"

"It's been a shitty night."

"Oh. What happened, Levi?"

And he'd told her about the cold fear that had gripped him and how he had been so furious with Trudy — so irrationally enraged that he had wondered what was going on with him and how Trudy could tear him up inside like that.

"You care for her. More than you want to and more than you probably are ready to admit. You can be overpowering, you know."

"She's the one with the power. I don't even know myself when I'm around her. It's nuts!"

She'd chuckled, and the sound had been warm in his ear. It had made him smile and had relaxed the tensed muscles in his neck and shoulders.

"Take a deep breath, Levi. Clear your mind. Better?"

He'd tried, but the strange feelings kept circling his heart, looking for a chink in the armor. "Did you see Sissy's show last night?"

"Of course. You know that I love to watch you. I'm your most devoted follower."

"Some calls came in afterward. I'll talk to Detective Sinclair later to see if anything came of the tips."

"There's something else. You're jealous of the detective?"

"He sure moved in on Trudy fast."

"Hmmm. What's good for the gander . . ."

"What's that mean?"

"How long did you know Sissy Franklin before you had her? An hour. Two?"

"You're listening to gossip again."

"I don't have to listen to gossip. I *know*." Laughter had threaded through her voice. "You're not the only psychic on speaking terms with Sissy."

That had gotten his attention. Quintara had been talking to Sissy? Shit.

"In her office lavatory?" Quintara had expounded. "Her sitting on the sink with the faucet biting into the small of her back? With your clothes on?"

"Christ, Quintara! I'm hanging up."

That low, naughty laugh again – classic Quintara. "Oh, yes. She told me all about it."

"You're not helping." He could handle Sissy. Trudy? Not so much.

"Oh, dear Levi. You're cross because I can get under your skin. And so can Trudy. You're used to calling all the shots with uncomplicated women. You give them one of your smoldering looks, tell them to drop their panties and spread their legs, and then you go to work on them. Then you quickly put them out of your mind. It's not so simple with Trudy, is it?"

Levi opened his eyes slowly to stare at the dark sky outside the plane. He recalled how quiet Quintara had been when he'd told her about Trudy asking if he'd be a faithful lover. They both knew that would be a tall order for him. No woman had ever asked that of him.

The overwhelming physical attraction he had for Trudy mystified him. He hadn't experienced this level of hard-on producing need since way back in England with Lizzie. He'd been young, randy, and totally inexperienced then. It was natural for him to want to bed Lizzie every day, every night, and three or four times every Saturday and Sunday. To be so fixated on one woman now . . . God! He lusted for Trudy. Smoking-hot, cock-driving, mind-blowing lust. What really singed his soul was that he couldn't stand the thought of any other man having her.

All he had to do was picture her soft, auburn hair, limpid, green eyes, and sweet, upturned mouth and he could drive nails with his dick. She was smart as a whip, winsome, a wise ass, and a touch wicked. And all of that turned him on in a big, big way.

He shifted in the seat, the heat pooling in his groin, making him lengthen and thicken. He gathered in a big gulp of air to clear his head. Goddamn, he had it bad for her! How the hell had this happened? It was so *not* his style. And why did it bother him so damn much that she couldn't wait to leave him after they'd fucked?

"Do you need anything, Mr. Wolfe?"

He sat up straighter and blinked. The flight attendant was leaning toward him, a frown puckering her brow.

"I'm fine." His ears popped. "Are we descending?"

"Yes. We'll be landing in a few minutes."

"Thank you." He buckled his seat belt, feeling hot and bothered and fucking miserable.

Chapter Ten

Sitting on the RV park's fishing pier the next morning, Trudy sipped coffee from a University of Tulsa Hurricane mug and held Mouse's leash in the other hand. The Chihuahua sniffed the weathered planks and Trudy wondered what gross scents she must be picking up on – fish scales, fish guts, bird poop, blood, bait. Mouse was totally absorbed in the aroma bouquet.

Trudy faced the water again and sighed as melancholy drifted around and through her. She watched a pelican fly just above the water, its feet skimming the surface, and then landing not too far from her on the shore. She smiled, watching it, thinking how funny it looked on land and how graceful it was in the air.

Swinging her feet over the side of the pier, she admired the sun diamonds glinting across the choppy water. She looked at her phone to make sure it was on and the ringer volume was as loud as it would go. Why hadn't Levi been in touch with her? Not a peep from him since he'd sent a text last night that he had landed safely and had given her his hotel room number.

Her eyes burned and she blinked, realizing she was still staring at her phone. Ring, damn you! What if something was wrong? Maybe he'd had a car accident and was in the hospital or . . . She mentally braked. God, was this what he had gone through when he'd been unable to reach her? Should she text him just to be sure he was okay? No, she was being silly. He was fine.

Earlier, she had plugged his name into the search engine and been dazzled by a wide array of photographs of him. Most of them pictured him at events, always accompanying a woman – many, many women. Mostly tall, blond, stacked women. Women who looked well-heeled, always in expensive clothes and wearing dazzling jewels at their throats, wrists, or earlobes. There were a few of him and Sissy Franklin and she was always looking at him with open adoration. Yep. She had carnal knowledge of him. No doubt about that, Trudy had thought, staring for too long at those photographs.

A few recent ones were of him and an Atlanta TV meteorologist named Nicola Bartlett. The weather girl he was linked with, Trudy surmised. Nicola was blond, extremely pretty, and stacked. She looked to be in her early twenties. In the photos, Levi usually had his arm around her waist. In one of them, he was bending near her ear, saying something to her that had made her smile and look up at him with shining eyes. He was wearing a tuxedo in one. Levi in a tux was orgasm worthy.

A couple of magazines had included him in their roundup of "Sexiest Bachelors" or "America's Most Eligible Bachelors." His bio info on Wikipedia was sketchy:

Leviticus David Wolfe, (birthday November 12), known professionally as Levi Wolfe, is an American television personality and professional psychic medium. He is best known for appearing on television shows such as "The Tonight Show," "The Sissy Franklin Show," "The Late Show," and "Psychic Detectives." Born in Carthage, Missouri, Wolfe says he realized he had special gifts when he was seven years old. He has written books about his psychic experiences, including bestsellers *Soul Searching* and *A Curse and a Gift*. He studied psychic and paranormal fields in England and has degrees in parapsychology and psychology from Duke University and Georgia State University. He became well-known when he assisted the FBI in capturing serial killer Vernon "Bud" Schneider, who murdered more than a dozen women in New York and Maine.

When did he have time to earn those degrees? He must have a high IQ, she thought. He's probably the classic 4.0 GPA overachiever.

And he knew he was psychic at seven years old . . . two years before he was in a "crisis mode" and Gregory had saved him. She tried to picture him as a dark-haired boy. Something terrible had happened to him and it must have been more than just realizing he was having visions. That was often upsetting, but he'd had inklings before then.

No mention of his parents or what his real name had been before he changed it to Wolfe. Did he have brothers and sisters or was he an only child? Another realization hit her. Hey, his birthday was in a few weeks! She recalled him saying something about not caring about his birthday or age. Wonder if he ever—.

"Are you fishing or daydreaming?"

She jumped and looked over her shoulder as her heart climbed into her throat. A man stood behind her, the sun at his back and obscuring his features from her. She lifted a hand to shade her eyes as she beat down the black wings of fear that rose up inside her. Then she recognized him.

"Jay." She let out a shaky laugh. "You scared me for a second there."

"I'm sorry," he said, softly. "May I join you?"

"Sure. Have a seat." She patted the planks next to her, then glared at Mouse. "Some watch dog! Not a peep from you."

Jay laughed and reached out to pet the Chihuahua's head. "What a cutie! What's her name?"

"Mouse." Trudy leaned back on her locked arms. Jay was wearing another Hawaiian print shirt, snug blue jeans, and sandals. "Visiting Mike today?"

"Yeah. I'm owed about three weeks of vacation. I've covered the hurricanes and stockpiled a lot of vacation days the past couple of years. My boss says I have to use it or lose it, so I'm taking this week off." He glanced around. "So you're not fishing. You must have been daydreaming."

"Yes. It's been a crazy couple of days."

"Still working on the serial murder case?"

"That's right. Do you know Detective Sinclair?"

He nodded and gave her a smile that deepened the dimples in his cheeks. "My dad said that Sinclair has been here and picked you up. You two dating?"

She decided to skirt that issue. "Did Detective Sinclair show you the sketch of Zelda?"

Jay nodded. "Yeah, but after I saw it on the Sissy Franklin Show. I filed a story about it. Did they find her?"

"Not that I know of." Trudy frowned. "I thought that the police would release that sketch immediately to the media." Why hadn't they? she wondered.

"Have you tried to reach Zelda . . . you know, with your mind?"

She shook her head. "That's not how it works for me."

"How does it work?"

She paused, not wanting to launch into a description of how the thoughts of strangers wove through her mind, unbidden.

He held up his hands. "If you don't want to talk about it, that's okay. I understand. Talking to a reporter is something that a lot of people are reluctant to do."

She nodded, glad for the reprieve. "Your father is a character."

He barked a laugh. "That, he is."

"He had quite a career, didn't he?"

Jay petted Mouse and didn't answer for a few moments. "He was gone a lot while I was growing up. Work, work, work. He loved his work. Even when he was home, he was writing, reading, doing class plans. Now he realizes that he should have taken more time to be with his family."

Trudy squirmed, feeling as if she were hearing something too personal. "So you two are making up for lost time now. That's great."

"Yeah, I guess so." He touched the short sleeve of her white eyelet blouse. "Where did you get this? It looks great on you."

"Thanks. I think I bought it at Sears," she said. She poked him in the side with her elbow. "I like your shirts, too. They remind me of Magnum P.I. You know that old TV show?"

He grinned. "Yeah, I get that all the time. A couple of the guys at AP call me Jaynum."

Her cell phone rattled against the planks between her and Jay. She snatched it up, her heart soaring, and then falling when she saw that it was Quintara's number – not Levi's. She brushed her finger across the screen, glancing at Jay as she did. "I should take this."

"Go ahead."

"Hello? Quintara?" Trudy scrambled to her feet, clutching the phone in one hand and Mouse's leash in the other.

"Yes, dear. How are you? Do you miss me?"

"Oh, Quintara, you have no idea how much I wish you were here this very minute. Hold on a second." She smiled at Jay. "Good to see you again, Jay."

"Nice to run into you, too."

Tugging on the leash to get Mouse moving, Trudy left the fishing pier and walked along the crushed seashell path toward her RV. "I'm back," she said into the phone. "You there?"

"Yes. Have you made any headway on the case since I left?"

"No, not really."

"Levi said you had been in contact with the murderer."

"You've talked to Levi? When? Today?" She realized her voice had hitched up with each question and she stopped in her tracks and forced herself to get a grip on her emotions.

"I spoke with him before he left for Los Angeles. You have him in a tailspin, dear."

"I . . . I what?" Trudy shook her head and started walking again. "I don't understand."

"He has risen above a terrible upbringing, Trudy, but he still has very tender spots that you must not poke or he'll lash out. He doesn't mean to be rude or unfeeling. It's just that some of the pain comes back and his defenses rise to protect himself."

Trudy realized that she was standing in front of the RV, frozen by Quintara's revelations. "What kind of terrible upbringing?"

"Someday he might tell you about it, but it's not my place to do so. I don't even know all of it because he simply shuts down when I probe too deep." Her sigh whispered across the miles. "I so want you two to get along and work together. You're both so dear to me."

"I like working with him, but—."

"No, no! Don't give up so soon, dear. It's only been a week."

A week? God, it seemed longer than that! "He's very draining."

"He says the same thing about you. But he also finds you exhilarating and exciting."

"He does?"

"Of course, he does. You challenge each other and there's nothing wrong with that. Makes life worth living, I say."

Trudy closed her eyes for a moment and felt a weight lift off of her. Maybe Quintara was right. She was expecting too much too soon. "You always make me feel better."

"That's why I'm here, dear. To lift you up and set you on the correct path. I do the same for Levi. Now you two must learn to do that for each other. But it will take longer than a week."

Trudy smiled. "Okay, okay."

"I must go now, dear. I'm expecting a gentleman caller."

"Oh?"

"Yes. A man I met yesterday at the grocery story. We both reached for the same avocado and I told him if he let me have it, I'd let him have it later."

Trudy couldn't help it. She burst out laughing because she knew

Quintara wasn't kidding and she wasn't exaggerating. "Poor man," she sputtered. "He has no idea what he's in for."

"Goodbye now, dear. Play nice with Levi."

*

At two o'clock, Trudy let Mouse out of the RV to do her business. She stretched and wished the hours would speed up. She missed Levi. Missed him like crazy. She had called Tom and asked him about the sighting of Zelda. He'd tracked down the notations about the call and said he would talk to the guard, too. Then she'd sent Tom her notes about what the guard had said to them.

She had opened her laptop and gone over the information on the case, the autopsy reports, and the photographs of the bodies. She had checked her phone over and over, unable to concentrate because she kept thinking about Levi. *Attractive wrapping paper. Nobody really sees me.* That's how he thought of himself? She shivered now, recalling how he'd said it and the self-contempt and vulnerability that had been so evident on his handsome face and in his expressive eyes that she had fought back tears.

Damn it! Why didn't he call her? Was he so flipping busy that he never gave her a thought? Out of sight, out of mind? Guess he was having a grand, old time with Lexi. Was he sleeping with *her*, too? Wait . . . didn't she read somewhere that Lexi was married and—.

A black wave engulfed her, almost knocking her to her knees. Trudy stumbled, momentarily blinded, and she felt her way to the picnic table bench, pulling Mouse with her. She sat down as words and images spread through her mind, blotting out everything else.

She was walking along the beach behind a shapely brunette. The girl had short hair that fluttered in the ocean breeze. It was sort of like her own – layered, covering her head with shiny curls. She wore a two-piece suit that was demur for the current barely there bikinis favored by most women her age. She sauntered toward a beach bar and slid onto a stool.

Yeah. I could do her. She thinks she's all that and a bag of chips, but she's clueless.

Trudy closed her eyes. Oh. No.

Want to be my friend? Want to play?

The girl sipped a drink. Orange drink. She turned on the seat and looked behind her, around her. She was young. Maybe twenty. She had a pretty face. Round face. Big, brown eyes. Small nose and mouth. The bar was colorful . . . on the beach . . . in front of a hotel. Parrots. Orange chairs. The Jolly Roger?

I'd like to fuck that mouth. Then I'd fuck your ass. Then your mouth again so you could taste your own shit. Yeah. That would be awesome. Tag, you're it.

Walking away now . . . along the beach . . . and the vision lifted from her eyes and Trudy fell back into her own frantic thoughts. She fought the urge to vomit. She had sensed more violence in him this time. His insanity was escalating, his need to inflict pain was more avid.

Flinging back her head, Trudy stared at the blue sky and breathed deeply, imagining the fragrant air chasing away the dirty, smutty feelings that the killer's thoughts had left in her mind. After a few minutes, she grabbed her cell phone.

With trembling fingers, Trudy crafted a text to Levi. "Please, please, please," she begged softly, hoping and praying he would answer her. She hit "Send".

Levi, are you there?

Then she hit the number to speed dial Tom Sinclair. He answered on the first ring.

"Tom, I just had a vision and I saw his next victim. Have you got something to write with or are you at your computer?"

"Uh . . . ummm, wait." Seconds ticked by and she could hear the rattling of paper. "Okay. Shoot."

"Is there a bar called The Jolly Roger?"

"Yeah, I know that place. On the beach."

"That's it . . ." Her phone beeped and she knew Levi had sent her a text, but she continued on, telling Tom about what she'd seen, what the girl looked like, and every detail she could pluck from her memory.

"Great, great," Tom mumbled. "I'm on it, babe. I'll dash over here right now and talk to the bartender. I'll be in touch."

She ended the call and looked at the text from Levi. *Yes. What's up?* No "Buttercup" this time, she noted with sinking spirits. *Where are you?* she typed.

His reply came within seconds. *Sound stage. Just wrapping up. Need something?*

He's back. I just saw his next victim. Her fingers shook as she pressed the "Send" button. God, she wished Levi was here with her! Or Quintara. No, Levi.

Her phone rang and she sucked in a little gasp, then laid her hand over her pounding heart. Levi's name floated across the screen. "Yes?"

"Tru, are you okay?"

She closed her eyes. Oh, she liked his voice! It was like a cooling night breeze.

"Yes. Thanks for getting back to me so quickly. I know you're busy and I'm sorry to bother you."

"Please, Tru." He sounded a little irritated. "You're never a bother. I'm going right to the airport as soon as I leave here. I'll be there in a few hours."

"Okay." She closed her eyes and tried to block out the echo of that other nasty, depraved voice that had been in her head a few minutes ago. "I called Tom and told him about it. He's on his way to the bar to talk to the bartender and find the girl."

"Good. Hey, remember to write down your impressions in the netbook. Do it as soon as you hang up. Every detail you can recall. Okay?"

"Yes, I will."

"I shouldn't have come here, damn it. I should be there with you. It's irresponsible of me to leave you when we're in the middle of this."

"It's okay."

"No, it's not." He sounded mad, but not at her. His voice also was huskier than usual.

"Are you okay?"

"Some kind of stomach thing – it's nothing. See you soon."

She pushed the "end call" button slowly, regretfully. But then a faint smile touched her lips. He was coming back . . . back to her.

*

The headlights of his car didn't sweep across the mostly empty RV lots until after eight o'clock. Trudy threw open the door to her RV, jumped to the ground, and sprinted toward the car that Levi parked in front of Cabin Four. It was a different car this time. The Nissan had been replaced by a sleek, black Jaguar. Although she wanted to rocket into his arms, she stood back a few feet from the car as he emerged, looking tired and achingly handsome.

"Hi. Welcome back," Trudy said, uncertain of how much to reveal to him about how positively, absolutely, freaking glad she was to see him.

"Thanks. It's good to see you."

She stepped closer and he placed an arm around her shoulders, giving her a hug. She looked up into his face and saw the paleness of his skin.

"Hey, you're really sick!"

"I'm okay. I'm just . . . it's jet lag mostly, I think."

"Did you see a doctor? Are you taking medicine? Have you eaten?"

"I ate some antacids earlier. I'm not hungry."

She shook her head. Men! "Stow your luggage and then come to my place. You should eat something besides Rolaids."

"No, really. I don't think I could keep anything down."

"Leviticus David Wolfe, do as you're told."

His brows arched and then lowered slowly. "Someone's been on the Internet reading about me."

"I don't know what you're talking about," she teased him. "I swear, you Scorpios!" Then she turned and went back to her RV. "Make it snappy. I have something to report!"

*

Levi took a swallow of orange juice, but shook his head when Trudy offered him another Oreo cookie or saltine cracker and cheese. His stomach did a pitch and roll.

He sat across from her on the banquette. Her netbook sat before him and he finished reading the last of her notes on what she'd seen and heard earlier. Forcing himself to concentrate on the task at hand, he glanced over her notes again. "Did you recognize the beach?" he asked, his voice echoing in his head. He flexed his jaw and his inner ears popped.

"Not really, but when I told Tom about the bar, he knew which one it was."

"So, he's there now."

She nodded. "He called again right before you got back. He said they were talking to the bartender who was on duty. I gave them a description of the girl. They're hoping the bartender will know her."

133

"Good. The sick motherfucker could kill her tonight."

"God, no!" She slammed her green eyes shut. "She's so young!"

"Hush." He rested his hand on hers. Just that slight touch made him want her. He'd thought of little else while he'd been away. "It's my fault that we're not on top of this case. I shouldn't have gone to L.A. I told Darla to cancel all of my public appearances for the rest of the month."

"You had other appearances scheduled?"

He nodded. "It's what I do, Trudy." Shaking his head, he resented the censure in her eyes. If only she knew how much he'd already altered his life for her . . . hell, she wouldn't believe him. He'd never wanted to work with anyone before, but since meeting her he'd been obsessed with the idea. And now he hated to be away from her. Postponing appearances, turning down money, changing appointments with people he needed to see. Even Darla had questioned him about some of the meetings he'd put off or canceled outright.

"Who is Darla?"

He ran a hand down his face. He felt hot and clammy. "My assistant."

"Oh. You have an assistant? Like a secretary?"

He leaned back and folded his arms. Was she really that clueless about him? Most women he knew had researched him thoroughly within hours of meeting him – if not *before* actually meeting him! "Yes, I have several secretaries and one executive assistant. I run a company, Trudy."

"Oh." She shrugged. "I admit that I know nothing about that side of you."

"I thought you were investigating me on the Internet today. I own Wolfe Enterprises, Inc."

"You have so many irons in the fire," she said, almost in a whisper. "I'm surprised you have time for this kind of thing."

"This is my passion," he said, and her gaze lifted to his. "This is my calling. The other things help pay for it." He looked at her netbook again. "I got a report from Sinclair this morning. Nothing has come from the tips called in to Sissy's show about Zelda. Several people said they had met her and confirmed that the sketch was accurate, but no one knew her last name or where she lives."

"You look tired. You should get some rest."

His eyelids were leaden and he rested his head in his hands, feeling jet lagged and drugged. "You said the girl is young?"

"Yes. Maybe twenty."

Rocking his forehead against the heels of his hands, he fought off the sense of helplessness and failure. He shouldn't have gone to L.A. If he'd been here when Trudy had experienced her vision, they could have set off right then and found the beach bar and maybe even have found the girl. *Fuck!* He forced his head up and his eyes open.

The cell phone on the table chimed and he automatically reached for it, thinking it was his.

"Hey, pretty lady," Tom Sinclair said before Levi could say anything. "I have some news for you and I'd like to deliver it in person and make good on that rain check you owe me!"

Ice cold fury blasted through him and it took everything in him not to throw the phone across the room and smash it to bits. His gaze snapped to Trudy and he could tell by her wide eyes and red face that she had heard each smarmy word. Knowing that if he opened his mouth right now he would call Sinclair every foul thing he could think of, he held the phone out to Trudy and nodded at it, silently bidding her to answer the detective.

"Hi," she said, her tone high and breathy. "What news? Levi's here."

"Oh, okay. Well, that's good. I guess."

Holding her gaze, Levi felt his upper lip lift in a snarl. *Stupid son of a bitch.* And he had thought he might like Tom Sinclair when he'd first met him. He'd even thought they might go out for a drink, play a game of pool, and talk shop. Now, as he imagined the man's hands on Trudy and his mouth and tongue on her and in her, he wanted to crush the phone he held.

His stomach muscles bunched and twisted. That damned tuna salad sandwich at the airport, he thought. It had tasted a little off. He should have stuffed it into the trash instead of into his mouth.

"Tom, can you tell me your news now? I'm really anxious to hear."

Levi put the phone down on the table and slipped out of the booth, unable to withstand any more of Sinclair's chit-chatting with Trudy.

"It was the Jolly Roger Tavern right on the beach. The barkeep knew the girl you'd described to me. She and her folks were staying at the adjoining hotel. Good work, babe! We talked to her and her parents. We thought they might stick around and let us put surveillance on the girl and maybe catch this guy that way, but they weren't having any of that. They've already booked a flight back to Omaha."

"I'm glad she's safe."

"Yeah. We either saved her life or ruined her family vacation. We'll never know for sure, I guess."

Levi stood at the kitchen sink with his back to Trudy, but he glanced around at that and saw her stiffen. She hitched up her chin in that way that made him want to kiss her until she was breathless. He could almost see the smoke coming out of her ears.

"We saved a life, of course," she snapped. "Do you actually think I made all that up? How could I have?"

"Okay, babe! Sorry."

"Thanks for the news, Tom. I . . . I have to go and . . . I'll talk to you tomorrow. Thanks again."

He heard her place the phone on the table, but he didn't turn around. He kept his eyes closed as he gripped the edge of the counter. Sickness rose in him and he realized he was going to spew. Pushing away from the counter, he thought he might make it to the bathroom, but then in the next second, he knew that there was no way. He spun back toward the double sinks and heaved up the crackers, cheese, cookies, and orange juice.

"Levi!"

He heard her, but he wasn't finished. More of the horrible tasting stuff filled his mouth and then the sink. His gut knotted, clenched, and knotted again. He groaned and felt something cool and wet touch his forehead and cheek. Reaching blindly, he took the wet washcloth from Trudy and pulled it down his hot, sticky face. It felt like heaven and he moaned appreciatively.

"Levi, you poor thing. You're going to take a shower and then you're going straight to bed." Her tone was as sweet and comforting as a lullaby and it did strange things to his heart and head.

He turned on the faucet and splashed water onto his face, then rinsed the sinks and his mouth out as best he could.

"Don't worry about that. Get in the shower."

He looked at her. She raised her brows and pursed her lips in a way that made him think of a strict schoolmarm. "Here?"

"Yes. You're staying here tonight so I can keep an eye on you."

"No." He shook his head. Was she nuts? *Now* she wanted to spend the night with him? "I'm leaving."

"Where do you think you're going?"

"To my cabin." His throat was on fire and his voice was almost gone. All he could manage was a rasp.

"Then I'm coming with you. Let me grab some things—."

"No, Trudy!" He snagged the hem of her blouse to keep her in place. "Let me be. I'm fine. I just need some rest."

"I agree, but you shouldn't be alone."

"I'm alone most of the time, so don't worry about me." He let go of her and ran the washcloth over his face again before tossing it onto the counter. "Sinclair's sweet-talking made me puke my guts out, that's all."

Disbelief flared briefly in her eyes, but then amusement tipped up the corners of her lush mouth. His gut knotted again, but this time with longing.

"Made me want to puke, too," she said, gifting him with a full-on, Trudylicious grin. "Stay here, Levi," she whispered. "Let me look after you."

She was tempting . . . so tempting . . . "No." He shook his head again, unwilling to be in her bed alone while she played Nurse Trudy. Even though her wanting to take care of him touched something foreign and tender deep inside him. For the first time in a long, long time he felt a yearning to be coddled, to be cared for . . . cared about. He touched the tip of his index finger to her freckle-dusted nose. "I'll see you in the morning."

Her fingers closed on his shirtsleeve. "Levi, please."

Gathering in a deep breath, he told himself not to grab her and kiss her like a caveman. Besides, his mouth tasted horrible. "Trudy, listen to me, please. You are the most infuriating woman. Did you know that?"

"I'm just—."

"I know what you're just trying to do," he said. "I feel like shit warmed over. So let me go, Trudy. For the love of God, let me go to my lonely, little cabin before I snap like a twig and try my dead-level best to take you again right this second. Right here. Right fucking now." He smiled at her wide-eyed, mouth-agape expression. Her fingers let go of his shirtsleeve. "Good girl. Thank you."

Then he turned on his heel and left before she could recover.

Chapter Eleven

Trudy carried a thermos of coffee and a wicker basket full of blueberry muffins with her toward Cabin Four. The door was standing open a couple of inches, so she leaned inside. "It's Trudy! You decent?" She gave a little yelp when the door swung open and Levi filled the threshold.

"No. Never. I thought we had already established that."

She gave him the once-over, taking in his jeans and blue t-shirt that was almost the exact color of his eyes. He'd already showered and shaved. "You look like you feel better this morning."

"Compared to last night, I certainly do." He stepped back and motioned for her to come inside. "What do you have there, Miss Tucker?"

"Coffee and muffins."

"You're an angel."

As she passed by him, he gave her a smack on her rear and she issued a startled cry, whirling to face him. "Hey! Watch it!"

His eyes widened and his lips formed an "O" at her reaction, then he grinned.

"You're a devil," Trudy said, but she couldn't keep from grinning back at him. "Next time you do that, I'll hit back."

"That wasn't hitting. That was patting. And it's your fault for having such a cute denim-covered ass."

"Whatever. It was uncalled for." She set the basket and thermos on the table where he had, undoubtedly, been working. His laptop and netbook shared the space with scattered papers and a compact printer. Cords snaked across the floor to the outlet. The wall behind the table was covered with information about the case. Each victim's photo was taped there along with maps, autopsy reports, notes, and timelines. Trudy issued a low whistle. "Somebody's been busy."

"It's how I work. I have to bring order to chaos."

"I thought you'd be resting. Taking it easy."

He flung her a *don't be stupid* glance and set two coffee mugs beside the thermos. "Will you join me?"

"Yes, thanks." She glanced around at the brass, double bed that dominated the space, the linens on it thoroughly mussed from a restless sleeper. A rumpled, damp towel, bar of soap, and black nylon travel kit lay at the foot of the bed. His Rolex, wallet, and a few other incidentals were scattered next to a digital alarm clock on the bedside table. She stepped around the bed and peeked into the bathroom. Some of his clothes hung from a metal garment rack on wheels. A toilet, a sink, a small rack filled with towels and washcloths were all crowded into the meager space.

"Where's the shower?" she asked, turning back to Levi.

He nodded at the front door. "Out there. The park's men's and women's restrooms have showers in them."

She sat at the table with him while he poured coffee into the mugs and helped himself to a muffin.

"Did you make these?" he asked around a mouthful.

"Yes."

He rolled his eyes in a swoon, earning him a smile from her. She was glad he was feeling better and in a good mood. She'd actually expected him to be as grumpy as a bear this morning. His cell phone danced on the table and he glanced at it. Sissy Franklin's name glowed on the screen. Trudy looked from it to him. He pursed his lips and shrugged.

"I'll let it go to voice mail."

"Answer it," Trudy urged. "You shouldn't keep Sissy waiting."

He cast her a scolding look before he answered the phone. "What's up, Sissy?" He continued to consume the muffin while he listened.

Trudy could hear Sissy's voice, but she could only make out a word or two. She thought Sissy was talking about her show. Levi drank some of the coffee and smiled at Trudy. He wagged his head, rolled his eyes, and made a talking gesture with his free hand.

"Sissy . . . Sissy! Take a breath, for fuck's sake," he said, cutting into whatever she was yapping about. "I can't. I'm still on this case in Florida." He listened to her for another minute. "I flew into L.A. and right back out." He finished off the muffin and grabbed another one. "No, I don't have time for that now." He sighed heavily. "It's hard to say, but for at least another week. I'll call you when I get back to Atlanta." His gaze flicked to Trudy. "Yes, she's still here. Sure, it's great. Okay." He swallowed hard, making his throat flex. "Same here. 'Bye."

Trudy arched a brow at him, noting that he seemed a tad flustered. "She keeps you on a tight rein, does she?"

He narrowed his eyes, trying to look menacing. "No. She was attempting to talk me into doing another remote or appearing on her show again this week."

"She asked about me?" Trudy took a bite of her muffin. She had to agree with him. They were delicious — and teasing him was even more delicious.

"Yes. She knows that we're working together."

"I bet she doesn't know that we're sleeping together."

He sent her a wry glance. "We haven't *slept* together."

"You know what I mean." She gave a shrug, dismissing the technicality. "Did she sign off with a 'Miss you like crazy and wish you were here'?"

"Not exactly." He leaned closer to her, a grin lifting one side of his mouth. "Are you enjoying yourself?"

"Immensely. I'm so glad I dropped by when I did."

He chuckled, but then glared at his phone when it buzzed. "Now what?"

Trudy craned forward, thinking it might be Sissy again, but "Unknown Caller" flashed on the screen.

Sighing dramatically, he answered it. "Hello. Who is this, please?" He listened and a frown line appeared between his eyes. "Yes, that's right. Who is this and how the hell did you get this number?" He pulled the phone away from his ear and pressed the screen, ending the call. "That's weird."

"What?"

"I don't know her." He held up a finger, stopping her next question, and pressed a number on the cell phone. "Hey, Gonzo. What? Oh damn, I forgot to tell you that I canceled that. Yes, I told Darla to cancel everything for the next couple of weeks so that I can devote my time to this Florida case." He listened for a minute. "Okay. Yes. Yes. That's good. Listen, Gonzo, I just received a call from a woman I don't know. She wouldn't tell me who she is or how she got my cell phone number. I blocked her number, but let me give it to you. I'd like for you to find out who she is and shut her down. Okay the number is . . ."

Trudy poured more coffee into his mug as he rattled off a telephone number. He glanced at her and gave her a quick, unfiltered smile that went straight to her heart.

"Keep me posted, Gonzo." He ended the call and sat back in the chair, deep in thought.

"An obsessive fan?" Trudy surmised.

"I suppose, but how did she get my cell phone number? That bothers me."

"Who is Gonzo?"

He smiled faintly. "Pete Gonzales. He runs the security firm that I use."

"What do you need security for?"

"For when I make personal appearances in certain venues," he said, lifting one brow at her. "There are a lot of crazy people out there, Trudy."

"Don't I know it." She set another muffin in front of him. "One more? They're small and it'll do you good. Blueberries are nutritious."

"Yes, Mom."

"Did your mother take care of you like this when you were a little boy and under the weather?" she asked in a teasing tone.

He examined the muffin before shoving it into his mouth and eating half of it at once. He took his time chewing and swallowing. As the seconds ticked by, Trudy thought he was going to ignore her harmless question and she wondered why.

"My mother is dead."

Trudy blinked as his answer sank in and she wanted to kick herself for letting her mouth get her in a pickle again. "I'm sorry, Levi." The fresh grief glinting dully in his eyes made her ask, "Did she die recently?"

"No. Twelve years ago."

She started counting back, but he was ahead of her.

"When I was seventeen. She died of cancer. Ovarian cancer." He finished off the muffin and wiped his hands together to dislodge crumbs.

"Oh." What else could she say? Uneasiness wound through her when he squared his shoulders and rocked his head from side to side as if to relieve bunched muscles there. One corner of his mouth kicked up in that way he had when he was about to say something with a punch to it.

"My father was unable to heal her."

She shook her head, baffled. "Heal her?"

"Yes. That's what he does." Hatred sparked deep in his blue, bruised eyes and it was so stark that it made Trudy wince inwardly.

"He heals people. But he laid hands on her and it didn't work. It really chapped his ass. But it wasn't his fault. Oh, no. It was *my* fault." His voice was scratchy, full of pain and scorn.

"How could that be?" Trudy asked, shaking her head, utterly confused by such a ridiculous assertion.

He looked at her as if she were thick-headed. "I didn't pray fervently enough, and of course, I consort with Satan. That's why she died. Because I'm a medium and my birth rotted her womb. Therefore, my father couldn't heal her." He ran a hand through his damp hair. "Sanctimonious bastard."

She cringed from his twisted explanation and the contempt embodied in his words. "That's a horrible thing to accuse your son of! Is your father still alive?"

A harsh, choppy laugh escaped him. "Oh, yes. He's alive all right. He has a new wife – a younger, bigger breasted, bigger haired, cancer-free, empty-headed piece of ass who makes him feel like a stud again. He's laying his self-righteous hands on desperate, pitiful people every day and *pronouncing them healed.* But *I'm* the liar. *I'm* the fraud."

"Who is he?" she asked, almost afraid to venture the question.

His gaze swept up slowly to confront her. A dark, disturbing expression fixated on his features before he finally whispered, "The Right Reverend John Comfort."

Trudy didn't follow evangelical preachers – or any preachers, for that matter – but she knew who that one was. You'd have to be totally divorced from the daily concourse of America to not have heard of the Reverend Comfort and the Hour of Comfort television show on one of the religious cable channels.

Much had been written about him and he was often interviewed when the subject was religion. He was a handsome man, not unlike his son, with a shock of white hair he combed straight back from his broad forehead, sky blue eyes, and a big, bright smile. He was a tall man, well-constructed, and he had a musical cadence to his deep voice. His good looks, mesmerizing voice, and alleged power to heal the sick and injured had made him a famous and wealthy man.

She also recalled images of his wife, AmyLynn, a bleached blond with a tiny waist and impossibly large breasts, who sang on the program and looked adoringly at her husband, muttering "amen" and "praise Jesus" every so often as he preached the Gospel according to Comfort. She couldn't recall any other wife of John Comfort's –

Levi's mother — so she must have stayed in the background or perhaps John Comfort hadn't been as famous back then.

"Oh." She realized her response to his revelation was sadly lacking, but he smiled as if he understood.

"Exactly," He nodded. "Dear Daddy has made quite a name for himself collecting money and popping people on the forehead with the heel of his hand to heal them on his TV show five fucking days a week. But, to him, I'm the only liar, the only cheat, the only charlatan in the family. It's so ironic, it's hilarious."

But he wasn't laughing. The pain in his expression squeezed her heart and Trudy reached out and covered his hand with hers. He flinched, but didn't move away from her sympathetic touch.

"He's quite the showman," she noted.

He gave a half-smile. "Yes. I suppose I come by it naturally."

"Do you ever see him?" she asked, gently.

"In person?" For a moment, he looked alarmed, then he scoffed. "Hell no! I want nothing to do with him and that's just peachy with him, too."

"So, you never had a good relationship with him? Even when you were a young boy?"

One corner of his mouth twitched into that sardonic grin he was so good at. His chest expanded as he sucked in a deep breath and then released it with almost a shudder. She thought she glimpsed revulsion in his eyes and perhaps even a sliver of fear before his lids fell slowly to shut her out. "No. No way. Oh, baby, you have no idea . . ." Then he pulled his hand out from under hers as if he couldn't stand to be touched at that moment — by anyone.

She wanted —needed — to lighten his mood. "I wish you had grown up in Mayberry with me," she said, giving him a wistful smile as she referenced a jest he'd made before about her own idyllic upbringing.

"Yes, so do I." Then he shrugged. "But I probably would have beaten the living hell out of the Beav and ended up being shipped off to reform school anyway."

They shared a smile and silence drifted between them for a minute before he drew in a noisy breath and flattened his hands on the table with authority. "I need to go to the police station around one o'clock. You want to come with me? Your boyfriend will be there."

It was her turn to roll her eyes at him. "Are you referring to Detective Sinclair?"

"I am."

"Why are you going to meet with him?"

"I called him to ask if I could look at some of the personal articles taken from each victim."

"Why?"

"I tried to reach each one of them this morning, but had no luck. I have to touch something before I can call them to me."

"Why were you trying to reach the victims?"

"Because I have this nagging feeling that each one of them was in the company of another woman shortly before they were killed."

"Zelda?" she asked, following his theory and feeling the truth in it resonate.

He nodded. "I think so. I didn't ask them about who they'd been with before because I didn't know about Zelda then. But now . . . I need to see if I can get one of them to tell me . . . show me like Shelly did. Maybe one of them will even let me see Zelda's face or tell me her last name."

"What would be the point of him working in concert with a woman?"

He folded his arms against his chest. "Perhaps she gets the trust of the victim. She sets them up for the kill."

Trudy frowned and warded off a shiver. "That's creepy. She would be as sick as him."

"Are you going to let Sinclair claim his rain check?"

She thought about telling him to go jump off a cliff, but clamped down on her sharp tongue. "No. I want to concentrate on this case."

"Not going out with him again has nothing to do with me and how much fun you have in bed with me?"

"No." She stiffened when his expression called her a liar. He could be such a delinquent . . . "You mentioned reform school. Were you in one?"

Muscles tightened in his jaw and she felt his shields click into place. She instantly wished she could take back the question.

"You probably should go now. I'll meet up with you later." He shoved up from the chair in a fluid motion that took her completely by surprise.

"Wait!" Trudy grabbed his hand. "I'm sorry. I shouldn't . . . I just want to know you better, Levi. That's all."

He looked down at their joined hands and he gave a little shake of his head. "There are things that I can't . . . I don't want to talk about," he said in a near whisper.

"I understand." She stood up, facing him.

"I doubt that." He trailed the fingers of his other hand through her hair and his smile was so sad that it chipped away at her heart. "I didn't go to reform school. Not the kind you're thinking of. But I did go to . . . I guess you'd call them faith-based schools for wayward children where I was supposed to be put on the righteous path. And I didn't have pleasant experiences in them. And that's all I want to say about it."

He had been abused, she thought, and it wrenched her heart. His childhood had been the exact opposite of hers. She had been treasured and he had been . . . what? Misunderstood? Outcast? Resisting the urge to wrap her arms around him in a vain attempt to protect him from his own memories, she brought his hand to her lips and kissed the back of it. "I'll leave you alone. I'm sorry for dredging that up. If you need anything . . ."

He slipped his arms around her. "I've liked being fussed over by you, but your time of playing Nurse Trudy has come to an end. I'm all well."

Her breathing quickened as a quivering sensation in her belly spread slowly through her. God he was barely touching her, but she was trembling and lightheaded already!

"Levi . . ." she whispered, suddenly wanting his mouth on hers.

"Yes?" His lips touched hers and then pulled back.

"Levi," she said again, her voice pleading.

"Tell me what you want, Trudy." He brought his hands up to touch her face and his fingers slid from her chin and then moved slowly, softly to her throat, his gaze following their progress. "Tell me."

"You," she breathed, and his mouth came down hard on hers. She groaned and nipped his lower lip.

He drove his fingers through her hair and tilted her head so that his lips could find better purchase and then his tongue had sex with hers – carnal, hot, tongue sex. She closed her hands around his wrists and felt her knees tremble as desire wound through her. Her body bowed into his, needing to mate, needing to melt into his.

Tearing his mouth from hers, he stared into her eyes as he gathered in a huge, shuddering breath. "Christ, Trudy! I lose my fucking head around you." His eyes darkened to blue/black. "You make me crazy and oh, baby, you can kiss."

Her? Not her! Him! She couldn't speak. Her heart throbbed in her throat.

His phone buzzed again and he flung it a withering glare. Trudy wiggled from his embrace and found her voice.

"Answer it. I'll see you in a couple of hours. If it's Sissy again, tell her I'm only borrowing you for a week or two and I promise not to damage the goods. Oh, and you can have the rest of the coffee and muffins."

"I'd rather spread you out on that bed and get a taste of you again."

The phone kept buzzing and Trudy sidestepped him and gave his tight butt a sharp whack with the flat of her hand as she darted to the door. She flung it open and looked over her shoulder at him. His grin was all salacious and sensual and his eyes were all hunger and tempered desire.

"Witchy, witchy woman," he said, rubbing his rump. He made a grab for her, but she let out a little shriek and dodged him. Laughing under her breath, she bolted out of the cabin and sauntered to the RV, letting her hips sway. She knew he was watching her.

*

"So, you're sure your tummy is okay now?" Trudy asked, peering into Levi's face as he held open the door to the police station for her.

He sent her a reassuring smile. "I'm fine."

She preceded him inside the police headquarters and through the security measures. Wearing their "Visitor" lanyards, they went up to the second floor where they stopped in front of the reception desk. The middle-aged woman who had greeted them the last time had been replaced by a young Latino who could barely take her eyes off Levi. Trudy couldn't blame her.

Levi was right, she mused. He was *fine*. Looking exceptionally handsome in a light weight, black pin-striped jacket over a dove gray shirt, he exuded masculinity.

"Hello, Mr. Wolfe," the Latin hottie purred. "How may I help you?"

Trudy smiled when she caught the girl's eye. *Yeah, I know,* she thought. *He's gorgeous. And what's more, he kisses like he invented it!*

"Good afternoon. Detective Sinclair is expecting us."

"He certainly is," the girl said, her sloe-eyed gaze sambaing slowly over Levi's face and body. "You know the way to his desk?"

"Yes, thank you." Levi reached back and grasped Trudy's hand. He sent her a quick smile before setting off with her to Sinclair's desk.

The moment Tom Sinclair noticed their clasped hands his face grew ruddy and his gaze snapped accusingly to Trudy. Feeling uneasy, Trudy pulled her hand from Levi's as unobtrusively as possible and held it out to Tom.

"Good to see you again," she said. Tom waited a beat, cut his eyes at Levi and then shook her hand.

"Hi, Trudy. You look great — as usual." His brown eyes moved swiftly and appreciatively over her mint green sundress that left her arms and a lot of her back bare.

"Thanks, Tom." From the corner of her eye, she could see Levi's cool regard. She instantly regretted taking her hand from his and then resented him for making her feel that way. "Do you have those personal items Levi asked for?" she asked, needing to get on firm footing again.

"Yeah, yeah." Tom tore his gaze from his appreciative perusal of her legs and turned back to his desk. "They're right here. You can't take any of this stuff out of the building. You understand that, don't you, Wolfe?"

"Yes, I understand." He sounded terse.

Trudy looked closer at him and when his gaze met hers, she realized that he was agitated and on the verge of being royally ticked off.

He glanced around. "Is there an interrogation room we can use? Somewhere quiet and private?"

"Yeah, sure." The detective gathered three plastic baggies and motioned for them to follow him. "Come on."

Levi stared at Trudy and she gave him a quizzical look that asked, *What's wrong now?* He lowered his brows and bobbed his head, signaling her to follow Sinclair as he took up the rear.

Sinclair stopped in front of a metal door. "You can use this room," he said, switching a sign that read *open* to *occupied*.

"Thank you." Levi took the evidence bags from him. He looked from Sinclair to Trudy, then back to Sinclair. "Does someone have to be in there with me or can I do this alone?"

Trudy hitched up her chin, knowing she had just been dismissed and felt Tom eye her warily.

"Uh . . . I guess it's okay," Tom said.

Refusing to succumb to his foul mood, Trudy fixed a smile to her lips. "Good luck, Mr. Wolfe."

His smile was as disingenuous as hers. "Why thank you, Miss Tucker, but luck has very little to do with it." His gaze flicked to the detective. "This shouldn't take long. Just try not to interrupt me. Thanks." And then he stepped inside the small room and shut the door with finality.

Tom issued a low whistle. "He's a double feature and tub of popcorn, isn't he? Is he always like that?"

She laughed softly at the description. "Yes, most of the time, he is." She motioned to a few chairs sitting against the wall. "May I wait here for him?"

"Sure! You want a cup of coffee or a soda?"

"No, thank you." She sat in one of the straight-backed, metal chairs. "Please, don't let me keep you from your work."

"This *is* my work." Tom sat beside her. "I have to wait until he comes out of that room and collect those evidence bags from him."

"Oh."

"So, what's he doing in there with them?"

She furrowed her brow. *Good question.* "He's touching each item and trying to summon the spirit of its owner so that he can ask her some questions."

"In other words, he's trying to talk to dead people," Tom drawled with a smirk.

Trudy stiffened and knew that if he said that in that way to Levi's face he would be lucky to keep his front teeth. Especially in the mood Levi was in right now! She drew in a deep breath and told herself to be professional and not bite the nice policeman's head off. "That's right. He's playing a hunch and he's hoping that he can confirm it by contacting the victims again."

"So, you've seen him in action, have you?"

"I have." She turned her serious gaze on Tom and was glad when he pulled the collar of his shirt from his wide neck as if he was suddenly uncomfortable. "He's the genuine article. No bullshitting. No grandstanding. No hocus-pocus. What he tells you, you can believe."

Tom's gaze moved from her steady stare to his clasped hands in his lap. "Okay. Yeah. That's good. So, are you with him now?"

"I told you, Tom. I'm concentrating on this case."

"So, you're not with him?"

"I don't know what you mean," she said, although she knew *exactly* what he meant. "You know that I'm working with Levi on this case."

"Yes," he said, drawing out the word. "But he's sort of anal about you. It's obvious that he thinks of you as more than just a co-worker."

"Anal about me?" she repeated and tried not to think of that in a sexual context. "I think you're reading more into it than there is."

"I don't think so. He's pretty much told me to keep my hands off you."

"What?" she turned her head sharply to examine his sheepish grin. "When did he say that?"

"This morning. He called me about wanting to set up a meeting and said that he hoped I behaved like a gentleman around you." Chuckling, he shook his head. "I told him that I didn't need advice on how to treat ladies from the likes of him. And he said that you belonged to him."

"He did not!" Trudy felt her mouth hang open and she forced her teeth to click shut. "I can't believe he would say such an audacious thing!"

"But you just told me that what he says I can believe," Tom said, almost slyly.

Trudy breathed in and out a couple of times before she trusted her voice again. "About work. About his psychic impressions. You can trust him about those – implicitly. But, like many men, he has a tendency to overstate when it comes to personal matters." She arched a brow. "My dad calls it 'pissing contests.'"

Tom laughed. "Yeah, I suppose he could have been doing that. You're a looker, Trudy, and I'm sure this isn't the first time a couple of men have wrestled over you."

Smiling, she didn't meet his gaze because it *was* the first time this sort of thing had happened to her. She had witnessed it happening to girlfriends and even to her sister a couple of times, but never to her. It was aggravating and . . . thrilling.

"How long have you two been working together?"

"Only a short time. This is our first case together."

"I hope you can tap into the serial killer's head again if he decides to attack another woman."

"Is there any doubt that he won't kill again? Of course, he's going to go after another woman. It's just a matter of who and when."

Tom's expression was suddenly weary. He leaned forward and propped his elbows on his knees. "Yeah. This case is getting to me. I thought for sure we'd find this creep in no time." He stared at his clasped hands hanging in the space between his spread knees. "I'll be so damn glad when we catch him."

"Me, too." She rested a hand on his shoulder and gave it a squeeze. "I know the police are getting a bad rap from the media about this. I don't know what else they think you can do to catch this guy. I mean, you're throwing everything you've got at it. He's going to mess up and you'll nail him."

That's when Levi chose to throw open the door. His gaze fell on her hand resting on Tom's shoulder and his eyes frosted over. Trudy's hand slid off of Tom as he stood up, his weary expression changing to expectant.

"Did you get new information? Trudy says you're playing a hunch."

Levi gave the evidence bags to Tom, but kept his gaze on Trudy. She felt the blood drain from her face and resented him for making her feel as is she'd wronged him somehow.

Levi drew in a deep breath and jerked his gaze away from her to confront Sinclair. "I'm fairly certain now that each of the victims was in the company of a woman shortly before she died."

"Oh, yeah? This Zelda woman, you think?"

"Yes. They'd made a new woman friend. They liked her and they invited her to their place for drinks or dinner."

"A lesbian thing?" Tom asked, earning Levi's wince of irritation.

"No." Levi drew in a slow breath and Trudy knew he was clamping down on his – pissyness. "Nothing sexual. Just girlfriends."

"You think Zelda is working with the killer?"

"I think it's too big of a coincidence that they all had made a new friend and invited her to their apartment or home and ended up murdered or kidnapped and then killed. The girlfriend is not always called Zelda. Barbie Allen and Debra Williams met a woman called

Zara. Jane and Shelly met Zelda. They both fit the description of the one we had before, so it's definitely the same woman."

"Those names aren't that common. I'll run a check to see if any women with those first names have been arrested for anything in Key West." Tom jotted the information into a notebook he'd pulled from his back trouser pocket. "Anything else?"

"No. But I'll go over everything again and I'll e-mail you if I recall anything more from the victims. Thanks for your cooperation, Detective."

"Sure thing, Wolfe."

Levi looked from Tom to Trudy. "If you're finished here, can we go?"

Trudy wanted to yell at him in utter frustration. Why was he making such a huge deal over nothing? He was being such a Neanderthal! And he had no right! "We came here for you, Mr. Wolfe," she reminded him coolly. "If you're finished, then we should be on our way and let Detective Sinclair get back to work."

He gave a curt nod, then held out his hand to Tom. They shook. Trudy smiled at Tom.

"See you later," she said and turned on her heel to follow Levi out of the detective division, past the smiling, hungry-eyed receptionist, down the stairs, and out onto the sidewalk. He didn't hold her hand this time.

She stopped beside him as he slipped on his tortoise-shell sunglasses. Okay, so he was mad, she fumed. Well, she was none too pleased herself!

"Are you hungry?" he asked, quietly, almost politely.

She eyed him warily. "Look, I know you're seething, so let's have it out and get it over with. I have a few bones to pick with you, too."

"I don't want to have a scene right now, Trudy," he rejoined, still quietly. "I just had a draining psychic session and I want to sit down somewhere, have something to eat along with a good, stiff drink. Does that work for you?"

She stared at him, feeling totally out to sea, then shrugged. "Works for me."

"Good." He set off for the car with her almost having to trot to keep up with him.

Chapter Twelve

Sprawled in a chair, his jacket draped over the back of it, his shirtsleeves rolled up to just below his elbows, his tie's knot loosened, and the collar button unfastened, Levi glanced around the patio of the Key West café. He drank some of the whiskey straight he'd ordered as he and Trudy waited for their nachos supreme to arrive. She sipped from her soft drink, her gaze flicking to him every so often.

Infuriating woman.

He wanted to throttle her one second and fuck her the next. Taking in a deep breath, he told himself to chill out as he came down off the fit of jealousy he'd experienced while watching her with Sinclair. Why the hell did he feel so possessive? It was nuts. But he couldn't shake it. The more he was around her, the more he couldn't bear the thought of another man touching her.

Christ! They hadn't even spent one full night together and she had him by the balls! Which was another bone of contention. Why didn't she want to stay and snuggle after they'd had sex? Every other woman he'd ever been with wanted to, but not Trudy. Oh, hell no. She had to jump and run as soon as he pulled out of her. And why should he care, anyway?

But he did. It rankled him. It festered in him. It had become a prime mission – to make her spend the whole night with him.

Observing her through the veil of his lashes, he felt that odd softening around his heart when he recalled her telling him at the museum that she saw him – saw past his face and saw *him*. He believed her. When she looked at him, he felt a connection like no other. And being inside her had felt so *right*. Judging by the brush-off she'd given him every time, she obviously didn't feel the same. How many orgasms did the woman require before she enjoyed herself enough to hang around for an entire night for a repeat in the morning?

"When did Quintara ask you to join the Roundtable?"

He jerked when she spoke – he'd been that deep into his own thoughts of her. He ran his fingers up and down the condensation on the drink glass and considered what she'd just asked him. Was she joking? He looked at her. Nope. She was serious. "Join? I've never joined. There was no Roundtable when I first met Quintara. In fact, it was my suggestion that she begin the Psychic Roundtable."

She blinked, obviously stupefied. "How did I not know this? I just assumed . . . well, that's the problem, isn't it? I've assumed too much and I actually know very little about you." She sent him an apologetic smile. "So, tell me about it, please."

He nodded, accepting her apology. She *had* assumed a hell of a lot about him and he suspected he had Quintara and the Psychic Roundtable participants to thank for that. He knew he was the source of gossip among them because Quintara had told him. Of course, he was used to people assuming they knew him when they didn't, but he wanted to get closer to Trudy. He was drawn to her and had been since the moment he'd first laid eyes on her heart-shaped, heart-stopping face.

"Are you going to tell me?" she asked, pulling him back to the present.

"Yes, sorry. Well, Quintara had quite a few people calling her and dropping by her place wanting to know more about their own experiences and what they meant. She's such a great teacher that I told her she should hold monthly or even weekly workshops for budding psychics and have a higher level for those with real promise." He chuckled at the memory. "She came up with the Roundtable theme and I got her a couple of gigs on radio programs. I called in a favor from a newspaper reporter to do a feature on her. Within a few weeks, she had people crawling out of the woodwork, waving money in her face, wanting to attend her workshops or be allowed in the Roundtable."

He finished off his drink as the waiter arrived with their huge platter of nachos.

"Would you like another, sir?"

Levi shook his head. The whiskey had done the trick. His head was clearer and his insane jealousy was under control. For now, at least. "I'll have a glass of ice water with lemon, please."

The waiter nodded. "Can I bring you another Diet Dr. Pepper, ma'am?"

"Yes, thanks."

Nodding again, the waiter left to get their drinks.

Trudy selected one of the cheesy nachos and popped it into her mouth. Levi took one off the mountain of them and munched it. Delicious.

"Anything else I can get you?" the waiter asked, returning with their beverages.

"No, thank you," Levi said, grabbing another nacho.

"So, where *did* you meet Quintara?" Trudy asked.

"In Oklahoma City at a psychic fair and conference," he said, wiping at his mouth and fingers with a napkin. "I was a speaker and I was also on a panel with her. She approached me later and informed me that I was extremely talented and that I was frittering away my gifts when I could be making money from them." He grinned. "She said she had big plans for me." He laughed, shaking his head as he pictured brassy, bawdy, bountiful Quintara – his truest, dearest friend. "I was intrigued. And I could tell she was absolutely serious. It had been a long time since anyone had shown any real interest in my psychic abilities. I couldn't refuse her."

"She's hard to refuse," Trudy agreed, helping herself to another nacho.

"She could see I was coasting through life. I was in my debauchery period."

"Debauchery?"

Memories of those days sifted through him like old, dog-earned photos. Those were days he never wanted to return to. "I was living out of a suitcase, drinking way too much, and balling a different woman every night. Back then I was what you seem to think I am today. I stopped even asking the women's names because I really didn't give a fuck. I'd lost every shred of my self-esteem."

"Was this after Lizzie?"

Lizzie? He met her curious, green gaze. She really was interested in Lizzie and he wondered why. His relationship with Lizzie was years ago . . . kid stuff, really. He ate another nacho before he answered. "Long after Lizzie. She had nothing to do with it. I dive-bombed all on my own."

They ate in companionable silence for awhile as the nacho mountain gradually became a nacho bump. Trudy watched as a waiter, holding two ice cream cones, moved past their table and handed them to a couple seated near them. When he started back toward the restaurant's entrance, she stopped him.

"What kind of ice cream is that?"

"Key lime sprinkled with graham cracker crumbs," the waiter said. Her eyes widened. "Yum!"

Levi chuckled. When she looked at him like that, he'd damn near give her anything she wanted. "We'll have two of them."

"They're our specialty. You'll love them," the waiter assured them.

"What sort of plan did Quintara have for you?" Trudy folded her arms on the table and leaned closer, obviously enjoying the stories about how he and Quintara forged their friendship. The top of her dress gaped a little, giving him a nice view of her cleavage.

"She wanted me to hire a booking agent and appear on television shows and radio programs. She said I should work with police on murder cases." He shrugged, grabbed one last gooey nacho, and moved the almost empty platter aside. "She told me I needed to be bigger than life, a real showman, and she helped me perfect my stage presence."

Trudy's mouth dropped open. "Are you serious? Quintara is the one who encouraged you to become the Great and Mysterious Levi Wolfe? She shaped you into a splashy, showy, psychic extraordinaire?"

He examined her large, green eyes and slack mouth. "You didn't know that she's responsible for my public persona? Quintara never told you?" He tipped back his head and laughed up at the blue sky "That is rich! Quintara is the mad visionary who pieced together this Frankenstein monster that you so distain and she doesn't tell you! Oh, yes, that is quintessential Quintara."

Trudy scowled at him and jerked up her chin in that way that made him want to kiss her hard until she whimpered. "I don't distain you, Levi. You must know that by now."

Pleasure heated his blood and he recalled vividly the softness of her skin and how her body responded to his. Yes, he knew she liked him. She just didn't like him enough to suit him. He wanted her to be as out of control over him as he was over her. And he meant to get her there, damn it.

"You still distain my showmanship," he corrected with a smile. He hooked one arm over the back of the chair and watched as she finished off another nacho. He really, really wanted to feel her mouth on his cock. Soon. "I thought I'd changed your opinion of me, but now I wonder. You're hot and cold. Loyal and disloyal."

"Wait a second." She held up a warning finger and her eyes threw sparks. "I am *not* disloyal." She pointed her finger at him. "*You* are misinterpreting every move I make and making mountains out of molehills."

"Oh, is *that* what I'm doing?"

"Yes."

He nodded, tamping down his anger as he watched people passing by the café. "So, when I was holding your hand and you yanked it away so that you could shake Sinclair's, I misinterpreted that move? And when I came out of the interrogation room and you were caressing his shoulder and looking at him with those big, moony, green eyes, I was making a mountain out of a molehill?"

"Yes. Exactly." She drew in a deep breath and plunged on before he could speak. "I don't want to see Tom anymore. Not like that. I *liked* that you were holding my hand, but I felt uncomfortable . . . and then it seemed that you might be making some kind of claim for Tom's benefit. And I was only commiserating about this damned case with Tom when you came out of the room. I actually had been telling him what a fantastic psychic you are and he was telling me that you claimed that I *belong* to you." She ran out of breath and had to stop.

His burst of anger dissipated. He crossed his arms on the table and met her level gaze. "You're right. I held your hand because I wanted everyone to know that you were with me – Sinclair included. When you pulled away from me, it felt as if you'd slapped me."

She closed her eyes for a few moments and he hoped to hell she regretted her actions. "Sorry. That wasn't my intention."

The waiter approached with their ice cream cones. "Enjoy," he said with a smile.

Levi nodded at the waiter and tasted the ice cream. It was rich and he was glad there was only one scoop of it. Trudy's tongue peeked out and she took a small lick of the frozen treat. She tasted it again, gathering more crumbs on her tongue this time. Levi's cock roused up.

"Good?" he asked, shifting uncomfortably in the chair.

"Ummm. Very."

While she had her eyes on him, he decided to give her a little show. He licked his ice cream all the way around, making swirls in the pale green confection with the tip of his tongue. He grinned as her eyes darkened to the color of emeralds.

Deliberately and slowly, she took the dessert into her mouth until her lips touched the cone . . . all the way in and then all the way out. Fuck! He hardened more and pressed against his fly as perspiration dotted his forehead.

"Do that again and I won't be responsible for my actions," he warned her.

She shrugged, the picture of innocence. "I'm just enjoying my ice cream."

He glanced around at the crowded patio and then sent her a scolding look. "Enjoy it a little less, okay?"

"You're fun to tease," she said, grinning.

"And you're a charming, little prick-teaser," he rejoined.

They finished the ice cream cones in silence, glancing at each other, then at the people milling around them and seated near them. Trudy brushed her hands together and sighed.

"That was delicious."

"I agree." He popped the rest of the cone into his mouth with a flourish and then captured her hands, turning them over to stare intently at her palms. "I see success in your future."

"Oh? Anything else?"

"Yes. Sex. Lots and lots of sex."

She pulled free of him, giving him a little smile. "Oh yeah?"

"Yeah." He folded his arms against his chest and settled back in the chair. Enough teasing. He wanted to get a few things straight with her. "Do you remember the first time we met at the Roundtable?"

She nodded.

"The moment I touched you – I knew I had to have you. You were wearing a green blouse and jeans that evening. Forest green."

She swallowed and he saw the pulse in her throat flutter.

"I felt this . . . this magnetic pull as if you were my true north." He placed a hand over his thumping heart and hoped to hell she appreciated his candidness because this wasn't easy for him. He usually avoided conversations about feelings and emotions – except when he talked to his psychiatrist and then it was necessary. But Trudy was different. He wanted to work with her and he also wanted very much to fuck her again and again and again. After that first time with her, it had been abundantly clear to him that one time with Trudy wasn't enough. In fact, she had taken over his fantasies, his dreams, and had become the only woman he wanted. He didn't know how long he'd feel this way, but he needed for her to know that she was more than a booty call.

She pulled her bottom lip between her teeth and her eyes grew luminous. He sat forward, resting his arms on the table, needing to be closer. "I couldn't stay away. I had to fly in every month or so to get my Trudy fix."

She wrinkled her nose. "You didn't attend the Roundtable just to see me."

"The hell I didn't! Why else would I? I get nothing out of it. I was there for you."

"You didn't drop by every so often just to see Quintara?"

"No. I usually only visit the Roundtable once or twice year. Until you showed up."

She swallowed hard and averted her gaze. "Why me?"

"I just told you. I felt an instant connection and I wanted to be with you . . . work with you. And now that I've been with you . . ." He glanced around at the other diners and lowered his voice. "I want you every which way and six times on Sunday."

She swallowed with an audible gulp. "No man has ever spoken to me like you do."

He shook his head, not buying it. "I find that difficult to believe."

"I like it." She sucked in a breath as if the admission surprised her.

Levi felt a grin overtake him. "Why do you like it?" he asked. "Tell me."

"You make me feel . . . wanted . . . sexy."

His cock strained against his fly and his chest tightened. "Baby, you are sex on legs."

She opened her mouth to speak, but then her face froze and her eyes grew large. A glassy haze seemed to drift over them, changing their deep green to a light olive color. She sat straighter and her head turned slowly away from him until she was staring at the street.

"Trudy?"

Nothing. She didn't acknowledge him in the least.

Levi closed his eyes. Shit. The crazy motherfucker had her again.

Feeling helpless, Levi glanced around at the other people on the patio, but no one seemed to notice the glassy-eyed girl sitting at his table, staring sightlessly at the street. Tentatively, he scooted his chair closer to hers and took her hands in his. This wasn't the greatest place for her to be in a trance!

A barely discernible quiver danced through her limbs and he wanted desperately to enfold her in his arms and shelter her. But that wouldn't help her through this. He closed his eyes for a moment, trying to tune into her as he searched through his years of training, schooling, and his bag of tricks to find the right tools.

"Trudy?" he whispered, opening his eyes and leaning closer to her. He ran his thumbs over the back of her hands, appreciating her soft skin, wishing fervently that he could see what she was seeing. "Where are you, Trudy? Talk to me."

"Walking to Mallory Square," she said, her voice flat, like a robot's.

Looking in that direction, Levi frowned. Naturally, he's going to Mallory Square a couple of hours before sunset where it will be jam-packed with people. The area was a big, open space near the ocean, full of locals and tourists where a stalker could get lost and stare at women without drawing attention to himself. "Is he alone?"

"Alone, but not for long," she whispered back to him. "Got my eye on someone." She scanned the area in front of her, craning her neck, furrowing her brow. "Where the hell is she? Here, kitty, kitty, kitty. Come rub up against me so I can run a knife between your tits and watch you bleed out."

Levi glanced around. A man and two women sat at the table nearest them and they were looking at them. He saw one of the women lean toward the man and say, "That's Levi Wolfe!" *Oh, Christ on a crutch.* Catching sight of the waiter, Levi let go of Trudy's hands and motioned for him to come over.

"Yes, sir?"

"How much is the bill?" Levi stood and pulled his wallet from his back pocket.

"I'll go print it——."

"No, just tell me how much. We have to go."

"Is there a problem?"

Impatience blew threw him like a hot wind. He looked at the young, pimply-faced waiter from beneath his lowered brows and shoved him with his mind. The waiter drew in a deep breath and blinked his hazel eyes. *Got your attention now? Just do as I say!* "Will this cover it and your tip?" He threw two twenties and a ten on the table.

"Yes, sir. Yes!"

"Fine." Levi shoved his wallet into his back pocket and then shrugged into his jacket. Leaning down, he took Trudy's hands into his again. "Stand up, Trudy. Stand!"

She moaned and shook her head.

He pulled her up to her feet. She swayed and he wrapped an arm around her waist and made her walk with him.

"We're going to Mallory Square," he said, close to her ear. "Walk, Trudy."

She moved more like a zombie than a lithe, young woman. He tightened his arm around her waist and they made their way jerkily along the sidewalk. He realized that she was stumbling more than walking, so he directed her toward a covered bench next to a bus stop. Anyone looking at them probably thought she was completely wasted. He let her slide down his body to sit on the bench and he joined her, peering into her flushed face and expressionless, olive green eyes. God, she was really gone!

"What's he doing now, Trudy? Where is he?"

"Mallory Square," she breathed.

He glanced in that direction and guessed they were about two blocks from the square – the acclaimed southernmost tip of the continental United States. Steel drum music drifted to him and then a violin sang out as musicians warmed up. He could imagine the scores of artists, clowns, jugglers, stilt-walkers, and even Gypsy palm readers and half-assed psychics joining crowds of natives and vacationers as they did every evening to watch the unobstructed view of the sun setting in the ocean.

Studying Trudy's blank expression, he wondered what was going on behind her sightless green eyes. Her experience might be similar to his, but it also *had* to be vastly different. He mingled with benign spirits. She had been taken over by a flesh-and-blood devil who was only a few blocks from where they sat. An icy chill clamped onto his heart and, not for the first time, he feared for Trudy's safety. They were close to the killer. If she could commune with him, could the killer sense her, as well? If the killer saw her, would he make the connection and realize she was a threat?

"What do you see?" he asked her, wishing she'd talk. He took her by the shoulders and turned her around so that she faced him on the bench.

"Her. I see her," Trudy said, her lips barely moving.

"What does she look like? What's her name?"

An unpleasant smile claimed her lush mouth. "See you later, cuntie. We'll have fun later. Yeah, laugh it up, bitch. I'll fuck your mouth and make you choke on my big, fat cock before I slice off your nipples. Yeah, I can see your nips sticking out under that thin shirt. You think you're such a pretty pussy, don't you? Fucking bitch. Later. After some girl talk."

Levi shook his head, disturbed by the ugliness falling from her lovely mouth. He winced, hoping she'd come back soon. Girl talk? What the hell? Was the woman already talking to Zelda while the murderer looked on?

Trudy blinked and blinked again. A shudder convulsed through her and then life blazed in her green eyes again. A whimper escaped from her.

"Thank God." Levi pulled her into his arms and rocked her back and forth. "Jesus, that scares the shit out me, so I can only imagine what it does to you."

"What?" Her voice was muffled against his chest.

Reluctantly, he held her a little away from him and met her questioning gaze. "What did you see? What does she look like? Do you know her name?"

Trudy drew in shaking breath and closed her eyes. "She's about my age, taller than me, white-blond hair and it's piled up on her head in a high ponytail. She's stacked. Big boobs – probably double D's – small waist, small hips, tanned legs. She's wearing cutoffs and a white t-shirt and she's barefoot."

"Is she with anyone? Is Zelda with her?"

She puckered her brow, deep in thought. "I think she's with a group of people, but I'm not sure."

"Let's go find her." He stood up, pulling her to her feet. "We're only two blocks away." Bending his knees, he ducked down to capture her gaze. Her cat eyes were swimming with unshed tears. "Are you okay?"

She nodded and wiped the moisture from her lashes. "I'm fine now. My head was foggy there for a minute, but I feel okay, I think."

Slipping an arm around her shoulders, he set off with her toward the crowds at Key West's most famous square where a woman had been marked for death by a madman.

Chapter Thirteen

For more than an hour they searched frantically, crisscrossing the square, looking into faces, and not finding her. Trudy couldn't believe how many women were wearing cutoffs! And not one of them was the blond she was desperate to locate. Occasionally, she had caught sight of Levi. Once, he had stopped and was signing the back of some woman's t-shirt! Another time, he was being followed by three giggling girls.

He's a mini celebrity! The realization was sobering. She had never considered that he would be recognized and approached so often by strangers and adoring fans. Did he like that kind of attention? she wondered. Or was it a nuisance to him? It certainly was off-putting to her when they were trying to find a killer's next victim!

Stopping in front of a red-and-white striped artist's tent, which she and Levi had designated as their "meet up" spot, she moved from foot to foot in exasperation as she waited for him to join her. Was he signing autographs for his fans or helping her look for the blond? She watched the mingling throng in front of her, hoping . . . hoping . . . to catch sight of a white-blond ponytail.

"He's dreamboat handsome, isn't he?"

Trudy started slightly, realizing that the brunette standing next to her was addressing her, although she was staring at someone straight ahead of them. Following her gaze, Trudy spotted Levi. He was chatting with several wide-eyed women.

"You're talking about Levi Wolfe?" she asked, and the woman nodded, still smiling.

"He's very kind and considerate, too," the woman added as she glanced quickly at Trudy before swinging her attention back to Levi again.

Trudy gave the woman the once-over. Wait . . . her attention fastened on the t-shirt she wore – the t-shirt Trudy had seen Levi signing the back of a little while ago. "He autographed your shirt," she said. "So, you're a fan of his?"

"A fan?" The woman laughed and shook her head. "Oh, honey, I'm so much more than a fan!" Still laughing, she sauntered away. Trudy watched until she lost sight of her in the crowd. The exchange left her feeling oddly unnerved, but then everything about this afternoon unnerved her.

Excitement grew among the celebrants as the sun began to dip into the ocean. It was almost palatable, shimmering in the slanting sunlight. Musicians blasted out tunes as all sorts of other performers from mimes to chimps wearing tuxedos entertained, some for money and some just to be part of the action. A spattering of applause lifted in the air as the huge orange orb dipped lower and lower. Instead of feeling the magic of it all, Trudy's insides twisted with annoyance. Why couldn't she find the woman in cut-offs? It should be easy. They had found the one before and saved her life.

As people around her "ooohed" and "ahhhed" and applauded the sunset's spectacle, Trudy shook her head. Everyone was going about their lives, oblivious to the fact that a monster was pacing among them, searching, sniffing, prowling, anxious to spill more blood, to extinguish one more life as if it were his right, his singular purpose on this earth.

"No luck?"

She jumped and then drew in a short breath when she realized that Levi was standing behind her. "God! Don't scare me like that!"

"Sorry. You're jumpy."

"And why not? He's around here somewhere!"

"Okay, okay." He ran his hands up and down her arms.

"I've seen no fewer than twenty-five blond women in cutoffs and none of them was the one I wanted to see. Maybe she didn't hang around for the big show, but why come here if you're not going to watch the sunset?" Trudy scanned the crowd again. "She must be around here somewhere!"

He rested his hands on her shoulders and pulled her back against him. "She might have met friends here and then scooted off to get a good table for dinner, beating the sunset crowds."

She sighed, resigned to yet another failure. "This is pointless. We should head back to the car. We need to let Tom know." She meant to push away from him, but he enfolded her in his arms, crossing them above her breasts, his hands closing warmly around her shoulders. His lips touched her hair.

"Wait a few minutes. We're here. Let's enjoy it."

"I can't. I don't want to." Frustration coiled inside of her.

"It's magic time in Key West."

"Not for me." She closed her eyes and tried to relax, tried to slough off the casing of failure and helplessness.

His breath fanned the side of her neck. "I'm in awe of you."

She stopped breathing, his statement making everything inside of her soften and glow for a few quiet moments. Suddenly, the world seemed peaceful and safe again.

"There goes the sun, Trudy," he whispered in that sexy, throaty voice of his. "Slipping slowly into the sea. You can almost hear it hiss and sizzle."

Why did that sound so sexual? He could make almost anything sound that way.

She opened her eyes to the glorious vision in front of her. The sky glowed in amazing bands of color and the ocean was a bed of liquid gold. From the corner of her eye, she saw a mime approaching them and she smothered a giggle when Levi rasped, "Oh, shit. A fucking mime."

The black-and-white faced performer was clad in a black suit, a white shirt, and a big, orange bow tie. His white-gloved hands covered his heart and he mimed a big, pumping organ and batted his lashes at them. Then he used one index fingers to paint a valentine in the air in front of him and glanced up in a swoon where the first bold stars were peeking out of the firmament.

"Can he be any cornier?" Levi groused.

Trudy sighed, thinking it was kind of cute. The mime swung around, placing his arms about himself, and pretended to be a couple embracing and fondling. Levi used those moments to melt with Trudy back into the crowd and away from the mime.

Resigned to the fact that they had failed to find the next victim, Trudy slipped an arm around his waist as he tucked her against his side. Natural. Like they walked this way together all the time, Trudy thought even as she was blazingly aware that it was the first time for them.

A sign ahead of her caught her attention. "Look, Levi. A palm reader."

"I've already read your palm," he said in a low and throbbing voice, his arm tightening around her shoulders and pressing her closer to him.

Oh. Right. Lots of sex in her future. She shook her head, her blue mood surfacing again. What good were visions if she couldn't keep someone safe?

She felt Levi's steps falter and then he stopped. She glanced at him. He was staring at a small cluster of tents ahead of them.

"What is it?" she asked.

"I think that's someone I know. Yeah, that's him. Come on. I'll introduce you." He strode confidently with her toward the open-sided tent that was, more or less, a canopy and smiled when the man looked up. "Hello, Glenn."

"Levi Wolfe!" The white-haired, gray-bearded man half-rose from his chair and extended his hand, pumping Levi's with unconcealed delight and gusto. "The last time I saw you was four years ago in New Orleans on that ghost tour! Of course, I see you all the time on television."

"I'm so glad I ran into you, Glenn. Please, allow me to introduce a friend of mine and a fellow psychic Miss Trudy Tucker. Trudy, this is Glenn O'Connell. Glenn is an excellent aura reader, among other talents."

"Hello." Trudy shook his hand and returned his warm smile. She glanced at Levi, finding his politeness touching. For a boy who was obviously rebellious enough to grow up in reform schools, Levi had acquired Ivy League manners.

"What are you doing in Key West, Glenn?" Levi asked.

"I live here now. I decided to sell my home in Eureka Springs. The spirits in that house were driving me nuts. It was getting really bad, Levi. One of them played the piano off and on almost every night."

Trudy looked at Levi to catch his reaction to talk of piano playing spirits. He seemed mildly interested. Suddenly, she recalled her own spiritual encounter. Ethel! She had seen Ethel right before the killer's thoughts had invaded her. And Ethel had been very, very upset. She hadn't been able to hear her, but Trudy was certain that if she could have she would have heard Ethel screaming. But about what? Ethel had disappeared and the murder's thoughts and sights had taken over.

"Trudy? Earth to Trudy. Come in, please."

She blinked away her thoughts and smiled reassuringly at Levi. "I'm sorry. Did you say something?"

"Her aura is incredibly strong . . . distinct and deeply colored," Glenn said. "But you are troubled, aren't you, my dear? There are disturbances in your aura that have no business there. You're doing fine, Trudy. Just fine. Keep on this path."

Trudy kept silent, not wanting to dwell too much on his revelations. Keep on this path? This rocky path she was treading with Levi?

"You are wrestling with a question," Glenn said, zeroing in on Levi, who looked tense, wary, and decidedly uncomfortable. "An important question about trust." Glenn smiled and glanced at Trudy. "The answer, my friend, is yes. With your life and with everything you are and have been. Yes."

Levi shot a glance at Trudy and then back at Glenn, giving a brief shrug. Intrigued, Trudy ached to ask for more, but she knew this message was not hers. Still, it bothered her that he hadn't decided to trust her yet.

Glenn sat behind a table that was strewn with pamphlets about ghosts, palm readings, and the paranormal. A tent sign read: Aura Readings $25. A slight scowl blanketed his freckled face as he stared up at Trudy, his gaze moving slowly above the top of her head, down her shoulder, back up, and down the other shoulder. She had seen mediums do this before. He was deciphering her aura. "You have a spirit following you."

Trudy gasped. "Yes! Ethel. She's a ghost I see now and then. But only since I arrived here in the Keys."

Looking from Trudy to Levi, Glenn's eyes softened as he swung his gaze back to Trudy. "She's not a ghost, young one. As I understand it, there's a difference between a spirit and a ghost. A spirit is here of its own volition. It's here to impart something or to guide someone. A ghost is a soul that's still anchored to this realm because it can't or won't find its way to the next dimension. Yours is a spirit."

"You can see her?"

"No. I sense her in your aura."

"Can you hear her? Because I can't."

Glenn's smile was patiently indulgent. "I can't hear her because she's not speaking to me. She's speaking to *you*."

"But what does she want?" Trudy spread out her hands in an abject appeal to the man, who seemed to know about mute spirits who popped up at inopportune times.

"That's for you to discover."

"But I can't hear her," Trudy repeated, desperation coloring her voice.

"You will when you fully accept her. You've been denying her existence and her purpose in your life and that's why you can't hear her. When you finally acknowledge her purpose, her connection to you, then you'll hear her voice. Levi was ready to accept Gregory when Gregory appeared to him, so it was an instant connection and communication. You've been blocking your spirit guide, making it difficult for her to reach you."

"Spirit guide?" Trudy took a step back before she could stop herself. Her gaze flew to Levi and she glared at him when he smirked. "No. Ethel isn't my spirit guide. She's a . . . she's attached to the RV park. Her husband is there."

"She's not there for him. She's there for you." Glenn shrugged. "But who am I? You can believe me or not."

"No, I'm not . . . I don't mean . . ." Trudy gathered in a deep breath. "I believe you're very gifted."

"Like every human, I can err." Glenn shrugged again and held out his hand to Levi, who clasped it and then extended some folded bills to Glenn. "Thank you for the reading."

Glenn held up his free hand. "You don't have to pay me."

"I want to," Levi said, his tone irrefutable. "I insist."

Shrugging, the man took the money. "Thank you. Rid yourself of some of that pain you hold so close to your heart. You believe that it protects you. But, my friend, it's poison, not a magic elixir. It keeps you from what you need most in your life – love."

The stark uncertainty and sadness evident in Levi's expression squeezed Trudy's heart. In the space of a breath, he inched up his chin and recovered his mask of cool composure.

"Take care, Glenn. Be seeing you."

"Fare-thee-well, Levi. Nice to meet you, Trudy. You two are after the killer, yes?"

Levi nodded, reaching out to capture Trudy's hand.

"Tread carefully," Glenn said. "I'll take evil ghosts over evil mortals every time."

They moved off slowly, Levi's fingers wrapped around hers, his thumb brushing across her wrist every so often. Still rattled by Glenn's assertion that Ethel was her spirit guide, Trudy drew in a deep breath. A spirit guide? No way. It just didn't compute.

"Let's go to the police station and brief Sinclair on the latest target," Levi said. "Then we'll go back to the RV park to regroup and compare notes."

She nodded.

"And you should try to connect with your spirit guide."

"She's not –!" She bit off the rest when she saw the teasing light in his eyes and the slow curving of his lips. "You love it, don't you?"

"I love the irony of it, yes."

"I'm not convinced," she said, knowing that she was being stubborn.

He chuckled. "You won't be able to hear her until you believe in her," he said in a sing-song voice.

"Oh, hush."

They walked the rest of the way to the Jaguar like that. Together, but separated by their thoughts.

*

Arriving at the RV park well after nine o'clock, Trudy wasted no time in letting Mouse out to do her business. The little dog was full to bursting.

"I'm a horrible mother, aren't I?" Trudy asked her, feeling inanely guilty for staying away so long. "I didn't plan on being gone all day and most of the evening. But what a good dog you are, Mouse. I don't deserve you."

She picked up the Chihuahua and smiled when the little gray creature gave her kisses after kisses. Ah, unconditional love! If only it could be bottled and clearly labeled so that no one would mistake it for that other kind – the kind that broke hearts and spirits.

Inside her RV, she scooped some peanut butter into a Kong toy for Mouse and let her go at it. She stood for a few minutes, watching the dog wrestle the toy and try to lick every bit of the peanut butter from its holes and crevices. That would keep her happily busy for at least an hour.

Feeling hot and sticky and afraid she would be too tired later for a shower, Trudy dashed into the bathroom, stripping off her clothes as she went, and turned on the faucets. Levi had insisted that she meet him in his cabin in an hour to review their notes and impressions. They'd already related everything to Tom Sinclair, but Levi wanted to go over it all again.

Whatever. She rolled her eyes as she stepped under the stinging shower spray. She was too weary to argue with him. Just do it and get it over with, she told herself. Then she would come back to the RV, climb into bed, and pass out.

Standing under the shower, scenes from the past few hours flitted behind her eyelids. She was still feeling dejected because they hadn't located the woman. She knew beyond a shadow of a doubt that the blond only had hours to live. Maybe a day, tops. Her thoughts moved, as they so often did lately, to Levi. He'd looked so vulnerable and wretched when Glenn had told him to let go of his pain so that he could experience love. But Glenn was right. As long as Levi refused to trust and open up, he was effectively making it impossible for real, everlasting love to enter his life.

After the shower, she pulled on a pair of tan capris and a white t-shirt and told herself she would make this quick so that she could get some shut-eye. As she was crossing the grounds toward the cabins, she noticed that the elderly couple in the mini was gone. A big Airstream and a 21-foot trailer and red pickup truck were the new additions in the park. There never seemed to be more than four or five RVs there at one time. Mike Yardley must be barely limping by financially, she thought, feeling pity for him. Maybe Jay was chipping in what he could to help out his old man.

She tapped on the cabin door and it swung open. Levi waved her in, turning and walking toward the dining table and mismatched chairs.

He leaned toward her and smiled. "You smell good."

She glanced at him. He'd showered, too, and shaved. His hair was slightly damp. He'd pulled on a pair of dark blue jeans and a black, V-necked t-shirt. His feet were bare.

"I meant to turn on the TV to see if they were running the sketch of the blond woman on the news tonight," Trudy said. At the police station, she had spent an hour with the sketch artist to create a mockup of the next victim.

"They won't. Not tonight."

"You don't think they could make the evening news?"

"They could, but they won't. I imagine they will give the sketch to their patrol officers tonight and tomorrow."

"Why do they wait to show the sketches to the public? Someone surely would recognize this latest woman and the police could remove her from harm's way – like the last one."

Standing in front of the wall and studying the materials spread across it, he turned slightly to look at her. A wry smile curved his mouth. "You're assuming the police believe us about the blond."

She blinked at him. "Well, of course, they believe us. They had me talk to the sketch artist so that they could get a rendering of her as quickly as possible."

"*They* did? Or *Sinclair* did?"

Trudy opened her mouth to answer, but then closed it as the import of his question stole her words. She realized what he was saying. "You don't think the police believe us?"

He shrugged, his broad shoulders stretching his t-shirt. "They seldom do. I don't imagine the good officers of Key West are any different. We're lucky we have Sinclair believing us – or at least trying to."

"Why would Tom work with us if he thinks we're full of crap?" Trudy sat on the bed.

"I think he wants to believe us, but he's surrounded by officers who think we're about as genuine as a three dollar bill. So, it's difficult for him. Like I said, we're lucky he's willing to give us the time of day."

"But there must be other officers who are giving us the benefit of the doubt."

"Oh?" He looked back at her again, arching a brow. "Did you see any of them glad-handing us and thanking us for our work today?"

She frowned. "No."

"Every time I call, I speak to Sinclair. And if Sinclair isn't in the building, I'm told to call back later. They don't even offer to transfer me to his voice mail so that I can leave a message."

"Oh. Well, that blows." She puffed out a breath of disappointment.

"It's the way it is most of the time with cops, Trudy. Get used to it."

"You really don't think they'll release that sketch to the news? Even after we saved the last young woman?"

"Saved her or alarmed her and her family for no reason?"

She stared at him, irritation at the police prickling her. "I know that's what they usually think. That we're just a couple of charlatans or mental cases."

"That's about the size of it." He sounded nonchalant, even uncaring.

"Doesn't that bother you even a little?"

"I try not to let it. If I allow the frustration and anger to consume me, it takes my focus off the case I'm working on. It's not worth the energy."

She shook her head, feeling weary again and oh, so tired. So, the Key West police were like other police departments she had worked with? Most of them pegged her as an opportunist or a kook. She wasn't all that surprised, but she was disappointed.

"I've been trying to figure out how he got into Shelly's apartment," Levi said.

Trudy propped herself on her stiffened arms and tried to concentrate on the case, even though her mind was getting fuzzy around the edges. "There was a window beside the door on the landing," she offered and then yawned.

"Yes, and it was locked and still sealed up with paint."

"Oh. How do you know that?"

"I read the police report. There were no signs of forced entry."

He was *so* focused! Trudy shook her head, feeling vaguely guilty for not being as thorough. She had read through the police reports, too, but obviously not as closely as Levi. She looked at the bed she was sitting on, fighting the urge to lie down.

"I think that the most logical explanation is that Shelly was one of those stupid people who never locked her door."

Trudy stifled another yawn. "There are a lot of them."

"Yes. Fools living in a fool's paradise, thinking that no one will invade their privacy."

The last of her resistance fell away and Trudy slowly crumpled sideways, unable to resist the bed any longer. She pulled her legs up, curling into a fetal position. Oh, it felt so good! She closed her eyes . . . just for a second.

"Something is niggling at me, Trudy." His voice floated to her and she tried to listen, but her exhaustion was winning. "It has to do with Zelda . . . ah, Trudy . . . you're worn out, aren't you, my beautiful witch?"

Something niggled at her, too. Glenn's words wove through her mind like a whiff of smoke. He had been talking to Levi about trust.

"You can trust me," she murmured.

"What?"

"You can trust me with your life and with everything you are and have been," she repeated and then sighed.

"Trudy . . ." His voice held a myriad of emotions that she was too tired to sort through. "I want to do that. I know that I should . . ."

"Then do it." She rubbed her cheek against the soft pillow that smelled of Levi, and floated on a shimmering sea of liquid gold.

Chapter Fourteen

Small, warm puffs of air tickled her eyelids, her ear, her lips, and then whispered words wound their way into her consciousness.

"Wake up, sleeping beauty."

She released a mewling grumble as she forced her eyes open to find Levi's face inches from hers. He closed the distance and kissed her softly on the lips.

"She wakes!" he whispered. "Finally." He kissed her again before leaning back a little to look down into her face. "Good morning."

Trudy blinked. Was she dreaming? Wait . . . where was she? She glanced around. Oh, the cabin. The cabin? Propping herself on her elbows, she blinked rapidly at the sight of Levi stretched out beside her, bare-chested, the sheet hiding him from the navel down. She glanced at the window. It seemed to be grayish outside the dirty panes. "What time is it?"

"Six-thirty. You have officially spent the night with me, Miss Tucker. We've slept together."

She peeked quickly under the sheet and was relieved to see that she was still dressed. "I need to get back to the Gypsy Spirit."

"The *what?*"

"My RV. That's what I named it." She moved to fling aside the sheet and eject herself from the bed, but Levi clamped a hand on her shoulder and pushed her back down.

"Oh, no you don't. Just relax. I've enjoyed watching you sleep and now I'd like to enjoy watching you when you're awake."

"Watching me sleep?" she repeated, then shuddered. "Did I snore?"

His grin broadened and his eyes sparkled with mischief. "No."

"I bet I drooled, didn't I?" She rolled her eyes. "Oh, God. I did. I drooled."

He tipped back his head and laughed and he looked so young and sexy that her heart tripped over itself. "No. No drooling," he assured her, still chuckling.

"I didn't say anything stupid in my sleep, did I?"

"Trudy, stop!" He shook his head and his teeth grazed over his full bottom lip. "Nothing happened. I don't think you moved even a pinky finger once you fell asleep. You're beautiful, you know. And you look like an angel when you're sleeping."

She covered her hot face with her hands for a few moments and studied him through her fingers. Even early in the morning, the man was sinfully delicious looking with the lower half of his face shadowed by stubble and his hair in a wild tousle. The fan of his dark lashes on his cheeks as he swept his gaze down her sheet-draped body sent a swirl of longing through her.

"Is that why you didn't want to spend the night with me? You were afraid you'd snore or drool?"

"No . . . I . . ." She shrugged. What could she say? That she didn't want to like him more than was absolutely necessary, but that train had already left the station because she was fairly sure she was halfway in love with him already? "Mouse! I need to—."

"I've already seen to her."

"You . . . you have?" she turned toward him and wondered if he had anything on under the sheet. When she'd peeked before, she'd only been concerned about her own body, not his.

"Yes. You left the door to your RV unlocked."

"I wasn't planning on being away all night," she defended herself.

"Still . . . you *must* take your personal safety more seriously or I'll have to do something about it!"

She blinked at him, realizing that he was actually serious. He was a little ticked off.

"Anyway, I found your keys inside the RV and I locked it behind me." He nodded to the bedside table. "Your keys are there. I took Mouse for a walk around midnight. She'll be okay for a few more hours."

"Oh. Thanks." She smiled, touched by his desire to protect her. He really could be so thoughtful. Levi Wolfe was a man of many, many moods. Wait . . . did he say . . . "A few more hours?"

"Well, yes." He walked two fingers up her arm to her shoulder. "We need to get these clothes off you. They're wrinkled."

She eyed him, warily. "What are you wearing?"

"Armani," he said around a grin.

"You are so bad."

"Oh, no. I'm good. Damn good." He leaned closer and kissed her mouth gently, softly. "I was wondering . . ."

"About what?" she asked, her lips brushing his with each word.

"If we were in the middle of doing . . . it." He smiled against her lips. "Would the crazy motherfucker be able to grab hold of your mind?"

"I've wondered about that myself," she admitted, angling back a little to see his pretty face better. "But I don't think he would be able to because my mind – not to mention my body – would be too fully engaged."

"Hmmm. But I *want* to mention your body," he murmured, his mouth slipping over hers again. "More importantly, I want to *see* your body." His warm hands moved up under her shirt and peeled it right off of her. "Because I'm addicted to your body," he whispered, dropping kisses over the top of her breasts as his nimble fingers unhooked the front clasp of her bra. It fell away and she rose up enough to wiggle free of it and fling it aside. He rewarded her with a devilish grin and unbuttoned and unzipped her slacks. She hitched up her hips and let him slide them and her panties down her legs, sending them sailing. "That's so much better."

"Much," she agreed. She gathered handfuls of his hair and pulled his mouth flush to hers. Her tongue went to work and so did his, vying for dominance. His won. Trudy moaned her surrender, parting her thighs to allow him to claim his spoils.

"Aren't you glad you spent the night with me finally?" His lean body slid between her thighs and he gazed longingly at her nipples and then took one into his mouth for a long, strong suckle.

Trudy arched up in sweet agony. "You're really proud of that, aren't you?"

Her engorged nipple slipped from his lips with a soft *pop*. "I am. I'm tired of you treating me like a dildo."

"A dildo!" She had to giggle at that because he was *so much more* than a dildo. He was all warm hands and wet mouth and taut muscles and she couldn't seem to get close enough to him. His mouth closed over her other breast and she arched up, rubbing herself against his hard cock.

"Mmmm," she murmured. The man was absolutely unparalleled when it came to foreplay. His fingers teased and plucked at her other nipple. She writhed against him, feeling his hotness sliding against her as he moved lower and lower, his mouth paying homage to her ribcage, her navel, and then her——.

"Oh!" Trudy slammed her eyes shut when he kissed her clitoris and the tip of his tongue gave it a tiny flick. "No, no, no, Levi."

"Yes, yes, yes, Trudy," he whispered against her hot, wet skin. His tongue lashed at her and he pressed his hands on her inner thighs and moved them farther apart so that he could get even more up close and personal. "Sweet Jesus, you taste so fucking good."

She couldn't form a sensible sentence if she tried. She could barely make a sound as his mouth continued to lay claim to her and she felt herself climbing, tensing, and writhing with unimaginable feelings. She'd never been with a man before who took her so audaciously, so unapologetically, and so completely. He just dove right in as if he owned her body, knew her intimately already, and had a right to invade every inch of her. His tongue plundered, dipping into her entrance and then rubbing against her clitoris until she thought she might die from pleasure. He pushed two fingers inside of her and worked them furiously in and out.

"Oh, God," she managed to grit out as she felt her climax shoot up through her like a ball of fire.

"That's right," Levi said, his breath hot against her already flaming skin as his fingers curved slightly to rub her G-spot. "Here she goes. Oh, yes, she's gone."

And she was . . . gone to that mindless place where all she knew was quivering, shuddering pleasure. His tongue continued to stroke her and his lips sucked her as she fell back to earth, back to the brass bed in Cabin Four.

Opening her eyes, she saw Levi's lopsided smile between her spread thighs. He licked his lips and rose up to his knees, sitting back on his heels. His gaze devoured her nude body as he sucked the fingers that had been inside her. It was the most erotic thing she'd ever witnessed and she thought she might come again right on the spot. His chest rose and fell and beads of sweat rolled down his lean torso. To her eyes, he was male perfection. He slipped on a condom as his gaze moved slowly over her body.

"Fuck, I'm a lucky bastard. Put your legs around me," he said, his eyes darkening to turbulent blue. He cupped her butt cheeks in his long-fingered hands and directed all of his concentration to the place where their bodies would join.

Trudy held her breath, feeling him slide his cock up and down her slit several times before gliding in, slowly, confidently, fully. She gazed up into his face and the look of undiluted pleasure there clamped down on her heart. He was so fantastically gorgeous. Muscles bunched in his arms as he moved in and out of her slowly, leisurely. She admired his wide chest, defined by muscle and sinew, and loved the swirl of ebony hair on his pectorals. She ran her hands across his chest and then lower to the V that bracketed his taut lower abdomen. He smiled at her as her fingertips delved into the mass of curly black hair.

"I'm in heaven right now, angel baby," he said, his voice raspy and seductive as he continued his steady, friction-building, orgasm-spawning pace. "This is my heaven."

For all its corniness, Trudy grinned, thinking he was irresistible when his shields were down as they were right now. No mask, no persona, nothing to keep her apart from the real man. His jaw tensed and his eyelids shuttered his beautiful eyes from her for a few moments before he began thrusting faster and harder, grinding his hips every time he drove in to the hilt. He growled low in his throat and that primal sound sent a flaming arrow of hot sexual arousal through her.

"I want you to come again for me, Trudy," he said, his breath escaping in little gasps and grunts as perspiration formed on his forehead and dripped down his cheeks. "You're going to come and you're going to scream my name when you do."

She shook her head even as the flicker of another orgasm came to life deep in her belly. The head of his penis shifted higher and touched that place inside of her that sent her reeling. "Levi," she gasped, digging her fingers into his upper arms. She tightened her legs around his waist.

"Louder." He shifted ever so slightly, just enough to fan the flames inside her. "You're almost there. I can feel it. I feel every twitch, every flutter, every heartbeat. You're there! My name, Trudy! My name."

"Levi! God, Levi!" His name was torn from her throat by a wave of ecstasy. The world tipped over and her body went weightless as she grabbed his shoulders and clung to him. She pulled him down to her, running her hands over his muscled back and through his hair. Kissing his neck, she bit his ear lobe, letting it slide through her teeth, and heard his breath hitch.

"Mine, mine! Ahhh, Trudy," he growled her name and his hips pumped hard into her. He trembled under her hands. Then he released his breath in a long sigh that tickled the damp curls on her forehead. "You're mine, you hear me? Mine," he whispered near her ear. "I don't even know myself when I'm with you like this."

With her eyes closed, she felt a single tear roll down her cheek as his words wrapped tightly around her foolish heart. Was he feeling things for her that were foreign to him? Were they enough to make him want to be hers and hers alone? She caressed him, running her hands over his shoulders and down his sides. He was lean muscle and warm skin, hard edges and leashed power. He commanded her body as if they'd been lovers for years instead of days.

Lifting to his elbows, he gently pushed curls of her damp hair off her forehead and kissed her eyelids, her nose, her cheeks, her lips. "You are just way, way too irresistible. That mouth of yours. Fuck, I have wet dreams about your mouth." He kissed her lips, sucking gently on her upper one until she smiled. "Hey, baby?"

She opened her eyes and her heart skipped a beat. His eyes were that beautiful, cobalt blue that made her think of the sea. "I used to hate for men to call me that."

"What? Baby?"

"Yes. It's always sounded demeaning to me. But not when you say it."

"That's because you know I would never demean you." His lips traveled down her cheek, over her jaw line, and down to her throat. He shifted his hips against her.

Oh, God. She stared at him. He was still semi-hard inside her. She shook her head. "You came."

"I did," he affirmed. "But I've told you. I can't get enough of you." He laughed at her shocked expression and pulled out of her, then rolled onto his side. "What? Have you only been with lightweights before me? One pump and they're done?" Chuckling under his breath, he removed the condom, tied it into a knot, and lobbed to toward the waste paper basket. It dropped in and disappeared. "He shoots! He scores!"

Trudy laughed and snuggled into him. His arms enfolded her and he kissed her hair. She closed her eyes and drank him in – his smell, the soft stroking of his hands on her back and in her hair, the strong beat of his heart under her ear. Enjoy it while it lasts, she told herself.

"Go back to sleep," he murmured. "I set the alarm for eight-thirty."

"What time is it now?"

"Seven-fifteen."

She sighed, rubbed her cheek against his chest, and happily obeyed.

*

When they'd finally rolled out of bed, Levi had announced that he was going into Key West for some printer supplies and to get some fresh cinnamon rolls for their breakfast. Loving that idea, Trudy had promised to make a pot of coffee. They'd also decided that, if she didn't make contact again with the killer, they would go to Mallory Square that afternoon to see if they could spot the blond.

Trudy went back to her RV to make good on the promise of fresh coffee and to let Mouse out to do her business.

While Mouse nosed around, Trudy took the opportunity to stretch out the kinks in her muscles. A tiny bit sore, she smiled as moments of her lovemaking with Levi flitted through her mind. Was it lovemaking? Would he call it that? Doubtful. Should she let him know that's what she wanted? He didn't want to be her dildo, so he obviously wanted something more. But how much more?

She bent over and touched her toes, then straightened and reached for the sky. A blue jay perched on a low limb in the tree near her and squawked loudly. Watching it, Trudy recalled that her dad insisted that jays were yelling, *Thief! Thief!*, letting other birds know that a nest-raiding cat was on the prowl.

Looking around to see if there was a predator in the vicinity, Trudy saw only Mouse and – *oh crap!* – Ethel. Trudy drew in a deep breath and told herself to chill out. Ethel seemed relaxed. Much more relaxed than she had been yesterday when she'd been hysterical.

"I hope you're feeling better today, Ethel," Trudy said.

Ethel smiled.

"Okay, here's the thing," Trudy said, looking down at her tennis shoes as she wrestled with herself about accepting Ethel as her guide. This was some cosmic joke, surely. Yeah, and the joke was on her.

Determined to see it through this time and connect with Ethel, Trudy cleared her throat. Obviously, Ethel was here for a reason and Trudy realized that she wanted to know why Ethel had chosen her.

"Let's start over, shall we? When I first saw you, I was startled because I've never seen spirits before. I thought you were here to hang out with Mike, but I've figured out that you're here for me. So, what can I do for you or what can you do for me?"

Ethel's form wavered, waffling from head to toe, and Trudy gasped, thinking that she was going to disappear like a puff of smoke. Then her form solidified as much as it could, still transparent, but clear enough for Trudy to see a smile wreathing Ethel's face. She really was a nice-looking woman. Her hair lay in gentle waves over her head and she had high cheekbones, a small nose, and big dimples.

"That's good of you, Trudy." Her voice was soft and melodious.

Trudy sucked in a noisy breath. Shocked, that the spirit's words were so clear, it took her a few moments before she could speak. Tears stung her eyes. "Ethel! I hear you!"

Do you hear me in your head now?

Trudy blinked at her, and after a few startling seconds, she nodded. Feeling positively giddy, she gathered in a deep breath and focused her thoughts, sending them forth like a laser beam. *Yes. You're in my head now. Do you hear me?*

Ethel nodded. *We'll talk like this from now on.* Then she turned slowly, giving Trudy a wave, and floated toward Mike's trailer.

"That's it?" Trudy called after her, feeling cheated. "No words of wisdom to impart?"

Ethel waved again. *Watch out for the jaybird!*

Trudy propped her hands on her hips, glaring at Ethel until she faded away like a memory. "Thanks. That'll save my bacon, for sure!" She kicked at a tuft of grass in a fit of frustration. How pointless was *that?*

Mouse barked at her, evidently not pleased that Trudy was taking it out on one of her favorite places to pee. Trudy shook her head and laughed at herself. What did she expect? The spilling of the secret of the universe? Foretelling of her future? Or maybe the name and address of the serial killer's next victim?

She looked up in the tree, but the blue jay was gone.

*

The cinnamon roll was paradise on a plate. Trudy had obviously relished every bite and closed her eyes on a long sigh when the last morsel went down, followed by a sip of coffee.

"Ahhh. It tasted as good as it smelled," she confirmed.

"I agree." Levi sat across the table from her. He'd finished his cinnamon roll ten minutes ago and had enjoyed watching her eat because he absolutely loved her mouth. The shape of it, the way the corners tipped up just so, and that full, curvy upper lip that just begged to be nipped lightly and sucked on.

He shifted uncomfortably on the bench seat, capturing her attention. She sipped her coffee again and her green eyes smiled at him over the rim of the cup. The witch.

Snuggling with her in bed had been incredibly satisfying. Almost as fantastic as the sex, which didn't make any sense at all. But there it was. Holding her, knowing she was all his in those minutes, those hours, were beyond satisfying. When he was with her like that he felt . . . what? Relaxed? No, more than that. Satiated? More than that. He'd have to talk to his psychiatrist about these new, indescribable feelings. Maybe Dr. McClain could come up with a word for them. He sure as hell was at a loss.

His thoughts meandered to Mallory Square. Glenn had told him that he could trust Trudy implicitly. Trudy had concurred. Complete trust was something he withheld, although there was something about Trudy that enticed him to take another chance. He'd have to discuss that with Dr. McClain, too.

"So, when should we leave for Mallory Square?" Trudy asked.

"Around five, I guess."

"Hopefully, we'll find her and then the police can protect her from him."

"That's the plan."

"Guess what? I talked to Ethel while you were away and I could hear her!"

"You accepted her, I take it." It gave him no end of pleasure that she was now saddled with an entity, especially since she had given him so much grief over Gregory. "Payback's a bitch, isn't it?"

She did that chin jerk thing that never failed to make his cock perk up. "Rub my nose in it, Wolfe. Anyway, I heard her when she spoke aloud and I also could hear her in my mind. It was so weird!"

"Why?"

"Because she spoke in complete sentences! I thought spirits sent impressions or some kind of signs. But she actually talked!"

"Gregory talks to me like that. My theory is that guides can communicate more fully because they have a special, deeper connection with us. The spirits *we* summon aren't there for us. They're there to impart messages to others *through* us, so they can't communicate as directly. Some mediums can't hear them. Spirits have to show them items that symbolize emotions or places and things. Others can hear bits and pieces, but it's never as clear as when a spirit guide communicates."

Trudy smiled and gave a little shake of her head, "When it comes to the paranormal, you're not just a practitioner; you're a scholar."

He considered this for a few moments. "I'm a student of it just like you. It's a field that no one can master."

"Why not?"

"Because we aren't meant to," he said, enjoying the way her eyes lit up with curiosity and the tilt of her head. His heart seemed to swell in his chest and he looked away from her to stare out the window, not wanting to give away too much of his feelings toward her until he could figure them out for himself. How could one look from her make him melt a little inside? How the hell did she do that? "Some mysteries shouldn't be solved. At least not now and not here." He cleared his throat and closed his eyes for a second to gather himself. "So, what did Ethel say?"

"Oh, right." She gave a little sigh. "She imparted some mind-blowing information."

He arched a brow, intrigued. "Oh? Do you want to share or must I beat it out of you?"

She pursed her lips to keep from smiling and her eyes danced with an inner joke. "She told me that I should watch out for the blue jay."

"The blue jay," he repeated, blankly. "And do you know what that means?"

"There was a blue jay squawking in the tree, so maybe she thought it might poop on my head." She sat back with a sigh. "Is that what you and Gregory talk about? Dodging bird shit and stuff like that?"

He grinned and then let the chuckle bubble up from his chest. It should be against the law for a female to be so damned cute. Women hardly ever joked with him, poked fun at him, or even made him laugh. Quintara did and that was one reason why he liked being around her. But Trudy? She was in a class by herself. In so many ways.

"I can see why you value Gregory so much now," she continued as serious as a judge, but imps danced in her eyes. "I can hardly wait to receive more priceless instructions from Ethel. I mean, it could be anything! Don't wear plaid with stripes. A couple of Long Island Iced Teas will knock you on your butt. Girls just wanna have fun and guys just wanna get laid."

He let go of a laugh and shook his head at her. Jesus, it felt good to laugh with her! The sound of her giggle enchanted him and made him feel young and carefree — something he had rarely been in his life. And for a few crystal clear moments he saw how it could be for them . . . if only he wasn't so damned fucked up.

He hadn't realized that his laughter had died abruptly until she reached across the table to touch his hand.

"What?" she asked, her green eyes studying him.

"You're funny, that's all."

"Yeah, I know. But what just happened? What made you stop laughing? You look so sad . . . so lost."

"It's nothing." He drew in a deep breath, not wanting to think too much about his regrets, his mistakes, all the shit that had hardened him. "So, we're set? We'll leave for Key West about five to find the blond woman." He slipped out of the booth. "I'm going to print out some things and handle a bit of other business. You spend quality time with Mouse."

"Yes, sir!" She looked up at him, her gaze searching his face, trying to find answers.

He closed his eyes to shut her out and leaned down, touching his mouth to hers. The magnetic pull was there like always. His Tru. His true north.

"See you later."

"Okay."

He was at the door of the RV when her voice reached out to him.

"Watch out for the blue jay, Levi!"

And he laughed again and chuckled all the way back to Cabin Four. He would definitely have to take this up with the good Dr. McClain, he thought. This carefree feeling was new to him and he wasn't sure he should trust it — or trust Trudy with the memories that burdened him and made him feel unworthy of her. He knew that his psychiatrist would have plenty to say about it, but he wasn't sure he wanted to hear it — yet.

*

After devoting a couple of hours to Mouse, Trudy was bored and so was Mouse. The Chihuahua let her know she had experienced all the quality time she could stomach by lying down at the very back of her crate and refusing to come out.

"Okay, I get it," Trudy groused. "Be that way." She peeked through the window toward Cabin Four where Levi was holed up.

Wonder what he was doing? Had he eaten lunch yet?

"Oh, my lord!" Trudy groaned, aggravated with herself. "Can you go ten minutes without thinking about him?"

She went outside with Mouse and sat at the picnic table. The sound of irregular footsteps coming closer turned her around. She squinted against the sunlight and spotted Mike Yardley standing near her RV.

"You staying another week?" he asked, leaning heavily on his cane.

"Probably. I'll know for sure in a couple of days. Do you want me to pay for another week now? I can."

Mike looked around at the empty spaces. "No. I doubt if I'll have an influx of folks clamoring for your space." He shifted and gave a wince. "Fantasy Fest is in two weeks and more people will be here for that. It's Key West's version of Mardi Gras."

"Hopefully, I'll be back home by then." Trudy motioned to the other bench. "Why don't you have a seat?"

"I'm sure you're busy."

Trudy shrugged. "Not really. Not right now anyway."

He shuffled forward, a bent-over man in chinos and a red t-shirt from Sea World. He lowered himself slowly, painfully onto the bench. "Damn knees are going out on me," he grumbled, but then a smile lit up his round face. "Got some good news today."

"Did you?"

"A man who looked at the park a couple of months ago is going to make an offer on it. I might actually unload this turkey."

"Great! And what will you do when you sell it?"

"Probably go back to Nebraska. I have a younger brother and sister-in-law there I'm pretty fond of."

"Won't you miss Jay?"

He frowned slightly and sighed. "He has his own life. I think I just get in his way."

"I thought you two were making up for lost time."

A shrewd expression covered his face. "He tell you that?"

"He mentioned that you were at work a lot when he was growing up."

"Yeah. I loved being a reporter and teaching at the university. The home fires had trouble competing with that. Ethel understood, but Jay . . ." He shrugged.

"He comes by fairly often to visit with you, so he's making an effort," Trudy ventured.

"Yeah, he drops by. But sometimes you just can't make up for lost time."

Not knowing what to say about that and sensing it was far too complex for her to comment on, Trudy nodded. "Well, I hope you get a good offer on this place, Mike. I know you're anxious to move on."

"Yeah, I need to get out from under it, for sure." A sly twinkle lit his eyes. "You see Ethel anymore?"

"Yes, I have. Quite a few times. Do you believe that I see her?" Trudy asked, dubiously.

"Awww, I don't know, and what difference does it make if I do or not? You think you see her, so that's all that should matter to you." He twisted around to peer behind him at the cabins. "You're working with that fella in Cabin Four, huh?" He caught her nod. "He's the one I saw on television. Are you two sweet on each other?"

Trudy felt color flame in her cheeks. "Why would you ask that?"

He shrugged. "Lots of coming and going between his cabin and this RV and I've seen the way he looks at you." He chuckled. "It's none of my business. I'm just an old man with too much time on his hands." With a grunt, he shoved up to his feet and planted the tip of his cane firmly on the ground again. "Gotta go. Nebraska is playing this afternoon on TV and I don't want to miss a minute of it." He moved creakily toward his trailer. "Be seeing you."

A jaybird squawked and Trudy looked up, searching through the leaves for a flash of blue. Jaybird. Not bluejay. Ethel had said jaybird . . . Jay.

"Mike!" Trudy called, and he stopped and turned back to her. "Did Ethel ever call your son Jaybird?"

He shuffled around to face her, leaning both hands on his cane. "Yeah. Jay was born two months early and he looked like a skinny, little bird. We started calling him Jaybird and it stuck." He studied her for a few moments. "Did he tell you that?"

She started to tell him a white lie, but she couldn't do it. "No."

A slow grin spread over his face. "Ethel told you?"

Trudy nodded and waited for him to call her crazy.

He chuckled, waved a hand, and then turned around and continued his slow stroll to his trailer.

Shoving aside thoughts of Ethel, Trudy put Mouse back inside the RV. She finally gave in to her curiosity and marched with determination to the cabin to tap lightly on the door.

"Enter." His voice floated out to her and she realized the window was open. The tacky curtains moved languidly in the weak breeze.

Trudy pushed open the door. Levi sat at the table, the printer humming and spitting out pages, the cell phone pressed to his ear. He smiled and motioned for her to come inside.

"What time does the auction begin?" he asked whoever was on the other end of the call and then he glanced at his wristwatch. His gaze lifted and locked on her. He held up one finger, asking her to wait. She nodded.

"I've toured the building and I want it, but the most I'll pay is four million two. I think it will go for around three-six, don't you?"

Four million two? As in, dollars? Trudy stared at him in shock. He wasn't well-off. He was freaking rich!

"Oh, more than that! Hell, the wiring will cost that much. I'd say we'd spend more like seven hundred thou just to get it up to specs. Did you see those lavatories? They'll have to be completely gutted. At least there isn't any asbestos to worry about like at the Greenwood Building." He listened and nodded. "Buy something this time, Monroe. Otherwise, why should I keep paying you?" He chuckled at something the other person said. "Call me as soon as the auction is over and let me know how it turned out. Right. Transfer me back to Darla, will you?" He moved the phone away from his ear. "Sit down, Trudy. I'll just be another minute."

She realized she was standing and staring at him, but who could blame her? He was throwing around huge sums of cash like it was nothing! Looking at her meager choices of where to sit — the bed or one of the dining table chairs — she opted for the softer bed. He started to say something to her, but then put the phone to his ear again. Trudy heard a woman's voice.

"Hi, Darla. Have you heard anything from Gonzo?" He scowled. "I tried to call him this morning, but I had to leave a voice mail. Get in touch with him and tell him to call me. I think I saw that woman again at Mallory Square yesterday."

Trudy sat up, galvanized by his words. That woman? The blond woman? Why didn't he tell her? She opened her mouth to ask him, but he shook his head, his expression telling her she had it all wrong.

"I want Gonzo to take this seriously, Darla. Tell him that and have him call me pronto. Anything else?" He tipped back his head and stared at the ceiling. His brows dipped down and he sat up straighter. "Oh? She did? From where?" He hunched his shoulders and turned slightly away from Trudy so that she couldn't see his expressive face anymore. "Oh, great," he said, derisively. "Just what I wanted to hear. Yes, yes. I know." He sighed. "Go ahead and wire the money." He sounded resigned and sort of defeated. "Just do it, Darla." He pushed the "End Call" icon and set the phone on the table. His blue-eyed gaze swept to her and she saw him make a concerted effort to put aside whatever had troubled him about the phone conversation. "What can I do for you, Miss Tucker?"

"You're busy. I'm bothering you."

"I've told you before, you're never a bother to me."

"What woman did you see in Mallory Square?"

"Not the blond," he said, reading her thoughts. "Someone else."

"Who?"

He shrugged and crossed over to the bed. "A woman I keep seeing around Key West and it makes me think she might be following me."

"An obsessed fan," Trudy said.

"Possibly." He sat beside her and hooked an arm around her waist as his mouth swooped to the curve of her neck. "What else has made you frown?"

"I didn't know you had that much money to throw around." She tipped her head to the side to give him better access to her neck. His lips felt like feathers on her skin.

"I don't throw it around. I invest it," he corrected her, kissing her jaw as he brought his hand up to the back of her head. "I buy older office buildings and retrofit them so that they're useful again for modern businesses. Then I sell them. It's been profitable for me."

She smiled as he continued to nuzzle her. "I think I know what Ethel was really talking about."

"Tell me."

"Her pet name for her son is Jaybird. Mike told me. Now I have to figure out why she wants me to watch out for him."

"I can take a wild guess."

She leaned away from him to look at his face. His eyes were hooded and he wore that brooding, sexy expression that made her want to ravage him. "Go ahead. What?"

"He wants to get you horizontal. Just like I want to right now"

"Oh, lord." She rolled her eyes. "That's your reasoning for everything."

"Why are you dismissing it so quickly?"

"Because I've only talked to Jay a couple of times and he was nice, but he's *not* interested in me."

"His mother begs to differ. And Mother knows best."

"Does she? You really believe that, do you?" She watched the shields snap into place, evident in his wary expression and the flexing of muscles in his jaw. "I've been wondering . . . were you always sent away to school?"

He nodded. "Except for a few years, yes."

"And your mother was okay with that?"

He let go of a humorless chuckle. "How the hell did we get on this subject? I don't want to talk. I just want you. I need you." He leaned into her, making her fall back onto the mattress. He kissed her over and over again, barely allowing her a second to breathe. She knew that he was giving her something else to think about besides his troubled upbringing – and it was working. Finally, he tore his mouth from hers and she stared into eyes that were dangerously dark and predatory. She ran her tongue across her throbbing lips and tasted him. He had such a determined look of lust on his face that she felt herself go from damp to sopping wet in a heartbeat.

He grabbed the hem of her t-shirt and pulled it up. "Lift your arms," he said, none to gently. She did and the t-shirt went up and over her head. He flung it aside and unbuttoned and unzipped her jeans. He dipped down and his mouth grazed the side of her neck, gliding lower to suck and kiss the tops of her breasts above her bra. He reached beneath her and unclipped it, removed it, and gave it a toss. Before she could form a thought about being nude from the waist up while he was still fully clothed, his lips closed around her nipple and fired her blood. She arched her back, her hips moving, her thighs parting in an age-old appeal. She was so glad she'd decided to interrupt his work.

"Yes," he hissed. His fingers closed on her waistband and he tugged once, twice, three times until her jeans cleared her hips, all the while sucking greedily on her breast.

"Oh, Levi . . ." She shook her head, enthralled with what he was doing to her.

He removed her shoes and dispensed with her jeans and panties in record time and then he was flinging aside his t-shirt. He stood beside the bed and shucked his jeans and jockey briefs. Reaching into the bedside table's drawer, he found a condom, his gaze traveling hungrily over her body.

"I haven't been able to get you out of my head today," he murmured, his gaze never leaving her body as he rolled on the condom with practiced ease. "You are one beautiful distraction." A smile tipped up the corners of his mouth and then he pressed a knee in the mattress and his warm body slid onto hers.

He sucked her nipples, bringing them to straining attention again. Trudy groaned and writhed. She reached down between their bodies and grasped his erect penis. Her fingers explored him . . . he felt big and hot and hers.

"Now," she whispered.

"You're so wanton, Miss Tucker," he breathed in her ear.

"I want it hard and fast, Wolfe," she whispered.

"Jesus," he groaned. Clutching her hips, he thrust into her. She cried out and clung to his shoulders. She whipped her head from side to side as he moved in and out, setting a blistering pace. Her feelings spun out of control as she was caught up in the wildfire of him. Before she knew it, she was coming and crying out his name as shudders racked her body. And still he kept slamming into her. She glimpsed his face above her, his eyes tightly closed, his teeth gritted, veins in his neck standing out in bas relief. Then he seemed to gather himself. He pulled out of her slowly, slowly, and then sank back into her . . . every inch of him. He touched her sweet spot and she trembled. It felt like the aftershocks of an earthquake. She felt him come inside her and her name whispered across his lips.

"Trudy . . . my Tru."

Levi sprawled half on and half off her. Trudy drew in a deep, mind-clearing breath, and stroked his shoulders and back. He rubbed his cheek against her breasts.

"God, Trudy, you're tearing me inside out," he panted against her hot skin. He rolled over and removed the condom, tied it, and dropped it in to the waste basket. Then he planted a kiss between her breasts before taking a nipple into his mouth and biting down gently.

Moaning, Trudy closed her eyes and tipped back her head in the pillow as he sucked and kissed. She writhed as the ache between her thighs moved from a simmer to a boil.

"Be still, baby," he said as the tip of his tongue flicked her straining, burning nipple as he massaged her other breast. "Be still and feel it."

"I do! And I can't be still!"

His hand skimmed down her body, into the nest of hair, and he slipped two fingers inside her. Her inner muscles grabbed hungrily at his fingers.

"Yes," he hissed. "You still want me inside you."

She nodded. Oh, yes. His fingers circled and pressed further into her. His thumb touched her tender, swollen clitoris. The man was a magician, pure and simple, she thought, her hips bucking as his thumb continued to rub her. Her orgasm gripped her ferociously and she came in a shudder of mindless, wordless bliss. What he could do to her . . . it was almost embarrassing!

Feeling him stir slightly against her side, she smiled as his erection nudged her. She wrapped a tight hand around the base of it and he became a statue. Oh, he liked that! Fisting him, she moved up and down the silken, steely length of him. She felt him expand against her palm and he shuddered. Shifting onto his side, he groaned and shut his eyes. He rested one hand on her hip, caressing and then tightening as he watched her manipulate him.

"Ahhh. Oh, Christ." He slammed his eyes shut. "Give me another condom, damn it."

She laughed, bent to kiss the tip of his cock, then let go to get a condom out of the bedside table's drawer. He held out his hand for it, but she kept it out of his reach. She kissed the crown of his cock again and then took it into her mouth. He grew still. Very, very still. She wasn't even sure he was breathing.

"Easy," he rasped, thrusting up. "You're killing me."

"Be still, baby," she said, throwing his instructions back at him and then gave him a lick. "Be still and feel it."

"Smart-mouthed witch," he groused, a smile tipping up one corner of his wicked, wicked mouth. He grabbed the condom out of her hand and tore it open with his teeth. "Now you're going to get it."

"I've already had it," she said, tossing him a cocky grin. "Several times."

He rolled the condom on and his eyes glittered dangerously. "Oh yeah? Well, you haven't had it like this." Getting to his knees, he gripped her ankles and brought them up to his shoulders, lifting her butt off the mattress. He slid his hands down her legs, turned his face to press a kiss to her ankle, and then guided himself straight into her.

Lights exploded behind her eyes and Trudy let out a little shriek as his swift invasion seared through her. He buried himself deep inside her and she was sure the head of his penis was knocking against her womb.

"Oh, God!" she gasped, reaching out blindly to grab his forearms and hold on tight because she knew he was going to start moving and it was going to shatter every sexual experience that she'd had before.

He pulled out and then drove right back in, his hands gripping hips and holding her exactly where he wanted her, high off the mattress and completely at his mercy. He ground against her, making her tremble, and then began pumping fast and furiously into her as sweat beaded on his forehead and slicked his body and hers.

"You like it hard and fast? Then, that's how you'll get it. Hard!" He rammed into her. "And fast!" Again, driving her hips up with his thrust.

"Levi . . . oh, God!" The words tumbled from her, but she was hardly aware of anything except the erotic savagery of his movements and the rapid build up of tension coiling in her belly. She was close . . . so close.

"Don't come yet," he ordered, the words falling from his lips along with his panting breaths.

"I'm coming," she moaned.

"No!" He gripped her hips and suddenly stopped, pulling out and leaving her gasping and her body throbbing for release.

"Don't stop!" She gripped his arms harder, her nails biting into his skin.

His eyes were molten blue and his chest rose and fell as if he'd just finished a marathon. "You'll come when I want you to come," he said, and then guided himself slowly, oh so slowly all the way into her.

Trudy shook her head. What game was he playing? Did he really think he could control her orgasms? But then, in the next clear thought, she realized he was doing exactly that. He closed his eyes and swiveled his hips again, rubbing his shaft higher against her as he brought one hand to her mound. His thumb slicked over her clitoris. A burning spasm branded her and Trudy let out a cry.

"Have you had it like this before, Trudy?" he asked, a cunning grin tipping up one corner of his mouth as one hand stroked her leg. He kissed her ankle again and shifted her legs higher onto his shoulders.

She shook her head, silenced by his mastery over her body.

"I didn't think so." He cupped her butt again, retreated, and rammed back into her. "Come, Trudy," he said, and she did.

Her body seemed to break apart with the longest orgasm she'd ever had. She trembled and quaked as Levi plunged into her again and again, prolonging the intense pleasure that had her gasping and crying out, unable to form any coherent words.

With one final thrust, he let her legs slip down off his shoulders and his body covered hers. She felt him expand inside her and then he released, growling against the side of her neck as he grew rigid. Slowly, slowly he relaxed.

She found his hands and laced her fingers tightly with his, bringing them up to either side of her head on the pillow as they both drifted down off the impossible high, their bodies still throbbing and pulsating.

"You're unbelievable," she said when she could form words again.

"I know," he said with a puckish grin. He kissed her shoulder and unlaced their hands. Moving off her, he broke their final connection.

Trudy groaned a protest and he chuckled as he peeled off the condom and tossed it into the waste basket. He held out his arms and she snuggled into his embrace.

"Conceited much?" she teased.

"It's only conceit when it's not true."

She considered this and rubbed her cheek against his damp chest in a nod. He was right, damn him. She pitied any man who would come after him and then bit her lip because the thought of being with anyone but him was too painful to even contemplate.

Chapter Fifteen

They were among the first people to arrive at Mallory Square. Levi and Trudy sat on a bench, sipped lemonade, and watched gulls and pelicans swoop and dive into the Atlantic. Around the perimeter of the open area, musicians tuned their instruments and artists set up their tents. After about an hour, the space started filling up.

"Look at all these people," Levi said, scanning the faces. "We could miss her so easily."

"I don't even know if I would recognize her," Trudy said. "She will have on different clothes and she might even wear her hair differently."

"It won't hurt to try." He took her hand in his and stood, pulling her with him. "We won't split up this time."

"Why not? We can cover more ground apart."

"I don't want to let you out of my sight tonight."

"Levi, please," she chided.

He glanced around and worry pinched the skin between his eyes as he tightened his grip on her hand. "Humor me."

"What's wrong? Why are you so edgy?"

"Are you watching the crowd, Trudy? Pay attention."

She sighed at his diversionary tactic. She could argue with him, but from the stubborn set of his jaw, she decided it wasn't worth it. "You're cutting off the circulation in my fingers."

"Oh." He glanced down at their clasped hands and eased his grip. "Sorry."

"Thanks. That's better."

Trudy walked with him, scanning faces, watching, hoping, failing.

"See anyone who marginally looks like her?" Levi asked after a while.

"No. Have you?"

He shook his head.

"Crap." Trudy sighed.

Levi slipped an arm around her waist and guided her toward two men who were playing steel drums. The song they tapped out with

193

their talented fingers and the heels of their hands was lazy, happy, and a little sultry – perfect for a Key West sunset.

"Dance with me."

Trudy took a step back, glancing around. "Here?"

"Why not?" He held out his arms and she stepped into them.

She focused on his liquid, lithe movements. He spun her and she laughed up into his face. The music swirled around her and she realized that other couples were dancing near them, smiling and laughing. She caught sight of several young women standing nearby and watching them – or, rather him. Their avid gazes followed Levi and she saw one of them say to the girl beside her, "He's hot!" Trudy admired his hip-rocking movements and the smile that overtook him when he looked at her and she couldn't agree more. And he was all hers – at least for now. He whirled her and pressed his front to her back, one hand holding hers and the other splayed across her stomach as he rubbed sensuously against her rump. She closed her eyes and rested her head against his shoulder. Her gaze met his and something deeper than sexual attraction sparked between them. His hand came up to cradle her chin and his lips parted.

"Trudy?"

"Yes?" she asked, her heart stopping because something important – something vital was in his eyes, in his expression.

"I don't know what's happening to me," he whispered, his voice roughened by emotion. "I shouldn't . . . but I want . . ."

Suddenly, a light flashed and a dark-skinned man was beside them, a camera clicking away as he took photo after photo of them. Levi glared at the pushy photographer.

"Hi, Levi," the intruder said, lowering the camera. "Just wanted a few shots for all your fans."

Levi's smile became brittle and cold. "You have them now and you've ruined the moment for us." He pulled Trudy to his side. "Let's go." He guided her away from the dancers and steel drum players.

"Sorry, Levi," the photographer called to him.

"Fucker," Levi growled under his breath.

"Shhh," Trudy cautioned as they walked past the clutch of girls who'd been watching them dance. "Do you know him?"

"He's taken my picture before – many times."

"You wanted attention . . . it's the price of fame."

"I know that," he snapped, his expressive eyes sparking with quick anger. "Believe me, I know!"

He was upset and irritated and she didn't want to rub salt into his wounds, so she slipped her arms around his waist and gave him a quick hug. His gaze softened almost instantly and surprise registered on his face. Trudy smiled at his reaction, finding it endearing that such a small gesture startled him . . . unbalanced him.

"Shake it off, Wolfe," she whispered as she leaned her head on his shoulder. She glanced away from him and saw a blond woman with large breasts and slim hips and her breath caught in her throat.

"What?" Levi asked, then spotted the same woman. "Is that her?"

But in the next second, the woman turned her face toward them and Trudy's heart started beating again. "No," she said. "No, it's not her."

"Let's keep looking for a few more minutes."

Something seemed to squeeze her brain and Trudy stopped in her tracks. She glanced suspiciously at Levi. "You didn't just do that brain poke thing, did you?"

He sent her a quizzical look. "No. Why?"

She took a deep breath as the odd feeling persisted. It wasn't as if someone was trying to take over her thoughts, but more like someone was thinking about her, concentrating solely on her.

"He's here," she said as her instincts crystallized.

"What?" Levi glanced around. "Who? Where?"

"The psycho."

"You know him? You recognize him?"

"No, but I sense him. He knows us."

"I don't get it." A frown line creased his brow.

She surveyed the crowd, trying to find one face that arrested her. "I don't understand it either," she admitted. "It's like when you were driving back from Miami that night and I could feel you."

"Feel me how?"

"In my head." She puffed out a breath of frustration. "This is new to me. I wasn't sure I could trust it." She continued to scan the crowd, hoping to zero in on one person. "I didn't know what you were thinking, but I could feel your energy. I sensed your urgency and I knew it was about me and that it was you."

"Okay." He gripped her shoulders and bent his knees to bring his eyes level with hers. "And what are you sensing now?"

"His excitement," she answered. "And his concentration. He's watching us."

"He is?" Levi straightened and slipped a protective arm around her shoulders.

"I think so." She felt his chest give a little jerk and she glanced up to see his scowl. "What's wrong?"

"I see that woman . . . the one I think has been following me."

"Where?"

He gave a directive nod. "Over there by the jugglers."

The jugglers tossed and caught bowling pins, hoops, and a bowling ball. Several women stood near them, watching and applauding, all except for one. She stared directly at Levi. There was something familiar about her—. Suddenly, sharp explosions split the air and Trudy nearly jumped out of her skin. She heard shouts and gasps and then Levi's arms tightened like bands and she was hauled roughly and possessively against his chest. His body curved around hers, shielding her. In the next moment, she saw colors streaking across the sky and his hold loosened.

"Fucking fireworks," Levi rasped.

She let out a sigh of relief and looked up at his frown. "We're a little jumpy."

He closed his eyes and let go of a short laugh. "We have reason to be. You're sensing a serial killer is near us, watching us, and I just spotted a woman who appears to be following me and somehow pirated my cell phone number." He opened his eyes and looked toward the jugglers. "And she's gone."

"So is the psycho," Trudy said, only just then realizing that she no longer experienced the odd, brain-crowding sensation. "I don't sense his presence any more. I'm not even sure it happened. It might just be a sinus headache coming on and—."

"No, Trudy. Don't doubt your feelings." He dropped a kiss on her forehead. "You're a gifted medium. Always trust your instincts. I do. Come on." He pulled her with him toward a place at the sea rail. People lined it, but there was just enough room for them to squeeze in. His arms wound around her and he held her against him. "Let's watch the sunset and forget all this other stuff."

Trudy closed her eyes and pressed her cheek against the front of his shirt. He smelled delectable – Armani mingling with Levi – and his heartbeats were strong in her ear. When she opened her eyes again, the sun was dipping into the ocean and people applauded and cheered. She looked up to see if Levi was watching the spectacle and her heart stuttered when she saw that he was gazing at her.

His eyes were deep-ocean blue. He kissed her and his tongue delved past her lips. He framed her face in his hands while he continued to place soft, tender kisses on her lips.

"Look at that, will you?" he whispered into her hair as he embraced her again.

She turned her head to see the lowering sun flood the sky with bold swatches of colors – orange and gold, pink and blue, red and purple. "It's so beautiful."

"It is, isn't it?" And then he let go of her and started clapping along with the other people around them.

Laughing, Trudy joined in, drowning in his smile, and she knew that she would never forget this moment in time when she realized, without a shadow of a doubt, that she was madly, gladly in love with Levi Wolfe.

*

They stopped at a seafood restaurant for dinner. Levi decided to try the seafood platter than included conch – something neither he nor Trudy had ever had before – and Trudy opted for salmon croquettes.

"How is it?" Trudy asked as Levi took his first bite of conch meat. She grinned as he chewed with exaggeration. "Tough?"

"Very." He forked another piece of it and held it out to her. "Try it."

She wrinkled her nose, but let him place the bite on her tongue. It was definitely chewy. "Not a lot of flavor."

"Nope." He shrugged. "These mussels and shrimp are good, though."

She cut off a piece of one of the croquettes, dunked it in the mustard sauce, and held it out to Levi. "Here you go."

He grinned and accepted the morsel. His brows lifted and sparkles flitted through his eyes. "Hmmm. That's good!"

She nodded. "I know what I'm doing when it comes to food."

"I'll remember that." He swallowed and drank some iced tea. "How old were you when you knew you were psychic?"

"Twelve," she answered. "I sort of knew that some thoughts were in my head that weren't mine before that, though."

"Did the thoughts belong to someone you knew?"

"No. It was a man who had kidnapped a young girl and raped and strangled her. I woke up screaming and I told my mother about my dream and . . .." Her voice trailed off, her words stolen by the pained expression on Levi's face. "What's wrong?"

He averted his gaze quickly. "Nothing." Staring at his plate, he pushed plump shrimp around with his fork. "What did your parents think about this nightmare of yours?"

He was playing it cool, but she knew she'd said something that had upset him and that he wasn't going to discuss. He could be so infuriating! Sighing, she tried to resign herself to the shields he was so adept at erecting. "My parents comforted me and said I must have watched something on television that I shouldn't have. But then two days later there was an article about the discovery of a girl's body."

"How old was the child?" His voice was low and tightly controlled.

"Four or five, I think." As she watched, she saw a shiver of revulsion pass through him. This was an old wound, she thought. "They arrested a man a couple of weeks later. Her mother's boyfriend." She sat back, irritated with his refusal to trust her with his thoughts. "What is it, Levi?"

"I was just thinking about the child . . .." He set his jaw and swallowed hard. "And of you as a young, frightened girl, of course. Did your parents believe that you had tapped into the kidnapper's thoughts?"

"No. But then it happened again and again and they sent me to a psychiatrist."

One corner of his mouth twitched. "Did that help?"

"Not much. My nightmares continued, but then things calmed down when I was about fourteen. I only had one or two episodes for the next few years, so I thought it would end. It all came back with a vengeance a few years ago. I couldn't sleep without nightmares and no one wanted to hear about my visions and the voices in my head."

"That's when you met Quintara."

"Yes. Thank God for Quintara."

"She's a saint," he agreed.

Trudy fell silent for a few minutes. Something about the child being kidnapped and murdered had opened up a wound within him. Something he flat-out refused to discuss.

"Are you all right?" she asked, dipping her head to snag his attention.

"Yes." He dabbed at the corners of his wide mouth with the napkin. "Of course."

"So, were you sent to a psychiatrist when you were young, too?"

"Not really. But I've been in therapy for the past six years," he said, quietly, haltingly.

"You have?"

"Yes." He looked at her as if challenging her to disapprove. "I have a degree in psychology, after all. Therapy has helped me cope." He issued a wry smile. "I'm a fucked up mess."

She didn't like the flinty expression on his face or what he'd said about himself. "How often do you see a psychiatrist?"

"Twice a month. I used to go at least once a week."

"That often?"

"Yes." His smile cooled. "Now you're wondering if I'm a head case and if there's hope for me."

"You're right," she said, and smirked when her agreement wiped the smile off his face. "You can't read minds because that's *not* what I was thinking at all."

He actually looked relieved. "Okay. So, what were you thinking?"

"That you have a lot of 'No Trespassing' signs pinned to you. You're very closed off and hard to get to know." She drank some iced tea, letting her words sink in and not surprised when he averted his gaze from her. "Trust is something you want, but you're not willing to give."

He looked out the restaurant window at the cars zipping past and his tongue moved inside his cheek. She could tell he was choosing his response to her carefully. Finally, he swung his attention back to her.

"You're right. I trusted someone once completely and I regret it to this day." He closed his eyes for a few seconds and shook his head. "Trudy, if I dump all my neuroses on you, it won't help me or you. Can you please just back off?"

She held his gaze for a few heartbeats before looking down at her plate. She didn't want to tread all over his feelings, but she was also getting tired of running into roadblocks. "I can do that," she said, quietly, grudgingly. "I do it all the time."

The waitress approached their table. "Anyone want dessert?"

Levi arched a brow at Trudy and she shook her head. "No, thanks. Just the check, please." He handed her a credit card.

"Okay. Be right back."

"Don't sulk," he said after the waitress was out of earshot.

"I'm not," Trudy said. "I'd like to know you better, that's all."

"I'd like that, too. And you can get to know me without dredging up all my hang-ups and screw ups. Leave that to my psychiatrist. She gets paid very well to hear it and try to help me make sense of it."

"She?"

"Yes. Dr. Althea McClain. I've been seeing her for two years."

"Two years and whatever it is still haunts you."

"She's very good and I've made a lot of progress since I've been her patient. Look, I'm not unique. I had a screwed up childhood. Lots of people do." He turned toward the waitress, taking the credit card and receipt from her. He added a tip and signed it before giving it back to her. "Thank you."

"Sure thing. Y'all come back and see us." The waitress flashed them a smile and hustled off to her other diners.

"What kind of progress have you made with Dr. McClain?" Trudy asked.

He shook his head and glanced around, effectively ending the conversation. "Ready to head back to our luxurious accommodations?"

"I am if you are," she said, placing a lightness in her tone she didn't really feel.

"Tell you what . . ." He reached across the table and captured her hand. "I'm willing to let you trespass all over me tonight."

She couldn't stop the grin from spreading across her face. "I just bet you are."

He shrugged. "That's just the kind of guy I am."

*

Somehow they ended up in the RV with their clothes scattered from the door and all the way into the bedroom. Trudy had shut the bedroom door to keep Mouse out and Levi had drawn all the curtains around the windows, making a dark cocoon for them. He had switched on a lamp to cast a glow across the room.

In the space of a minute or two, they were on the bed, their naked bodies touching, their mouths clinging, their hands roaming.

"Where are my jeans?" Levi said, lifting away from her.

"Why? Do you think you're going somewhere right now?"

He chuckled. "No. I have some condoms in my pocket." Finding the jeans on the floor, he shoved his hand in the pockets until he located the strip of packets. "Are you on birth control?"

"No."

"Why not?"

"I haven't . . . needed any lately and I didn't renew my prescription." She shrugged, then made a face at him when he grinned. "I'm not as promiscuous as you, Wolfe. I'm much more particular about who touches me."

"And I'm grateful for that." He climbed onto the bed and crawled up her body, kissing strategic places on her as he went. "But it would be nice if you got on birth control. It would be so much more fun."

"You don't like condoms?"

"I'm glad we have them, but I don't particularly like them, no."

"They prevent STDs," she reminded him.

He raised his head from her breast and frowned at her. "And you're worried about that with me? Don't be. I always use a condom and I just had a physical a month ago."

"But you just asked me to get on birth control, so how could you always use a condom?"

"Right. I asked *you* to get back on birth control." He stared at her, waiting for her to understand him.

Trudy held her breath for a moment, weighing his words and not sure what to make of them. Was thinking long-term with her? She arched a brow, silently asking him.

"Do you think I'm going to stop wanting you when this case is over?" he asked in a chiding way. "Really? You feel this?" He nudged her belly with his iron-hard erection. "This won't go away when the psycho is caught and put in prison."

"You'll be in Atlanta and I'll be in Tulsa. Will this . . ." She reached between their bodies and clamped her hand around him, making him suck in his breath and his eyes grow larger. ". . . stretch that far?"

He laughed and rested his forehead against hers. "There are things called airplanes, Trudy. You should hop on one sometime instead of rolling around in this big tin can of yours."

She ran her thumb across the wet tip of his penis and he tensed all over. She grinned.

"You think that's funny?" he asked, a little breathlessly.

"I think I've got you right where I want you . . . almost . . ." She pressed a hand into his shoulder and pushed. "On your back, Wolfe."

He followed orders, his brows knitting and the foil packets falling from his hand onto the mattress. "What are we doing?"

"I believe we're having sex . . . and I'm having you," she murmured. "Or, at least the parts you'll let me have." She smiled when a frown tipped down the corners of his wide mouth, and she was glad she'd made her point. Now to make another point . . . she laved her tongue across the wide crown of his penis and he shuddered. The next lick drove his head back into the pillow and gritted his teeth against a growl.

Delighting in her sexual prowess, Trudy imagined a Key Lime ice cream cone as she let her mouth slide over him until he nudged the back of her throat, then she swirled her tongue around him as she pulled him back out, sucking hard on his length.

"Jesus!" he groaned, every muscle in his body tightening and his cock growing even harder in her hands. "That feels way too good. I don't think I can stand it."

"Try," she said, taking him back into her mouth to trace the thick vein running the length of him with the flat of her tongue.

"Harder, Trudy. Suck harder," he whispered, roughly.

"Nobody asked you for instructions, Wolfe. Zip it." For once, she wanted to do something in bed with him that didn't require him telling her what to do and when to do it. "I'm in charge here." And just to prove it, she fisted him and began stroking him, hard and fast.

"Oh, God!"

"No, it's just me," she said, smirking, and getting a glare from him. She pressed quick kisses on the tip of his shaft as she continued to fist him, stroke him, fire him up. His breathing grew labored and choppy. When she took him in her mouth again, she tasted him on her tongue and knew he was close. Very close. She tightened her lips around the head of his cock and sucked until her cheeks caved in. Then she let her teeth scrape lightly along the silky, hot length of him as she gently cupped his scrotum. Something sweet and salty dribbled from him onto her tongue.

"*Fuuuuck!* Get a condom," he gritted out between clenched teeth. "Get one now or get ready to swallow."

She let him slip from her mouth and massaged the head of his shaft with her thumbs, feeling him lengthen and thicken. He narrowed his eyes to smoking slits and his breathing became choppy. After another minute, she grabbed one of the foil squares. Ripping it open, she pinched the end of it and slid it over his straining member. Excitement showered through her like a downpour of fireworks. To bring him to such a quivering need elated her, made her want him with a fever pitch. He clamped his hands on her waist and would have shoved her onto her back, but she wouldn't allow it.

"Uh-uh," she said, shaking her head as she tightened her thighs against his hips, straddling him. She rose up, poised over him as she gripped the base of his cock and then directed him into her. Slowly, she drifted down onto him. He felt incredible . . . full to bursting. He sucked in a huge breath as his glassy-eyed gaze held hers before lowering to her breasts. His hands followed, lifting the globes, his palms rubbing against her diamond-hard nipples, making her wetter so that the slide of him was like satin.

He shook his head and managed a tight, tense smile. "It feels like your body was made to fit mine."

She couldn't respond with words. The feel of him stretching her, throbbing in her was all she could concentrate on. Plunging down on him again and again, she wiggled against him, and he bucked up into her. It was exquisite and she let out a cry that was almost a scream of pure ecstasy. His hands moved down to where his body joined hers and his clever fingers found her swollen, throbbing nub and pinched it.

Trudy thought her head would explode as her climax trampled through her. "Levi!" His name split the air, following by her sobbing groans as the orgasm shook her tenaciously and then, finally, tenderly. She felt him buck beneath her and she opened her eyes to see him bare his teeth and squeeze his eyes shut as he came. His chest heaved up and down and she could see his heart thumping beneath his skin. It was one of the most savagely beautiful sights she'd ever experienced. More beautiful even than a Key West sunset. She wanted to applaud.

"That's right. It's so fucking right," Levi crooned, his hands on her hips. He bent his knees and his thighs supported her back as she came down off her orgasm and slumped against him. "You milked me dry, Tru. I've got nothing left."

She smiled and lifted up off him, then snuggled into him, resting her cheek on his chest and breathing in the citrus, clean scent that was Levi. Stroking a hand across his chest, she enjoyed the afterglow. After a few minutes, he gave a little jerk, then chuckled.

"I fell asleep," he murmured. "You've worn me out."

"I doubt that." She lifted her head and looked into his sleepy eyes. "Do you remember the first girl you kissed?"

"Yes," he said, drawing out the word. "Why?"

"I was just wondering. You do it so well. The best, actually. Wayne Simpson was my first. He was a bad boy."

"Oh?"

"Yes. He was always getting into trouble, but I thought he was brave and I loved his wicked grin."

"Sounds like a pattern developed early."

She kissed the indentation at the base of his throat. "I believe you're right about that. So, who was your first?" When he didn't answer immediately, she examined the muscle ticking in his jaw and the wariness in his eyes. "Levi, come on! You're honestly not going to tell me something as trivial as that?"

He sighed and rolled his eyes. "Lizzie."

"Lizzie?" How could that be? He didn't meet Lizzie until college. "Lizzie in England?"

"Yes."

"How old were you?"

"Nineteen."

She rose up on her elbows to see him better in the semi-darkness of the room. "Your first kiss was when you were nineteen?"

"I was a late bloomer."

Something just didn't add up. Nineteen and never been kissed? And looking like he looked? Had he been shut up somewhere alone with no females around until he made his way to England? The silence grew heavy. Trudy propped her head on her hand and studied his face. He looked uncomfortable.

"Why did you wait so long to kiss a girl?"

"Because I went to schools where there were no girls to kiss."

"Ever?"

"Not until my senior year when I came home to be with my mother in her final months."

"And you didn't kiss a girl then either?"

He shut his eyes and his long lashes dusted his cheeks. "I had other things on my mind."

She pushed locks of hair off his forehead as the sadness in him touched her heart. Sometimes it seemed that he adored his mother and sometimes it seemed that he lumped her in with the hatred he so obviously felt for his father. "So, Lizzie was the first girl you kissed. And she was the first girl you had sex with, too. Right?"

He nodded, cutting his eyes sideways at her.

"She's a very important person in your life."

"It was years ago and I'm a very different person now then I was back then."

"Aren't we all? So, you and Lizzie were college lovers."

"Yes, but I wasn't her only bed mate." He angled a glance at her. "Lizzie was promiscuous. She'd gone to Catholic all-girl schools and she was making up for lost time, too."

She sighed, content that he'd spilled a few tidbits about his past. From the moment he'd mentioned Lizzie to her, Trudy had sensed that theirs had been a complicated relationship and he'd just confirmed it. "Do you still see Lizzie?"

He didn't answer for a few moments. "No. Not in a long time."

That news made her way, way too happy. She rubbed her cheek against him and then kissed his flat nipple. "The inquisition is over, Levi," she told him, her voice emerging husky. "You can relax now."

He sighed. "Thank you." He kissed the top of her head and nuzzled her hair. "By the way, I'm spending the night with you again."

"I'll allow it this time." She smiled and knew he was smiling, too.

Chapter Sixteen

Levi awoke with a start as Trudy's knee jerked up into his groin. "Hey, hey," he whispered, moving back. "Watch out for the family jewels."

She thrashed again and froze suddenly. A foreboding coated him and Levi sat up and switched on the table lamp. Trudy lay on her side, her knees drawn up, her body tensed. She furrowed her brow and a whimper of distress flexed her throat.

Watching her for another minute, he saw her eyes moving under her eyelids and he suspected that this was not a dream she was experiencing.

He sat up and ran his hands through his hair. She needed to remember whatever was going on in her head right now, which meant that she needed to be awake. He went around to her side of the bed and touched her shoulder. She was as tightly wound as a top. Every fiber of her was fighting off the intrusive thoughts of a serial murderer. Not of the stalking kind, he thought, but of the killing kind. The kind that she had learned to avoid because they were too raw, too horrific. He glanced at the glowing numbers in the bedside clock. 2:16. Last call was over. The bars had closed. Murder time.

Grasping Trudy by the shoulders, he hauled her up to a sitting position. He gave her a little shake that made her head bobble. She screwed up her face, fighting him off.

"Wake up, Trudy. *Now!*"

Her sable lashes fluttered and then lifted to reveal glassy, green eyes. But he was familiar with that look now. She was awake and seeing through another's eyes.

"What's happening?" He pulled her into his arms and rocked her gently. "Look around and tell me what you see. You're safe in my arms. You don't have to be afraid."

"No, no, no." She whimpered, reminding him of a child. He grimaced and ran his hands up her back. She gripped his shoulders, her nails sinking into his skin.

"You can do this, Trudy. Where is he?"

"He's . . . got her by the throat and she's begging him not to kill her." She trembled and then grew very still. Levi eased her away from him so that he could see her face. The smirk on her lips told him that she was totally gone, completely immersed because it wasn't Trudy's smirk. It belonged to a madman.

"I'm going to kill you, bitch," she said, her voice low and deadly. "Beg! That's right. Beg me!"

"Where are you?" Levi whispered. "Living room? Bedroom?"

"See this knife? This is going to slice you up real good. Fucking cunt! I'll fix you." Trudy closed her eyes and tears spilled onto her cheeks. "And he shoves the knife into her right eye. Oh, the screams! They hurt my ears." She covered her ears with trembling hands. "The blood gushes and he shoves the knife into her other eye. She's still screaming. He shoves the knife into her throat." Tears washed her cheeks.

Levi fought off the urge to awaken her. He had to let her go through it. All of it.

"There! There! There!" Her voice was low again and manic. "Shut up, you squealing pig. There! Into your black heart. Now the nipples and those big tits. You didn't appreciate what God gave you, did you? Had to get bigger ones. You're dressed in these threadbare jeans . . . and look at this shirt. It's a man's shirt! Ungrateful, ugly bitch."

Levi breathed heavily through gritted teeth, the words stabbing him and worry for Trudy twisting in his gut. He knew what it was like being in the middle of a murder, but not like what she was experiencing. She was wielding the knife right along with the sick motherfucker!

"Oh! I'm coming all over you, fuckhole. It feels so good!" She sighed and smiled. "The come mixed with the blood. So pretty. So pure. So right. Yes. One more squirt. Ahhh." She relaxed and her head lolled back.

Levi slammed his eyes shut against the horror of it.

"Love this part. Squirting my swimmers all over you while your blood spills out," Trudy said, her voice low and guttural. "Okay. Back inside the barn, stud. You're tame now. Nice and flexible. Need to get my stuff in the bathroom."

Flexible? Levi frowned. He had applied many colorful descriptions to his own dick, but flexible had never been one of them. This fucker was truly weird. Or maybe that had been Trudy's impression – her description.

"Did I get everything? Yeah. Got it. I'm wiped out. Got to get up early for work."

"What work?" Levi gripped her upper arms and stared into her heart-shaped face. Her beautiful mouth was slack and her eyes were dilated, swimming in tears. Her short, auburn hair was in disarray, sticking up here and there, curling onto her forehead. This needed to end tonight. Right now. "What's his name, Trudy?" He gave her a little shake. "Please! Where does he work? Who is he?"

She went limp, her head falling forward, and she moaned. *Shit!* Levi settled her back on the bed. Her lashes fluttered. "Hmmm," she murmured and her pretty lips pursed in a pout. "I'm sleepy."

"Angel baby?" He let her lie back on the bed again and leaned down to kiss her because he simply couldn't stop himself. She was so delectable, even when she was coming out of a living nightmare. He swept his thumbs across the wetness under her eyes. "You awake?" One hand shot up to grasp his wrist and a scream climbed up her throat. He looked into her frightened green eyes. "It's okay, Tru. It's me."

A shudder snaked through her from shoulders to hips before she turned onto her side and curled into a ball. "I saw him murder her," she choked out. "Oh, it was terrible! I don't think I'll ever be able to . . . oh, God!"

"I know, baby, I know." Levi lay next to her, curving his front to her back. He kissed her hair and caressed her shoulder and arm. She trembled and sobbed. "Deep breaths, Trudy. Think of your family, your friends, your favorite memories. Let them wash your mind clean of that psycho's thoughts and feelings."

"Stay here with me," she whispered.

"I'm not going anywhere," he promised. And he held her, wrapping his arms around her and fervently wishing he could protect her from all evil, all pain.

"I'm thinking of us . . . of you," she murmured on a sigh.

Levi held his breath as a sweet, tight feeling latched onto his heart.

*

A little after seven in the morning, Trudy sat at the RV's kitchen table and sipped coffee while Levi poured Cherrios into two bowls, sliced bananas on top of them, and added milk.

"Do you want sugar?"

"No."

He set one of the bowls in front of her "Eat."

Sighing, she picked up a spoon and obeyed. He sat across from her and tucked into his own bowl of cereal. He'd gone to his cabin while she'd been in the shower, she surmised, noticing his change of clothes. He was watching her again, his navy blue eyes full of concern.

"You're staring again," she murmured.

"Sorry. Are you feeling better after your shower?"

"Yes."

"I've been on the phone with Sinclair again. He's read through the report we sent him about the murder you witnessed. They haven't turned up a body yet."

"She's out there," Trudy said, closing her eyes a moment to ward off the depravity that threatened to engulf her again. "I hope they find her soon."

She felt drained, but the crunchy cereal, sweet banana, and cold milk were actually giving her a burst of energy. After her connection with the murderer, she had slept fitfully, startling awake several times. The last time she had insisted on getting out of bed, taking a couple of aspirin, and standing under the stinging shower spray.

"We've done everything we can, Trudy."

"I know. It just sucks that it hasn't been enough."

"You understand why it's important for you not to sleep through those visions, don't you?"

"Yes, of course. If it helps to actually see the murder, then that's what I have to do." She noticed that he released a little sigh of relief. "Don't worry about it, Levi. I'm okay. When I first came to Quintara I was a mess," she said, trying to make him understand why she hadn't wanted to experience the murders before. "I was having trouble sleeping and I was exhausted. Murders happen mostly late at night or early in the morning. They'd wake me up and I'd be terrified and couldn't sleep for two or three days at a time. It was affecting everything in my life – my work, my relationships, everything. But I've learned how to cope and I think I'm stronger now."

"Trudy, you *are* strong," he assured her, reaching across the table to rest his hand on her forearm. He gave her a squeeze before letting go. "You saw a lot important things like the fact that she seemed to recognize him."

"He was furious when he thought she'd made him. That's when he . . . he . . ." She shook her head, blocking the heinous scene.

"Where did she know him from?" He pushed aside his empty cereal bowl and folded his arms on the table, his blue eyes alight with interest.

"I don't know. He just saw something in her face that told him she recognized him. Or maybe she said something . . . I'm not clear on it yet. Hopefully, you'll be able to shed more light about that when you're able to connect with her."

"Did you get any inkling of what kind of work he does?"

"An office type area with computers."

He gave a dismissive wag of his head. "Well, that won't help very much."

Mouse barked and jumped up on the bench seat beside Levi. She turned in a circle three times before settling against his leg and resting her head on his thigh. He looked from the dog to Trudy, his brows arching in amazement.

"Like most females, she finds you very attractive and wants to sleep with you," Trudy noted, wryly, then finished the rest of the cereal while Levi stroked Mouse's small head and consulted his phone, sorting through messages and e-mails.

She thought back to the waking dream, her mind returning to it like a tongue seeks a paining tooth. Something kept nagging at her . . . after he'd killed the woman he had done something . . . oh, yes.

"Can I ask you something?"

Levi nodded, not looking up from the cell phone.

How to phrase this? "After you ejaculate . . ." She paused as his gaze leapt to hers. Ah, she had his attention *now!* "Are you relieved that your penis isn't – um, hard anymore?"

One corner of his mouth quirked up. "That is an odd question, Miss Tucker. Is this something that you've been curious about for a long time or a recent study? Something to do with last night when we . . ?"

"No, nothing to do with us. Just answer me," she said with exasperation.

He tipped his head to one side and she could tell that he was considering the question. "Well, as we both know, after *I* ejaculate, I'm often still hard." He grinned at her. "But, no, I can't say that I think of it like that. I'm usually floating in 'just came euphoria' and enjoying being buried balls deep inside such a beautiful, warm, receptive woman." His smile was tender and personal and it made her heart expand. Then his gaze sharpened and his brows lifted as if he'd been struck by an idea. "This is about the murderer. He referred to his junk as being flexible, right? I wasn't sure that was his thinking or yours."

"No, it was him. He was glad it was flaccid again. Flexible."

"Yes, well, he's screwy, for sure. Certifiable." He set aside the cell phone. "What did he have in the bathroom? You said he went back in there to get his stuff. Did he leave more weapons in there?"

"Oh, I forgot about that! I need to send that information to Tom." She pointed a finger at him. "See? That's why it's good you're here. You help me sort through it all and recall things."

"Yeah, I'm not just a pretty face and a stiff cock."

She returned his grin and then shook her head, slinging her thoughts back in order. "No weapons. He had clothes in there, I think."

"Clothes? Are you sure? What the hell was he doing? Did he take some of her clothes as a souvenir?"

Trudy sorted through the images. There was a wig. Designer jeans. Pretty, pink shirt. A padded bra. A woman's clothes. He'd stuffed them into an over-sized shoulder bag. With a jolt, everything slammed together like a jigsaw puzzle. Trudy sucked in her breath as the last pieces locked into place, letting her see the whole, crazy picture. "Levi!"

"What? *What?*" He leaned toward her, his eyes wide with alarm as he clamped his hands around her wrists.

"Zelda!"

"Zelda was there? In the bathroom?" His voice rose with each word.

She nodded and then shook her head. She took a deep breath to steady her pounding heart. "*He* is Zelda."

Levi stared at her and she watched in fascination as his expression changed from confusion to realization. His hands slipped away from her. "*What?!*" He fell back in the padded booth. "*He* is Zelda? You mean, he dressed up like a woman and . . . oh, Christ!" He stood up, making Mouse jump down and bark furiously at him as he paced, the heel of one hand plastered against his forehead and his eyes wide and unseeing. "*Fuck me!*"

She nodded as it solidified in her mind "He dresses up like Zelda, gets to know the women, gets an invitation to their home, and then he goes into the bathroom, changes clothes, and comes out a man!"

"Oh, my God!" Levi's eyes were wide and a bright, intense blue. "He is so fucked up! This is nuts to the nth degree!"

His excitement was infectious and Trudy found herself grinning as she watched him piece it together. His movements were jerky and full of pent-up energy. He turned his back to her for a few moments and then whirled around to face her again, his blue eyes blazing, his dark brows lowered.

"So, is he a transvestite or a . . . a transgender or is this simply his M.O.?"

"I don't know." She examined the thoughts that had invaded her and the feelings associated with them. "He doesn't seem to view his penis as pleasurable. It's more like a weapon or a tool. He was angry at the women because they . . . I don't know for sure. It doesn't make sense to me." She chewed her lower lip and tried to decipher the jumbled, twisted feelings. "They don't appreciate their own bodies?"

Levi propped his hands on his hips and stared down at the carpet, his fingers drumming across his hips bones. He exuded deep concentration. She could almost feel the information whizzing through his nimble, brilliant mind.

"He's envious," he said, glancing at her, his breathing rapid and choppy. "They have what he wants and they don't appreciate it . . . or he doesn't think they do. It's like Dr. Karen Horney theorized."

Trudy shook her head. He'd lost her.

"The feminist psychoanalyst," he said. "Autogynephilia, a love of oneself as a woman. Dr. Horney said that men experience womb and breast envy more powerfully than women experience penis envy because men need to disparage women more than women need to disparage men."

Trudy raised her brows. "I like this psychoanalyst."

"Yeah, well I think Dr. Ray Blanchard actually coined the name for the condition." He ran a hand through his hair. "Anyway, this guy might have a tendency to be sexually aroused by the thought or the image of himself as a woman. It's very complicated and I'm not doing the theories justice."

Trudy marveled at the complex man standing before her. One moment he was going on about "nuts to the nth degree" and the next he was spouting psychology terms that made her eyes cross. She couldn't keep the grin from spreading across her face.

He noticed and tilted his head. "What?"

"You. Levi, the psychologist!"

A shy smile overtook him, but then he shook it off. "My degrees are showing." He rested his fists against the edge of the table and his eyes locked on hers – blue to green. "Trudy! Do you know what you've done? You have broken this sonofabitching case wide open!" He kissed her hard, but then in the next moment his lips softened on hers and his hand came up to cradle the back of her head. She parted her lips and his tongue skimmed across them before dipping inside. Her heart kicked into overdrive and she lifted her hand to caress the side of his face. His morning whiskers tickled her palm.

He ended the kiss and she opened her eyes. His were dark blue now, desirous blue. "You're amazing, did you know that?"

She shook her head.

"Well, you are. Call Sinclair and tell him what you've figured out."

"What *we* figured out," she amended.

He shook his head. "No, it was you. Own it. I would." He brushed his lips across hers and his smile was sweetly salacious. "Save my place. I'll be back in a little while."

"Where are you going?"

He grabbed his cell phone. "To the cabin. I want to call Dr. Franz Wooten in Geneva. He's a gender specialist and he'll have some good psychological insight into this crazy motherfucker." He started out, then hesitated and looked over his shoulder at her. "I just had a thought."

"What?" she asked, twisting around in the booth to look at him.

"He was glad his cock was flaccid . . . flexible . . . because he could tuck again."

"Tuck?" she repeated, shaking her head. "What's that?"

"Tuck his penis. It's what female impersonators do so that their packages won't show under slinky or tight dresses and skirts. They shove their testicles up inside them, then pull their cock back and wrap the excess skin around it to hold it in place."

She blinked at him. "Good grief! You can shove your balls up inside you?"

"Yes. Sure. After all, testicles start as ovaries that fall out of us when we turn into males. They can be shoved back inside."

213

"But doesn't that hurt?"

He shrugged. "Doesn't sound comfortable to me, but I don't know. I've never tried it. Even though he was dressed as a man again, he might have wanted to tuck because he likes the feeling. I'll ask Dr. Wooten about it."

"How did you know about tucking?" she asked, giving him a ribbing grin.

He glanced up and tried to keep the smile from overtaking him. "I read about it somewhere."

"Oh, sure," she noted, dubiously. "Probably in a professional journal of some kind."

"Probably. The Psychology of Female Impersonation and Manipulation of the Male Apparatus," he rejoined. "Get some rest, you brilliant witch, you."

She made a face at him, but he didn't see it. He was already out the door with Mouse barking after him, still irritated at him, no doubt, for dumping her.

*

A rapping on the RV's door roused Trudy from her nap. She scrambled from the bed and padded through the RV, glancing at the digital clock on the oven. Half past noon. She opened the door to Levi.

"I woke you?" he asked, stepping inside.

"Yes." She pushed her fingers through her hair, giving it a rough combing. "Do you have news?"

He nodded. "They found the body a couple of hours ago."

"Oh." She rested a hand against her heart where the news had sent an arrow of pain. "Well, thank God. Who found her?"

"Her boyfriend stopped by to check on her. She's a waitress and she didn't show up for work this morning. Her name is Amanda Duncan."

Trudy slumped onto the sofa, feeling drained and still a little groggy. "How horrible for him."

"That's the bad news."

"You have good news?" she asked, dubiously.

"I do. I have an invitation from Captain Delbert Phillips to meet with him at police headquarters. If he thinks I'm sane, then he's going to allow me to check out the murder scene today." He sat on the couch beside her.

She gripped his arm, turning to face him. "No kidding? So soon? Maybe you can find out how she knew the perp and hopefully get his name!"

"That's exactly what Sinclair told Captain Phillips. So, let's hope I make a good impression."

"I'm sure you will. You look sane to me."

He grinned. "Well, considering the source . . ." He kissed the tip of her nose. "You're not upset that you weren't invited, too?"

"I don't need to be there. You can handle that all by yourself. In fact, while you're at the police station, I might take a break from all this ugliness and go shopping."

"For what?"

"Key West souvenirs for me and my family."

He placed a hand on her thigh. "Don't you want to go to the crime scene with me?"

"I'll pass this time."

"I understand." He slipped an arm around her and drew her against him.

"So, when are we going?" She smiled and thought about how easy it would be to get used to being held by him, comforted by him.

"My appointment with the captain is at two."

"Oh! That's great. I'll get ready." She sat up and gave him a once-over, taking in the shadows under his eyes. "Are you sure you're up to this? You didn't get much sleep last night either."

"I'm up for it." He leaned in and gave her a hard, smacking kiss. "I'm always up for it."

Taking in his wiggling eyebrows and devilish smirk, she narrowed her eyes. "No, Levi. Not now." She pulled him up from the couch with her and pushed him toward the door. "Out!"

*

Sitting in the back of the police cruiser, Levi checked his wristwatch. It was almost half past noon. His meeting with Captain Phillips had taken longer than he'd expected. Phillips was the standard issue cop – bald, brown chevron mustache, hooded gaze, built like a tank, polite but giving nothing away. He had questioned

Levi about the cases he had worked, his books, how often he got things right, and when he had been wrong. The usual questions that Levi had answered many times before. Levi had learned to be honest but modest, candid but careful when dealing with police officers.

Phillips was shrewd and he hadn't been on board with Levi visiting the murder scene, so Levi had downplayed all the hocus pocus of psychic work and had focused on gathering evidence. He had taken note of the signed baseball sitting in a dome on the credenza behind the detective's tidy desk.

"I know your department is on this like white on rice," Levi had told him. "I know you're going to catch this sick sonofabitch. I just want a chance at bat . . . to see if I can possibly help. If I fan out. . ." He had smiled. "Well, it sure as hell won't be the first time and it won't affect your investigation."

That had broken the ice and Phillips had chatted with him about the case for a few more minutes before phoning Tom Sinclair, who was at the murder scene.

"Sinclair, is the evidence collecting done?" Phillips had asked. "Good. Stay put. I'm sending Levi Wolfe over." Then he'd pinned Levi with a steady, squinty glare. "I don't want to hear any shit from you on TV or anywhere else about us not cooperating or not doing a good job. You got that, Wolfe?"

"Loud and clear," Levi had said, holding onto his temper. "I think you have me confused with someone else, Captain. I work *with* the police. Never against them."

Asshole. Levi yanked at the knot of his tie, agitated as he sat in the back of the squad car and wished that Trudy was next to him. She would have made this more pleasant, more tolerable. He closed his eyes for a few moments as scenes from last night replayed in his mind. She was everything and more than he had dreamed she'd be. His connection to her was so strong, it floored him. He couldn't shake the intense possessiveness he felt for Trudy or the ever-present concern that she would get so close to him that she'd be able to really know him and then leave him. And he'd be destroyed.

Shifting uncomfortably, he tried to shrug off a nagging feeling that had been dogging him all morning. It made him uneasy and he kept worrying about Trudy. He checked his phone. No text or call from her. He decided to text her.

Heading for the crime scene. Should be back to the station in an hour or so.

He stared at the back of the heads of the two cops in the front seat. They chatted amiably, laughing and smiling, joshing each other. It made him miss Trudy even more. His phone vibrated and he read the text.

All shopped out! The murder spree is ending. I feel it. See you soon.

Slipping the phone into his breast pocket, he hoped she was right. Something was going to happen . . . he just wasn't sure what.

The squad car turned into the driveway of a small, pale pink house with a red roof. A white picket fence ran around the front yard. The sight of this scrap of Home Sweet Americana tightened Levi's throat. So perfect on the outside, he thought, and so hellish on the inside. Sort of like the homes he'd known as a kid.

With a heavy sigh, he opened the car door and unfolded his frame from the backseat. He stretched and gathered his composure, preparing himself for the horror to come.

The porch was just big enough for two chairs and a small table. The railings were draped with yellow police tape and an officer stood at the front door, checking credentials.

"This is Levi Wolfe," one of the squad car cops told the front sentry. "Phillips sent him over."

"Right." The other cop moved aside. "Sinclair's in there waiting for you."

"Thank you." Levi stepped into a small living room of Amanda Duncan's home. He glanced over the white walls decorated with cheap art and framed family photos, the ubiquitous leather couch, rattan rocker, and tweedy recliner, an area rug, and a 52-inch flat screen TV that dominated the whole space. Straight ahead he glimpsed a dining room and kitchen. Sinclair stepped into view from a hallway off the dining room. He nodded at Levi and motioned him over.

"She was killed in the bedroom back here," the detective said by way of greeting.

"Where's the bathroom?"

"Uh . . . right here between the two bedrooms," Sinclair said, giving Levi a quizzical look.

Levi stepped into the bathroom first, knowing that "Zelda" had probably been in there changing clothes. "Did they dust for prints in here?"

"I guess so." Sinclair stuck his head in. "Yeah, there's some dust here on the door and over there above the sink."

Levi nodded. "Okay. Which bedroom?"

"Here, to the left."

Gathering in a big breath, Levi moved into the room where sunlight poured into two large windows, spotlighting a king-sized bed that took up most of the space. A narrow chest of drawers and a bedside table were squeezed in. A double closet took up one whole wall. The murder had happened on the bed. It was blood-stained, now dry and crusty. Levi removed his camera from his leather satchel and snapped a few photos as he regulated his breathing and started clearing his mind of all superfluous thoughts.

"As soon as you're done here, we'll take all the bed linens and other things as evidence. Try not to touch anything. What do you need?" Sinclair asked.

Levi put the camera into the satchel and shook his head. "Nothing. It will help if you just stay out of my way and don't talk to me."

"Oh. Okay."

Taking out the e-notebook, he opened it and jotted down a few impressions. The huge bed. A broken lamp. Sheets ripped. Pillows stabbed over and over again. Candles scattered across the top of the bureau. Jewelry box overturned. Probably something taken from it as a souvenir. He closed the netbook.

Show time, Wolfe, he thought as he moved to stand next to the bed, his knees bumping against the box springs. He inhaled and exhaled three times as he slowly closed his eyes and let it come . . . let the images swirl and dip and skitter through his mind until they finally stopped . . . focused . . . sucked him in.

Amanda appeared behind his eyelids. She was lovely, emanating light. He smiled at her and held out his hand. *May I? Will you take me back there, angel?* She grasped his fingers and pulled him inside her. He became her.

"This is wrong," he murmured. "I should be in the hallway." And so he turned and nearly ran over Sinclair as he walked from the bedroom to the hallway . . . just outside the bathroom.

"Zelda?" he called, looking at the bathroom. Although he could see into it, his mind could not. The door was closed. Zelda was in there. "Are you okay in there?"

The door swung open and . . . a shadow moved . . . a man! Who . . . how . . !

Levi felt the man's fingers close on his throat and force him back, back, back to the dark bedroom. His eyes widened and he tried to talk, but only garbled sounds escaped. He was bent backward onto the bed as he clawed at the hand that was closing off his airway and stared at a man with a baseball cap pulled low onto his forehead. A Gators baseball cap? It was hard to see anything. What's that? A knife's blade glinted in the feeble light leaking in from the living room. In his other hand . . . a big knife with a serrated blade.

Fighting now. Kicking, fingernails breaking, life being choked out of him. Wait. Oh. She knows him . . . her . . . him? Those dimples. Yeah. It's *him!* The man cursed.

"Fucking bitch! Don't look at me. Stop . . . looking . . . at . . . me!"

Sudden, excruciating pain dropped him to his knees and he covered his eyes with the heels of his hands. He felt blood gushing from them like hot water, covering his fingers and making everything slippery. Then the dull, lurching, tearing plunges of the knife into his breasts . . . chest . . . across his throat.

He was dying . . . dying . . . rising up to the light . . . the bright, beautiful light. Then Amanda let him go, let him float back down. *Thank you,* he said to her. She smiled and her image faded.

Levi?

Everything in him stilled. Peace washed over him. A familiar peace he had come to rely on in his darkest hours.

Gregory? Is something wrong?

Levi, Ethel is here with me.

Ethel?

She's worried.

About what?

Levi, check your phone.

Okay.

And Levi?

Yes, Gregory?

Ethel has lovely dimples.

He felt the heat of the sunlight pouring through the windows. Levi opened his eyes. He was lying on a bed that reeked of blood and chemicals. Why the hell had Gregory contacted him? He hardly ever showed up at a murder recreation. Maybe three or four times before . . . tops. And those were in the early years when the murders sometimes had affected him so deeply or he he'd been so drunk that he'd had trouble moving away from the light and back to the living. Gregory had popped up and guided him, showed him the way.

But he'd never brought another spirit with him before.

"You okay, Wolfe?"

Sinclair. Levi closed his eyes again for a few seconds, coming back all the way before he tried to stand.

"Yes." His voice sounded hoarser. "I'm fine, thank you."

"Did you see him? The murderer?"

"Not much of him. I saw the lower half of his face and then he took out my eyes – *her* eyes. He's about my age and a little shorter than me. He's a nice looking guy and he . . . he has . . . dimples."

"Dimples?"

Levi turned around to face Sinclair. "Yes. Deep dimples in his cheeks." *Ethel has dimples.* "Oh, Christ!" He slammed his eyes shut again as bits of visions that weren't his, but were borrowed, zipped through his head like a movie that had been fast-forwarded. . . a guy in an Hawaiian shirt and a baseball cap in an outdoor café, smiling at him . . . no, her . . . Amanda. Smiling at Mandy. Asking if he knows her. Maybe he interviewed her once? No? Then at Mallory Square again, but this time Mandy is sharing a joke with Zelda. Her boyfriend is in St. Petersburg and won't be back until tomorrow. Mandy says she's glad they ran into each other. She invites Zelda to have a drink . . . at her house. The All American house.

"She'd met him before," Levi said, putting it all together. He realized he was trembling and his eyes felt as if they were pulsating in their sockets. The visions had come so quickly, they'd hammered his brain. "She knew Zelda, but she didn't make the connection until he came out of the bathroom." He opened his eyes and stared at Sinclair, the knowledge bursting through him like a mortar blast. "In as Zelda and out as the guy with the dimples."

Watch out for the jaybird. Levi stared at Sinclair, excitement making him jittery and full of nervous energy as it always did when he knew – when he *knew* he was right. "I've identified him."

"Who is he?"

"Jay Yardley."

"Jay . . . the AP reporter?"

Levi nodded. "It's him. You need to bring him in for questioning. Search his place and you'll find evidence."

"Let's get back to the station and you can run this up the flagpole for Captain Phillips," Sinclair said, his eyes wide and his movements suddenly jerky. "Yardley? Really? Hot damn. If this pans out . . ."

"It will," Levi said, his heartbeat returning to normal and certainty bringing him blessed peace. "Find him and arrest the son-of-a-bitch before he can kill another woman."

"Right. Come on. You can ride back with me."

Following him through the house and out to a black Camero Coupe, Levi folded himself into the passenger seat and glanced around the interior. The car smelled new. He grinned at Sinclair.

"Nice ride."

"I've only had her two weeks."

"How does she handle?"

"Like she's on rails." He gunned the engine.

"Sounds good."

"What's *your* chariot of choice?"

"I'm driving a Jag right now. Leased. In Atlanta, I have a couple of cars. A fully restored 1937 Cord 812 SC Sportsman and a new Corvette Stingray."

Sinclair whistled. "You take your rides seriously, my man."

Levi grinned. "You gotta take something seriously. Why not cars?"

Sinclair chuckled and gave the car the gas, smashing the speed limit and zipping around slower traffic because he was a cop and he could.

Automatically, Levi reached into his inside pocket for his cell phone. He had to text Trudy and tell her . . . *Check your cell phone.* Gregory's remembered directive sent a sliver of terror through him . . . almost like the kiss of a knife blade. The cell phone screen lit up. He had a text message. His finger shook slightly as he tapped the screen. It was from Trudy.

You're not here yet. Jay Yardley's going to buy me a beer. Be back in a few.

It felt like the blood in his veins ground to a halt. For a few seconds, he saw double and then his heart kicked and lodged in his throat. "Oh, no. Oh, Jesus, no."

"What?" Sinclair glanced at him with a worried scowl. "Goddamn, Wolfe! What's wrong?"

A sticky sweat coated him and his gut knotted. "Trudy is with Jay Yardley."

"She's *what?* How? Where?"

"Hell, I don't know!" Then his fingers tightened on the phone. "Wait . . . wait. We can trace her through her cell! The GPS is switched on." What the fuck was he doing talking cars and acting cocky when Trudy was . . . was . . . oh, Jesus. He had known something bad was going to happen . . . he'd felt it . . . and ignored it . . . and if she was with that sick fucker . . . oh, Jesus God no. "Let's go, Sinclair! Floor this bitch!"

Chapter Seventeen

The Conch Queen Bar and Grill was dark inside and Trudy couldn't see well enough to navigate, so she stopped just inside the door. Jay Yardley bumped into her.

"Oh, sorry." His hands came up to grip her shoulders and keep her from stumbling forward.

"I'm blind, coming in here from the bright sunlight." Trudy gave a short laugh. "I think there's an empty booth over there."

"I see it." Jay's hands moved down her arms. He stepped to her side, gripped one of her hands, and pulled her toward the booth. He waited for her to slip onto the padded bench before he sat in the seat opposite her.

Trudy released her pent-up breath, realizing only then that she'd been holding it as she'd waited to see if Jay would try to sit next to her or across from her. His hands brushing down her arms had sent a little alarm through her. For a few moments, she'd wondered if Levi had been right about Jay wanting to get her horizontal. But he'd done the right thing by giving her some personal space and she was relieved. She placed her shopping bags and purse beside her. A waitress came forward, arching her penciled brows.

"What can I get y'all?" she asked.

"Do you have Guiness?" Jay asked.

"Sure do."

"I'll have one of those."

"Make that two," Trudy said. "It's been years since I've had a Guiness."

"Then it's high time for another," Jay said, smiling to show off his dimples. "I'm glad we ran into each other. You've been shopping?"

"Yes. I grabbed a few things. I was actually hanging around the police station waiting for Levi when I spotted you."

"Where is he?"

"At the latest crime scene."

"Oh? I was at the station getting some info on that." He shrugged. "The cops couldn't tell me much. They're no closer to catching the guy."

"Not so! I think they're getting really close to making an arrest."

"Oh, yeah?" His arched brows rose and his hazel eyes gleamed with surprise. "From what I heard, they're completely stumped."

She shrugged off his impression and leaned back to allow the waitress to set two beers on the table. A group of five or six people left the bar, all laughing and poking at each other.

"Anything else?" the waitress asked, also leaving a bowl of peanuts in the shell for them to share.

"That's all for now. Thanks." Jay looked at the woman from head to toe as she walked away and frowned slightly. He took a sip of the dark brew. "Seems like this guy you're tracking is always one or two steps ahead of you and the police."

"It might *seem* that way from the outside, but the reality is different," Trudy assured him. "We're right on his heels. Get ready to write an article about his arrest, Jay." The strong, cold beer reminded her of her college days when Guiness had flowed between her and her small circle of friends. Realizing that it was much quieter, she glanced around. Only two or three other people were in the bar now.

Jay drank half of his beer in a few long gulps. Setting the glass down with a flourish, he pinned her with his hazel eyes. "So, you speak to the dead?"

"No, that's Levi's territory."

"Well, that's odd, because Dad said that you speak to my dear, departed mother." His expression shamed her, calling her a liar.

She bit her lower lip to keep from telling him to go to hell. "True, but that's unusual for me. I'm normally in touch with the pervs."

"The *what?*" He craned his head closer to catch her words over the wail of Reba McEntire on the sound system. "I don't think I heard you correctly."

"Pervs. Perverts."

He fell back in the booth and stared at her for a few seconds before taking another long drink of beer. "That's what you call them?"

"Yes, among other things." She grinned and took a swig of the ale. "I share their thoughts and sometimes I see through their eyes when they — well, when they murder their victims."

He averted his gaze from her to stare thoughtfully into the Guiness glass. "That must be fascinating. Like watching a film."

Fascinating? A cold finger slicked up her spine. "A snuff film – and it's gross to the max, believe me."

He examined his fingernails in the low light. "If you can see all of this, why haven't you identified him?" His tone was pointedly bland as if he were trying hard not to sound too interested or . . . too smug? She rarely heard actual voices in her head – she heard words in her own voice or a modified version of her voice. But the cadence . . .*his* cadence set off alarms in her and amplified the heightened tension she'd felt all day.

Trudy's sixth sense quivered to life. Something had changed in Jay's demeanor . . . something almost imperceptible, but her keen senses had caught it. Whose side was he on? This conversation was pissing him off, making him do a slow burn. She took note of the sheen of perspiration on his brow even as her own skin dampened under her arms and between her breasts. Yes, a storm was brewing and danger quivered in the air between them. She regulated her breathing and told herself to navigate carefully.

"I can't identify him unless he looks in a mirror or in some other reflective surface," she explained. "I see what he sees – his hands . . ." Her gaze moved of its own accord to Jay's hands and . . . yes, they were familiar. A sick feeling corkscrewed in her stomach. She swallowed the knot that formed in her throat as she forced her eyes back up. "Mostly I see the victims because that's who he's looking at."

"You see through his eyes," Jay said, softly, pensively. "And you know what's going on in his mind."

"Yes."

"That must be amazing."

Trudy sipped the beer, stalling as she decided how to respond to him. At first, she thought the lights had dimmed even more in the bar, but then she realized the dimness was internal. Someone was trying to delve into her thoughts. Was it Jay? Was he testing her? She resisted, needing to focus on the odd turn of conversation. Looking at him, she didn't like the supercilious grin on his lips.

"Amazing?" she repeated, determined to wipe the grin off his face. This wasn't funny. *She* wasn't funny. "No way, no how. They're all the same, more or less. Sick and twisted, so whatever they're thinking is totally crazy."

Jay's lips curved into a V shape, but Trudy couldn't actually call it a smile. There was no pleasure in it. It was more like a clownish sneer. "I've read about these men and a lot of them are geniuses."

Trudy rolled her eyes and released a sound of contempt. She was baiting him, goading him, she knew. But she couldn't help herself. She wanted to strike out at him. "I'm sure they think they're very clever, but they're delusional. They're insane, immoral, and depraved."

"If they are so delusional and depraved, how can they elude the police, you, and Levi Wolfe so easily?" Jay asked, his voice low and almost sing-song. His gaze flicked to hers and his eyes were expressionless, like a doll's eyes.

A shivery finger of fear trailed down Trudy's spine, making her sit up straighter. His lips pursed and his dimples disappeared as he waited for her to answer him. There wasn't a shred of friendliness in his expression. Something was off . . . something depraved lurked in this man.

Trudy cleared her throat. Her skin felt sticky, but she noticed that Jay wasn't sweating anymore. He looked as cool and as slick as a snake. "They always get caught," Trudy said, using every bit of her concentration to sound nonchalant. "In fact, I think they want to be stopped. It must be a terrible burden to carry around with them."

"Burden? What burden?"

She lifted her gaze slowly to him, wise to his misstep by asking that question. Only someone with no conscience, no empathy would ask such a thing. "The burden of pure evil and multiple sins, of course."

Jay's burst of distain struck her like a fist and it took everything in her not to flinch. His gaze intensified to the point that his pupils quivered and she felt the pressure of it in her mind. He *was* doing that! The realization stilled her heart for a moment and then it raced like a frightened, wild thing as she remembered this same feeling at Mallory Square. He had been there. He had been watching.

"That is a simplistic way to view the world, don't you think?" Jay asked, smoothly. "Good versus evil? Sin and redemption." He scoffed. "It's so childish. Like believing in angels and elves. People are far more complicated than that."

She finished the beer and set the empty mug down slowly. She hadn't been careful enough and had sailed into dangerous territory with Jay Yardley. The boyish, affable man she'd walked into the bar with was gone. Something maniacal and predatory sat opposite her now and the fine hairs on her nape rose and quivered.

"I believe there are people who are evil to their core," she said, moving the conversation along on cat feet. "How could someone gouge out another person's eyes and slit her throat . . . slash her breasts, cut off her nipples . . . and not be totally consumed by sadistic evil?"

"How, indeed?" Jay flicked his fingers through the side of his hair in a gesture that was decidedly feminine – the way a woman would push back her long hair from her temple, except that Jay wasn't a woman and his hair was too short to shove back behind his ear or over his shoulder.

Intrigued, Trudy remembered a few moments ago when he had held his hand out, examining his nails – not like a man, who would curl his fingers toward his palm. No. Jay had spread out his fingers, palm facing away from him.

Staring at him in the low light, she imagined him wearing a wig and heavy makeup. He'd be pretty, she thought, her heartbeats increasing as a clamminess coated her skin. She was absolutely certain that she was chatting with Zelda *and* the Key West serial killer. A cunning, cold, calculating, murdering machine.

Trudy looked away from him and grappled with her mounting fear. She knew that she was a terrible bluffer. Every emotion she experienced was usually stamped boldly on her face. She wouldn't be able to camouflage her feelings for long. He would see. He would know.

Her gaze wandered to the bar entrance. Could she simply stand up and leave? Once outside, would he chase her down or let her go? Or would he allow her to go outside? Did he have a knife or gun that he could draw and make her do his bidding?

"How many of these men have you helped to put in their graves or behind bars?" Jay asked. He tipped back the mug and finished drinking the dark ale.

Trudy watched his throat flex as one escape scenario after another played in her mind. She decided that excusing herself to go to the women's restroom might be best. Once in there, she could call Levi and tell him to bring the police to the bar and arrest Jay. Feeling Jay's expectant gaze, she realized he was waiting for her to answer him.

"I'm thinking . . ." she said, stalling again. "I just started working with police on these cases, so I haven't been involved with that many. I helped with one other serial killer case in Ohio a few months ago." But this was the first time she'd had a beer with one, she mentally added.

"An arrest was made?"

"No. The police were closing in and he killed himself."

"I know the case you mean. He took out his wife, then his mother-in-law, his mother, his boss, his sister, and then himself."

"That's right."

"Benjamin Andrew Elsworth," he said, nodding. "I remember him well. But he was easy because he focused on people he knew. Why did the cops need you?"

"They were having trouble locating him. I helped them find him. They surrounded him, but then he shot himself." She shifted uneasily, perspiration making her skin feel sticky. The air-conditioner was blasting and cooling the bar, but she was perspiring as if she'd been working out – or as if she was discussing murder with a monster. "You find serial killers interesting?" she asked, wanting to keep him talking until she could form a concrete plan.

"Very interesting." His smile was close to being inhuman.

"Then you'll be interested to know that Levi made himself famous by tracking down Vernon "Bud" Schneider. He murdered women in––."

"New York and Maine," Jay cut in, nodding. "Yes, I read Wolfe's book about that case. I believe the title was *Soul Searching*?"

"Yes, that's right."

"I wasn't impressed. He certainly didn't cover any new ground."

Under the table, she slipped her hand inside her purse and removed her cell phone. It was too big to palm, but she closed one hand around it to conceal it as much as possible.

"Wolfe communes with the victims," Jay mused. "That's not *nearly* as interesting as what you're able to do." He crossed his arms on the table and leaned closer. "To hear their thoughts . . . to understand their purposes . . ."

"Oh, I don't understand them," Trudy said, amazed that she could actually chuckle when her throat and mouth were as dry as dust. "They're cracked and there's no putting them back together again." From his scowl, she knew he was growing tired of this game and so was she. Trudy motioned for the waitress and lifted her empty glass. "Another round, please?" She smiled at Jay. "That was so good, I'd love another one. My treat." Then she glanced around and behind her. "Ah, there's the restrooms. Excuse me. I'll be right back." To convince him even more that she was returning and that her trip to the restroom was nothing to be concerned about, she patted her purse and shopping bags on the bench seat beside her. "I'll leave my things here. Watch them for me, okay?"

He nodded and she slipped from the booth, holding the cell phone low against her thigh and hoping he wouldn't see it. Making her way to the corridor that gave access to the restrooms, she willed herself to move unhurriedly and not look back. She breathed a sigh of relief as she pushed open the door and stepped inside. It was a two-stall affair, the toilets to her right and a sink straight ahead of her. Lifting the cell phone, she pushed the button on the side and the screen lit up. She ran a finger over the screen, unlocking the phone, and pressed the "1" key to speed-dial Levi.

Hurry . . . hurry . . . answer the phone, Levi . . .

The door at her back was suddenly pushed forward with a force that sent her stumbling into the sink. Her cell phone slipped from her hand and clattered across the tile floor. Whirling, she saw Jay leaning against the closed door. He extended an icy smile.

"Jay, what the hell are you doing?" Trudy said, managing to sound miffed instead of scared spitless. Her heart thrummed in her throat and her gaze moved of its on accord to Jay's right hand. His fingers flexed around the hilt of a knife and a long blade flicked out of it with the touch of his thumb against a button. "Why do you have that?"

"You know why," he said, his voice soft, almost dreamy, more feminine than male.

"Get out of my way. I'm leaving."

He shook his head and the dimples in his cheeks deepened. "You know what kind of women they were because you were with me, right? Pretty women who were too stupid to know it. They had perfectly fine tits, but they had to get them reshaped and make them bigger. They had good figures, but they wore ugly clothes that swallowed them or god-awful swimsuits they must have bought at Wal-Mart. No makeup or gobs of it. Their hair was tangled or wadded into a haphazard pony tail. Disgusting." He dipped his chin, his eyes glinting as they took her in. "Do you always buy your clothes at Sears? Don't you ever want to wear something high fashion . . . a designer's dream?"

"Of course, I do," she said, playing along. "If I had more money, I would wear nothing but designer labels." She ran her hands down her belly and along the top of her thighs. "I love being a woman."

"But you think I'm a pervert. You think I'm insane." The smile vanished from his lips and his voice had roughened. He sounded like a man again. "I bet you think I'm a fucking genius now, don't you? Right now you'd agree to anything I said just to keep me from slicing your throat open and cutting out your heart."

A scream clutched at her throat. She parted her lips.

"You scream, you die." He lifted the knife. "Simple."

"I scream, someone comes running, and then you get arrested . . . or dead."

"You want to die?" He backed her up against the sink. The blade of the knife tapped her throat and then he lifted it away so that she could look at it. "Did you see me gouge out that bitch's eyes when she recognized me?" His breath was soaked in Guiness.

Trudy nodded, her mind whirring, plotting her survival. She had to time it perfectly. She had to commit totally or it wouldn't work. Looking past him, she smiled. He frowned and she felt his confidence falter.

"Your mother is here," she lied.

He shook his head. "Who's crazy now, bitch?"

"You two were very close. She told me that she knew about you. All about you. But she protected you. She kept your secrets, Jaybird."

A muscle pulsed in his jaw and his eyes narrowed minutely. It was all she needed. Ramming her knee up into his groin, Trudy grabbed the wrist of his knife hand and pushed it away from her. Then she jabbed the thumb of her free hand into Jay's eye.

"Fucking whore! You're dead! I'll cut out your goddamned . . ."

She sidestepped him and lurched for the door. The knife arced, whistling up, nicking and burning her shoulder, and then the bathroom door flew open, slamming into the side of her face and sending her backward . . . backward . . . tripping and falling into Jay. She scrambled off him and saw the knife sweeping toward her again. She lost her balance, her feet sliding out from under her.

"Trudy! No!"

Levi!

Something hard banged against her head and all the lights in the world were doused.

*

A voice wound through her mind. A dream? Real?

"Hello, Trudy. I'm Dr. Drumright. You can open your eyes. Come on. I know you're conscious. What color are they? We all want to see for ourselves, don't we, people?"

She tried to lift her lids, but they wouldn't obey.

Murmuring. Chuckling. A hand on her face. Something sticking her. Her arms and legs being lifted. The rip of fabric. Cold. She was freezing cold. Her eyes popped open. Owww! The light!

"Oh, look, everyone. They're green. Your head hurts, I know. You're going to X-ray to see if you cracked it. Hey, Carol, take a look at her shoulder. Yeah, go ahead and clean and close that wound . . ."

Trudy shut her eyes and shut out the voices and that hurtful, cold light.

*

"Get your fucking hands off me, Sinclair! I want to know how she's doing and I want to know now!"

Levi? Trudy tried to call out to him, but she had no voice. Her lips and tongue wouldn't move.

Hands lifting, moving, pressing down on her. Humming machinery. Soft voices, but none of them Levi's. He had sounded so mad! Mister Moody Blues.

*

The shadowy figure came closer until she could see his dimples and his cold smile. Trudy backed away from him, but then the ground disappeared from under her feet. She reached out and the knife . . . oh, the knife! It plunged into her flesh, ripping, tearing, the tip finding her heart and cleaving it in two.

She screamed.

"There, there," a woman soothed. "Settle down. You're in the hospital. Lie back. Are you awake now? Sir, please, you have to step out so that we can attend to her."

"I'm not leaving."

"Sir . . . Mr. Wolfe . . . please."

"No!"

Trudy forced her eyes open to slits and glimpsed him standing at the foot of her bed. He was so far away. They were separated by a white and gray ocean. She lifted one hand. "Levi." Had she spoken? It didn't sound like her.

"Trudy! I'm here."

Was that him? His voice was husky . . . broken. Sighing, she fell back into the darkness.

*

Trudy?

Ethel?

I failed you. I placed you in danger.

I'm sorry about Jay. You knew about him?

Yes. I knew he was different, but I didn't know how sick he was until after I left him. I should have talked to him about his . . . tendencies, but I didn't. I love him, Trudy. He's my son.

I understand.

Do you?

Totally. We're good, Ethel. How's Mike?

Mike will be okay. Mike had his work . . . and his other women. I had Jay. I told myself it was just a phase my boy was going through — wanting to dress up in my clothes and tell me what to buy, what to wear. I failed him, too.

I understand. Ethel, did you guide me to the Stirring Palms? It couldn't have been a coincidence that I ended up there.

I don't believe in coincidences and neither should you. You're a remarkable young woman. Take my hand, dear, and I'll guide you back to where you belong.

*

The world positioned itself under her again. She felt its solidness. Trudy stared at the shadowy room with its silver blinds obscuring a large window. A tray on wheels was near her and a pitcher and plastic cup sat on it. Oh. She was in the hospital and she was incredibly thirsty!

Snatches of conversations returned. Suddenly, she was back in that restroom with Jay Yardley and his knife and his madness. She closed her eyes, blocking out the memory because it made her head pound furiously. Taking a couple of deep, head-clearing breaths, she pried her eyes open again and looked to her left, sensing that she wasn't alone. Levi sat slouched in a chair, his head resting in his hand, his elbow propped on the chair arm, his eyes closed. The lower half of his face was dark with stubble. His clothes were wrinkled. Oh, he looked so uncomfortable!

His chin slipped off his palm and his head fell forward. His whole body jerked and his eyes flew open to stare at her. At first, his gaze was unfocused, but then in the next second he was out of the chair and clutching her hand.

"You're awake!"

"Yes," she croaked out.

"Thank God in heaven." He pressed her palm to his lips and she curled her fingers against his whiskered cheek. His eyes drifted shut for a few seconds and his lips moved as if in prayer against her skin. When he looked at her again, concern swam in the blue depths. "How are you feeling? How's your head?"

Imps played bongos between her temples. "It hurts."

He reached across her, fumbling with something. "I'll call the nurse. Do you remember why you're here? You hit your head on the sink. That motherfucker was—." He turned as a wide beam of light fell into the room. "She's awake," he told someone. "Her head hurts."

"I'm sure it does." Another man stood next to her bed. "Let's take your temperature and get some other vitals." He glanced at Levi. "You'll have to shove over, friend, and let me do my job."

Levi frowned, but let go of her hand. "I'll be right over here, Trudy. I'm not leaving."

"You can believe that," the man said, shaking his head and chuckling. "That's his mantra. 'I'm not leaving!' and everyone on staff has started to chant it with him." He glanced toward Levi and chuckled again as he tightened a blood pressure cuff around her upper arm. "I'm Travis and I'm your nurse for this shift. You hit your head and you have a knife wound on your shoulder, but it's not deep. They stitched you up. You have a concussion, but you're doing great. Just great. Nothing to worry about."

"What time is it?" Trudy asked. It seemed to be very late.

"It's seven thirty."

"At night?"

Travis smiled. "Yes."

"I've been unconscious since this afternoon?"

"Uh . . . no, you were admitted yesterday afternoon."

"Yesterday?" She swallowed and coughed. Her throat and mouth felt like they were fur-lined. "I need some water."

"Certainly. Let me finish taking your blood pressure and I'll let you have a drink of water."

Her eyelids were too heavy to hold up. The blood pressure cuff tightened around her arm. She had been unconscious since yesterday? It felt odd to have no concept of time or of time lost. Levi . . . where was he?

"Levi?"

"I'm right here, Trudy." He stepped to the other side of the bed and filled a plastic cup with ice and water from the pitcher. Selecting an ice chip, he placed it between her lips, smiling faintly as she closed her eyes briefly on a sigh. Then he directed the straw to her mouth. He held the cup while she took several long sips of the cool, bracing water. It chased aside the remnants of fog from her head and moistened her mouth so that she could use her tongue again.

"Go see to Mouse for me," she said, motioning one hand weakly at Levi. "Get some sleep."

"Mouse is okay," Levi said, setting the cup down on the tray where she could reach it. "Mike Yardley is taking care of her."

"Mike?" She swallowed a sob. "Oh, dear. Mike. Jay. Oh, no." Tears welled in her eyes. "Does Mike know about Jay?"

"Yes."

"Where's Jay?"

"In jail. You're safe, Trudy."

She relaxed as Travis bustled around her, marking things on her chart and removing the needle from the back of her hand. Feeling a familiar burning pressure, she shifted. "I need to go to the bathroom."

"You think so?" Travis glanced at Levi. "I'm pulling this curtain for privacy while I remove her catheter."

Mortified, Trudy averted her gaze. She felt Levi's scowl, but he walked to the other side of the room. Travis yanked at the curtains, enclosing the bed with them.

"Just relax," Travis said, lifting the sheet. "You're going to feel a little pull and a slight sting. There. That's it. You still want to use the restroom?"

Trudy nodded, staring at the ceiling, feeling exposed and embarrassed. Travis patted her shoulder.

"Okay. Let me help you sit up. Swing your legs over. That's good. No, don't try to stand yet. Get your bearings first."

She blinked, realizing she was shaking and weak. Her head pounded even more furiously until she thought she might black out. Closing her eyes, she took several deep breaths, trying to force strength into her quivering muscles.

"Are you okay?" Travis asked. "Are you dizzy?"

"Kind of."

"Let me support you. Just lean on me. That's right . . ."

Travis assisted her as she moved with the alacrity of a turtle to the bathroom where she found blessed relief. He waited outside the door with Levi. When she was finished and began shuffling back to the bed, she heard Levi swear under his breath. Then she was lifted off her feet. Gasping, she automatically flung her arms up and around Levi's neck as he carried her to the bed and gently placed her in it.

"Are you okay?" he asked, concern etched on his handsome face.

She bit her lip, finding him damn near irresistible. "Yes. Thanks."

"Well!" Travis glanced from Levi to her and grinned. "Okay, then! Once you eat something and get a little more rest, your strength will come back," he assured her. "I'll have a food tray sent up." Travis glanced at Levi and winked. "Don't leave her, okay?"

Levi sent him a damnation glare, making Travis chuckle as he left the room. Taking Trudy's hand in his, Levi kissed the back of her fingers and closed his eyes on a long, weary sigh.

"I almost got you killed," he whispered. "I shouldn't have brought you here. Quintara was right. You could have died."

Trudy gasped. "Don't say that! It's absolutely not true. You didn't bring me here. I came on my own. Look at me." She waited for him to open his eyes. There was nothing but pain and self-loathing in them and her heart wrenched. "Hey, Wolfe, give me some credit, will you? I handled the situation, and if you and the police hadn't barged in and sent me sprawling, I would have made a clean escape."

"You're incredibly brave," he said. His mouth thinned into a hard line. "He could have grabbed you before you could've escaped and sunk that knife into your heart. And it would've been my fault and it would've fucking destroyed me."

"Stop it!" Irritation surged through her. Then, in the next heartbeat, she fought back tears because he had just revealed the depth of his feelings for her. She gathered in a deep breath before she trusted herself to speak again. "Leave it to you to latch onto the worst scenario. I'm *fine*, Levi. I bumped my head and scratched my arm."

"That's a knife wound. Not a scratch."

"The tip of the knife caught me when he was waving it about. Don't be so dramatic."

"Don't be so cavalier. This is dangerous business, Trudy. You faced a man with a knife who has murdered five women, that we know of."

"And I lived to brag about it," she added, clutching at his shirtsleeve. "We did it! We kicked ass. We caught the bastard!"

A reluctant smile touched his lips. "*You* caught the bastard."

"No, we did. How did you know I was in the bar?"

"We tracked you through your cell phone."

"Brilliant! Did you know it was Jay? Did the last victim identify him?"

"Not exactly. I was able to piece it together. But I was almost too late and I—.

"Wolfe!" she interrupted him.

"What?"

"Shut up and kiss me."

The tension around his mouth faded a little. With a defeated sigh, he leaned over the bed railing and brushed his lips across hers once, twice, and then kissed the tip of her nose.

"That's it?" she asked when he straightened away from her. "That's all you've got?"

"For now. Yes."

She winced against the pain in her head. "Go on back to the RV park and shower and shave and—."

"No." He sat in the chair to drive home his intention. "I'm not leaving. Hopefully, you'll be released tomorrow."

"Levi . . ." she whined.

"No."

"Please?"

"This is where I want to be."

"I'm going to sleep and you have spent enough time watching me sleep." She clasped her hands together and shook them at him in a silent appeal. "Please go get some rest!"

He sighed again, but she felt him waver.

"It's a good thing you're so gorgeously male or I'd kick your stubborn ass," she grumbled, closing her eyes and releasing a long sigh. "You are dismissed for now, but I expect you back here in the morning." She heard his soft chuckle before she drifted off to sleep.

Chapter Eighteen

Loading the fork with a big bite of scrambled eggs and bacon, Trudy held it out to Levi. He shook his head.

"Quit being such an ass and eat this." She kept the fork suspended, refusing to give in. With a roll of his eyes, he leaned forward to accept the bite of her hospital breakfast. "Thank you," she said, giving him a scowl. "I swear, I don't know what I'm going to do with you."

"I have some lewd suggestions, if you're interested," he said with a quirk of an eyebrow. "Anyway, the food is for you. Not for me."

"I'm sure you have had very little to eat. You can have the eggs and bacon. I'll eat the cereal. You can have the coffee. I'll drink the juice. Don't argue with me. Just do it."

"You're bossy this morning." He sat on the edge of the hospital bed and took the fork from her.

"Your bossiness and pissyness are rubbing off on me."

He slanted a narrowed glare at her. "It's nice to know that you think so highly of me."

He shoveled eggs and bacon into his mouth. Trudy shook her head. The man was starving just as she had suspected.

"You should call your parents."

Trudy almost choked on the cereal and milk she had just spooned into her mouth. "Why?" She eyed him, warily.

"Because they're worried about you."

"You . . . you didn't tell them that I was in the hospital, did you?" Her heartbeats slowed.

"No."

She placed a hand to her fluttering heart. "Oh, thank God!"

"Quintara told them for me."

"Oh, crap!" Trudy dropped the spoon, her appetite sufficiently snuffed. "Why? Why did she do that?"

"I asked her to." He raised his dark brows, clearly puzzled by her reaction. "They deserve to know when their daughter's in the hospital, don't they?"

"I'm sure they're worried out of their minds," Trudy said, already picturing her father and mother upset and swearing that they would talk her out of any more of this crazy psychic work.

"All the more reason to call them." He finished the last of the bacon and eggs and reached for a triangle of buttered toast.

"Hand me my phone," she said, telling herself to get it over with. She frowned at Levi and took the cell phone from him. "You shouldn't have troubled them with this."

"Troubled them?" He shook his head and went to stand by the window to look at the bright morning while he sipped coffee from a Styrofoam cup. "They love you, Trudy. You're lucky to have people who love you."

His simple statement made her wince with guilt. She studied his profile and wondered if he would ever accept her love or allow himself to love her. With a sigh, she punched in her parents' number in Tulsa. There will be crying, she thought, and the moment she heard her mother's voice, she sobbed.

*

Outside Trudy's hospital room, Levi paced in the wide hallway. He stopped to stare at the door to her room. She was in there crying. Sobbing on the phone with her parents. He had left her because he couldn't bear watching her distress. God, it was his fault. He'd almost gotten her killed. Stupid, stupid, stupid.

His cell phone buzzed in his trouser pocket and he pulled it out, staring at the screen for a few seconds before his eyes focused. It was Quintara.

"She's crying," he said, not bothering with civility.

"Why?" Quintara asked.

"She's talking to her parents on the phone."

"Oh, well. That's to be expected."

"Is it?" He shook his head, not following that reasoning. "Why?"

"Because . . . well, it's her parents and she knows they're worried and she's female."

"I almost got her killed. You know that, don't you?"

"Is she being released from the hospital today?"

"Yes. We're waiting for the doctor to sign the papers."

"When is she coming home?"

"In day or two, I guess. I don't want her driving that damned motor home."

"Well, good luck with that. She's a grown woman and I imagine she'll do as she pleases, whether you approve or not. Levi, stop pacing."

He stopped, wondering how she knew.

"Listen to me. Get off the guilt train! The chances of Trudy ever confronting a serial killer in person again are slim. It was a fluke. How many psychics do you know who have actually seen a serial killer whom isn't already behind bars? Hmmm? Answer me."

"One. Trudy."

"That's right."

"You didn't want her to work on this," he reminded her. "You said we should start with something less dangerous."

"She handled herself admirably from what you've told me. She kneed that bastard in the gonads and poked him in the eye."

"It could have so easily gone all wrong."

"Yes, but it didn't. Remove your sackcloth and ashes. You should be rejoicing instead of moping around!"

He ran a hand through his hair. "Yes, you're right. I don't know what to do with these feelings I have for her."

"You'll sort them out, dear. They're normal. Maybe not for you, but they're normal for most people."

He spied Tom Sinclair striding down the hall. "Thanks, Quintara. I have to go. I'll keep you posted." Ending the call, he shoved the phone into his trouser pocket and met Sinclair in the hall in front of Trudy's room.

"She's talking to her parents," he said.

"They're here?" Sinclair asked.

"No. On the phone."

"Oh." Sinclair nodded. "How's she doing? They're releasing her today, right?"

"Yeah." Levi angled forward to see into the room. Trudy was off the phone. She was blowing her nose in a tissue and her eyes were red-rimmed. "Trudy?"

She looked at him.

"Tom Sinclair's out here."

She motioned for him to come in. Levi stepped aside and let Sinclair enter first. He was right on his heels.

"Hi, Tom. Thanks for dropping by." She nodded toward the big bouquet of flowers sitting on the window sill. "And thank the department for those, will you?"

"Sure thing. How are you feeling?" Sinclair gave her a worried look. "Is your headache gone yet?"

"Yes, almost. I was talking to my folks and . . . well, I'm okay now." She smiled brightly and her gaze flickered from Tom to Levi. "We're waiting for the doctor to sign my release papers and then I'm outta here."

"Going back to Tulsa?"

She glanced from him to Levi and a shadow of regret darkened her eyes. He knew just how she felt. "Yes."

Sinclair rested a hand on top of hers. "We got him, Trudy. Way to go."

"It was a group effort."

A scoffing sound escaped Levi before he could stop it. Trudy scowled at him and he shrugged. "Jay Yardley would still be on the streets of Key West if not for Trudy."

"And you," Trudy said. "I don't know why you keep acting as if you did nothing, Levi. You figured out who he was probably at about the same time I did."

"Your discovery that the killer and Zelda were the same person put us on the right track." Levi crossed his arms and stood at the foot of the bed. He felt like a sentry, guarding his woman from all suitors. The image brought a smile to his lips. His woman. Wonder what Trudy would think of that?

"Did you see Captain Phillips on TV this morning?" Sinclair asked.

"No." Trudy looked at Levi and he shook his head.

"He gave you and Wolfe credit for helping identify Yardley as the serial killer."

"That's nice of him, isn't it, Levi?" Trudy asked, sending him a *be gracious* look.

He nodded, not feeling magnanimous since he hadn't seen the TV news and didn't know what Phillips had actually said about them. "Why weren't you interviewed?" he asked Sinclair. "It's your case."

Sinclair shrugged. "You know how it goes. When the boss wants to address the media, then everybody else stands aside. Yardley has confessed to everything. He's actually proud of it."

"Sick fucker," Levi growled, and Sinclair nodded.

The detective turned back to Trudy. "I have to run. I just wanted to thank you. If you're ever in Key West again, Trudy, look me up."

"I will. Thanks, Tom."

Levi raised his brows at the lack of invitation extended to him by Sinclair. Tom leaned toward Trudy and kissed her temple . . . the side of her face that wasn't bruised. Levi looked away, stabbed by jealousy even though he knew it was unreasonable. Trudy wasn't enamored with Sinclair, but he still had to fight the urge to tell the detective to keep his paws off her. He realized he'd fisted his hands at his sides and he was grinding his teeth.

Sinclair stuck out his hand to Levi and he shook it. "Thanks, Wolfe. Be seeing you."

"Right." Levi forced himself to be civil. "Thanks for everything. I'm glad we could help. I'll send you a final report for your files in a few days."

As Sinclair left, a doctor, wearing scrubs and round eyeglasses, came in. He smiled cordially at Levi and then devoted his attention to Trudy.

"Hi, there." He grasped Trudy's hand. "I'm Dr. Dawson. How are you feeling?"

"I'm fine," Trudy assured him. "I'm ready to check out of here."

Dr. Dawson patted her shoulder. "A nurse will be in to get your signature on some forms and to give you the prescriptions that have been written for you."

"What are they for?" Trudy asked.

"Muscle relaxants and high voltage Advil to take the edge off any headaches you might experience."

"When can I drive home?"

"You don't have to drive," Levi said. "She can fly home. I can hire someone to drive the RV to Oklahoma for you."

"No, *I'm* driving the RV to Tulsa," she said, sending a quelling glare toward him. He fought back the urge to bark orders at her. *Infuriating woman!*

"Tomorrow is soon enough," the doctor said. "If you develop a headache that won't subside after you take pain medication, come back to the hospital immediately."

"Will do."

He patted her shoulder. "Have a safe drive home."

"I will. Thanks."

He nodded at Levi and left. Levi studied Trudy for a few moments, wondering what tactic to take to bend her to his way of thinking.

"Why don't I hire a private jet to fly you back to Tulsa? I can arrange for someone to drive your RV."

"A private jet? Get real, Wolfe." Her green eyes widened as if he'd offered her a magic carpet ride. "Look, I know you mean well, but I'm going back to Stirring Palms and – What?" She frowned at him because he was shaking his head.

He drew in a breath, knowing she wouldn't like his next news. "The motor home isn't there anymore."

She folded her arms. "What have you done with it, Levi?"

"I moved it." He held up his hands. "It's parked at the Hyatt."

"The Hyatt Hotel? Why?"

"Because that's where I'm taking you. We're staying in a suite there."

"And what have you done with Mouse?"

"She's waiting for you at the Hyatt." He let out a long breath when she smiled a little. She was warming to the idea.

"Oh." She pushed out her bottom lip. "You could have asked me first if I wanted to stay in a hotel."

"Yes, I could have if I wanted to argue about it," he allowed. "But I didn't. Trudy, I want to spend a day and night with you totally relaxed. We deserve it."

A slow smile lit up her face and made his heart do a back flip "Yes, I suppose we do."

*

The hotel suite was luxurious. It was, hands down, the swankiest one Trudy had ever been in. There was a sitting room, a small dining area with French doors that opened onto an outdoor balcony that provided a breathtaking view of the ocean, a big bedroom, and a spa-like bathroom.

Trudy fell back onto the king-sized bed and patted Mouse's round head as she listened to soft music coming from speakers placed strategically around the suite. Propping her head in her hand, she looked toward the bathroom where Levi stood in front of one of the sinks. Peering in the mirror, he carefully and efficiently dragged a razor through the shaving cream on his cheek.

He wore a white terrycloth robe provided by the Hyatt, loosely belted at the waist. She wore one, too. Warmth spread through her and she wanted to purr and then growl as her gaze drifted over him. In a hotel suite with Mr. Wolfe. Lucky, lucky girl. His gaze moved sideways, catching her watching him.

"Enjoying the show?" he asked, swishing the razor in the water-filled sink.

"You look sexy," she said, smiling.

He chuckled and shook his head. "That bump on your noggin scrambled your brains, sweetheart."

"False modesty doesn't become you, Levi. You know you're hot." She fell back on the bed to stare at the ceiling. "Women grovel all over you. You say, 'panties' and they strip them off."

"What drugs did they give you at the hospital? I want some."

She laughed, lightly, "Are you hungry?"

"Yes. Order us something."

"What?"

"Surprise me."

She pushed up from the bed and went to the dining table. After consulting the menu and trying not to notice the outrageous prices, she ordered two cheeseburgers, shoestring potatoes, and a pitcher of lemonade. Moving out to the balcony, she sat in one of the chairs and gazed at the ocean. A few minutes later, Levi strolled out to join her, using a towel to wipe away the vestiges of shaving cream from his face and neck. He looked more rested and less like a man who had been to hell and back.

"I'm going to tell you something that's going to blow your mind," he said.

Trudy was starting to smile, but froze. Uh-oh. "Don't keep me in suspense."

"Ethel contacted Gregory."

For a few moments, she couldn't get her mind around what he meant. "Ethel and Gregory? How? Why?"

"I don't know how . . ." He chuckled and stood behind her chair. He placed his hands on her shoulders and massaged the bunched muscles there. It felt so good that she closed her eyes and let her head loll forward. "After I had experienced Mandy's murder, Gregory spoke to me and said that Ethel was with him. He said she was worried and that she had lovely dimples."

Trudy's eyes popped open. "No! Really?"

His fingers pressed into the tops of her shoulders and his thumbs moved in small circles against her nape. "And he told me to check my cell phone. Of course, when I did, I found your message."

"Gregory and Ethel joined forces to put you on the right path?"

"Looks that way." He placed a light kiss on her bruised temple.

"Meanwhile, they left me in the lurch."

She leaned forward and he kneaded the muscles along her spine. He was really good at this masseuse thing! She wondered how many women he'd practiced on to become so adept at it. Another thought occurred to her and she released a short bark of laughter.

"Leviticus David Wolfe, you've even turned Ethel's head! Instead of assisting *me*, she found a way to help *you*!"

"And she helped you, Trudy Louise Tucker." His lips touched her cheek and then he nipped her earlobe playfully, sending a tingle of pleasure racing down her neck and arms. "I don't understand it either. Maybe she was so close to Jay that she couldn't directly intervene." His fingers stopped circling for a few moments before continuing their firm but gentle pressure against her neck muscles. "I don't know how it all works over there."

"Over there?"

"The place they now inhabit," he explained.

"Ethel guided me to that RV park. She wanted me there. She wanted us there."

His lips slid along the side of her neck and his tongue wet a patch of skin on her shoulder. "I'm just very, very grateful you're here with me and in one lovely piece." He nuzzled the back of her ear.

Someone knocked on the door and Levi jerked his attention from her. "Ah! Food!" He strode to the door and threw it open to allow a food cart to be wheeled into the room by a uniformed waiter. "Smells great. What did you order?"

"Cheeseburgers and fries," Trudy answered, coming back inside the suite.

His gaze bounced to her. "You're kidding."

"You have something against cheeseburgers?"

"No." He chuckled as he went into the bedroom and came back with his wallet. He handed the waiter a tip and saw him out. "It's okay," he said, lifting the covers off the food. "In fact, it's perfect. Only you would order cheeseburgers and fries at the Hyatt in Key West when you're given carte blanche." He stared at the pitcher of lemonade and grinned. "No dessert? No Key lime pie?"

"Well, I noticed there are some chocolates and fruit in that basket over there, so I thought . . . since they're free we might as well eat them for dessert." She shrugged.

He glanced at the complimentary basket of goodies and shook his head. Hooking an arm around her waist, he hauled her to him. "You need to be spoiled, Trudy Tucker."

"Spoiled? Why?" She pressed her mouth to his and bit down lightly on his lower lip. "Want to work up a real appetite?"

He grinned against her grin. "Let's eat."

"Oh, piffle!"

"Piffle?" Chuckling, he moved away from her. He placed the food on the table, a burger for her and one for him. "Sit down. This is exactly what I need."

She settled in one of the chairs and took a bite of the burger. It was thick and juicy and she realized she was ravenous. The broth, Jell-O, and cereal at the hospital just hadn't cut it. She swallowed the first bite and wiped her mouth with a linen napkin that had an H embroidered on it.

He dabbed at his mouth with his napkin. "I've liked being with you."

She stared at him, almost afraid to breathe. "I've liked being with you," she allowed, dreading what would come next. Was this the brush off?

"I've never been in a monogamous relationship. Have you?"

Trudy sat back in the chair and tried to stop her heart from throwing itself at her ribcage. "Not really. I mean, I dated a guy for about four months a couple of years ago and – well, I assumed we were monogamous."

"Did you two live together?"

"No. It wasn't that serious."

He enjoyed the burger and fries for a few minutes, leaving Trudy to twist in the wind. How could he eat after firing that volley at her? If he didn't say something else very soon she was going to hurl the rest of her burger at him.

"I like the idea of having one with you," he said, glancing at her from under his sooty lashes.

Trudy resisted the urge to shove her index fingers into her ears and wiggle them in a show of getting them back to working order because she really wasn't sure she'd heard him right.

He held up a cautionary hand. "But you'll have to cut me some slack because I don't know the rules of conduct."

Realizing that she was holding her breath and about to pass out, Trudy released a long sigh. "I think we make the rules as we go along. Levi, what brought this on?"

He glanced out at the ocean and his jaw hardened. "The thought of you being with another man makes me want to haul off and beat the shit out of someone and I'm trying very hard to keep my brawling days behind me."

Her eyes widened at his vehement admission. She knew he saw red every time she was around Tom Sinclair, but . . . wow! He had a huge possessive streak running through him. "Brawling days? You used to fight?"

One corner of his mouth kicked up. "Daily."

"Was this recently?"

"No, in school. Well, I did have some bar fights in my mid-twenties . . ." He shrugged. "But nothing in the past two or three years. When I was a kid, it was either fight or be the bitch."

When she winced, he made a swipe with his hand.

"But back to the present!" He pinned her with his beautiful blues. "What do you think? You want to give it a whirl?"

She managed a nonchalant shrug, even though her heart was full to bursting. "I'm game. But you should be clear on what this mean."

"It means you won't let another man touch you."

She nodded, finding it charming that he was so focused on her behavior instead of his own. "What about oral sex? Is that cheating?"

"Oral sex . . ." He gave her a sidelong glance. "No, not really."

"Why not?"

"There's no penetration . . . exactly." Confusion flitted across his face as if he didn't even believe what he'd just said.

"Okay, say I walked into a hotel room and I saw some woman giving you a blow job. Would you feel guilty? Embarrassed? Or would you just zip up and introduce me to the woman kneeling before you?"

He arched a brow at her. "I'd feel guilty and maybe embarrassed. So, what you're saying is that I shouldn't do anything that I wouldn't feel perfectly fine having you see me do."

"Exactly. Same goes for me," she hastened to add so that he wouldn't feel picked on. "If you get in a bad way, you can masturbate, but I'd rather you let me take care of you."

He looked away from her quickly and drew in a quick breath. Trudy knew she'd just stumbled upon another "No Trespassing" sign. She closed her eyes and tried to stop herself from questioning him, but failed.

"What's wrong? You have something against masturbating?"

His eyes slid sideways toward her. "Not really."

"But?" she asked. He pressed his lips together and ignored her. She walked her fingers across the table and rested her hand on his, drawing his attention fully to her. "What are you thinking about? Don't trust me enough to tell me?"

"It's not a question of trust—."

"Oh, yes, it is," she interrupted him. "It's all about trust. I don't know why and you may never tell me why you're so secretive about what haunts you, what happened to make you so guarded, but I know *for certain* you don't trust me."

He closed his eyes for a second and pulled his hand out from under hers. "It's nothing, really. When I was sixteen I was caught masturbating by a school counselor."

"And you were punished for it?"

"Yes." The smile he managed was neither pleasant nor amused. "Three grown men held me down and I was beaten with a thick paddle. Really, it was more like a club. They broke my collarbone, my right wrist, and three ribs."

Her hand flew to her gaping mouth. "My God!"

"It actually turned out to be a good thing because one of my busted ribs punctured my right lung and they had to rush me to the hospital before I croaked. That caused the police to investigate and the school was shut down."

She let her hand drop slowly from her mouth. "Did your parents know what was happening there?"

He nodded. "I told them every time I was allowed a phone call, but I guess they thought I was exaggerating. Or that's what they wanted to believe." He waved a hand, batting away the subject. "Who knows? I was allowed to come home after I was released from the hospital. My mother had been diagnosed with cancer by then."

Trudy breathed through the pain she felt for him, since he obviously refused to feel any of it himself. "Where was this school?"

"That one was in the Dominican Republic." He gave a careless shrug.

She couldn't stand it. She had to touch him, so she scrambled from the chair, went around the table, and sat in his lap. Looping her arms around his neck, she hugged him, rubbing her cheek against his.

"What's this all about?" he asked with a mixture of humor and puzzlement.

That he had to ask her told her how void his life had been of tenderness and compassion. "This is because you deserve a hug," she said, kissing his forehead and breathing in the intoxicating scent of him. She pulled aside his shirt and kissed his collarbone. "Imagining what you must have gone through makes me feel ill, Levi."

"And that's why there's no point in telling you any of this shit." He leaned back to capture her gaze. "It doesn't do either of us any good."

"You're wrong about that," she said, running her hands through his hair and admiring the inky waves. "Shutting me out only makes me feel farther apart from you. And I want to feel close to you." She kissed him and let her lips linger on his for a few moments. "So, we're going to be a couple?"

"I think we already are, aren't we?" He settled his hands on her waist and scooted the chair back to give them more room.

"I suppose. You think you'll be any good at fidelity?"

"I don't know. I hope so." He gave her a quick kiss and lifted his arm to check his Rolex. "Right now I need to call my office."

"Oh. Okay." She pushed up from his lap and moved aside so that he could stand. He dropped a kiss on the tip of her nose.

"Thanks. Tell you what, put on your bathing suit and we'll go to the beach in a little while. Then, later, I'll show you how I close out a case. We'll go over our notes and everything. We need to compile a final report and send it to the police."

"Sounds great," she said, although she wasn't that enthused. She sighed as he strode from the room. Mister Moody Blues was back.

He wanted a monogamous relationship because he didn't want her to have sex with anyone but him. That was it in a nutshell. If she had to make a bet, she'd wager that he wasn't at all sure he could follow through with his end of it. Well, she had today and tonight to make him understand that his faithfulness to her could not be in question. *Trying* to not be with another woman just wouldn't cut it.

Uh-uh. Nope. No friggin' way.

Chapter Nineteen

Opening her eyes, Trudy stared at a shaft of starlight falling across the wide bed. Where was she? Oh, right. The Hyatt. She squinted through the dusk at the alarm clock beside the bed. Seven-thirty! She'd been asleep for almost three hours!

The walk on the beach and then the work on the Yardley case – sorting through notes and photos, and compiling a comprehensive file – had worn her out. She'd decided to take a nap before dinner while Levi caught up with more e-mails and phone calls.

Speaking of Levi . . . where was he? She sat up, her gaze darting toward the living/dining room area.

"I'm over here, baby."

Levi's raspy voice emerged from a shadowy corner of the large bedroom. Whipping around, Trudy saw him sitting in a wing chair.

"What are you doing?"

"I went down to the gym for a run on the treadmill. And I've been watching you sleep, which seems to have become a hobby of mine."

She stretched and let out a groan. "That's a fascinating hobby you've got there. Sorry I slept for so long." She waited a minute, thinking he'd join her on the bed, but he seemed to be glued to the chair. Scooting off the bed, she went to him and he opened up his arms to receive her. He wore nothing but a pair of dark blue workout shorts. She sat in his lap and looped her arms around his neck and his circled her waist. His skin was warm and damp, his muscles more defined. He *had* been exercising!

"You talked to Mike Yardley?" she said.

"That's right."

"How is he?"

"Devastated and confused."

"Poor man."

"He's selling out and moving."

"He told me he thought he had a buyer for the Stirring Palms."

"Yeah, he does." He tightened his arms around her. "He had no clue about Jay."

"Jay fooled a lot of people."

"He's confessed to everything. He thinks he's a fucking genius. He'll be a fascinating case study for psychologists and psychiatrists."

"Maybe material for a new book by you?"

He shrugged. "Maybe."

"I could tell that he thinks he's superior to most of us foolish mortals," she said, her voice dripping with the scorn and contempt she felt for Jay Yardley.

He nodded. "I've been thinking . . . "

She stiffened a little. When he said that, she never knew what to expect.

"After you knew the score with Jay, why didn't you play dumb and get the hell out of there?"

She leaned back to witness the worry lingering in his eyes and wished he would let it go. "About the time I puzzled it all out, he could tell I knew," she said, making her tone light and matter-of-fact. "I thought it would be safer to shine him on until you and the cops could get there, rather than try to make a run for it on my own."

He rested his forehead against hers and rocked his head back and forth, closing his eyes. "So dangerous, baby."

"Shhh. Let's not rehash it again." She smoothed her hands through his hair where it was damp at his temples. "Have you booked your flight to Atlanta?"

He nodded and then stood up with her in his arms. A yelp escaped her and she let go of a laugh.

"Levi! Wait . . . I can walk!"

He laid her on the bed and then slid in beside her. "I don't want to talk about leaving you." Unknotting the belt at her waist, he pushed the robe off her shoulders, exposing her body to his heated gaze. "I like being here like this with you."

She bit her lower lip, touched by his admission as she took in the beauty of his face. He kissed her lightly on the lips and then reclined on his back. She cuddled close to his side. He really was the most handsome man she'd ever met. The bridge of his nose was straight and his mouth was wide and . . . oh, what he could do with it! Her gaze moved to his hands, resting on his flat stomach. Those hands were magical, too.

"Can I ask you something?"

"Shoot."

"You never met Jay before the arrest, right?"

He looked at her from the corner of his eyes. "I saw him a couple of times from the cabin window, but I never actually met him or talked to him."

"If you had shaken his hand, would you have sensed that he was our murderer?"

"I doubt it."

"But you knew that the guy at the motel had been the one looking at us through the sliding glass doors that night. Oh! And there was that cowboy at the bar you bumped into and you knew he'd been with Zelda."

"Occasionally, I can get flashes of insight, but serial killers are closed off. Their evil surfaces when they're contemplating a kill. Most of them compartmentalize their lives and open up that trapdoor to the depravity in their souls when they have a prey in their sights. That's how Jay fooled everyone."

"If I can determine who is a murderer by touching mug shots, does that mean I'm touch sensitive, too?"

A frown line creased his forehead for a few seconds. "You're concentrating on the photos, but what you're really doing is acting like a beacon for the killer's psyche to navigate to and open up to you. These men you're accessing are still alive. Correct?"

"Yes."

"Okay, so you're concentrating and reaching out with your mind, and when a murderer reaches back, you make a connection. *You're* the mind reader. Not me."

She smiled and looked down the length of his tautly muscled physique, then smiled and wondered if he could read her mind now. "Changing the subject . . . but do you know what I love most about your body?"

"I'll take a wild guess. Is it between my legs?"

She slapped his shoulder playfully. "No! I mean . . . I like that, but it's not what I was thinking about. I'm glad you're tattoo free. It's such a joy to see a beautiful male body with no graffiti on it."

"I'm glad you approve." He shifted onto his side and propped his head in his hand.

"No old girlfriends' names, no dragons, hearts, knives, guns, skulls, and cryptic messages. Why do people think they have to stamp images of their lives onto their bodies as if their minds are incapable of holding onto and recalling memories without visual reminders or clues?"

"Further evidence of the 'dumbing down' of America? All I know is that there's very little of my life that I would want to commemorate," he said, dryly.

His simple statement sent an arrow through her heart. She kissed him, then let her lips skim down the center of his chest. He smelled musky and tasted salty. When he groaned appreciatively, she continued her gentle assault and gripped the waistband of his shorts. She pulled them down along with his briefs and slid them off his legs and feet. His cock bobbed up, growing stiffer by the second. She gripped its base and her gaze met Levi's. His eyes were on her, dark and hungry. He stared at her for a few heart-stopping moments before he fell onto his back, giving himself over to her.

She smiled and bestowed a long, lush lick. He clutched the sheet at his sides as she took him inside her mouth and sucked hard, letting him slip in and out. He groaned and squeezed his eyes shut even tighter. She took him in deeper and ran her teeth lightly along his satiny skin. A low growl rumbled from him and he clutched at her hair and moved her head, directing her mouth to take more of him. She flexed her throat to accommodate him and then she held still to allow him to revel in it.

"Christ, that feels good," he murmured. "You don't have to be so gentle. It won't break."

Smiling against him, she moved faster, her tongue swirling across his hot skin. She sucked on the glistening tip. She heard his breath grow choppy as his erection thickened and lengthened. He was getting close. She tongued the throbbing vein that ran down the length of his cock and he shuddered.

"That's enough," he whispered, his voice strained, urgent. "Have to get a condom." He reached for one lying on top of the bedside table, but Trudy snatched it from his fingers.

"I'll do it," she said, tearing open the foil packet and removing the tacky contraceptive. She pinched the top of it and rolled it onto his lovely, large, erect penis.

"Do you remember the first woman you made love to?" she asked, shrugging out of the hotel's complimentary robe and flinging it aside.

"I told you already."

"Lizzie?" She gave him an *oh really?* look. "You were in love with her?"

He frowned. "You want to talk about this *now?*"

Laughing a little, she draped herself on top of him and kissed his lips. His hands roamed her body, over her butt and up to her shoulders. "I was just wondering because I'm going to make love to you." She smiled and arched her brows at his slight frown. "Don't worry. You don't have to reciprocate in kind. But there's a difference between intercourse and making love. You know that, right?"

He glanced up as if seeking divine guidance and then heaved a weary sigh. "Yes, Trudy. I know that most women think there is a big difference. I'm not dense."

She wanted to bite a plug out of him for being so arrogant and clueless, but she refrained. "You're not dense, but you also don't know what you're talking about. Women don't *think* there's a difference, we *know* there's a difference. And lucky you are going to experience that right now."

Not waiting for a response or to see the next expression on his way-too-handsome face, she kissed his parted lips again and then his throat and along his collarbone – his broken and mended collarbone. Even thinking about the horror he'd experienced being beaten like a defenseless animal made her redouble her desire to make him feel treasured and loved. She wanted desperately for him to share the tenderness and compassion banked in her heart just for him.

Taking her sweet time, she caressed his body with light fingertips and left little wet spots on his skin with her lips and tongue. She blew softly on the nest of curls below his navel and grinned when his cock inched even higher against his stomach. She ran her hands down his taut, muscled, hair-roughened thighs and left kisses there.

"I love your body," she whispered. "And I love your mind. I see your heart, Levi, and I want to know it more intimately. I want to know *you.* And I want you to know me like no one has ever known me."

Just when she was about to work her way back up his beautifully toned and muscled torso, he sat up and took her face in his hands. He shook his head slowly and she saw him swallow – hard.

"Something wrong?" She could barely manage a whisper. The look he gave her – as if she was the most gorgeous, most precious thing in the world – made her heart swell. He brought her mouth to his in a kiss that was tender at first. Then he parted his lips and his tongue swept through her mouth in a show of dominance. He was taking over and she decided to let him because, truthfully, her body demanded it.

"This love-making . . ." he said, his voice husky and his eyes smoking. "I think it's supposed to be mutual."

She nodded, struck mute by the desire flooding through her at the sound of his sexy voice and the clear intent in his eyes.

"Okay, then I should participate. You can't expect me to lie here like a statue." He gripped her waist and in a quick move that never got old, he had her on her back and his mouth was on her breast. One of his legs settled between hers and he rubbed against her. She was damp with desire.

He hooked his ankles with hers and forced her legs further apart. He reached down and guided the head of his penis to her portal, but he didn't enter her. Instead he shifted his hips, rubbing against her as he bent his head and his tongue wrapped around her nipple and tugged.

"Oh, God," she whispered, smiling to herself at how he had so skillfully turned the tables on her. "Levi, please." The feelings were so intense that it was hard for her to form words.

"I want to please," he whispered, his voice gruff and raspy. "That's all I want to do. To please. To show you what you mean to me."

She had to see his face. Clutching at his hair, she pulled his mouth away from her breast and stared into his beautiful blues. He knitted his brows, silently asking her what she was looking for, what she wanted from him.

"I want you inside me," she said, unable to think of anything else but to have him fill her, possess her wholly and totally. The tender, tremulous longing for him was almost more than she could bear. She quivered inside and out. "Now!"

"Gladly." He moved slowly, giving her inch by slow inch of him, stretching her, making her feel every inner muscle, every nuance of his invasion, his gaze never releasing hers. "This is mine," he said, rocking his hips and thrusting deeper. "You are mine. Say it, Trudy."

"I'm yours," she whispered, kissing him, circling his tongue with hers. His words thrilled her. She released his hair and clutched at his shoulders and back, needing him to move, to drive in and out of her, to make her come.

Resting his forehead on hers, he pulled out of her, all the way. She felt bereft and her inner muscles clutched and flexed. He closed his eyes for a few seconds and when he opened them again passion burned brightly, fanning her flames higher and higher. With a quick intake of breath, he shifted and drove into her.

"Oh, yes," she said, her voice lifting along with her hips.

He stopped, not moving other than his chest rising and falling with his rapid breathing. "Again?" he asked.

"Yes!"

He withdrew and then plunged into her again, showing no mercy. His momentum lifted her hips off the bed once more and she grabbed his upper arms and held on. Oh. Oh! Her body clutched at him as the glorious tension tightened deep inside her where he was, where he seemed to grow and stretch her.

"Again?" he whispered, his breath stirring the damp curls on her forehead.

"Yes!" She almost screamed the word because she was building . . . on the brink.

He slipped one arm beneath her back and his other hand curved under her knee, hiking her leg up, angling her sideways a little. And then he plunged deep, impossibly deep, and something wild and carnal burst within her and she cried out until her throat ached and her breath sawed in and out of her burning lungs.

"That's right, baby," he rasped near her ear. "Let go. Let go!"

He increased the tempo, driving in and out while he held her gaze. As her climax diminished, she closed her eyes on a long sigh. Then he stilled and took her face in one hand.

"Look at me, Tru. Look at me!"

She stared into his dark sapphire eyes.

"See me," he rasped. "Feel me."

"I do," she breathed.

"Say my name. Say it!"

"Levi!"

"Keep your eyes open. You always want to know more about me. Know this. This is *you* owning *me*." He drew in a chest-expanding breath and moved slightly inside her. The infinitesimal movement sent spokes of burning pleasure out from her core to her extremities.

Staring at him in wonder, she realized he was letting her see him fall apart. Fall apart for her. He let go of her face and braced himself above her on stiffened, muscle rippling arms. Parting his lips on a sigh of sublime surrender, he gave a little shake of his head and gritted his teeth. A muscle fluttered in his jaw. His body grew hotter and harder against hers. A crease appeared between his brows and his eyes were unfocused, a hazy, soft blue she couldn't recall ever seeing before. He shook his head again as if it was all suddenly too much to bear and she knew he was on the brink and that he was beyond rational thought.

She ran her hands down his sides and hooked her ankles at the base of his spine. He was all feeling, all hers – his whole being reduced to the part of him buried inside of her. The veins in his neck stood out and he shuddered and pumped wildly inside of her. Then he stilled as his release came.

"God, God, God." It was a moaning, low chant. He rocked his hips forward in one final climax that made her sex clutch hungrily for him, tighten around him. "*Fuck*, Trudy!"

Trudy felt tears sting her eyes from the raw rapture of Levi Wolfe. Clinging to him, she fought back more tears. Who knew that loving someone so much could almost hurt?

His breath soughed in his throat and his lips were soft against hers. He sucked gently on her upper lip and smiled. "This mouth. Jesus God, I can't get enough of your pretty, pouting mouth." He rested on his elbows and looked at her, pushing a few locks of her hair out of her eyes and off her forehead. "Did you see what you do to me?" he asked, a thread of desperation in his voice. "This is how it feels for me every time I'm with you. Every single time."

She didn't know what to say, how to thank him for the unexpected gift he'd just given her, so she kissed him, deeply and ardently.

"I want you to know that this is new for me," he said against her lips. "You're beauty and light and everything good in my life, Tru."

The sweet pleasure of his words overwhelmed her, humbled her, overjoyed her. "It's the same for me," she spoke against his mouth.

He lifted his head to meet her gaze and gave her the lopsided smile she had come to love so much. "And as much as I hate to admit you're right . . . I did feel the difference."

She gave him a smacking kiss. "Proving once again that you're not just a pretty face."

"Exactly. And neither are you." His lips touched hers, softly, lovingly as he eased himself out of her and fell sideways onto the mattress.

Trudy flung one leg over his hip and pressed her face against his chest. He ran a hand up and down, from her nape to her backside, stroking, caressing. His fingertips brushed over the square bandage that covered the stitches from the knife wound.

"Does this hurt?" he asked.

"Not at all."

"Sick motherfucker," he growled.

"Shhh." Trudy closed her eyes. He had lowered his shields and let her see the effect she had on him . . . the power she could wield over him . . . the ability he had given her to hurt him if she so desired, trusting that she wouldn't. She had seen the once-shattered, now pieced-together heart of him.

"When is your flight?" She felt his heart kick.

"Tomorrow, mid-morning. But it's still today, so let's take a shower. I'll wash you and you can wash me and then I'm going to bury myself inside you again and I might just fucking stay there forever."

"Sounds like a plan," she said, then jumped up and raced him to the bathroom.

*

The VIP airport lounge was quiet, although there were six other people there besides Trudy and Levi. A woman was getting a chair massage from the masseuse and an older couple read sections of USA Today. Two men in business suits sat enthralled with their netbooks and a businesswoman listened with closed eyes to her iPod.

Sitting side by side on a two-cushion couch tucked into a corner and partially obscured by a pillar, Trudy looked at Levi. His features were tense as he checked messages on his cell phone. He seemed distant, already gone from her. Reaching over, she covered the cell phone screen, making him look at her instead.

"Hey."

"Hey," he rejoined.

"I'm going to miss you."

He released a short, choppy breath. "Oh, Christ, Trudy."

"We'll call each other," she assured him. "We'll text each other. We'll e-mail each other."

"Right," he said, a faint smile touching his mouth but not quite making it to his eyes. "I don't know how I'm going to handle a long-distance relationship. I'm not cut out for it."

"You haven't had one yet. Let's give it a try before we throw in the towel."

"I'm not throwing in the towel," he said, emphatically.

She kissed his frowning mouth. "We'll see each other again soon, right? We'll catch up on our business back home and then we'll make time to visit each other."

"Right," he agreed again, but he still looked uncertain.

Trudy sighed. How many times had he been sent away by people who were supposed to love him? "I'm looking forward to you visiting me in Tulsa. You can see my home and meet my folks."

His eyebrows shot up. "Meet your parents?"

"Well, of course, And my sister and brother and their families."

"Hmmm." He stroked his chin that was darkened by stubble and grinned. He hadn't taken time to shave because he'd wanted to spend every possible minute in bed with her. "I've never met a girl's family before."

Leaning back to get a better look at him, Trudy realized he meant it. "No kidding?"

"No kidding."

"Don't worry. You'll bowl them over."

"Even though I'm a medium? And a show-off?"

"Oh, they won't care about that. They'll only be interested in how you treat me."

"That's nice. That's how it should be."

"And I'll visit you in Atlanta. Especially on your birthday." She ran her fingertips down the lapel of his dark blue jacket. He was flying today as a businessman in a suit, black shirt, and the dark tie with the yellow flecks in it. She wondered if he'd go straight to the office when he landed.

"I don't celebrate my birthday, Tru."

"Oh?" She regarded him with mild surprise. "Well, I do. I celebrate it in a big, big way."

"You do?" A smile teased the corners of his wide mouth.

"Yes. From this year on, I do." She grabbed his tie and pulled him closer to her to whisper in his ear. "And I have a very special gift for you. I'll tell you what it is now so that you can look forward to receiving it when I visit you in Atlanta."

"Okay. Tell me." His voice had roughened and become huskier. She was getting to him.

"Well, for your birthday I will be on . . ." She lowered her voice to barely a sound. "Birth control." Then she leaned away from him to catch his reaction. His eyes sparkled with immediate interest and a slow, sexy smile claimed his lips. "You like?"

"Yes, I like that very much. In fact, that might be the best birthday gift I will ever receive." His mouth warmed hers in a slow, sucking kiss. His arm came around her and he caressed her back, revealed by the cut of her peplum blouse. "Skin on skin."

A delectable shiver of anticipation feathered up her spine and she wondered if he could feel it. When he deepened the kiss and she felt his heart kick against the palm of her hand resting on his chest, she had her answer. "You're going to miss me, aren't you?" she asked, not really needing his reply, but wanting it.

"Like shadows miss light." His voice was so husky, so Levi.

She tipped her head to one side. "Do shadows miss light?"

He pressed a kiss in her palm. "Shadows can't exist without light."

"Oh." The unfettered, unfiltered romance of his statement wrapped around her heart and tugged. "Levi . . . I . . ."

The public address system announced that first-class passengers for his flight should now board. Regret crept into his eyes.

"Fuck," he whispered into her ear, the word rife with frustration. "Ignore it. I'll board last."

"You'll be so busy in Atlanta that you won't have time to miss me very much."

"That's bullshit, but I'm sure I'll be wishing it was true." He shook his head, almost in a scolding way. "You have no idea how much I'll be trying to get my mind off you."

Reluctantly, they stood up. He released a long sigh as he gazed into her eyes. His hands settled on her upper arms and he dipped his head and kissed her. The kiss wasn't for the faint-hearted. It was demanding, desperate, and full of longing. When his mouth finally released hers, Trudy blinked at him and fought a sudden urge to beg him to stay one more day, one more night with her.

The tinny voice sounded over the speakers again, urging first class passengers to board. Last call.

"I'll text you as soon as we land," he said.

She nodded, emotion clogging her throat.

"Stop every couple of hours while you're on the road and text me. I want to know you're safe until you get home."

"I know," she said, for he'd already gone over this and over this with her. "I'll be fine," she assured him. "But I'll keep in touch. I promise."

"You do that." He kissed her bruised temple gently and gave her a fleeting smile. "If you want to keep me sane and happy, that is."

"Oh, I do," she assured him. "I'll see you soon."

"Soon," he agreed and attempted another smile. "But not soon enough." With a scowl and a helpless shrug, he grabbed his carry-on luggage, and strode away from her.

She watched him go and shook her head when he didn't look back, but moved confidently down the jetway. Only when she lost sight of him did she allow the sob to emerge from her thick throat and the tears spill from her eyes. God! She never believed it would hurt this badly to see him go!

Wiping aside the hot tears, Trudy turned and made her way through the airport and to the parking lot where she'd left the Gypsy Spirit. It would be a long, wretched trip back to Tulsa, she thought, but tried to buoy herself with thoughts of e-mails and phone calls with Levi. But she knew they would be weak substitutes for the flesh and blood Mister Moody Blues. She promised herself that she'd convince him to come visit her in Tulsa within the next week or two and then she'd make plans to see him in Atlanta for his birthday. In between those visits, she would have to find some work. The Key West case was exciting in so many different levels, but it had added not one dime to her bank account.

Once in the RV, she let Mouse out of the dog crate and checked her e-mail and was astounded to find at least a dozen messages from people she didn't know. Reading a couple of them, she discovered that they were from people asking to hire her. She sat back in the driver's seat, stunned and elated.

She was about to log out of her e-mail when she spotted a message from Levi. When had he sent this? Just now? The subject line was; "I'm a Coward." Shaking her head at that, she opened the e-mail. It had been sent at seven o'clock that morning when she'd been sleeping. She glanced at her wristwatch. It was almost noon. Gathering in a deep breath, she read the message.

Tru;

I have to get this off my chest or I'll explode and I don't think I can say it to your face – yet. I don't feel worthy of you.

You know a little bit about my past, but I've hidden much of it from you because I don't want it to taint what we have and, frankly, it's embarrassing. But, believe me when I tell you that I'm improving. I'm trying. I want to be a better man for you.

Last night confirmed what I've known almost since the day I met you, my true north. And that is that I'm yours. And you're mine. Don't fucking forget that!

Your L.

Trudy read the message twice, each time finding more in it to make her ache with love for him, make her hurt for him. Jeez. Did he have any idea what this e-mail would do to her? She felt herself unravel and she sat in the RV for a good half hour crying and cursing him for leaving her and knowing she was making absolutely no sense.

"Levi, damn it!" She swiped at her eyes, rubbing away her tears with the heels of her hands. "I didn't want to blubber over you! Like it's not already hard to separate from you, even for a few days, and then you write something like this!"

But she was glad for his e-mail – glad that he was, at least, trying to explain himself to her.

With a sigh, she hit "reply" and typed:

My L.;

Thank you for lowering your shields last night and this morning to let me glimpse your hidden heart. I don't want to get too flowery here on you, but it meant a lot to me. Trusting me with your past disappointments, regrets, and demons isn't a burden and won't taint my feelings for you. I trust that I can tell you anything and that, someday, you will trust me, too.

Missing you already,

Your Tru (north)

She hit "send" and hoped he took her message to heart.

Being without him would be difficult, but she would have to persevere because she needed to concentrate on acquiring funds. She had to work and, thank God, she had people who, evidently, wanted to pay her!

It won't be so bad, she told herself so that she wouldn't start crying again. She'd consult with Levi about her next case. They'd talk on the phone. Maybe they'd even "sex-text" each other. That could be fun.

"Oh, piffle," she grumbled, swinging around in the driver's seat to face front. She turned the key in the ignition and the RV rumbled to life. "Time to hit the road, Mouse. The sooner we get home, the sooner I can accept a new case or two, and the sooner we can make plans to see Levi again."

Levi was right, she thought. Soon. But not soon enough.

*

The elevator doors opened onto the penthouse floor and Levi gathered up his luggage and stepped out of the compartment. The doors closed behind him with a soft hiss. His unit took up the whole top floor and the elevator didn't arrive at this floor without an access code.

He always secured the black lacquered double doors leading into the penthouse when he was going to be away for longer than a day, so he knew they'd be locked. When he'd landed, he'd texted Trudy as promised. Trudy had left him two messages – an e-mail answering the one he'd sent her early that morning and a text letting him know she was on the road and having no trouble.

The e-mail had stolen his breath and made his heart swell almost to the point of pain. Was this love? Could he actually be falling in love with her – already in love with her? It had taken all his concentration to put her sweetly worded e-mail out of his head long enough to text his assistant and VPs to let them know that he was headed home. Since Wes Statler, his housekeeper and personal chef, wouldn't show up again until tomorrow, he'd probably send out for a pizza or go grab a burger somewhere later.

Fumbling for his keys, Levi noted that it was almost three o'clock. His heart felt like a lead weight in his chest. He missed Trudy so much he decided to move up his next appointment with Dr. McClain. He had a lot to sort out now that he was home.

Finally fitting the key in the lock, he pushed open the doors and carried his luggage inside, dropping it beside the long, crescent-shaped sectional that faced the fireplace and flat-screen TV above it.

He stretched from side to side to work out the kinks in his muscles as he stared out the glass wall at Atlanta's skyscrapers and Olympic Park. He glanced around and then straightened slowly when he saw the newspaper sections folded on the coffee table and a ceramic mug sitting beside them. What the hell?

His eyes widened as he looked around, seeing other things out of place. The large urn beside the fireplace was full of lilies and greenery – all fresh. A big, plush pillow lay on the hardwood floor – blue velvet with gold fringe. He'd never seen it before.

He started to back up, realizing that someone had been in there. Someone might *still* be in——. A clatter of dishes sounded from the kitchen – a room he couldn't see from where he stood.

"Levi?" a woman's voice floated out to him and his heart kicked and then froze solid with dread. "Is that you, babe? Are you finally home?"

The End

Dear Reader,

Don't throw the book against the wall! I know you're wondering, "What the heck?" You can find out right this minute. THROUGH HIS TOUCH is available on Amazon. So go get it! Levi and Trudy's tangled love affair continues, along with their powerhouse psychic skills. I know many of you don't like cliffhangers, but you don't have to wait to find out what's going on. Each book in this series will conclude a case Levi and Trudy are working on, but their relationship will evolve with each book.

Let me know what you think. Leave a review on Amazon and/or Goodreads. Drop me a note. I'm writing these books for me and for you, so let me hear from you.

Happy Reading,

Deborah

About the Author . . .

Deborah Camp is the author of more than 50 romances, both contemporary and historical. Her books have been praised by reviewers, bloggers, and readers who love complex characters and clever plotting. She always mixes in a bit of humor, even in her romantic suspense novels.

She lives in Tulsa, Oklahoma, where she makes a comfortable home for her dogs and the "Levi" in her life. She volunteers her time to the Animal Rescue Foundation (ARF) that rescues dogs and cats from kill shelters and finds them loving homes.

www.deborah-camp.com
www.facebook.com/officialdeborahcamp
www.pinterest.com/debbycamp44
www.deborahcampwritersdesk.blogspot.com
www.twitter.com/authordebcamp

Also by Deborah Camp
All available on Amazon

<u>Novella</u>
The Madcap and the Miser

<u>Historical Romances</u>
Blazing Embers
Primrose
Fire Lily
Black-eyed Susan
Fallen Angel
Cheyenne's Shadow
My Wild Rose
Lady Legend
Master of Moonspell
Solitary Horseman
Too Tough to Tame
Tough Talk, Tender Kisses
A Tough Man's Woman
To Seduce and Defend
Belle Star, Bandit Queen

<u>Contemporary Romances</u>
To Have, To Hold
Devil's Bargain
For Love or Money
This Tender Truce
In a Pirate's Arms
Just Another Pretty Face
Vein of Gold
Right Behind the Rain

After Dark
The Butler Did It
Wrangler's Lady
Hook, Line, and Sinker
Love Letters
Weathering the Storm
The Second Mr. Sullivan
A Newsworthy Affair
Destiny's Daughter
Taming the Wild Man
Oklahoma Man
Sweet Passion's Song
A Dream to Share
Winter Flame
Midnight Eyes
Riptide
Tomorrow's Bride
They Said It Wouldn't Last
Strange Bedfellows

More novels in the MIND'S EYE series...

Through His Touch
Through His Heart

65567179R00166

Made in the USA
Lexington, KY
16 July 2017